Anything *You* Can Do...!

The question hung in the air like a challenge.

Indeed, it was a challenge that Lane Brooks, best of the best in terms of newspaper people, wasn't about to refuse. She didn't have the first clue concerning cat shows, but she enjoyed being around cats, so an investigative piece featuring such an event would be a snap.

"I want to do the story," Lane answered quickly before her arch nemesis, Clay Crawford, could. "But I understand if Clay isn't up to it."

He bristled, and she reprimanded herself for forgetting one of her father's cardinal rules: *If you issue a dare, you better prepare for a rousing affair.*

"Of course I'm up to it," Clay said, and Lane's gaze automatically flew to his lap. She closed her eyes briefly and was glad that he couldn't read her mind.

Their would-be boss, Marcus Miller, finished issuing his challenge by offering them a satisfied, catlike smile. "Then may the best man—" he paused and bowed in Lane's direction "—or woman win."

For more, turn to page 9

"Without me, the show would be a bad talk show with a laugh track."

Renata paced. "It needs the solid foundation of my counseling experience. I know you're entertaining and witty, but..." The look on Hawk's face stopped her. "What's so funny?"

"You. I agree. The show needs the man-woman thing."

She paused, momentarily stunned. "Okay, then, we need to get you up to speed on marriage counseling. I have lots of books and videos you should study—"

"Hold it. What we need is for you to lighten up. A lot. You've lost your flair. So, forget research. If you cheer up, we'll be fine."

Renata shook her head. "That's not..."

"Let's flip for it. Heads we do it my way, tails yours."

"You want to flip for the fate of my show? Why don't we just wrestle for it?" she said dryly.

"You into wrestling?" Hawk asked, stalking closer. He stopped inches from her.

Renata's breath caught in her throat. *He wanted to kiss her!*

For more, turn to page 197

HARLEQUIN DUETS

ISBN 0-373-44143-6

Copyright in the collection:
Copyright © 2002 by Harlequin Books S.A.

The publisher acknowledges the copyright holders
of the individual works as follows:

ANYTHING *YOU* CAN DO...!
Copyright © 2002 by Darlene Hrobak Gardner

ANCHOR THAT MAN!
Copyright © 2002 by Daphne Atkeson

This edition published by arrangement with Harlequin Books S.A.

® and TM are trademarks of the publisher. Trademarks indicated with ® are registered in the United States Patent and Trademark Office, the Canadian Trade Marks Office and in other countries.

Visit us at www.eHarlequin.com

Printed in U.S.A.

Anything You Can Do...!

Darlene Gardner

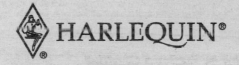

TORONTO • NEW YORK • LONDON
AMSTERDAM • PARIS • SYDNEY • HAMBURG
STOCKHOLM • ATHENS • TOKYO • MILAN • MADRID
PRAGUE • WARSAW • BUDAPEST • AUCKLAND

Dear Reader,

I didn't have to look farther than across the dinner table for a model for my competitive heroine in *Anything* You *Can Do...!*

When my daughter was younger, the foolproof way to get her to finish everything on her plate was to pointedly eye her little brother's meal. "Would you look at that," I'd say, ever so casually. "I do believe he's going to finish before you." It didn't matter if my son's plate was piled high with food or contained nothing more than a few peas. She'd finish off the rest of her meal with gusto. Anything to finish first.

Lane Brooks also has that burning desire to win. I put her in the competitive world of journalism, paired her with a yummy hero and let her loose. Lane learns important lessons along the way to the most important victory of her life. I can only hope that one day, after the games have been played and the goals scored, my daughter, too, realizes that it's love that conquers all.

Enjoy!

Darlene Gardner

P.S. Online readers can write to me at darlgardner@aol.com.

Books by Darlene Gardner

HARLEQUIN DUETS

1

OH, NO! Say it ain't so!

Lane Brooks's brain screamed the words, but no sound came from her lips. She dragged her gaze from the man standing at the entrance of the coffee shop and inclined her head, ever so slightly, toward the woman seated next to her.

"Would you please hand me that newspaper on the next table, Stacy?" she asked in perfectly modulated tones, adding a cool smile.

"The newspaper?" Stacy reached over to retrieve it, then flipped the paper over to look at the masthead. "But isn't this a copy of the competition?"

Resisting the urge to snatch the paper from her sister, Lane very calmly removed it from Stacy's unresisting fingers and ducked behind it.

Her eyes fell on the story stripped across the top of page 3-B, one she'd already read twice and had overheard the ladies at the next table laughing over.

"Did you read the story in the *Miami Courier*? About the thief who gave a clerk his driver's license to prove he could legally drink the beer he was stealing?"

Lane had worked the police beat last night for the *Fort Lauderdale Times,* but she hadn't gotten that story. Why hadn't the desk sergeant at the Miami

PD told *her* the kid was spending the rest of his twenty-first birthday in a jail cell?

It could be because Lane hadn't picked the report out of the stack and delved deeper, but she suspected that Clay Crawford's unfair physiological advantage had charmed the information out of the female sergeant.

Her sister craned her head so she could peer around the paper at Lane. At twenty-three, Stacy was a year younger than Lane and a more athletic version of the same blond-haired, brown-eyed theme. Her long, straight hair was pulled back in a ponytail instead of cut in short layers like Lane's, the better to keep it out of her eyes in case she decided to go out for one of her frequent runs.

"I know you live and sleep newspapers, Lane, but do you have to read one while we're having coffee?"

"You're drinking bottled water," Lane pointed out in a stage whisper. "And I can't help it. I need it for camouflage."

"Camouflage? Why on earth do you need camouflage?"

"Remember the story I told you about when I got off work after my first day at the *Times?*"

Stacy's eyes went wide. "You mean when you had sex with Clay Crawford on a crowded beach minutes after you met him?"

Lane cringed inwardly both at Stacy's description and the volume of her voice. A well-heeled woman at the table behind them shot her a shocked glance and shook her frosted hair in dismay while nudging her cappuccino-drinking companion. Lane smiled radiantly at both of them.

"It was *almost* sex on a *secluded* beach *hours* after I met him,'' she whispered, struggling hard to maintain her unflustered exterior. ''And I'd appreciate it if you'd refrain from announcing that juicy tidbit to everyone here.''

Looking anything but contrite, Stacy gave her a broad, knowing smile. ''At least you admit it's a juicy tidbit.'' Nevertheless, she lowered her voice. ''Are you going to tell me why you brought up that story now?''

''Only if you promise not to look toward the entrance of the coffee shop.''

''Clay Crawford is here?'' Stacy's blond ponytail whipped around with her head at the declaration, and Lane had to strain to keep the newspaper in place.

''You promised not to look, Stacy.''

''I did not.'' Stacy said, making Lane regret asking her to meet at the coffee shop to talk about her ambivalence over her impending job interview. ''You asked me to promise, but I didn't get around to doing it.''

''Stop looking, Stacy.'' Lane tried to sound pleasant, but she could have been talking to the newspaper for all the attention Stacy paid her.

''Wowzer!''

Lane didn't mean to lower the newspaper, but the connection between her brain and hands seemed to have gone haywire. Her eyes met with a sight as delicious-looking as the piece of double-chocolate fudge behind the cashier's glossy glass counter.

Sex on two legs.

That's how she'd thought of Clay Crawford ever since he slanted her his devastating smile and she'd temporarily put her brain on ice to follow him into the most sensuous experience of her life.

A single glimpse was enough to remind her why she'd succumbed to temptation. Clay was everything she didn't want in a man and everything, unfortunately, that sent her pulse rate shooting through the roof so that she half expected plaster to rain down on her head.

The privileged son of the *Miami Courier*'s wealthy publisher, he was hotter than the sun that beat down on Miami Beach. But as he stood inside the doorway, he acted as cool as an iced café latté.

The top of a reporter's notebook stuck out of the pocket of a tawny sports jacket he wore with an exquisitely cut pair of khakis, clothes probably tailormade for him. They covered a body that was certifiably drool-worthy. She was qualified to know. She'd seen the glorious length of him all but naked, had caressed the sleek skin over his sinuous muscles, had pressed her lips against his warm flesh.

His thick, slightly wavy hair was inky black. His back was to her, but she knew it fell over his strong, wide forehead in charming disarray.

The teenage girl behind the counter eyed him from under her flapping lashes as she took his order, giggling at something he said.

"Golly!" Stacy said. "Don't tell me that's your Clay."

"He's not *my* Clay," Lane said with false calmness as she got back behind the cover of newspaper.

"As far as I'm concerned he is." Her sister kept talking, obviously no longer bothered by the black-and-white newsprint between them. "I know you, Lane. You're the least promiscuous person I know. You don't have sex with just anyone."

"It was a year ago, Stacy. And I keep telling you

it was *almost* sex. I stopped him before we got that far," Lane whispered, but the entire truth was that he'd been the one who'd stopped. She'd wanted... Well, Lane wasn't going to let herself think about what she'd wanted.

She needed to focus on the next morning when it had been driven home to her exactly why she needed to stay far, far away from Clay Crawford.

"Sex is sex," Stacy said, then stopped abruptly. "Oh, my. Would you look at that?"

"At what?" Lane asked, but she couldn't see anything through the newspaper.

"At the hunk-a-thon. Another one just walked in. He's talking to your hunk. I think they're together." Stacy swore. "I'm going to ask the man at the next table to move his head so I can see around it."

"No, don't!" Lane implored. "And please stop staring. I don't want to draw Clay's attention."

"Maybe I could see better from here," Stacy said, and Lane heard a scratching noise as her sister repositioned her chair. "Oops."

An instant later, Lane felt a warm splash of liquid hit her lap and heard her sister's shouted apology. Trust Stacy to knock over Lane's cappuccino instead of her own water. She pushed her chair back and got to her feet, automatically soaking up the mud-colored brew with the first thing available, which happened to be the newspaper.

With a feeling of doom, Lane raised her eyes toward the front of the shop. They locked with Clay's, which were a grayish shade of blue that reminded her of the ocean on the misty night she'd lost herself in his arms. He grinned and inclined his head in acknowledgment. She tried to swallow, but found that she couldn't.

She gave him a curt nod and very calmly, very deliberately broke eye contact while ignoring her pingponging heart.

She returned her attention to Stacy as she continued to blot her skirt. "Please tell me he's not coming this way."

"I can't." Stacy grinned. "Because he is. And he's bringing the other hunk with him."

Lane braced herself for the sound of Clay's voice, which was as low and rich as the chords of a cello.

"I know you don't like the *Courier,* but I didn't realize you considered it a rag," he said.

"Hallo, Clay," Lane said airily, ignoring the way the sound of his voice sent vibrations through her. "Fancy meeting you here."

She groaned inwardly. She sounded like a snotty society miss instead of a sophisticated reporter about town.

"I keep telling you, Laney, I'll meet you anywhere. Any time," Clay drawled, and she caught the full impact of his devastatingly attractive face.

His eyebrows were thick and regular, his nose long, his jaw strong and square. The entire effect might have been too harsh if it hadn't been for his mouth, which was wide and full-lipped and heart-stoppingly luscious. He smiled, and her heart stopped.

He set his cup on an adjoining table and extended her a couple of thick napkins. "I don't suppose you want me to dry your skirt for you," he said, sounding hopeful.

"Smart man," she drawled as she took the napkin

and blotted the liquid from her cream-colored skirt. With the brown stain, it resembled the coat of a Holstein. Her job interviewer would probably moo when he saw her coming.

"If I were that smart," he whispered for her ears alone, "I'd have thought of a way to finish what we started last year."

His gaze was much hotter than the liquid that had spilled in her lap. She looked away so as not to get scorched. The well-dressed woman with the frosted hair, the one who had appeared so disapproving when Stacy announced that Lane had sex with Clay, caught her eye.

She silently mouthed four words, so slowly that Lane made out every one. *I don't blame you.*

Lane turned back to the table, where a waitress had begun mopping up the spill. She called over her shoulder that they should move to an empty table.

"Mind if we join you?" Clay asked.

We? Belatedly, it dawned on Lane that Stacy had mentioned a secondary hunk. Funny, she hadn't noticed anybody but Clay. She swiveled her head inches, and there he was standing next to Stacy. A good-looking blond guy in jeans and a T-shirt that proclaimed football life's greatest pleasure. His eyes were riveted on her sister.

"Of course we don't mind," Stacy said before Lane could object. She beamed her megawatt smile first at the blonde, then at Clay. "We'd love the company. I'm Lane's sister, Stacy Brooks."

Clay introduced the guy with the delusions about football as Ted Green, then waited as he and Stacy exchanged a too-long handshake. Clay had barely enunciated the first letter of his own name when Stacy interrupted him.

"Oh, I already know who you are. Lane's told me all about you."

Clay gave Lane a sexy, sidelong glance and a very male smile as he held out a chair for her at the table. "So you talk about me, do you, Laney?"

"I do not." Lane desperately cast about for something to explain her sister's comment as she sat down. "I might have mentioned you once ages ago. Stacy's mind is like a net. Whatever goes inside stays there."

"Nets are made of mesh," Ted pointed out.

"With lots of tiny little holes," Stacy added helpfully.

It took a supreme effort for Lane not to glare at Stacy. "Like a steel lockbox, then."

"So what did Laney say about me?" Clay asked Stacy, but he was watching Lane. She did her darnedest not to cover her face with her hands and duck under the table.

"She said," Stacy began deliberately, and Lane offered a rare prayer, "she used to see a *lot* more of you."

The corners of Clay's eyes crinkled as he smiled at Lane. When his attention was diverted, Stacy took the opportunity to give her a ribald wink, which caused Lane to picture Clay's glorious body naked and poised above hers. She willed her cheeks not to burn.

He repositioned his stool a good two inches closer to hers, and she considered moving out of thigh-brushing range. But then he might guess she was trying to get away from him before she did something stupid. Like make a dash for the fire extinguisher to douse the heat that was rapidly spreading through her body.

"Laney has this odd idea that I'm the opposition because our newspapers are rivals," Clay said, neglecting to add that as general-assignment reporters who often worked on the same stories they personified the rivalry.

Stacy waved a hand. Lane noticed that Ted followed her every move with avid interest. At the rate he was going, he'd soon change his mind about life's greatest pleasure.

"It's not such an odd idea when your father is a high school football coach," Stacy said.

"Did you hear that, Clay?" Ted pumped his fist as though he'd just scored a touchdown. "We're with women who have football in their genes. It doesn't get any better than that."

"Anyway, Dad was forever warning us about hanging out with the competition," Stacy said, sneaking a flirty glance at Ted that told Lane she was flattered by his attention. "What was it he always said, Lane?"

"If you get cozy with the competition, you might as well sit down in a Barcalounger," she repeated without hesitation.

"That's it," Stacy said. "Why, one time when I was running track in high school, I tripped and Izzy Collier beat me. Dad wanted to blackball her from my birthday party!"

"You ran track?" Ted snapped his fingers and pointed at her. "I thought I recognized your name. Didn't you make All American at UM in the 1500 meters a couple years back?"

Stacy had the kind of face that showed her every emotion. Now it flushed with pleasure. "How'd you know that?"

"I'm a sportswriter at the *Courier*. I cover pro football, but I remember reading about you." He paused significantly while he ran his eyes over her sister's delicate features. "Of course the stories never said how gorgeous you were."

Stacy let out a giggle that was more flirtatious than jolly.

"Please tell me you don't work for the *Times*." Ted put his hands together as though he were praying. "I couldn't stand it if you couldn't get friendly with me."

Her sister giggled again. "I'm a physical education teacher at a high school in Hialeah. And get this. I have a unit where I teach the students the rules of football."

Ted placed his hand over his heart. "That settles it. You have to go out with me. It would be too cruel if you said no."

"I don't think that word's in my vocabulary where you're concerned," Stacy said, looking at him through lowered lashes. "How about tonight at eight o'clock?"

"Seven," Ted said quickly.

"Six," Stacy retorted.

"They remind me of us when we first met. Before things got complicated," Clay whispered into Lane's ear, his breath rustling her hair and sending shivers the length of her body. "Why don't you meet me tonight, too?"

She was tempted. Oh, so tempted. Especially when he laid a warm hand over hers. She turned to find his face inches from her, his delectable mouth close enough to kiss. She called on her willpower.

"Because it *is* complicated," she said smoothly and slid her hand out from under his. The smell of coffee in the shop was strong, but Lane still got a whiff of something clean and heady that might have been either shampoo or soap or just plain Clay. She decided she'd subjected herself to temptation for long enough. She rose, surprised when her legs supported her weight.

"Stacy, we need to get going," Lane said loudly enough to break her sister out of her Ted-induced trance. "I have to change my skirt."

"But you don't have time to go home and get back here before your interview," Stacy protested, tearing her eyes from Ted so she could look at her watch. "You only have a half hour."

Clay raised a dark brow, and Lane could sense his reporter's curiosity going to work.

"It's just a routine on-the-job interview," Lane said quickly, sending Stacy a silent plea to shut up. As sneaky as Clay was, he might try to horn in if he knew she was up for another job. Never mind that she wasn't entirely sure she wanted said job. "The subject of which I don't intend to discuss with you."

"I wouldn't ask." Clay kept his extraordinary eyes on her. "Remember, *I* think we can keep our professional lives separate from our private lives."

"I don't consider my professional life to be separate from my private life," Lane said. "Now we really must go. Ta-ta, Clay, Ted."

Her back straight and her head high, she glided away as Stacy said her goodbyes. She was horrified that she'd actually said ta-ta. Maybe she was carrying this grace-under-fire thing too far.

She walked out of the cafe into the blinding Florida sun, giving herself the mental pep talk she always called upon after running into Clay. Her attraction to him was purely physical and, therefore, resistible. He'd grown up pampered and rich, with all life's advantages. He simply didn't appeal to her on a deeper level.

"Isn't he dreamy?" Stacy gushed when she came through the doors. Her palms were pressed to her flushed cheeks.

"Well, sure, but I told you I wanted to avoid him."

"Not Clay. Ted." Stacy did a pirouette, her arms raised to the crystalline blue sky. "We decided we couldn't wait until six to get together so he's picking me up at five. I think I'm in love."

"You can't be in love. You just met the guy."

"Oh, yes, I can be. Unlike you, I don't believe in suppressing my emotions." She waggled her eyebrows. "Or my desires."

"I don't desire Clay Crawford."

Stacy laughed. "Rubbish. If you didn't desire him, you wouldn't have had sex with him."

"Almost sex," Lane corrected. "And even if I did desire him, I can't get involved with him. He's the competition."

"Ahhhh, but he won't be the competition if you decide you want to work at that magazine." Stacy shook a finger at her. "Then he'll just be an eligible man you've had sex with."

"*Almost* sex," Lane muttered, gazing down at the sidewalk to avoid her sister's too-perceptive gaze.

Her soiled skirt came into view. "Besides, who's going to hire a woman whose skirt looks like a cow should be wearing it?"

"You won't have one during the interview," Stacy said.

"What? A skirt?"

"No, silly. A stain. You should be glad my jeans were all in the wash so I had to pull this skirt out of the back of the closet. You and I are about the same size, right?"

Lane examined her sister's narrow hips. "Not really."

"Close enough," Stacy said dismissively. "That building across the street must have a bathroom where we can switch."

Stacy hooked an arm through Lane's and started walking away from the coffee shop, but Lane couldn't resist one look back at the scene of her latest close encounter with Clay Crawford.

She spotted him through the glass window, making no secret that he was watching her. Before she could turn back around, he blew her a kiss that made it feel as though a legion of wing-flapping butterflies had just been let loose in her stomach.

"Leave me alone, butterflies," she muttered.

"I don't see any butterflies," Stacy said, inspecting the air around them. "A couple of gnats, sure, but no butterflies."

"That's because I've gotten rid of them," Lane said.

But, even as she walked determinedly away from temptation, she knew she was lying. Not only that, but she didn't have a clue how to make the dratted things go away.

2

THE RECEPTION AREA of *Splash!* magazine was Florida to the core. The furniture was white, the carpeting deep blue and the walls decorated with paintings and photographs of the ocean. The magazine's logo, prominently displayed behind the circular reception desk, featured a leaping dolphin poised above a deep-blue wave.

Clay Crawford's pulse jumped with anticipation as he approached a smiling, dark-haired receptionist. Within the hour, he fully expected to be offered a job on the slick new general-interest magazine.

He yearned for the position of staff writer so badly he'd thought of little else during the past month. Well, that wasn't exactly true. He'd thought of Lane Brooks, too, but then he always did.

It was ironic that she was meeting with a source in the same vicinity as the interview that could eliminate the professional barrier between them. He wanted no barriers at all—not even clothes.

"Clay Crawford to see Marcus Miller," he announced cheerfully. "I have an appointment."

"You can go right in, Mr. Crawford," the receptionist said, batting eyelashes so coated with mascara he wondered how she had the strength to blink them. Her smile faded and her voice grew husky. "And next time, feel free to come in to see me."

He grinned, not taking her seriously, but her comment proved that women generally liked him. So why did Lane treat him like a pariah?

He could have sworn he and Lane had discovered passion and each other the night they met, but his perception of what had happened grew less certain with each passing month.

Was Lane as immune to him as she'd seemed in the coffee shop or was she merely wary of cozying up to the competition?

He rapped on the office door and pushed it open, eager for the Editor-In-Chief of *Splash!* magazine to offer him the job so he could find out.

Marcus was standing behind a white Formica desk as smooth as the scalp he surely shaved daily. The floor-to-ceiling windows in back of him made him look even smaller than his five feet two and afforded a view of an azure sky dotted with puffy white clouds and the startling blue of Miami's Biscayne Bay.

"Clay, my man." Marcus smiled, his teeth white against his sun-bronzed skin. His all-black clothes made him look out of place in the office, like an oil stain on a wedding dress. "Come over here and meet my little girl."

"Afternoon, Marcus." Clay scanned the office for the other man's daughter but couldn't find her. "I don't see your girl."

"She's under my desk," he said, crouching so not even the top of his bald head was visible. "Here, Prune. Come to daddy."

Clay winced. A girl named Prune was almost as bad as a boy named Sue.

Long moments passed before Marcus finally

yelled "Gotcha" and stood up. But instead of a girl, he was holding a...

"What *is* that?" Clay asked.

"A cat," Marcus said, his compact hands stroking the animal's slender, elongated body. It had ears like a bat's wings, a wedge-shaped head and piercing emerald eyes that were focused on Clay. Its body was as hairless as its owner's head, which brought up a frightening possibility.

"Did you shave it?"

Marcus threw back his head and laughed.

"It's a Sphynx." He buried his nose in the cat's wrinkled skin. "You're not supposed to have hair. Are you, Prune?" As an aside to Clay, he said, "Her name's actually Faline Prunella, but I call her Prune for short."

He carried the cat to an overstuffed white armchair in the corner of the room, rhythmically stroking its skin as he sat down.

He would have looked like a villain in a James Bond movie if his cat hadn't been bald.

"You're probably wondering why I called you into my office," Marcus said, crossing his short legs.

The cat bore such a striking resemblance to its owner that Clay half expected it to cross one of its naked legs, too. He blinked to get the image out of his mind and focus on more important matters.

"I figured you wanted me to see the operation up close and personal," Clay said, barely refraining from adding *before you offered me the job.*

Marcus had already interviewed him twice over dinner and drinks at Bayside, Miami's waterfront entertainment complex. If he intended to turn him down, Clay figured he would have done so with a phone call.

"I did, but I also wanted to talk to you about your father," he said, still stroking the cat. Four eyes focused on Clay. "I hear that Charles Crawford isn't pleased that his star reporter is looking elsewhere for a job."

Ah, his father. Try as he might, Clay couldn't escape the fact that his father was the principal player in Miami's most illustrious journalism family. Or that too many people thought his position at the newspaper depended upon that fact. But what was the best way to get that across?

"My full name is William Clay Crawford."

Marcus gave a slight nod, but he clearly didn't understand the point behind Clay's revelation.

"Behind my back, my co-workers call me Prince Willy." He cleared his throat, finding the next part difficult to repeat. "Heir to the throne."

"Oh, but it's an awfully prestigious throne."

"Not if people are under the impression that I didn't have to work to get there. If I'm to command respect, I have to earn it first. That's awfully hard when it's my father sitting in the glass office making personnel decisions."

"So you want to make a name for yourself on a publication that isn't owned by someone named Crawford?"

Clay felt himself relax. "Exactly."

"And your father's going to let you go without a fight?"

"I can handle my father," Clay said, suppressing a tinge of unease. His father had a history of angina trouble, and there were indications that a flare-up might be in the making. But he'd deal with that when—and if—it came.

"I'm quite impressed with you, Clay. You're a professional any magazine would be proud to have on its staff." Marcus paused for breath and Clay waited for the words he yearned to hear.

"Mr. Miller, your two-fifteen appointment is here," announced a voice over an intercom.

Those weren't the longed-for words, Clay thought wryly as he waited for Marcus to inform the receptionist that she was mistaken. Clay's appointment had begun just minutes ago so Marcus couldn't possibly have arranged a meeting with anyone else. The editor walked over to the intercom and pressed a button.

"Send her in."

Before Clay could question him on the identity of the mystery guest, Lane Brooks walked—er, shuffled—through the door. Clay's mouth dropped open and his blood ran hot. Her stained skirt had been cream. The va-va-voom one she was wearing was red and a size too small.

The skirt hugged her body so tightly that the outline of her shape, from her rounded hips to her sweetly shaped rear, was clearly visible. He shifted uncomfortably and glanced down at his lap.

Oh, great. Just what he needed after trying to impress upon Marcus how professional he was.

"Ah, Miss Brooks, it's nice to finally meet you in person," Marcus said. "I'm Marcus Miller, this is Prune and..."

"She's a hairless cat," Lane exclaimed excitedly, walking over to Marcus and reaching out to stroke Prune's smooth head. She didn't so much as glance in Clay's direction. "I've never seen one of these in person before. She's absolutely lovely."

No, thought Clay. Lane was lovely. She had a classic heart-shaped face with a cherry of a mouth and a pert little nose that he knew was dotted with freckles underneath her makeup.

She'd covered her brown eyes with stylish little glasses he thought she wore more to convey the image of a professional than because she needed them. Her figure was curvaceous without being overweight, and her blond hair was cut in short, sophisticated layers. She seemed to have forgotten that a pen was tucked behind her ear, and her fingertips, as usual, were ink stained.

Clay wouldn't have changed a thing about her, except the aversion she seemed to have for him.

"Thank you," Marcus said, obviously pleased. "At least you're not going to accuse me of shaving him like our friend Clay here did."

"Clay?" she repeated, then swiveled her head very slowly until her brown eyes locked with his. He thought he saw a flicker of surprise, but it was gone before he could be sure.

"Lane Brooks, I'd like you to meet Clay Crawford. Clay, Lane."

Clay rose, keeping his briefcase strategically placed.

"We've already met," Lane said as he felt a smile spread across his face. He couldn't help it. She was just so darn pretty.

"Lane," he said, then added mischievously. "Fancy meeting you here."

The corner of her mouth twitched, telling him she wasn't quite as humorless as she wanted him to believe. But it *was* strange to see her here in Marcus's office.

Did she intend to interview the editor for a story about his new magazine? Yes, that must be it. But why had Marcus scheduled the interview on Clay's time? Unless...he wanted to give her the opportunity to talk to *Splash!* magazine's newest reporter. It would be the perfect opportunity to point out that their dueling jobs no longer stood in the way of their pursuing a relationship, Clay thought happily.

"You're both probably wondering what the other is doing here," Marcus said. "I won't keep you in suspense. You know, of course, that I'm about to hire a staff writer for my new magazine."

Clay glanced at Lane, a terrible certainty growing in his gut. He saw in her eyes that she, too, had guessed what Marcus was about to say.

"Congratulations, Clay, Lane. The search is down to two. You're the finalists for the job."

LANE KEPT HER LIPS carefully curved in a smile, but her thoughts were anything but cheerful.

Trust Clay Crawford to figure out she was up for the *Splash!* job and go after it himself. After all that talk in the coffee shop about competition being no impediment to a relationship, no less.

He'd been plotting to slide under her defenses and beat her out for the job even then. Just as he'd schemed to scoop her on that story about the corrupt mayor the first day they'd met.

Oh, she was so angry she could stamp her foot! Right on his.

"I couldn't ask for a more worthy rival," Lane

said smoothly, keeping her feet planted firmly on the ground while she offered Clay one of her hands.

"Likewise," he said. Watching her warily, he engulfed her hand in the warmth of his much-larger one. She ignored the heat that blasted up her arm and slid her fingers from his.

"Either one of you would make a fabulous employee, but unfortunately I have to choose," Marcus said. "That's why I'd like to propose a competition."

Clay ran a hand through his dark hair, which Lane absolutely would not let herself remember as being luxuriously silky. Instead, as she sat down in the wing-backed chair Marcus indicated, she focused on Clay's hair color. Black, like his scheming heart.

"I'm going to assign both of you the same story," Marcus continued. "The journalist who comes back with the best one wins."

Lane sat up straighter as her father's voice echoed in her head. *If winning isn't everything, how come losers cry?* Her competitive juices flowed like precipitation in the rain forest.

"I like winning," she said.

Clay sent her a concerned look. "Marcus didn't mean to say 'win.' He meant that one of us would 'get' the job. Didn't you, Marcus?"

Marcus shook his head. "No. I'm pretty sure I meant to say win."

"Great." Lane clasped her hands together in what was nearly a clap. "What do we write about?"

"An investigative piece on a new organization threatening the integrity of a thriving industry."

"Sounds serious," Lane said. The bigger the story, the better she liked working on it. And the more satisfying it would be to scoop Clay. "Tell us more."

"I want you to delve into the underbelly of the FFF to weed out corruption and expose it for the sham it is."

Clay scooted forward to the edge of his seat. Lane could tell he was as intrigued as she was. "What kind of organization is the FFF?"

Marcus bounced Prune on his lap as though she were a baby and lowered his voice. "The Florida Feline Federation."

Even though Lane had no intention of getting cozy with the competition, she exchanged a glance with Clay at the editor's use of the word *feline*. He looked as befuddled as she felt.

"It's a new group that's luring Floridians by the hundreds to the shows it's putting on throughout the state." Marcus's expression hardened. "I have good reason to believe it's fixed. I'm thinking kickbacks."

He went to his desk and picked up two manila folders, which he handed to Clay and Lane. She opened hers, staring down mutely at the FFF name, which somebody had circled with a red magic marker and drawn a slash through.

"These are dossiers about the FFF, which is holding a three-day extravaganza beginning on Friday in Lake Haven," Marcus continued as he paced across the room. "I'd like the two of you to infiltrate the show."

He smacked the desk with the palm of his hand. "We must protect the people of Florida from these swindlers."

"Excuse me," Clay interrupted. "But are we talking about cats?"

"Not just any cats," Marcus said, rapping the desk again. "Show cats. Cats like Prune that have a right to be admired and recognized as outstanding examples of their breeds."

Lane bit her lip as a suspicion formed. Marcus's presentation was way too passionate to be unbiased. "Prune didn't enter one of these FFF shows by any chance, did she?"

Marcus held up the cat by its midsection and thrust it into the air, the way the king of the lions did in that Disney movie when introducing his heir to its subjects. Prune's long pointed tail dipped as she stared at them with her green gaze out of her oddly shaped head.

"Does this look like a cat that should finish out of the ribbons to you?" Marcus asked. "Especially considering other organizations have bestowed her with the title of Grand Champion?"

"Every cat has its day," Clay said carefully. "Maybe it wasn't hers."

Marcus shook his head vehemently. "No. The FFF shows are fixed, I tell you. I know it. I just need proof. Now, do you want to do the story or not?"

The question hung in the air like a challenge, which Lane wasn't about to refuse. She didn't know anything about cat shows, but she enjoyed being around cats. It would be a snap.

"*I* want to do the story," she answered quickly, before Clay could, "but I understand if Clay isn't up to the challenge."

He bristled and she cursed herself for forgetting one of her father's cardinal rules: *If you issue a dare, you better prepare for a rousing affair.*

"Of course I'm up to it," Clay said, and Lane's

eyes automatically flew to his lap. She closed her eyes briefly, glad he couldn't read her mind. Of course her father hadn't meant that kind of an affair.

Marcus gave a satisfied, catlike smile. "Then may the best man..." he paused and bowed in Lane's direction, "or woman win."

IF THERE WAS A SINGLE SUBJECT Clay wanted to avoid writing about, it was cats. He didn't have anything against them, but they were the enigma of the animal world.

Now, dogs. That was a different story.

Dogs let you know when they were hungry or playful or sleepy. Dogs slobbered over you and were always glad to see you, no matter what offense you'd committed. They didn't make you try to figure out what was going on inside their heads.

In short, dogs acted pretty much like human males. Cats were like women: alien and impenetrable.

Take Lane, for example. She was standing next to him in the *Splash!* lobby, her eyes straight ahead as they waited for the elevator, as though she had absolutely nothing to say to him.

Well, he had a few things to say to her. The elevator doors opened and she sashayed inside, looking so delightful in that tight skirt that he forgot what those things were. When the doors started to close, he realized he'd also forgotten to move.

He stuck out a hand to stop the doors and slipped in beside her. "You can't get away from me that easily," he said with a grin that elicited nothing but a glare.

He almost asked her what sin he could have possibly committed considering *she* was the one going after *his* job. But starting an argument seemed unwise when he was still set on knocking down the ridiculous professional barrier that she was keeping between them.

"This assignment would be a lot more pleasant if we weren't at each other's throats," he told her when they were shut up in the elevator car. "Don't get me wrong. I'm not about to concede the job, but I'm up for calling a truce when we're not working."

"Oh, please," she said as the elevator slowed to a stop. "Like I'm naïve enough to believe that."

Before Clay could reply, the doors slid open and a teenage boy with more holes than a lousy alibi walked in. His nose was pierced, a ring ran through one eyebrow and each earlobe sported three or four earrings. One side of his head was shaved, and the other sported long black hair dyed red at the ends. He slouched against the back of the cage, a study in black leather, as the doors closed on the three of them.

Clay leaned closer to Lane. He noticed that she didn't move, not away from him or toward him. He could smell the strawberry-scented shampoo she used on her shiny blond hair. "What did you mean by that crack?" he whispered.

She brushed a piece of lint off her skirt. When she spoke, she sounded so composed she could have been discussing the weather. "I let you sidetrack me from doing my job once, Clay. I don't intend to make the same mistake twice."

"What?" The word erupted from him, and the teenager straightened and stared openly at them. Clay made himself lower his voice. Once they got to the lobby floor Lane would be gone, along with his chance to talk to her. "When did I ever stop you from doing your job?"

"I figured out a long time ago that your ulterior motive the night we met was to keep me from finding out you were about to run an exposé on the mayor."

One of the mysteries of the past year was suddenly closer to being solved. Lane had repeatedly told him she considered their jobs on opposing newspapers to be a problem, but he'd never understood her obstinate refusal to try to overcome it.

"That's not true," he blurted out.

She tapped her foot, as though she couldn't wait to get off the elevator and away from him. That did it. He hit the red button on the elevator panel, and the car screeched to a halt.

"I should point out that there's someone inside the elevator with us," Lane said. She didn't seem the least bit alarmed. Darn it, why was she so unruffled when he felt like kicking something?

"Hey, don't sweat it," the kid said, loudly smacking his gum. "Soap operas are where it's at, man, and this is like a live performance. I'll be so quiet you won't notice me."

Hoping the kid kept his vow, Clay looked deep into Lane's inscrutable brown eyes. "Listen to me. I didn't know you were working on a story about Mayor Quintana when we met."

She raised her eyebrows no more than a fraction of an inch. "So it was a happy coincidence that your story on the corrupt mayor came out the same day as my feature on his vintage collection of Ink Blot Man comic books?"

"Ink Blot Man. I love that dude," the teen exclaimed excitedly. "Hey, does he have issue 616? That's the one where Blotto squirts Armageddon Man in the eye so he can't see where he's aiming the nuclear weapon."

"I thought you were going to be quiet," Clay said.

The kid made a zippering motion across his mouth. "Like a corpse."

Clay returned his attention to Lane. "Yeah, it was a coincidence. You and I never got around to talking about what we did for a living."

Hell, when he'd run into her outside City Hall, the attraction had been so overpowering he hadn't been able to think of anything but asking her out. She'd said yes, they'd met at a downtown restaurant and gone on from there. "Remember, we had other things on our minds that night on the beach."

"What kinda things?" the teen asked.

Clay glared at him, and the boy put three fingers against his mouth. His nails were painted black. "Sorry, man. Go ahead. Explain why you lied to her about that mayor dude."

"I did not lie to her," Clay said, trying to hold on to his temper. Lane's expression hadn't changed. How did she do it? How did she maintain her composure like that?

"So you didn't want to scoop the *Times*?" she asked.

"Of course I did," Clay said. She gave him a smug look and restarted the elevator. He felt like whining along with the sound the gears made.

He rubbed the back of his neck and tried one more time. "You've got to know that night on the beach didn't have anything to do with newspapers."

"Cut the suspense," the teen complained. "How can I follow the plot line if no one tells me what the deal is with the beach?"

"Corpses don't ask questions," Clay snapped as the elevator car came to a stop on the lobby floor.

"What happened on the beach didn't matter," Lane said with a weary, bored air. "What matters is that we're up for the same job and I intend to get it."

She walked away in her too-tight skirt, and Clay couldn't think of anything to say to bring her back. He shot a look of annoyance at the black-jacketed teen.

"Hey, man, what you lookin' at me for?" the kid asked. "You're the one who blew it."

STACY PLOPPED DOWN on the black-and-white comforter Lane had special ordered to make her bed resemble a giant sheet of newspaper. She grabbed one of the red accent pillows, hugged it and closed her eyes as though imagining something human in her arms.

"Did I tell you that Ted and I had such a good time on our date that we're seeing each other again tonight?" she gushed, a breathy sigh in her voice.

"Only about fifty times," Lane said, trying not to grumble. She was happy for Stacy, but why was her sister lucky enough to fall for a strife-free guy while she had the hots for her archenemy?

She examined the clothes hanging in her closet, deliberately passing up her sexy little black dress for a staid black pantsuit. She was packing for a cat show, not for seduction.

"His lips are as soft as marshmallows," Stacy

said as Lane folded the pantsuit and laid it in her suitcase. "When I kiss him, I just want to eat him up. Yum!"

"Sounds painful," Lane said. "For him, I mean."

Lane needn't have added the clarification, because Stacy didn't seem to be listening.

"We're thinking of going to the beach tonight," she said dreamily, then suddenly became more lucid. "Oh, I remember what I needed to ask you. How did you and Clay manage without getting sand in all kinds of unwise places? Did you use a blanket or what?"

Lane's face felt as though it had been blasted by a furnace. She pulled a couple of ultra-modest blouses off their hangers and shoved them in the suitcase. For good measure, she added some vests. If she layered her clothes, she'd be more apt to come to her senses before Clay could coax her into taking all of them off.

"Stacy, I am not going to get into this with you."

Stacy grinned and got to her knees on the bed. "Why, Lane, is that a blush I see?"

"It is not," Lane denied, angry at herself for reacting. It was her rotten luck that the merest mention of Clay caused her body to attain ovenlike temperatures. When he had leaned close to her in the elevator the other day, she'd gone so weak in the knees she'd thought she was melting.

"How are you going to get through this weekend without ravishing him? Have you thought about that?"

Instead of answering, Lane threw a modest cotton nightgown into her suitcase. If she'd owned a chastity belt, she would have added it to the stack.

Stacy promptly plucked out the voluminous long-sleeved gown. She shook her head, her pretty face contorted in a grimace.

"No, no, no. This won't do at all," she said, walking over to the open drawer where Lane kept her night clothes. She rummaged through it and took out a black lace teddy that Lane had bought on a whim and never worn. "This is more like it. Believe me, Clay won't be able to resist you."

"Give me that," Lane said, grabbing for the teddy. Stacy laughingly held it out of reach. Lane crossed her arms over her chest. "I'm going to Lake Haven to expose deceit in the cat show industry, not to seduce a man."

"Oh, really." Stacy wagged her eyebrows suggestively. "I've never been to Lake Haven, but it sounds impossibly romantic. What's going to stop you from multi-tasking while you're there?"

"My desire to write for *Splash!* Do you realize what a fantastic opportunity this is, Stacy? I can make a giant leap in my career instead of taking the usual baby steps."

"I thought you wanted to build a career in newspapers. It's all you've ever talked about. You're so wrapped up in your job, you work every weekend and hardly ever take a vacation."

"I'm not working the next three days."

"Yeah, but two of them are Saturday and Sunday, which most normal people have off. You work so much overtime you barely ever date. Clay's about the only man you've shown any interest in."

Lane pointedly ignored her sister's comment about Clay and focused on what she'd said about her career. "I'm only twenty-four, Stace. I wouldn't have to stay at *Splash!* forever, just long enough to build my portfolio so I can move to a really top newspaper.''

''Moving over to a magazine so you can get a job at a newspaper when you already work for one seems convoluted to me. That's what I was going to tell you in the coffee shop before we got distracted.''

Lane refused to dwell any further on the things about Clay that had distracted her—his hard-muscled body, those misty ocean eyes, that low, sexy rumble in his voice when he…

''Are you listening to me, Lane?'' Stacy asked, and Lane realized she must have missed her sister's last few sentences.

''Sure, I am. Now listen to me. Marcus Miller approached *me*, Stace. He challenged *me* to write a better story than Clay. And you know what Daddy always says about a challenge.''

Stacy frowned, as though she couldn't recall. Lane could hardly believe it.

''If you're not up to a challenge, you're down for the count,'' Lane supplied. ''I'm definitely up for the challenge. All I need to do is get the right cat fanciers to talk to me.''

''And how are you going to do that?'' Stacy dropped back down on the bed and drew her legs under her. ''The people at the show might open up to you if you were one of them, but you don't have a show cat.''

''I most certainly do,'' Lane proclaimed. As if on cue, her precious pet entered the room with slow, deliberate steps. ''How could you have forgotten Marigold?''

"Oh, I didn't forget," Stacy said. "But don't you think she's a bit...portly to compete in a show?"

"She's not portly." Lane grunted a little as she picked up the cat and hugged her. "She's on the pleasantly plump side. Some judges like that in a female. Right, sweetheart?"

Stacy cleared her throat. "But wouldn't it be better if you had a purebreed?"

"It's abundantly clear that Marigold's an Angora," Lane said while she stroked the cat. "She looks exactly like the pictures of those beautiful cats in the breed books."

"She's not even white. She's gold. Sort of."

"The breed books say Angoras don't have to be white anymore to compete in shows."

"But what about her coarse fur and those eyes?" Stacy asked. "And that face? Isn't it a little, uh, squashed for an Angora?"

Lane burrowed one of the cat's ears against her chest and covered the other with a hand. "Shhh. You don't want to upset her. Especially because she has a gorgeous face."

Though not as gorgeous as Clay's, a wayward thought made its way to her brain.

"If you really want the job, Marigold might not be the way to go," Stacy said. "You'll already be distracted enough by Clay. How are you going to expose fraud if you spend the rest of your time fussing over Marigold?"

"Mr. Miller arranged for a professional cat handler to meet us in Lake Haven," she said, ignoring her sister's comment about Clay. "He'll get the cats in show condition so we're able to circulate more freely."

"Thank goodness," Stacy muttered. "Let's hope he can do for Marigold what Henry Higgins did for Eliza Dolittle."

"Nothing against Professor Higgins, but Marigold has more class than Eliza could ever hope to have," Lane said, putting down her cat. One of Marigold's beautiful milky-green eyes gazed back at her before the cat gurgled, gagged and coughed out a hairball.

Lane shut her suitcase with a thump. It wasn't until the next morning, during the long drive to Lake Haven, that she realized she'd neglected to remove the sexy black teddy Stacy had packed.

3

"SO, GIRL, what should we do next?"

Clay didn't expect the tiny cat making herself at home on the hotel's king-size bed to answer, but he wished she'd stop staring at him. Her eyes were so yellow he felt like he was drowning in a vat of butter.

Even if the cat could speak, there wouldn't be much to say. They'd checked into the hotel an hour ago, and already they'd exhausted just about everything there was to do.

Although Clay had ridden by dozens of scenic horse farms on the six-hour drive from Miami, the landscape had changed into a low-lying wasteland of scrub and burnt-out sky as he got nearer to Lake Haven.

The town, if you could call it that, didn't have a discernible center. Its main landmarks were the community college where the cat show was taking place and a couple of hotels. For urban sprawl, Lake Haven boasted a gas station, a convenience store, a pizza parlor and a barber shop.

He'd hung around the hotel lobby for a while, hoping to meet some cat owners before the show began tomorrow. Or, better yet, to run into Lane. But he didn't have any luck on either front. It turned out the other hotel in town, one of those no-frills motor inns where guests parked an arm's length from their doors, was offering a cat-lover's rate.

He shifted uncomfortably, awash in the cat's amber gaze. Even if the other hotel hadn't been full, he wasn't sure he'd qualify for the special.

"How 'bout you and me play a game?" he asked, searching the hotel room for something resembling a stick. He came up with a striped mixing straw that had been left by the mini-bar.

He tossed it across the expanse of thick green carpet, which had a passing resemblance to grass.

"Fetch," he said, adding enthusiasm to his voice. "Go on, fetch."

The cool stare the cat slanted him reminded him of the ones Lane Brooks was so fond of giving him.

He rubbed the back of his neck, aware that he hadn't been able to fully exorcise Lane from his mind since the night they'd met. He'd dated plenty in the past year, but had yet to meet a woman who stirred him as much as she did.

Despite the ludicrous charges she'd made in the elevator, he still thought the weekend was the perfect opportunity to improve relations between them. Once Lane got to know him better, she'd realize he'd never resort to underhanded tactics to get a story. She might even grow to like him.

"After all, I'm a likable guy. Everybody says so," he told the cat. He reached over to pet her, hoping to make friends, but her eerie gaze was so unwavering that he drew back his hand.

It was amazing that such a tiny animal could make him feel so uncomfortable. His cat of choice would have been a dog-size Maine Coon, but Ted's sister

Heidi was the only cat breeder he knew and she bred the diminutive Singapuras.

"So what do you think is keeping this professional cat guy?" Clay asked aloud. He'd left Wade McCoy word through the hotel's messaging system ten minutes ago that they had arrived. He shifted nervously. "Okay, I realize you don't know where he is any more than I do. But could you stop staring at me?"

The cat didn't so much as blink her yellow eyes. Clay rubbed his mouth. Maybe he should have spent last night reading up on cat behavior instead of the workings of cat shows.

"I don't suppose you want to learn how to roll over?" he asked. She looked supremely bored by the prospect. "Nah, I didn't think so."

The knock on the door sounded like salvation. He leaped to his feet so quickly that the sudden shift of weight caused the cat to bounce. He was across the room, pulling open the door, before his visitor could knock again.

The tall, rangy man standing there was in his fifties with sun-weathered skin, a ten-gallon hat and worn leather cowboy boots. He looked like he had just ridden in off the range. "Howdy," he said.

Clay's spirits sank. "You must have the wrong room, pardner," he said, tapping the room-number plate on the door.

The man's friendly grin didn't waver. "You Clay Crawford?"

Clay nodded, and the cowboy stuck out his large, callused hand. "Wade McCoy. Professional cat handler."

He engulfed Clay's hand in a viselike grip that

was mercifully brief, then brushed by him into the room. He walked on bow legs, the spurs of his boots jingling. "Now where's that little darlin' of yours?"

For an instant, Clay thought he'd said *dogie*.

The cat was lying on the bed in the same bored pose, but the pint-size traitor rose on her delicate legs and purred when she saw the cowboy. She moved toward him without hesitation.

Wade plucked her off the bed and brought her face close to his. "Hello, little lady." She looked no bigger than a mouse in his oversized hands. He examined her short-haired coat, which was predominantly ivory with bands of brown on the hair shaft.

"She'll be in good show shape once I bathe her," Wade announced.

"Don't they use their tongues for that?" Clay asked, and Wade threw back his head and let out a laugh that sounded more like a merry roar.

"A greenhorn when it comes to cats, are you?" he asked as he moved across the room and picked up the phone. "You don't mind if I use this, do you?"

Clay didn't have a chance to answer before Wade requested that the operator connect him to Room 214. A moment later, he was bellowing, "Gosh, darlin', stay put for a minute and lemme try something."

Wade set the cat down and strode to the locked outer door that connected Clay's hotel room to the one next door. He unlocked it, drew it open and banged on the inner door as though hammering on a fence that needed mending.

Disturbing the peace probably wasn't something

he thought about while enjoying the wide open spaces of the range.

"Hey, easy there," Clay said before he heard the unmistakable click of a door being unlocked.

He winced, hoping the person whose peace Wade had been disturbing wasn't ill-tempered.

The woman who stood in the doorway holding a telephone was silhouetted by the light behind her, but Clay would have known Lane Brooks even if she'd been shrouded in darkness.

Her pantsuit looked like it had been designed to hide her curves, but it'd be a sub-zero day in Miami before he forgot what was underneath those clothes. She shifted slightly, bringing her exquisite features into focus. Her trendy glasses were perched on her nose, and it looked as though she'd been running her fingers through her fair hair. It made him wish he'd been the one who'd mussed it.

"I figured you were next door when I heard the meowing through the wall," the cowboy said, sticking out a hand after Lane replaced the phone on its cradle. "Wade McCoy, P.C.H. Nice to meet ya."

"Lane Brooks." Her brown eyes lit up with a smile bearing no resemblance to the arctic ones she gave Clay. She took Wade's hand as though she noticed nothing strange about a cat-handling cowboy but winced until the shake was over.

It wasn't until Lane spotted Clay that her expression cooled.

"Oh, hallo, Clay," she said in that unruffled voice he was beginning to hate. "What are you doing in Wade's room?"

"My room," he corrected. His body had begun to heat at the idea of nothing but a thin wall separating them while they slept, but the notion either hadn't occurred to her or didn't phase her. "Wade's here to collect Rover."

At their twin expressions of confusion, he gestured to the diminutive feline who had jumped back onto the mattress and was methodically licking its paws.

"Her registered name's Whisker Hamlet Roderica Verbena of Oszechowski," Clay said, surprised he remembered it all. Ted's sister had explained the naming system. Whisker Hamlet was the cattery where the cat was bred, Oszechowski the last name of the owner and Roderica Verbena the cat's actual name. "I thought that was too much of a mouthful for such a dainty little thing, so I call her Rover."

He assumed from Lane's polite expression that she didn't think much of the nickname, but, as usual, she kept her thoughts to herself. She turned to Wade.

"You probably want to meet Marigold." She put slight emphasis on the name, as though it were better suited for a cat. "I'll get her for you."

"Marigold," she called. "Come here, Mari."

Her voice held such reverence that Clay prepared himself for one of those beautiful, pampered cats that acted as though the world owed them something for gracing it with their presence.

Instead, the homeliest cat Clay had ever seen waddled into the room. She was both pigeon-toed and bowlegged, a painful-looking combination. Her coarse hair was vaguely golden but it wasn't thick enough to obscure her pug features and crossed eyes. Clay fought an urge to turn his head.

"Laugh's over." Wade threw back his head and chortled so that the gold cap on a back tooth was visible. "Where you hiding the real contestant?"

"Marigold is the real contestant," Lane said at the same time Rover let out a great meow and sprinted across the room, straight for the Homely One.

Before Lane could react, Clay bent down and scooped up Marigold, who probably weighed as much as a hardcover copy of an unabridged dictionary.

Hissing, Rover dug her tiny claws into Clay's pant leg as though he were a tree she was trying to scale to get to a particularly juicy morsel of fruit.

"Down, girl," Wade said, prying the cat off Clay. He shook his head in consternation. "This one's gonna need behavioral modification."

Lane's lightly perfumed scent and strawberry shampoo, a combination he sometimes smelled in his dreams, enveloped him as she came up beside him. She hadn't been this close to him since their sexy night a year ago. Too bad it was her cat who had enticed her to cross into his territory instead of him.

"Roderica's probably just jealous," she said, taking her cat from Clay and hugging the lucky creature to her perfectly formed breasts. "That happens a lot considering Marigold's an Angora."

Wade snorted in what sounded like disbelief. "You have papers calling that cat an Angora?"

Lane licked her luscious lips. "Well, no, but only because I got her at the pound. I'm sure she had papers at some point."

"I hate to break this to you, darlin', but that cat's no Angora. She's a..." Wade stopped and walked around Lane, examining her cat. "Heck, I don't know what she is. Domestic Long Hair's about the closest I can come. But she's no purebreed."

Lane's face fell at Wade's pronouncement. She

was hugging the cat, her face buried in its fur, as though she really loved it. As though she didn't realize it was the ugliest thing since Medusa.

"Look. On account of my reputation, they're letting us enter your cats in the show late. But there's no way that cat's competing against the Angoras," Wade was saying. "I think it'd be better if—"

Clay stepped between Wade and Lane. "I've been doing some reading up on cat shows, and it seems to me you could enter her in the household pets category."

"Well, sure I could, but I can't be expected to—"

"Yes, you can," Clay interrupted. "So Marigold isn't in show shape yet. So what? Isn't that what Marcus is paying you to do?"

"But I'm—"

"Supposedly the best darn cat wrangler in the business."

"Cat handler," Wade corrected, but Clay's strategy had worked. The cowboy was flattered. "All right, all right. I'll see what I can do."

Clay turned back to Lane and her ugly cat. For the first time since the night they'd met, he didn't feel as though he was slamming into an iceberg when her eyes met his.

Dare he hope that the thaw had begun?

LANE SPENT the next fifteen minutes listening to Wade's directions, gathering Marigold's supplies and puzzling over what Clay had just done for her.

She'd proved over the past year that she could resist his potent sex appeal, but that had largely been because she'd convinced herself he was shallow and self-serving.

But how did those impressions fit into the way he'd taken her side against Wade? Clay obviously had the good sense to recognize that the cat wrangler was wrong about Marigold's appeal, but why hadn't he kept quiet and watched Lane squirm?

"Okay, I give up," Clay said when he'd shut his hotel room door on Wade, their battling cats and assorted supplies. "Why have you been looking at me like I have an algebra problem tattooed on my forehead?"

She almost smiled at the analogy, but she couldn't let him know she appreciated his sense of humor.

"I've been trying to figure out your ulterior motive in talking Wade into keeping Marigold in the show."

He crossed his arms over his chest. He was wearing a short-sleeved Henley that was the perfect complement for his dark slacks, and she couldn't help noticing how the action made his biceps ripple. "What makes you think I *have* an ulterior motive?"

"Oh, come on, Clay. If you throw the competition a lifeline, you can't count on winning the tug of war."

"I take it that's another one of your father's sayings?"

"As a matter of fact, it is."

"So you can't believe I'd do something nice for you just because I wanted to?"

"What I can't believe is that you'd jeopardize your chances of working for *Splash!* by helping me."

He winced. "You don't think very highly of me, do you?"

"No, I don't," she said, telling herself the wince

didn't bother her. She absolutely, positively was not going to let herself like him. She was attracted to the man's body, not the man himself, and she'd do best to remember that.

Especially when they were in a confined space where the most prominent piece of furniture was a king-size bed. All she'd have to do is sit down on the mattress, cock a finger and she could live out those year-long fantasies of what it would be like to make love to him.

She doubted he'd object to stripping out of his costly clothing so she could run her hands over his smooth, powerful muscles. So she could feel her naked flesh against his. So she could press her lips wherever the urge struck her. So she could...

Stop it! the sane part of her brain screamed.

She shook a finger at him mostly so she could get the benefit of some air on her flushed face. "It took a lot of gall for you to be nice to me like that. See that you don't do it again."

"Because of the ulterior motive?" he asked.

"Exactly." Her mind shouted retreat when he moved across the room toward her, but she held her ground and raised her chin.

"Okay, you got me," he said, lifting his palms. "I admit it. I did have an ulterior motive."

"Aha! I knew it all along," she said, trying to dislike him. But when she looked into his gray-blue eyes, they didn't seem devious. They seemed...kind. And hot. Oh, so very hot.

"But you're wrong about what I hoped to gain." His fingers came up to lightly trace her lips. His ocean eyes ran over her face. "What I want has nothing to do with the magazine."

Her heart beat so crazily that she was afraid he might see it jumping against her chest wall. With an effort, she made her voice airy and light. "What do you want then?"

"A kiss," he said, and she could feel his warm breath against her lips. "Just one kiss."

She forced out a laugh. They were alone with a bed in a hotel room, for heaven's sake. Did he honestly think they'd be able to stop at a single kiss?

"I hardly think what you did warrants that drastic a thanks."

His eyes twinkled as he settled his hands on her shoulders and gazed down at her. She was so used to keeping her distance that she hadn't realized how very tall he was. The top of her head came no higher than his nose.

"Then think of it as a competition," he whispered. "After we're through, we'll decide which of us kisses better."

She could kiss better, of course, and she'd prove it. Lane narrowed her eyes in determination, whipped off her glasses and tipped up her chin. She was prepared to move her mouth forward when she noticed the corner of his mouth jerk upward.

"You're trying to trick me, aren't you?" she accused.

The rest of his beautiful mouth curved into the smile. "Yeah," he admitted. "And, for a minute there, I thought it was going to work."

She backed up, and his hands fell from her shoulders. Keep retreating, she told herself firmly to stop her feet from reversing directions and rushing forward. But she wouldn't gain anything by letting Clay know how very much she desired him.

"Ah, Laney, don't look so distrustful. I want to kiss you because I want to kiss you, not because I want to beat you out of a story."

"Don't do it again," she warned.

"Want to kiss you?" He laughed, and the low sound vibrated through her. "Sorry to break this to you, sweetheart, but I can't stop wanting to kiss you."

"I meant don't *try* to kiss me, and you know it."

"But if you don't try, you can't win," he said logically. "Doesn't your father have a saying about that?"

Skip the coin toss, and nobody will carry you off the field on their shoulders.

"If he did, I wouldn't tell you about it," Lane retorted, and he let out another sexy laugh. She could get used to that laugh. And the smile that started at his lips, reached his eyes and seemed to draw her into it.

From somewhere, a knock sounded.

Exactly what she needed, she thought. Someone to knock some sense into her.

"Aren't you going to get that?" Clay asked.

She blinked. "Get what?"

His smile grew, telling her the question was a tactical error. "Somebody's knocking on the door. The one in your hotel room."

"I knew that," she said breezily and crossed through the set of connecting doors, chastising herself for staring at him. Glaring at him was all well and good, but she didn't think that's what she'd been doing.

"Surprise!" Stacy said when she pulled open the door. Her sister clapped her hands and bounced on her toes. Ted Green was standing next to her, his arm flung over her shoulders. "You'll never guess who we ran into in the hallway. Marigold. With this great big cowboy and this wee cat who was hissing at her. That's how we knew where to find you."

She turned toward the man at her side as though he was the sun and she a flower that had been in the shade too long. A frisson of alarm skittered through Lane. She'd taken Stacy's effusiveness about Ted in stride before now, but she hadn't expected her to show up in a strange city with him.

"You remember Ted Green, don't you?" Stacy asked. "Turns out he's just as spontaneous as I am. Tell her what you said when I suggested driving up here for the weekend, Teddy Bear?"

"Let's do it," he said, pumping his fist. Lane remembered he'd also done so the first time they'd met, suggesting that he watched far too many football games.

"Isn't he cute?" Stacy gushed.

Ted leaned down and gave her a quick kiss on the lips. "Not nearly as cute as you."

Stacy basked in the glow of his compliment. "We thought the name Lake Haven sounded terribly romantic. Moonlight swims and that kind of thing."

Lane raised her brows. "If there's a lake anywhere around here, it must've dried up in the Florida sun."

"Then we'll find a hot tub. Or a bathtub." Stacy sounded positively giddy. "Anything can be romantic if you're with the right man."

"Hey, you don't happen to know where Clay is, do you?" Ted asked, as though, heaven forbid, he thought his friend was the right man for Lane.

"Right here, buddy." Clay's voice drifted from

behind her, making Lane realize he must've followed her into the room when he heard the commotion.

"Oh, my heavens," Stacy exclaimed, covering her mouth with her hands. She elbowed Ted. "I told you they had the hots for each other, but I never thought we'd find them sharing a room."

"We are not—" Lane began.

"This is so great." Stacy opened her arms and enveloped Lane in a hug so tight that for a moment she had to gasp for air. "We're dating best friends."

"Clay and I are not dating," Lane denied in a strangled voice.

Stacy drew back, her features clouded with concern. "It's none of my business, hon, but maybe you should rethink sleeping with him if you're not dating."

"I'm not sleeping with him, either," Lane said through clenched teeth.

"Much to my sorrow," she heard Clay say, much too close to her ear. She swiveled her head, and he gave her that confident, nearly irresistible smile. "Although I'm working on getting her to agree to an open-door policy."

"No way, José," Lane said sweetly as Stacy pulled Ted by the hand into the room and started exploring.

"Oh, look, Teddy. Their rooms have connecting doors. Did you ask for them this way, Lane?"

"Hardly," she said under her breath. "Clay and I are competing for a job, remember? The cat wrangler opened the doors. They'll be shut the rest of the time."

"On the contrary, the door on my side will be wide open at all times," Clay whispered so only she could hear, the words sending a sensual shiver through her that she tried desperately to hide.

Lane crossed her arms over her chest at the same time that Stacy wrapped her arm around Ted's waist. Her sister was dressed in an unremarkable ensemble of blue jeans and a cropped shirt, but happiness shone out of her eyes, making her look even more beautiful than usual.

"The cat show doesn't start until tomorrow morning, right?" Stacy said. "Teddy and I are already unpacked, so how about all of us going out for pizza?"

"I'll pass," Lane said quickly, horrified at the prospect of spending more time in Clay's presence. She could only carry this self-control thing so far. Besides, she had work to do.

"If you're thinking about hanging around the hotel to make contacts, I already tried that," Clay said. "Seems like almost everyone else is staying at the other hotel."

Then she'd see about switching her accommodations, which would eliminate the problem of their side-by-side rooms.

"You won't get a room over there," Clay said as though he'd read her mind. "I tried and it's booked."

She gave an imperious toss of her head. "I prefer to check that out for myself, thank you very much."

"Lane," Stacy said, making her name sound as though it had two syllables. "Clay wouldn't lie to you. He's not the type."

"Yeah, Clay's as honest as a ref who's not on the take," Ted chimed in like the loyal friend he undoubtedly was. "If he says the hotel's booked, it's booked."

"Don't give her a hard time, guys. Laney's a professional. She needs to do what she thinks best." Clay wasn't touching her, but his gaze was so intimate it felt as if he was running his long, strong fingers over her sensitive skin. "But think about this, Laney. People with cats have to eat, too. Your best chance of running into them is probably at the pizza parlor."

"That makes sense, Lane," Stacy said. "I bet the place will be crawling with people. As far as I could see, it's the only restaurant in town."

Clay cocked a dark eyebrow. "You don't want me to get the advantage before we even start to play, do you?"

Lane chewed her bottom lip while she considered what he'd said. It made sense, but it also reeked of trickery.

"You're trying to play on my competitive nature to get me to come to dinner, aren't you?" she asked.

"Guilty as charged." He grinned unrepentantly. "But doesn't it make sense to stick close to the competition so you know what you're up against?"

Much as she hated to admit it, he was right. She couldn't believe he wanted her along at dinner purely for the pleasure of her company, so that meant he was up to no good.

Unfortunately, the only way to unearth his nefarious intentions was to do as he wanted.

"I'll get my purse," Lane said, eyeing him closely for a sign that he was gloating. She was absurdly glad when she detected the merest glimmer of smugness in his smile.

She worked up some healthy resentment, successfully distracting herself from her somersaulting stomach and the joyful anticipation rushing through her body.

If she had to suffer through a meal with Clay Crawford to achieve her ultimate goal of beating him out of a job, so be it.

LANE FOUGHT BACK the hormones that raged whenever Clay Crawford so much as moved one of his sexy muscles as she sent a dark look around the interior of the pizza parlor.

Red vinyl booths rimmed a dimly lit room that was dotted with a couple of pool tables, a jukebox and a table in the center of the room earmarked for the all-you-can-eat buffet.

Not that it looked as though the buffet table got much action. Aside from their foursome, the only diners were an elderly couple two booths away and a teenage girl staring sullenly into an open textbook.

Considering that the couple wasn't speaking English and the girl looked as though she barely spoke at all, Lane doubted any of them would be founts of information on cat shows.

Clay caught her eye and gave her a grin that managed to be both friendly and sexy at once, plunging her into a darker mood.

She tried to slide farther away from him but her side was already plastered against the cool brick wall. The other side of her body, the one inches from his, was hotter than Hades. A dichotomy that must be bad for her health, just as Clay Crawford was bad for her.

"And here I was hoping you were going to stick

close to the competition," he said, his ocean eyes twinkling.

Lane's response was automatic. "Get too close to the competition and prepare to get smacked upside the head."

Clay screwed up his face. "What's that supposed to mean?"

"Daddy's a football coach, remember." Stacy put her elbows on the table and leaned forward. "Although I never did think that particular saying made sense. I mean, how are you supposed to tackle someone if you're not close to them?"

"He meant it figuratively, not literally," Lane said. "Tackling's got nothing to do with it."

"Too bad." Clay waggled one of his sexy brows at her. It told her too clearly that his form of tackling wouldn't hurt at all.

She clenched her fists to ward off the all-body tremble she felt coming on and made a point of giving their surroundings a leisurely perusal. When she felt sure she'd shaken off the tremble, she swept a hand to indicate the rest of the restaurant.

"I thought you said this place would be crawling with people," she accused. Even though she knew that the dearth of clientele wasn't Clay's fault, it made her feel better to blame him.

"*I* said that," Stacy piped up helpfully. "Clay said you'd have a better chance of running into people here than you would in your hotel room."

"Thanks for clearing that up, Stacy," Clay said. "Lane doesn't always give me the benefit of the doubt."

"I don't know why," Stacy said brightly, reaching across the table and covering his hand. "You're absolutely delightful. Deep down, I'm sure Lane thinks so, too.''

Lane's inclination was to snap at her traitorous sister for defecting to the enemy's camp, but instead she composed her features and picked up her menu. Sometimes feigning ignorance was as close as you could come to bliss.

She was about to open the menu when the name printed across the top of it registered. It was Clay's fault she hadn't noticed it before. She would have if she hadn't been so focused on resisting him.

"Don't you think Mahatma's Pizzeria is an odd name?" she asked, whispering so her voice wouldn't carry across the barren landscape of the restaurant.

"It's a darling name," Stacy said. She'd removed her hand from Clay's and was gazing at Ted. She looked so mesmerized Lane was tempted to count to three and snap her fingers.

A middle-aged waitress wearing a pumpkin-colored Eat at Mahatma's T-shirt that hugged her ample breasts and clashed with the brassy red highlights in her hair approached the table.

"Sorry I didn't get over here sooner, but I'm not used to working a crowd," she said.

"This is a crowd?" Lane looked around in case she'd missed a hungry horde demanding to be fed. She caught a glimpse of the backs of the elderly couple before they slipped out the door, reducing the number of other diners to one.

"It's a crowd for us," the waitress answered. "We don't usually get anyone in here 'cept for Mahatma's folks and my girl over there."

"You must be pleased that your daughter enjoys the food here," Lane said politely.

The waitress let out a guffaw so great it nearly exposed her tonsils. "Are you kidding me? Bambi doesn't eat here. She's just not allowed to leave 'til she finishes her homework."

"Are you trying to tell us the pizza isn't good?" Clay asked the question that would be on the mind of any good reporter, not that Lane was ready to admit that he was a good reporter. At least not aloud.

"Depends on what you consider good food," the waitress said mysteriously, prompting Lane to flip open the heavy plastic menu. Clay, Stacy and Ted did the same.

The listings were enough to make watering taste-buds dry up like dew in the Great Indian Desert. The house specialty pizza featured toppings of pickled ginger, minced mutton and tofu. Another suggested choice was the Mayo Jaga Pizza, a combination of mayonnaise, potato and bacon.

"Mahatma's from India, and his wife's Japanese," the waitress explained. "I keep telling them rural Florida's not ready for this, but they're resisting. We got squid ink pizza and eel pizza. If those don't strike your fancy, we got green-pea pizza from Brazil and curry pizza from Pakistan."

"How about pepperoni?" Lane asked hopefully.

"Sorry, hon. The best I can do is tomato sauce and cheese. That's the only concession Mahatma's making to the masses."

"I read somewhere that squid is an aphrodisiac," Stacy said excitedly. "Let's get that."

"I thought it was oysters that were aphrodisiacs," Ted said.

"Close enough. They're both sea creatures,"

Stacy said, practically dancing in her seat with culinary anticipation.

"Then let's go for it." Ted nuzzled her sister's neck, proving he was already feeling amorous enough. Clay shifted. His hip bumped Lane's, infusing her with warmth. She had a mad urge to make a grab for him, drag him off to a back room and have her way with him. Obviously, she didn't need an aphrodisiac, either.

"I'm game," Clay said, staring straight at Lane as he closed his menu with a thump.

"Then so am I," Lane said, although it wasn't what she'd been prepared to say a moment ago.

After the waitress was gone, Ted leaned back in the booth, his arm casually draped around Stacy's shoulder. Another alarm sounded inside Lane. She had no doubt her sister's feelings for Ted were genuine, but what did Stacy really know about him? He could be a player with a dozen women on the side, and Stacy could be headed for heartache.

"Just our kind of place, huh, Clay?" Ted asked.

Lane couldn't keep her eyes from rolling. "I would've thought a five-star restaurant with a maitre d' was more Clay's kind of place," she muttered, much more loudly than she intended.

Ted let out a loud, boisterous laugh. "You sure you're talking about my man Clay? This man worships at the altar of the pizza god. I bet we've hit every dive in Miami searching for the ultimate pie. We're talking some seriously bad pizza."

"Pizza's never bad if you wash it down with beer," Clay said, as though he were a regular guy instead of a socialite who'd grown up rich and pampered.

"Oh, yes it is," Ted said. "Remember that pizza place in Gainesville you liked when we were in college? The one owned by the oil company? That was some greasy pie."

"You went to the University of Florida?" Lane looked at Clay directly for the first time in five minutes. Considering his family's riches, she'd have guessed Dartmouth or Brown.

"We both did," Ted answered for him.

"I bet you were cuuute in college," Stacy said before Lane could question Ted further about Clay. She stroked a hand down Ted's face. "Wasn't he, Clay?"

"He was never my type," Clay joked, but spent the next fifteen minutes patiently answering Stacy's endless questions about Ted Green as Lane worried about her sister's fixation with the man.

By the time the waitress arrived with the squid pizza, Lane almost forgot she'd been dreading it—until she got a look at the pie. Pale squid floated atop an inky sauce that had been sprinkled with chopped tomatoes.

"It's black," she said.

"Of course it's black." The waitress began slicing the pizza with a large knife, cutting into it with gusto. "It's not called squid ink pizza for nothing."

"Let me try." Stacy eagerly took a piece and bit into it. She'd barely finished chewing when she started making eyes at Ted. He picked up a slice, chomped down on it and stared back at her just as lustily.

"Oh my gosh," Stacy exclaimed. "It works!"

"You don't mind if we leave, do you?" Ted asked them, already half rising. Lane was about to object but was struck dumb by the fact that the inside of his mouth was stained black.

"But we can't leave the pizza," Stacy said. "It has magical properties."

"By all means, take it," Clay said, echoing Lane's thoughts. In short order, their waitress had boxed the pizza and promised she'd come back with a simple tomato sauce and cheese pizza for Clay and Lane.

Stacy had always had a gift for speed, but she might have set a personal-best time on her way out the door. Ted wasn't far behind.

"Maybe we should have made them leave the pizza here."

Lane wasn't aware she'd said the words aloud until Clay turned toward her, his eyes probing. She prepared herself for a crack about aphrodisiacs, but he surprised her.

"You're worried about Stacy," he stated simply.

She was about to deny it, but something in his expression stopped her. Something that crept past her defenses and made her want to confide in him.

"I wasn't worried until she showed up in Lake Haven with him." She ran a hand over the bottom of her face. "You don't know Stacy. When she finds something she likes, she throws herself into it."

She leaned forward, wanting to make him understand. "You should have seen her when she was falling in love with running. She ran everywhere. Upstairs when it was time to take a shower. Through the halls at school. Down the aisle in church."

A hint of a grin stole across his face. "How old was she?"

"Nine, but that's beside the point. Her basic personality hasn't changed. She can still be obsessive."

"So you're afraid she's running after Ted?"

"Yes," Lane said, nodding. "Exactly."

He picked up the hand closest to him and laced his fingers with hers, giving a soft, comforting squeeze.

"From what I've seen, I'd say Ted wants to be caught."

"But for how long? Stacy's gone out with a lot of guys, but I've never seen her like this before. You don't know her, Clay. Once she makes up her mind about something, that's it. And I think she's already made her mind up about Ted."

"I still don't think that's a problem."

"But what if this is just a fling for him?" She heard her voice crack. "What if he's toying with her?"

Clay gave her hand another gentle squeeze. "Ted's not like that."

"But how can you be sure what another person's really like? I know you went to college together, but how well do you really know him?"

"I know him as well as I'd know a brother," he said, his expression serious. "I should. He spent more time living with my family when he was growing up than he did his own."

Lane cocked her head. "What do you mean?"

He bit his lip and gazed down at the table, making Lane realize the story wasn't one he'd be confiding if she weren't so worried about her sister.

"I met Ted in the sixth grade when we played for the same youth football league." He seemed to be weighing his next words and this time it was Lane who squeezed Clay's hand. That seemed to give him the encouragement he needed to continue. "He didn't have the most stable family life. So when things flared up at his house, he lived with us. Sometimes for months at a time.''

Lane felt her mouth drop open. Clay's family was so loaded with power, prestige and money that she felt sure he'd grown up in a beautiful house in an exclusive neighborhood. She couldn't reconcile his family opening such a home to a troubled young boy who wasn't a blood relation.

''But why would your parents allow that?'' she asked, forgetting to cloak the words in politeness.

''Because I asked.''

Her heart turned over as she imagined him as a child, so concerned about a friend that he'd convinced his parents to make a little boy's life better.

''Ted's good people, Laney,'' he said, and this time she couldn't doubt his sincerity. ''I don't know for sure how he feels about your sister, but I can tell you he wouldn't deliberately hurt her.''

''Thank you,'' she said and smiled at him.

His lips curved into a smile that reached his misty blue eyes, and she'd never seen him look so handsome. ''You're welcome.''

The silence between them stretched a beat, and Lane became aware that he was still holding her hand. A bolt of warmth, lightning quick and just as powerful, traveled up her arm. The smile faded from his eyes and they became darker, more dangerous. A heavy sensation weighed down her limbs, pressing on her heart, making it difficult to breathe.

He was so close that she could hear him inhale and exhale, feel his soft breaths on her face, smell the clean scent of him. Space. She needed space.

''We'd have more room if you moved to the other

side of the booth,'' she said, trying desperately to hide her reaction from him.

For a moment, he just stared at her with those dreamy, sea-blue eyes. She tried to get her heart to stop thundering and held her breath so he wouldn't be able to tell how quick her breathing had become. It dawned on her that the only place she wanted him to move was closer.

Just when she was convinced he'd refuse her request, he slid off the bench seat. When he was on his feet, he leaned over the table and smiled. A lock of his dark hair fell over his forehead and she had to clench her fist so she didn't brush it back.

''I'm going to play something on the jukebox,'' he told her in a soft voice. ''You don't suppose there are any songs on there about squid, do you?''

She tried not to be amused, but the corner of her mouth twitched and then it was too late. Her smile broke free and there was no hope of reining it back in.

Clay gave her an exaggerated wink and walked away, leaving her more confused than a dog at a cat show. What had just happened? One minute she was successfully resenting Clay for maneuvering her into having pizza with him and the next she was pouring out her worries over Stacy's new romance.

She'd let him hold her hand, listened to his soothing words and lost herself in his sympathetic gaze. When the story about his association with Ted had slipped out, she'd even forgotten to dislike him.

Heck, who was she fooling? She'd been so touched at his generous display of friendship that her heart had swelled with tenderness. For Clay Crawford, the bane of her existence.

She laughed softly to herself, amazed at the curve-ball life had thrown her. Maybe she'd been wrong about Clay all along. Maybe he was as handsome underneath his skin as he was in it.

She swung her head around, suddenly hungry for the sight of him. He wasn't at the jukebox, but at a booth deep in conversation with an elderly man with long, flowing white hair who seemed to have appeared out of nowhere. The man was wearing a base-ball cap picturing a cat and proclaiming "Grand-paw Power."

Lane's racing heart nearly slammed to a stop before it resumed a slow, painful beat.

She was the worst kind of fool. She'd been moon-ing over Clay for the last five minutes while he'd been cultivating a source that would elevate his story over hers.

How could she have let him slip under her de-fenses that way, especially because their past history had taught her he'd stop at nothing to get a story?

She took a fortifying breath and edged out of the booth, determined to find out what the source had told him. She was even more resolute to not be so easily duped the next time.

She wouldn't forget, even for a moment, that Clay Crawford's ultimate goal was to beat her out of a story.

"BELIEVE ME, it's not for lack of trying," Clay told the old-timer, "but unfortunately Lane's not my lady."

"What do you mean she's not your lady? I have eyes. I saw the two of you together. Why do you think I called you over here?"

"To tell me how you figured me for a cat man." Clay repeated what Elliot had told him when he'd beckoned him to his table with the crook of his pudgy finger. "Something about our kind knowing females need as much attention and admiration as felines."

"Exactly," Elliot said and meowed. At least Clay thought it must have been Elliot who meowed, because no cats were anywhere in sight. Elliot continued as if hadn't heard a thing, "My wife, God rest her soul, used to say, 'A cat man can make a woman purr.'"

He'd no sooner finished uttering the sentence before he made another cat sound, which this time might have been meant to drive home his point. Except it hadn't been a particularly happy sound, definitely more meow than purr.

"Did you hear something?" he asked Elliot.

He shook his head, and the long white strands of his hair looked like they were blowing in a breeze. "Nope. Nothing. Nada. Not a thing. Nuh-uh."

"I was sure I heard something. Something that sounded like a cat."

"Maybe it's because you have purring on the brain," Elliot supplied.

"But what I've been trying to say is that I can't figure out what would make Lane purr," Clay said, then shook his head in bewilderment.

Here he was, faced with the perfect opportunity to gather information about the cat show scene, and instead he was talking about Lane. He hadn't meant to. When the old man called him over to the table, he'd had every intention of talking cats. His future with *Splash!* depended on it.

But as soon as Elliot mentioned Lane, the cats faded in importance and Clay started spilling his soul. Maybe it was because, with his round face, short neck and long, flowing white hair, Elliot reminded him of Santa Claus.

But it was a good thing Clay was too old to sit on Elliot's knee, because he'd probably crush it. Elliot had padding to spare, but judging by how low he sat, he wasn't a whole lot taller than an elf.

"Let me see if I got this straight," Elliot said. "You and she are here for the cat show, only not together. You're not strangers, but you're not sweethearts, either."

"That about sums it up," Clay said.

Elliot rubbed the white stubble on his chin while he considered Clay. Finally, he rapped the table. Clay thought he heard another meow, but was half convinced he was hearing things.

"Seeing that you're a cat man, I might be able to help you get her to come around to your way of thinking."

The offer was so unexpected that Clay couldn't help but be intrigued. Elliot professed to understand women and had obviously had a good marriage. What would it hurt to accept his help? He caught sight of the menu on the table.

"If you're going to recommend the squid ink pizza, it won't work," Clay said, his taste buds already rebelling. "I'm not convinced squid's an aphrodisiac anyway."

"No, no, no." Elliot waved his hand back and forth like a human fan. "Squid's got nothin' to do with it. I was a PR man 'til I retired a few years back. All we need to do is implement a strategic plan to get this gal to fall for you.''

''How 'bout you run that by me again in plain English?''

''We think up stuff that'll make you look good in her eyes,'' he said, then lowered his voice. ''Shhh. Here she comes now. We don't want her to know what we were talking about.''

Clay turned, prepared for the sensual punch that hit him whenever he looked at Lane. His gaze traveled up to her face, hoping she'd smile at him again. She was smiling, all right, but he definitely wasn't the recipient.

''I'm Lane Brooks.'' She shouldered past him to stick out a hand to Elliot. ''I couldn't bear to sit over there by myself while the two of you were chatting about my favorite subject.''

She glanced over her shoulder to level Clay with her coolest look yet. It was clear that she thought he'd been pumping Elliot for information. The conclusion shouldn't have bothered him. It might be beneficial for his story if Lane believed Elliot had plied him with cat show particulars, but Clay suddenly couldn't stomach the psychological warfare.

''But we were talking about—''

''Cats,'' Elliot interrupted, tipping his hat and introducing himself. ''What else would two cat men like us be talking about except for cats? Yep. That's what we were talking about. Cats. Felines. Furry things with four legs.''

''But we weren't—''

''Cats is where it's at.'' Elliot shot Clay a warning look, and Clay nearly groaned aloud. Taking on a geriatric PR man suddenly seemed like a very bad idea. "That's what my wife, God rest her soul, used to say."

"My daddy always says that when the cat's away, you don't have to change the litter box."

Clay, who'd been about to make another stab at convincing Lane he hadn't been working on the story, stopped short. "What's that got to do with football?"

"Make everything about football, and you'll find yourself sleeping on the couch," Lane said. "And no, that's not one of my dad's sayings. That one's all Mom."

Lane smoothed the short blond hair back from her face and turned her attention to Elliot, who basked in the glow of her smile. "I would love to talk cats with you."

"Then by all means, join me," he said, then added as a seeming afterthought. "Both of you."

Elliot scooted over on the bench seat to make room for Lane, clearly forgetting that he was supposed to be throwing her together with Clay. Some PR man he was turning out to be.

Clay blew out a frustrated breath and took the opposite bench, noticing how Lane wouldn't look at him and how Elliot had started meowing again. Which made no sense, unless...

"You have a cat in here, don't you?" Clay asked Elliot.

As if on cue, the broad head of a snowy white cat peeked out of the canvas bag Clay belatedly noticed was resting on Elliot's lap. The cat had small, tufted ears set low on its head, and long, thick fur.

"Shhh." Elliot put a forefinger to his lips. "What are you trying to do? Get us thrown out of here?"

"Oh my gosh," Lane said in hushed tones, reaching over to stroke the cat's head. "This is one of the sweetest-looking cats I've ever seen. What's its name?"

"He's Persian, so I call him Kublai Khat, after the great ruler."

"Kublai Khan was Mongolian, not Persian," Clay pointed out.

"It's a wonderful name and don't let anyone tell you differently," Lane said, then shot Clay one of her patented glares. The precious moments they'd shared back in the booth seemed like they'd never been.

"I didn't say it wasn't a wonderful name," Clay said.

"Then you think that it is?" Lane challenged. How had he gotten himself into this situation? He looked to his PR man for help, but Elliot had his arms folded over his chest. His brows were drawn so tightly together they resembled a strip of snow.

"I think that Kublai Khat has a better ring than Aga Khat," Clay said, refraining from explaining that naming the cat after the Aga Khan made more sense. Aga was from India, which was closer to Persia than Kublai's China.

She dismissed him with a chilly toss of her head and went back to stroking the cat. "I bet Kublai Khat does very well in shows."

"Never finished out of the top three yet," Elliot said, puffing out his chest.

"I would have been shocked if he had," Lane said.

Over the next forty-five minutes, Clay marveled at the way Lane got Elliot to open up about himself and his cat. The cynic in him wanted to believe that she was more interested in getting a good story than she was in Elliot, but the realist knew that wasn't the case.

Over the past year, when he and Lane had been assigned to the same story, she'd scooped him as often as not. Now he'd figured out her secret. People talked to Lane because they sensed she was as genuinely interested in them as she was in what she was writing about.

"So you approve of the way the FFF is running the cat shows?" Lane asked when the waitress had cleared away the remains of a surprisingly tasty tomato-sauce-and-cheese pizza.

"Indeed I do. With a president like Pup, it can't go wrong."

"Pup?" Clay sat up straighter. "I thought Peter Doggett was president of the FFF."

"That's right, but most people call him Pup," Elliot said. "That's on account of the wooden puppy on wheels he used to pull around when he was a kid. He got so obsessive about it his mother eventually had to hide the thing from him. Pup cried like a baby."

"Poor thing," Lane said. "It's hard on the little ones when you take away their toys."

"Pup already had peach fuzz growing above his lip," Elliot said, "but my wife still felt sorry for him. She talked our son into letting him have a kitten and that was the end of his dog days."

"Are you saying the FFF president is your grandson?" Lane asked.

"And a fine grandson he is. Not to mention a staunch cat man. All us Doggetts are cat men."

Clay considered the ramifications of what the old man had revealed. He'd had a hard time swallowing Marcus's story of cat corruption but there might be something to it if Elliot's cat was prevailing in the shows his grandson ran.

But was Kublai Khat getting special treatment? Clay never shied away from a tough question, and he didn't intend to now.

"Doesn't it get sticky when Kublai Khat wins a ribbon? Aren't you afraid people think you're using your family connections to further your cat's career?"

Elliot gasped and placed a hand over his heart. "I was a PR man for twenty-five years. I go to the FFF shows, but I don't enter Kublai Khat. Pup wouldn't allow it anyway. I've taught him to avoid even the appearance of impropriety."

"So you're saying the FFF shows are clean?" Clay asked.

"As a cat," Elliot answered. "That's the way I taught Elliot junior to live his life, and that's the way he taught Pup. When we Doggetts win, we win fair and square."

"Then do you send out a press release letting everyone know you've won fair and square?" Lane asked, which seemed to puzzle Elliot. "I mean, because you're in PR?"

"Oh, yes, PR. You can never underestimate the power of good PR." Elliot jabbed at the air to drive home his point. His gaze slid to Clay, and a strange light came into his eyes.

"What do you say we play that game of pool right now?" he asked. "I can't let a challenge go unmet."

Alarm skittered through Clay, rendering him

speechless. He was fairly good at the game, owing to the hours he and Ted spent bent over a table at a neighborhood pub, but he and Elliot hadn't discussed that.

"What kind of challenge?" Lane asked suspiciously.

"I told Clay here I play pool like Liberace played the piano. He challenged me to one game." He winked at Clay with the eye farthest from Lane. "To the winner goes the glory."

And the girl, he could have added. But Clay wasn't so sure. He'd agreed to let Elliot come up with a strategic plan to help him win over Lane, but he'd have liked to know what it was before heading to the pool table.

He had a sinking feeling the plan might not bring him glory...but grief.

WHAT COULD CLAY possibly hope to prove by forcing a sweet old man like Elliot Doggett to demonstrate his pool-hall prowess?

Lane tapped her foot as she pondered the question, the canvas bag holding Kublai Khat's warm, white body cradled to her chest.

Competition usually energized her, but watching Clay and Elliot prepare for this test was like observing David and Goliath. That is, if long-haired David had been a little old man and Goliath a handsome, dark-haired hunk who liked to fool women into thinking he was a nice guy.

He'd almost had her duped with that heartwarming tale about Ted. But if Clay really did have a shred of decency, he wouldn't try to beat up on a man fifty years his senior. The top of Elliot's white head barely reached Clay's magnificently formed chest, for goodness sake.

Elliot picked up a cue nearly as long as he was tall and gave it a coating of chalk so thick it looked like green rain was falling to the floor.

"You want to break or should I?" Elliot asked, and Clay indicated the table was all his. Probably, Lane thought darkly, because there was some hidden advantage to going second.

"Here I go," Elliot said.

He placed the bottom of his palm on the table and pulled his hand back as though getting ready to wave. Even Lane, who never played pool, knew that wasn't the proper way to make a bridge. Before she could tell him so, he put the cue between his thumb and forefinger, pulled it back—and missed the cue-ball entirely.

"Your turn," he told Clay.

"You sure you want to play?" Clay asked, a sentiment Lane was positive he didn't mean. He was the one who'd challenged Elliot, wasn't he?

"Show me what you got, Sonny Boy," Elliot said.

Clay leaned over the table, looking sleek and athletic, and sent the cueball into the racked balls with maximum force. They scattered, and two solid-colored balls went into the corner pockets. He quickly sank another two.

"He's beating my behind, yessiree, he is," Elliot, the poor thing, said. "My wife, God rest her soul, used to say the only thing better than a cat man is a cat man who can play pool."

"She was proud of how well you played, then?" Lane asked, feeling sorrier for him by the minute. It was a blessing Mrs. Doggett wasn't alive to see her dear old husband get embarrassed by a young, strapping bully.

Clay sent a troubled glance their way, probably because he wasn't yet comfortable with his lead. He lined up the next shot, moving so naturally and effortlessly that Lane suspected him for a ringer. She almost wept with relief when he missed.

"Didn't leave me much, did you?" Elliot said as he examined the table. After an excruciatingly long time, he sent the cueball careening off the side of the table. It smacked into one of Clay's balls, which sped straight into a side pocket.

"Darn," Elliot said, slapping the side of the table. "The whipper snapper's lucky as well as good."

Clay's luck didn't hold as he missed more shots in the next fifteen minutes than he made. Elliot was even farther off the mark, making Lane's heart hurt for him. When Clay finally sunk the eight-ball, the game came to a not-quite-merciful end.

Embarrassingly, three of Elliot's striped balls were still on the table.

"He's some pool player, isn't he?" Elliot asked, nudging Lane with his elbow. She'd been so busy shooting visual daggers at Clay that the nudge took her unexpectedly. Her elbow collapsed and the squirming bundle of cat dropped to the floor.

She'd done it now. The cat was out of the bag.

Looking thrilled to be free, Kublai Khat dashed across the restaurant. For a moment, his destination was unclear. But then he sprinted toward the waitress, who was sitting at a booth taking a dinner break.

"I sure hope her pizza doesn't have anything fishy

on it,'' Elliot said a moment before Kublai Khat jumped onto a chair and then hopped onto the table.

The waitress screamed and jumped to her feet, which didn't faze Kublai Khat. He made himself comfortable on the tabletop, picking what looked to be anchovies off the pizza like a conquering hero. Ghengis Khat, Lane thought, might have been a more fitting name for him.

''Take that cat and get out of here,'' the waitress shouted, pointing a shaking finger at all three of them. ''And don't let me see any of you darkening Mahatma's door ever again.''

And that, Lane thought with a heavy dose of sarcasm, was a fitting end to an evening that had gone to the dogs.

5

CLAY PICKED HIS WAY through the too-narrow aisle, so tired of talking cats that this time he swore he wouldn't stop walking until he reached Rover's cage.

The Roman coliseum probably didn't have as many cats as the Lake Haven Community College Cultural Center. The benching area of the spacious hall was lined with row after row of cages filled with a dizzying array of felines.

Cats that were spotted, bi-colored and tri colored. Cats with slick hair, wavy hair and no hair. Cats with big ears, small ears and bobbed ears. They were all represented.

Clay needed a break, not only to think about whether any of the dozens of cat owners he'd talked to that morning had said anything of value, but also to figure out how to get Lanc to say anything to him at all.

She'd given him the silent treatment after they'd gotten the boot from Mahatma's Pizzeria the night before, speaking only to Elliot on the drive back to the hotel.

By the time she'd disappeared inside her room and promptly shut the connecting door that led to his, he'd regretted offering the old man a ride. Elliot could have at least had the decency to be staying at the other hotel in town like everybody else.

Clay had hoped that Lane's disposition toward him would improve when dawn broke, but she'd left the hotel before he'd showered and moved out of the vicinity when she saw him coming.

Some truce this was turning out to be.

He passed cages draped with gold lamé, cages covered with ribbons and cages on which hung plaques that said things like Feline Pen and Paws but don't touch. Still he kept going until a breed name on a cage stopped him.

"Why is your cat called a Munchkin?" he asked a woman who couldn't have been more than five feet tall.

She took a feather teaser, inserted it between the slats of the wire cage and tickled the short-haired cat until it stood up. Except it still looked as though it was sitting down.

"See his front legs. They're no more than three inches long," the woman said in a voice so high it sounded like she'd been sucking helium. "But don't worry. He'd still be able to follow the yellow brick road."

Clay smiled and kept walking, nearly collapsing from mental fatigue when he got to Rover's cage. The tiny cat immediately vacated her spot in the corner, walked to the front of the cage and stared.

"Now is not a good time, Rover," he said irritably. "The cat wrangler's already chewed me out for the way you were meowing at Marigold last night. You think that's going to win me any points with Lane?"

"Speaking of Lane, how'd it go last night?" Elliot Doggett was suddenly beside Rover's cage, Kublai Khat in his arms. The cat yawned, and for a moment

Clay thought he got a whiff of anchovies. "Did the plan work?"

"I've been meaning to talk to you about that," Clay said, about to tell him the brand of PR he'd performed last night was Perfectly Rotten.

"She loves a winner, right? Everybody does." Elliot was practically brimming with excitement. Evidently, it hadn't occurred to him that nobody liked the bully who clobbered the underdog. Even if the purported bully had deliberately missed shot after shot to avoid winning.

Clay sighed. There was no point in hurting Elliot's feelings, especially when he'd only been trying to help. "Everybody but Lane," he said.

The tinny female voice over the public-address system, which had been making nonstop announcements all morning, cut into their conversation. "Household Pets numbers one through eight to ring three for judging."

"Laney has an entry in Household Pets," Clay told Elliot. "I'm going over there to show my support."

"Hmmmm. Show her you can be caring. That's an excellent plan," Elliot said, making Clay think that maybe it wasn't. But Lane couldn't run away from him if Marigold was on stage, which might give Clay an opportunity to explain what had really happened during last night's pool game.

Ring three, which was actually rectangular in shape, was one of eight judging areas set up in the hall. Most cat shows were six-ring shows that covered two days, but by the end of the three-day Lake Haven extravaganza each cat would get its turn in all eight rings.

A thin, red-haired woman wearing a white lab coat stood behind a lighted table, a dozen cages lined up behind her and three rows of chairs in front of her. Lane was standing in the spectator area, looking as calm and as cool and as beautiful as she always did.

"Hey, Laney," he said as he walked over to her side, preparing to be blasted by her glacial gaze. The eyes that met his, however, weren't frosty.

"Marigold's next," she said in a voice that trembled.

Clay had seen Lane stand up at a crowded city hall meeting and accuse a slippery councilman of lying. He'd seen her cross police tape to get the goods on a double murder. He'd never seen her nervous. Until now.

He reached for her hand, which felt small and cold in his. "Relax," he said, moving closer so she knew he was on her side. "She'll do fine."

She gave him a shaky smile before returning her attention to the judge. The redhead put another cat back in its cage and unlatched the one containing Marigold. A gasp went through the crowd when Marigold was out in the open.

"Oh, gosh." Elliot's voice, tinged with dismay, drifted from behind them. "I wonder who owns that unsightly thing."

"Laney does," Clay whispered. Luckily, Lane was so focused on the judge that she appeared oblivious to their exchange.

Clay heard her suck in a breath as the judge set Marigold down on the table. He had to give the redhead credit. She took only seconds to recover from the initial shock and then gave the cat an earnest examination.

"The judges interpret a written standard describing the ideal specimen of a breed when they judge the purebreds. But the Household Pets category is entirely subjective," Lane whispered.

Clay had already researched cat show judging, but he thought it a testament to her nervousness that she was sharing information. He knew, for example, that Marigold was being judged against solid-colored, longhaired cats. If the judge designated her among the top three, she'd compete against longhaired cats of any pattern.

The judge winced when she looked into Marigold's crossed eyes but otherwise kept up her professional demeanor. Ten minutes later, after she'd judged all the cats, she took out three ribbons and headed toward the cages.

She hung the red ribbon and yellow ribbon designating the second- and third-place finishers fairly quickly, but took her time with the blue winner's ribbon. Lane's hand tightened around Clay's when she neared Marigold's cage, but the judge didn't pause. She walked past the fat cat and awarded the final ribbon to a cute tabby.

"Marigold didn't get a ribbon," Lane said, her voice steeped in disbelief.

"There are two more days and seven more rings to go," Clay reminded her, thankful that each ring held its own mini competition, complete with ribbons. He reached up and touched her cheek. "I'm sorry, honey."

Her lips seemed to tremble and her brown eyes soften before she visibly got hold of herself. As though just realizing he held her hand, she slipped it from his.

"I appreciate your concern, but I'd prefer you not call me honey," she said, tipping up her chin. "Now if you'll excuse me, I need to get Marigold."

Her back was regally straight when she walked away but her shoulders dipped, hinting at her dejection. At the moment, Clay wasn't sure what he wished for more: Lane to rush back so he could take her in his arms and properly comfort her or a judge who'd see in Marigold what Lane did.

LANE WOULD BET Marigold's firstborn that Clay Crawford was up to something.

"I'd say it was a sneak attack if he wasn't being so obvious about it," she told the cat, who didn't seem to be listening.

But who could blame Marigold for dropping down in her cage and covering her face with a thick paw? The first round of judging had been a terrible ordeal and she was justified in being exhausted from it. Within seconds, she was emitting the adorable little wheezes that meant she was snoring.

Okay, Lane amended. She'd never have the heart to bet something as precious as Marigold's kitten, but she was still certain Clay was plotting something.

Why else would he have turned on the sweetness a little while ago when she and Marigold had to put up with the treatment of the clueless judge?

She knew this trick, because he'd tried it on her many times in the past year. He invaded her personal space, dazzling her with his sex appeal. Then he had the nerve to go for the double whammy and pretend to be Mr. Nice Guy. She was sure he meant to scramble her brains so her focus would be on him instead of the all-important story.

Well, it wasn't going to work.

Lane half rose in the seat she had stationed beside Marigold's cage, positioning her head so she could see over and around the two rows of cages that separated her from Clay.

Finally, at long last, he was standing, which gave her a clear view of him. Unfortunately, she also had a view of *her*. Not any her in particular but the latest in a long line of hers who seemed to gravitate to Clay like cats to catnip.

Why couldn't he try to cultivate male sources, she thought crossly, disregarding that most of the attendees at the show were female.

This one was a petite blonde so top heavy she looked like she might topple over. Against her ample bosom she cradled a sleek, black cat that reminded Lane of Clay's luxurious head of hair. It had been a year, but she still remembered what it felt like to thread her fingers through that hair and pull up on tiptoes to kiss the hard mouth that could turn so incredibly soft...

He unexpectedly swiveled his head and, with unerring accuracy, looked straight at her. Then he gave her a slow, devastating smile that set off a conflagration inside her body.

Lane ducked so quickly she banged her elbow on the side of Marigold's cage. She rubbed it, silently cursing Clay while she made a mental note to talk to the blonde with the black cat.

Her conversation with Clay might have been innocent but Lane couldn't take the chance that the busty blonde knew something.

She also couldn't afford to get too close to Clay for the rest of the day because of that darned inferno raging in her body. How was she supposed to think when her insides were snapping, crackling and popping? Which was probably exactly what the cunning man intended.

"This is a disgrace. The FFF should be flunked out of the cat-show business," a shrill, female voice sounded nearby, jarring Lane from her musings.

A few feet away, a tall, slim woman was packing up her belongings, muttering to herself. She scuttled a cat Lane recognized as a Siamese into a carrying case, her movements quick and jerky.

Finally, Lane thought, a break in the story.

Everyone else was giving the woman a clear berth but Lane crossed to her side, close enough to tell that the woman's eyes sparkled with angry tears. Hating to see anyone in pain, she placed a hand on her arm.

"I'm a good listener if you want to tell me what's wrong," she invited.

"Nothing's wrong with me. It's the FFF that's the problem." The woman indicated her Siamese, which had dramatic Seal Point coloring, its coat light-colored and its extremities inky black. "Anybody can see she's a beauty, but she's gone through three rings and hasn't gotten a ribbon yet. There's only one explanation for that."

"What's that?" Lane asked, hanging on her words. Was this the information she'd been waiting for?

"The FFF shows are fixed," she said as she gathered up the rest of her belongings. She picked up the case with her beautiful cat, which gazed up at Lane through blue eyes that somehow reminded her of

Marigold. "I can't prove it, but I won't stand for it. We're leaving."

Before Lane could question her further, she took off, her steps long and quick, her heels clicking on the linoleum floor.

Lane's newspaper training kicked in as she plotted her next moves. She'd talk to the owners of the Siamese who'd been judged against the angry lady's cat, especially the ribbon winners. Then she'd interview the judges to get their side of the story and finally...

"Gosh darn, you were brave to get close to that filly. She's touchier about that cat than a buckin' bull about the cinch in his side." Wade McCoy's voice registered upon Lane before the clink of his spurs as he joined her. "I've about given up hope she'll ever accept a judge's decision."

Lane slanted a sharp look at the cat wrangler, suddenly doubting that he was as shrewd about the animals as his reputation indicated. Hadn't he gotten a good look at the woman's stunning cat? "It seems to me she has a reasonable gripe."

"It's the same one she has at every cat show," Wade said. "She reminds me of my Aunt Mabel. Every year, Aunt Mabel entered her blueberry pie in the baking contest at the county fair. Every year, she got madder than a stallion without a mare that she didn't win. Never occurred to her it was on account of her leaving out the sugar."

"Why?"

Wade took off his ten-gallon hat and ran a massive hand through his thinning hair. "Something wrong with her taste buds is my theory. I learned right quick that you'd best be sayin' no if she offered you lemonade.''

"I wasn't asking about the sugar," Lane said. "Why does the lady who just stormed out of here remind you of your Aunt Mabel? It sounds like your aunt didn't have a good reason to be angry, but she does. Her cat's gorgeous."

"Can't argue with that," Wade agreed, restoring some of Lane's confidence in his cat sense. "I reckon he'd be a ribbon winner for sure, maybe even a Grand Champion. If he didn't have that nagging problem with his eyes."

"What nagging problem?" Lane asked even as a part of her brain figured out why the Siamese had reminded her of Marigold. The eyes. It had something to do with the eyes.

"He's a wee bit cross-eyed. Oh, not as much as your cat. But enough to get marked down for it. The judges, they have a mental checklist of the characteristics of a breed. Anything left of center, they take off points."

Lane stared at him openmouthed. Now that he'd pointed it out, she could call up a mental picture of the angry woman's cat and see that it was cross-eyed. But Marigold? Speechlessly, she crossed to her beloved cat's cage and tapped on the wire slats.

Marigold opened one sleepy eye, then the other, neither of which focused on Lane. It was true. Her beautiful cat was cross-eyed.

"Marigold's never going to win a ribbon, is she, Wade? No matter how many rings there are in the show?"

He didn't answer, but then he didn't have to. He

merely rubbed her shoulder, but the contact provided little comfort.

There is none so blind, she thought, as one who could not see that she had a cross-eyed cat.

LANE SHUT her hotel-room door behind her, kicking off her shoes as she crossed to the bed. She dashed sections of the three newspapers she'd bought to the floor before flinging herself on the mattress. Her eyes were dry, but her chest was heaving.

How could she have been such a fool as to delude herself into believing Marigold could compete with the exquisite cats that filled the Lake Haven Cultural Center?

She'd not only set herself up for humiliation, but Marigold as well.

Three times, she'd brought her cat to one of the judging rings with hope beating in her heart. Three times, that hope had been dashed into a million painful pieces. Marigold hadn't gotten past the first round of judging in any of the rings. Not one of the judges deemed her pretty enough to beat out the other solid-colored longhairs.

To think Lane had been so hopelessly naïve that she hadn't realized the result was a foregone conclusion.

Meanwhile, Clay's tiny cat had been bedecked with ribbons. It was bad enough that Roderica was entered in the championship competition while Marigold was designated as a household pet, but the cat wrangler had relayed that the tiny cat had been named best of the breed by two of the three judges who looked at her.

And there were still two more days and five more rings to go.

Lane buried her face in the mattress. She needn't have worried about Clay witnessing Marigold's mortification the other two times she'd been judged, because Roderica had been wowing the judges in a separate ring at the same time. So it had been easy to avoid being the subject of any more of Clay's false sympathy.

No matter that it hadn't seemed false at the time or that he'd managed to make her feel...cherished.

Silly woman, she thought crossly. Clay Crawford found her attractive, of that she had little doubt, but the only thing he truly cherished was the opportunity to beat her out of a job.

He was probably plotting his next move even now. She thought she heard a sound in the adjoining room and flipped over on her back, holding herself perfectly still while she listened to silence. Had it been a hanger scraping against a rod. Was he changing his clothes?

She imagined him shrugging out of his shirt, baring that beautiful chest that had exactly the right touch of brawn. She hadn't seen it clearly that night a year ago because of the darkness, but she remembered that his chest hairs felt silky against her fingers...and her lips.

Soft footfalls seemed to grow louder, as though he'd read her thoughts and wanted into her room. Into her bed. Into her...

A heavy knock sounded, not on the connecting door but on the front door. It was followed by her sister's voice, "Open up, Lane. It's Stace. I gotta talk to you."

Disappointment crashed through Lane. Not, she told herself, because she wanted to fling open the connecting door and make mad, passionate love to Clay. But because she would have liked the satisfaction of ignoring the knock.

"Yeah, right," she muttered in disgust as she walked to the front door. "Maybe this self-delusion thing has always been a problem for me. Why else would I have believed Marigold was getting a ribbon?"

She opened the door to find Stacy alone in the hallway, a smile as big as a Norwegian Forest Cat on her face. Her rosy lips looked well-kissed and her face was flushed from health. Or was that from whisker burn?

Stacy didn't wait for an invitation but fairly danced into the room, shutting the door behind them and giving Lane a smacking kiss on the cheek.

"Ohmygosh." She threw up her hands and let out a delighted, little yelp. "Did you know that you can stay in bed making love all night and half the day when you're with the right man?"

Lane's insides seized up at her sister's words before she remembered Clay had said Ted was a good person, not a player out to hurt Stacy. She forced a smile. "I'm glad you're happy."

"I'm not happy. I'm ecstatic." She hugged herself, then grabbed Lane by the shoulders. "I want ecstasy for you, too. That's why I think you should test my theory by getting horizontal with Clay. If you want to stay in bed with him forever, he's Mr. Right."

A wave of heat swept through Lane at her sister's words, but she ignored it. "Don't you mean Mr.

Write Me Out of a Job? That's why he's here, and I can't forget it."

"You're forgetting that I've seen the way you two look at each other." Stacy waved off Lane's comment. "Besides, there are more important things in life than work. I'm not convinced you want to write for *Splash!* anyway."

"Of course I do. Why else would I be here?"

"To win. That's your usual motivation, isn't it?" Stacy said. Before Lane could deny it, there was a rap on the connecting door.

"Oh, goody. That'll be Teddy Bear and Clay with our food," Stacy crossed to the door, chatting amiably. "We ran into Clay in the parking lot and he offered to help Teddy carry it up."

Never mind her fantasies of a moment ago when he hadn't even been in his room, Lane wasn't going to be railroaded into having dinner with her too-sexy nemesis. She positioned herself between Stacy and the door.

"I'm not eating with Clay," she said.

Stacy patted her cheek. "I know you'd rather do other things with him, honey, but that'll have to wait until you two are alone."

While Lane was stunned into immobility, Stacy slipped by her, opened the door and propelled herself into Ted's arms as though they'd been apart for a millennium.

Lane averted her eyes when the couple locked lips, and her gaze collided with Clay's. Before she could call upon her vaunted control, her eyes slid downward to his mouth and she remembered the dizzying pleasure of kissing him.

"Hey, Laney." The kissable lips were not only forming words, but smiling. "Are you game?"

For kissing him? Or for doing as Stacy suggested and testing to determine if he were the Horizontal Mr. Right?

"For what?" she managed to croak.

Only then did she notice the cartons of Chinese food he held. The aroma of fried rice and spicy beef filled the hotel room.

"For Chinese," he said. "Ted and Stacy brought takeout."

"Stacy was feeling guilty that we were neglecting you two, so she wanted to make it up to you," Ted explained, his arm flung over the back of her sister's neck.

Without asking Lane's permission, Stacy directed Ted and Clay to drag a table and chairs from her room into his so they could set up a dining area for four. Lane wasn't sure exactly how it happened, but moments later she was sitting down to dinner with Clay. For the second night in a row.

"Sorry we didn't get to the cat show today," Stacy said as they opened the fragrant cartons. She sent a lascivious look in Ted's direction. "But we were busy."

"We'd love to spend more time with you two, but we're going to be busy later, too." At Ted's words, Stacy nodded, as though the two of them had rehearsed the speech. "That's why we have to eat and run."

As if on cue, they each reached for one of the paper plates the Chinese restaurant had provided and piled on Moo Shu Beef and Kung Pao Scallops.

"We asked for squid or oysters, but scallops were

the best they could do,'' Stacy said as she and Ted bypassed the chopsticks and went straight for the forks. They dug in, like entrants at a speed-eating contest.

"So how'd it go at the cat show?" Stacy asked between mouthfuls. "Did Rover win any ribbons?"

Lane noticed that not only did Stacy use Roderica's nickname, but she didn't ask about Marigold, probably because she knew better. She averted her eyes and helped herself to some Chicken Chow Mein while she waited for Clay to boast about his Wonder Cat.

"She did okay."

Her head snapped up as she waited for Clay to expand on the statement, but he was taking a long drink from his soda can. Amazing. He intended to downplay the cat's accomplishments. Lane was tempted to let him, but then she remembered what her father always said.

The only thing a sore loser's good for is losing.

"Wade told me she won ribbons from every judge. I'd say that was more than okay, especially because Marigold didn't win any." Her voice broke but she pasted on a smile. "So you win this round."

"Everything's not a competition, Laney." Clay put down his fork and leaned closer to her. She backed away. "So what if the judges gave Rover some ribbons? That doesn't mean she's a better cat than Marigold."

"Oh, please. Spare me the rhetoric."

"I mean it," Clay said, his handsome face so serious she was tempted to believe him. If she was naïve enough to fall into that kind of trap. "Rover might be a pretty cat, but Marigold has her beat in lots of ways.''

Lane would have wholeheartedly embraced those sentiments before today's show, but a day among the feline elite had made her more jaded. She set her jaw.

''Do you hear this? He says that Marigold can beat out his champion show cat.'' She looked over at her sister and Ted to discover they'd been so intent on speed chewing that they hadn't paid attention to the conversation.

Stacy set down her fork beside a plate that was more than half full. ''I'm finished,'' she announced.

''Me, too.'' Ted got to his feet and pulled her sister up with him. Their arms wrapped around each other, octopus style. ''I did mention we had to eat and run, didn't I?''

The couple raced for the door, this time not bothering to ask if Clay and Lane minded if they left. Not that their answer would have made any difference.

''There go the world's lousiest dinner companions,'' Clay remarked lightly when the door shut behind them. Lane felt her lower lip tremble and immediately sucked it into her mouth. His expression turned serious. ''Oh, geez. You're not still upset about their relationship, are you?''

Remarkably, she wasn't. Clay had vouched for Ted and, for some mysterious reason she didn't care to analyze, that was good enough for her.

''I'm not upset about anything.'' Lane pushed her chair back from the table and stood. ''But I've had enough.''

Clay had the audacity to look as though he hadn't

a clue what she was talking about. He stared at the food on her plate, then back up at her. "You've hardly eaten a thing."

"I meant I've had enough of your pity." Even though her heart was trembling, she kept her voice even and her eyes dry. "I've accepted that Marigold will never win any ribbons so you can stop lying about her being superior to your fancy show cat."

"I'm not lying," he said, sounding sincere even though she was sure he wasn't. "I was pointing out your cat can do some things better than Rover."

She crossed her arms over her chest, because it made her feel better. As though his words would have to penetrate another layer before they could hurt her. "Name one," she challenged.

"Eat," he said quickly. Far too quickly.

"So you think Marigold is fat?"

"I didn't say that." He seemed to be searching his brain for an explanation. "She's *full-figured*. Like that actress who promotes clothing for big, beautiful women."

"Big cats eat more than little ones, so eating doesn't count." Lane squared her shoulders, getting ready to issue another exit line. She should have done so already instead of standing there, listening to his nonsense.

"I bet Marigold is faster than Rover," he blurted out.

She stared at him, surprised he'd noticed that Marigold was light on her feet. On the surface, pitting her against the tiny, tidy Roderica seemed like more of a mismatch than the tortoise and the hare.

"For a full-figured cat, she can scoot when she wants to," she said, then sighed. "Maybe she is faster than Roderica, but unfortunately we'll never know.''

''I wouldn't be too sure about that,'' he said, then crossed the room and picked up the phone. He stole a quick look at her as he dialed. ''I'm going to ask Wade to bring over our cats.''

She watched while he made the request, noticing he didn't tell the cat wrangler why he needed the cats. When he hung up, he gave her a smile that got the butterflies in her stomach flapping again.

''All set,'' he said.

She tapped the side of her mouth with a finger, trying to figure him out. ''Mind telling me what you have in mind?''

His blue eyes twinkled. ''We're going to have ourselves a cat race.''

6

CLAY LAID DOWN two paper towels on the hotel room floor, then glanced up to a wonderful sight. Lane had her lips determinedly clamped together, but her eyes were sparkling with laughter.

He winked at her, and her cool exterior collapsed. Her lips parted, and she giggled. Actually giggled. He knew she thought the notion of a cat race was silly, but the moment felt so intimate that he was glad he'd suggested it.

His rash contention that Marigold could outrace Rover went against every law of speed known to man or animal, but maybe, just maybe, his bargain would pay off. Rover had such dainty paws that she looked as though she'd fall over at any moment.

He only hoped Marigold lived up to her part. He'd long ago figured out that Lane hated to lose, but was only now realizing she hated it more when someone—or something—she loved lost.

"One of you care to tell me what's going on?" Wade McCoy tapped a booted foot on the grass-green carpeting.

Next to Wade were the carrying cases containing Marigold and Rover, which Clay had instructed the cat wrangler to place side by side across the room from the paper towels.

Lane giggled again. "Clay wants to race the cats to see which one is faster."

Wade shook his head so vigorously Clay was afraid his cowboy hat might fall off. "Now if that isn't the most foolhardy notion I've ever heard. Cats are too ornery to race."

"Greyhounds race."

"Greyhounds are dogs. They can be trained to do as they're told. Cats do what they darn well want to."

"They'll want to race after I get through with them." As he talked, Clay plucked scallops from a Chinese food container, wiped them clean of sauce and set them on the paper towels. When he was through, he speared a fat scallop with a fork and walked across the room with it.

"Ever heard of an incentive?" he asked before waving the scallop in turn in front of Rover and Marigold. "Cats like fish, right? And scallops are fishy."

Lane let out another delightful giggle and Wade shook his head. "Son, have you plumb lost your mind?"

"Bear with me here," Clay said. Cheering up Lane was his primary objective, but he wasn't convinced the race would be a bust. "Okay, Laney. When I count to three, you open Marigold's cage. Wade, you do the same for Rover. The cat that reaches the scallops first wins."

"Nuh, unh. No way I'm opening your little darlin's carrier," Wade said as color crawled up his face. "As your Professional Cat Handler, I'm going on record as sayin' this is a very bad idea. Not only won't it work, but if you let the cats out of those carriers you're gonna have a—"

"If you won't open the latch, I will," Clay interrupted impatiently, stooping behind Rover's carrier. "Get in position, Laney. Ready?"

"But I didn't finish what I was sayin'," Wade protested at the same time that Clay began his countdown. "You're asking for a—"

"On your mark, get set, go."

At Clay's signal, Lane lifted the gate on Marigold's carrier and Clay did the same with Rover's. The cats burst out of the enclosures like race horses at the starting gate at the same time Wade finished his warning.

"Cat fight!" the cat wrangler shouted.

The cats ignored the scallops and veered sharply left over the green expanse of carpeting. Marigold was in the lead, her portly body moving at Cheetah speed, with Rover in hot pursuit.

The gold cat's short, chubby legs were a blur as she bounded across the room, jumped onto a chair and used it as a launching pad to hurl herself onto a dresser. Her girth bumped a lamp, sending it crashing to the floor.

Rover emitted a meow that sounded more like a growl as she continued the chase, trailing Marigold onto the dresser and then leaping after her to the floor.

"Stop that mini maniac," Lane shouted. Since Marigold hadn't been miniature since her kitten days, and perhaps not even then, Clay assumed she was referring to Rover.

He raced across the room after the cats, keeping low, and made a grab for the tiny Singapura. She zigged when he zagged, slipping past him as he lost his balance and fell to the floor.

From flat on his back, he watched the two cats easily evade first Lane's, then Wade's grasping hands as they dashed toward the bed. The felines scampered across the king-size mattress, their paws slipping on leftover newspapers that were strewn over the quilt. Some of the sections slipped off the bed along with the cats.

Marigold appeared dazed for a moment as she thudded to the floor, but then she was off again, this time leaping onto and over the bedside table. Another lamp fell, along with an alarm clock, which erupted into an obnoxious, monotonous blare.

The sound seemed to panic Marigold, who raced across the room toward their dining area as Clay regained his footing. The fat cat passed over the paper towels, scattering the scallops. She was on the table in a flash, her thundering paws knocking over one container of Chinese food after the other.

Clay reached the table at the same time as Rover, who was slipping and sliding in the mess of Moo Shu Beef and fried rice. Taking advantage of her momentary distress, Clay plucked the cat off the table by her midsection.

Her short legs windmilled in an attempt to get away as she hissed and writhed. Marigold ran straight for Lane, who gathered her up and hugged her close.

Clay looked around at the shamble of a room and the I-told-you-so gleam in Wade's eyes before his gaze once again fell on Lane. Desperately, he racked his brain for anything that would counteract the cat-race fiasco.

"See," he said after a moment, raising his voice to be heard above the deafening blare of the alarm clock, "I knew Marigold was faster than Rover."

HOURS LATER, Lane stood with her fist poised to knock on the door that linked her room to Clay's. She was fairly certain he hadn't yet turned in for the night, because she'd heard him moving around moments ago.

She should be in bed herself, but she wouldn't be able to fall asleep until she had an answer to her question.

She started to draw her fist forward, but stopped its progress when she noticed her hand was shaking. Drawing in a deep breath, she counted to three. She rapped lightly on the door, her heart hammering harder than her knock. Moments that seemed like an eternity passed before she summoned the courage to knock again, louder this time.

His voice, velvet soft in the semidarkness, traveled through the door. "Laney, is that you?"

She cleared her throat, softly so he wouldn't pick up the sound of her nervousness. "It's me," she said. "Can I come in?"

"My door's already open, like I told you it'd be. Your door's the one that's closed."

Squaring her shoulders for courage, Lane pulled open the door and was treated to the sight she'd been fantasizing about the night before. Clay's naked chest. It was bronzed and muscular, with exactly the right amount of dark hair sprinkled on it.

Her eyes dipped. Oh, Lordy. His long legs and feet were bare, too, his body more sculpted and muscular than it had any right to be. He worked behind a desk, for pity's sake. He shouldn't be the perfect candidate for *Playgirl* magazine. He'd look even better if he wasn't wearing a pair of boxers decorated with tiny...

"Are those cats?"

"Kittens, actually," he said, then blushed, adorably so. The calico kittens were depicted in a playful tumble, their paws raised skyward. "I forgot to bring a change of underwear so I bought them today at the show."

She swallowed, trying to lubricate her suddenly parched throat. "So you sleep in your underwear?" she asked, trying to sound sophisticated.

His smile kicked up, sending awareness shimmering through her. "Actually, no, I don't."

"But..." Lane began, then lapsed into silence. He meant he slept naked, that he'd pulled on the underwear so he wouldn't offend her. As though anything about his body were offensive.

He leaned closer to her, his breath soft and warm on her face. "I can put on a shirt if you want."

And cover up all that gorgeous brawn?

"No," Lane nearly shouted, then clamped her lips. She had to get control of herself. "I mean, there's no need. This'll only take a minute."

He shifted his weight from one bare foot to the other and leaned against the door just inches from where she stood. The lateness of the hour added to the intimacy of their positions. She pulled her terrycloth robe tighter around herself, aware that all she wore underneath was the black lace teddy Stacy had packed. Why she had put it on, she didn't want to know. Neither was she going to analyze why she'd left her glasses on the bedside table.

"Sorry I didn't help you clean up the mess," she said. "Marigold was pretty spooked, and it took a while for me to settle her down."

"Don't give it another thought. I understand that Marigold needed you."

Silence stretched between them. She wet her lips, trying to summon the nerve to ask the question that had been bothering her. A lock of hair fell into her face and he smoothed it back, his fingertips seeming to transmit an electrical current over her skin.

"Whatever it is you want, you can tell me," Clay said.

I want you. The unbidden thought carried such a wallop that Lane stepped back, away from his touch.

"Not that I mind standing here talking to you." His wide mouth curved upward into a smile that could stop hearts. For a moment, before it resumed a slow, painful beat, she thought it had stopped hers. "I'll talk to you all night if you want."

What she wanted was to tumble onto one of their beds and make love to him until morning.

"No," she said, more to the notion of making love than to his offer to talk all night. "That won't be necessary."

She dropped her gaze to the floor, composing her thoughts before she finally gazed up at him. His blue-gray eyes were beautiful in the semidarkness as he waited for the reason she'd sought him out.

"Why were you so insistent that our cats race?" Finally, the question was out.

"You mean because it was such a dumb idea?" He grimaced, rubbed a hand at the back of his neck, the motion outlining his perfect biceps. "Okay, you caught me. I've researched the hell out of cat shows, but I don't know squat about cat behavior.''

She shook her head. ''That's not what I mean at all. It's just that, well, I got the impression that you wanted Marigold to win.''

''I did,'' he stated readily.

''But why?''

He stepped forward and put a hand that felt warm and wonderful against her cheek. ''Because I don't want you thinking your cat is a loser because some judge can't see that she's beautiful.''

''You think Marigold is beautiful?''

''I think,'' he said, his other hand moving upward so that both of his hands cupped her face, ''that you're beautiful.''

''You do?''

He nodded solemnly.

''I have since the moment I saw you come out of City Hall.'' His low voice set off vibrations in her body. ''The sun peeked out from behind a cloud, and I realized I'd forgotten my sunglasses. I turned around, and there you were standing on the steps, like you were waiting for me to turn and notice you.''

''I wasn't waiting for any such thing,'' she said, although the opposite was true. She'd spotted him the second she'd exited the building. He'd been standing by the curb, patting the pocket of his sport jacket, a dark-haired, blue-eyed man who touched something inside of her merely by existing.

''I noticed you anyway,'' he said, bringing his mouth closer to hers. ''I can't help noticing you, Laney. Whatever you do. Wherever you are.''

He shifted, and at long last, his mouth met hers.

Lane closed her eyes, fighting against the wealth of sensations that hit her as hard as a powerful ocean wave. *Don't respond,* she told herself, but his lips were coaxing hers apart, the heat from his bare chest radiating into her.

Think of something nonromantic, she commanded herself, and dredged up a song from childhood. Something about globs of greasy gopher guts, dirty piggy's feet and french-fried eyeballs. Images distasteful enough to kill any lustful tendencies.

His tongue slid against hers, and the images flew out of her head on swift wings, replaced by that of the darkly handsome man she'd resisted for far too long.

She sighed into the kiss, giving up to the inevitability of the moment and the intense pleasure of kissing him. He fisted her hair in his hands and angled his mouth over hers to deepen the kiss, sending hot fingers of sensation shooting toward her center.

Feelings she had kept buried for the past year burst to the surface and she wondered how she had ever dredged up the strength to resist him. How she would ever resist him again.

His mouth left her lips and he buried his face in the crook of her neck while his hands untied the belt at her waist. He edged the robe off her shoulders, exposing the black teddy to his gaze.

His eyes darkened, his mouth went slack, and she knew why she'd put on the teddy, had known she wanted to even when she'd argued with Stacy for packing it.

"Make love with me tonight, Laney." His was the voice of temptation.

Somewhere, in the recesses of her mind, lurked a

reason she should refuse. She tried to summon it, but he was backing her into the room, his hands on her body, his mouth once again fastened to hers, and she couldn't think clearly.

What was there to think about when she had the half-naked man of her daydreams in her room? It was useless to deny that she wanted him, that she always had.

She broke off the kiss, prepared to tell him so, when a loud, inelegant noise sounded in the darkness. Clay's head jerked up.

"What's that?" he asked. "It sounds like it's coming from your bed."

The room was dark except for the faint glow that was escaping from the crack in the bathroom door. Lane's eyes had adjusted enough to the darkness that she could see Marigold's body undulating on the bed as she let out loud, strangled coughs.

The display went on for a good fifteen seconds until, with a final hack, Marigold got her desired result. Exhausted, the cat promptly dropped down on the bed.

"Marigold just spit up a hairball," Lane explained.

Clay laughed softly and trailed kisses down her neck. "Let's leave your cat here and go to my room."

Marigold. Her cat. One of many that had converged on Lake Haven this weekend for the cat show extravaganza. Cats, she thought numbly. That was it. That was the reason she couldn't make love to Clay.

"No," she said, wondering where she got the strength to utter the syllable. "I can't do it, Clay."

Confusion clouded his face before his expression

cleared. "Marigold's asleep, Laney. She won't mind if you leave her. We can keep the door open between the rooms if you like."

"No," she said again, more insistently this time.

"Then we can close the door," he said, "but I've never heard of a cat with voyeuristic tendencies."

"That's because you don't have one."

"Okay. A closed door it is."

"I didn't say I can't do it in *front* of my cat, although I probably couldn't. I can't do it *because* of the cats." She stepped back from him and rearranged her robe, which was gaping open. "Because of the magazine story."

He ran a hand over his lower face, which was still moist from their kisses. "So we're back to that again?"

"We can't get away from it, Clay. We're competitors trying to beat each other out of a job."

"We're also two consenting adults who want each other."

"I'm not consenting," Lane said, fighting the urge to wrap herself around him. "For all I know, if I sleep with you, I could be setting myself up for emotional sabotage."

"What the heck is that?"

"That's where one person gets the other so mixed up emotionally that they lose sight of their goal."

"And that's what you think I'm doing? Worming under your defenses so *Splash!* hires me instead of you?"

She frowned. Put that way, it didn't sound quite the way she'd intended. "I can't forget what's important, Clay."

"Which, in this case, is beating me?"

"Exactly," she said.

Hurt flashed in his eyes before he banked it. "In that case, you're right. It would be a very bad idea if we slept together."

He pivoted and walked away from her, increasing her ache with every step he took. She swallowed so that she wouldn't call him back.

Then she crossed the room and shut the door, unsure of whether she'd been saved by a hairball or doomed by it.

7

CLAY TURNED the elegant, solid-gold pin over, admiring the detail the craftsman had put into the work. It was a depiction of a cat, appearing sleek, sophisticated and aloof.

Which was pretty much the way Lane looked whenever he was in the vicinity.

"That's a very wise choice," the middle-aged saleslady said, obviously eager to keep him from roaming to one of the other merchants who had set up kiosks in the cultural center. They were selling everything a cat owner could ever want or imagine. The saleslady was a walking advertisement for her wares. She wore cat-encrusted glasses and a T-shirt plastered with feline faces and the saying, It's a purr-fect world.

"I'm sure your lady will love that piece," she pressed. "Any cat lover would."

Except what Lane loved was Marigold. Clay frowned down at the gorgeous cat, which didn't resemble Lane's pet in the slightest.

"Do you have anything a little...fuller-figured?" he asked. "Maybe with eyes the color that reminds you of slime and a face that seems like it might have been bashed in by a baseball bat?"

The woman made a face and scrunched up her nose. "Now why in the dickens would I carry something like that? I'm in business to sell things, not to scare people.''

He handed her back the pin, shaking his head when she asked if she could wrap it for him.

"Let me show you something in some earrings then,'' she said. "I have the most adorable pair of Ocicats.''

"I'm not sure Ocicats will do the trick,'' he muttered.

"Had a fight with your girlfriend, did you?'' the woman asked shrewdly. "Well, then, you're at the right place. Nothing will get you back in her good graces faster than jewelry.''

He wished it would be that easy. But not only was Lane not his girlfriend, but he'd never been in her good graces in the first place. Clay stood at the counter while the cat vendor pulled out a selection of earrings on a black velvet tray and half listened while she chatted about Havana Browns, Russian Blues and York Chocolates.

What was he doing here anyway? He should be working on the *Splash!* story instead of trying to win Lane's affections with baubles. The jewelry probably wouldn't have the desired effect anyway.

"The yellow eyes on this Abyssinian earring glow in the dark,'' the vendor was saying, "which makes it handy for locating someone at night.''

Oh, he could find Lane all right. His challenge was getting her to come anywhere near him. Today's portion of the cat show had begun hours ago, and she'd steered well clear. She'd obviously meant it when she said she wasn't going to consort with the enemy.

Nothing short of him dropping out of the race for the magazine job would get her to change her mind.

Dropping out of the race. He turned the possibility over in his mind. Now there was an idea that made a lot more sense than a gift of Ocicat earrings.

"Maybe later," Clay said when the woman offered to take out her selection of necklaces. He turned away from the counter, distracted by his thoughts. He hadn't taken a dozen steps when he spotted Ted barreling across the floor, thrusting his upper body out in preparation for a chest bump.

Clay planted his feet and took the blow, grunting a little on impact. He liked Ted, but the man had watched one too many touchdown celebrations.

"Hey, bud, I've been looking all over for you." Ted indicated the vast hall with a swipe of his hand. "This place is like a football field with players dressed in tiny fur coats."

"Speaking of felines, where's yours?" Clay asked.

"If you mean Stacy, she's back at the hotel packing."

His statement didn't make sense. Stacy had made it clear she and Ted intended to stay through the weekend and now she was leaving. After Clay had assured her sister Ted would never deliberately hurt her.

"Please don't tell me she's leaving because you broke up with her," Clay said.

"Are you kidding? I think I'm falling in love with her," Ted denied quickly. "We're both leaving. The Dolphins' quarterback just announced that football isn't his destiny, and I got to do a story about why he's quitting."

Clay's heart started beating normally again, and

he clapped Ted on the shoulder. "Thanks for dropping by to let me know."

"That's not all I came to tell you. I got news about Dewey Markowitz."

The managing editor of the *Courier* for more than a decade, Markowitz was a hardworking dynamo with an unparalleled drive for success. Clay privately thought he was a Type A-plus.

"Don't tell me he had another heart attack?"

"More like a shock attack," Ted said, walking with Clay to a more isolated corner of the hall. "But who can blame him? It's not every day a man wins the lottery and becomes a millionaire."

Clay whistled long and low. "Good for him. And lucky for Dad. Anybody besides Dewey wouldn't stick around after winning that kind of money."

"Are you kidding? Word is it was all your dad could do to get the Dewster to give one week's notice. Money does strange things to a man, my friend."

Clay let out a short puff of air. "So what's Dad going to do for a managing editor?"

"Oh, come on," Ted looked at him and laughed. "Nobody's wondering *who* is going to be named the next managing editor, they're wondering *when.* I hear the betting in the newsroom poll is heavier on the sooner rather than the later."

Ted gave him an elbow that would leave bruises on a less sturdy man. "I was thinking about getting in on the action, so give me the inside scoop. Has your dad called you yet?"

Clay sighed. "He doesn't know where I am. He's been trying to talk me out of the *Splash!* job for weeks. I left my cell phone at home so he wouldn't get another chance.''

''I hear you, buddy,'' Ted said. ''I love your dad, but that man's a genius at getting what he wants. Not that I'm complaining. I like having you at the *Courier.*''

''I'm at the *Courier* because it suits me, not because it suits my father.''

''Oh, really. So why did you pass up the job at the *San Francisco Examiner* when we graduated?''

''You know why,'' Clay said. ''Dad got sick and I needed to stay close to home in case he and Mom needed me.''

Ted raised his eyebrows. ''And it never seemed strange to you that his angina cleared up when you started working at the *Courier?* And that it only flares up when you make noises about leaving?''

Clay thought back eighteen months to the last time his father hadn't been well. He'd been so worried about his father's health that he'd given little thought to the *Philadelphia Inquirer* editor who'd called to see if he was interested in a job.

''Are you saying that Dad's faking it?'' Clay asked.

''Not necessarily. Maybe the pains are psychosomatic. You're his only kid, bud. He's grooming you to take over. The managing editor position's the next step on the ladder.''

''But I don't want to climb that far up the ladder. Not yet. I'm only twenty-eight. I don't want a career people think I got only because of who my father is.''

''What do you want?''

''The *Splash!* job. The opportunity to make a

name for myself," Clay said. Silently, he added one more item to his list. Lane.

"Go for it then." Ted flung an arm around his shoulder so enthusiastically that Clay nearly collapsed under the heavy weight of it. "Because if you stay at the *Courier,* your dad will have you in the front office before you figure out how you got there."

LANE SHIFTED the cat carrier in her aching arms and trudged determinedly ahead, intent on reaching the hotel where most of the other cat owners were staying before night fell.

Finish what you start, her father always said, *or start finishing last.*

He probably hadn't been thinking of hiking a mile with a carrier full of squirming cat when he'd coined the saying, but the sentiment still applied.

She had a reporter to scoop, and by golly she was going to scoop him.

Sure, the job would have been easier if she'd left Marigold alone in the hotel room, but her sweet, still-ribbonless cat had suffered enough rejection at the second day of the cat show.

So, for that matter, had Lane.

How dare Clay Crawford have the unmitigated gall to act as though nothing had happened between them last night? Hadn't he heard the fireworks and felt the slow, sweet burn when they'd been in each other's arms? Hadn't he lain awake the entire night long unfulfilled and aching? Didn't he realize that everything had changed between them?

How could he have accepted her refusal to get involved with him as the final word?

Discounting his barely perceptible nod when he'd run into her that morning beside the "Cats are People, too" counter, he'd completely ignored her.

Instead of sending her those slow, sexy smiles that got her all worked up, he'd worked on the story. Every time she'd glanced his way, he'd been chatting up one cat person or another, no doubt gathering the information he needed to win.

"No way I'm letting that happen, Marigold," she told her cat. "You know what Daddy always says. When the going gets tough, the tough dig in and kick up some dirt."

Although she was a good ten feet from the corner, the sidewalk came to an abrupt end, as though the city had run out of funds to finish paving it. She stepped off the cement and promptly sank into the soft earth. She pulled up a foot and valiantly tried to shake off the mud that had seeped under the toe of her sandal.

"Kicking up some mud doesn't have quite the same ring to it, does it, Marigold?"

She marched purposefully on, reviewing her strategy. Because she was getting nowhere on the story, some after-hours work was in order. The logical place to conduct it was the Lake Haven Motor Inn.

She'd simply hang out in the lobby or at the hotel restaurant, making contacts and talking cats until she made headway on the story.

Best of all, Clay Crawford wouldn't know where she was. Her candy-apple red car was easy to spot, so she'd left it in the hotel parking lot to throw him off track.

Five excruciating minutes later, she rounded a bend and saw the sign adjacent to the motor inn advertising its cat lovers' special. *Cheap rates for catty lovers,* it read. She winced. The copy desk chief at the *Times* had been right when he claimed the world needed copy editors.

The motel was two stories with twin banks of rooms jutting off from a lobby too small to accommodate loiterers. Neither could she tarry in the non-existent motel restaurant. The motel was as isolated as the one Norman Bates and his mother ran.

Lane crossed the two-lane highway, surveying the scene. The parking lot was full but there wasn't a soul in sight. Resigned to waiting it out, she searched for a place to park herself and Marigold's carrier.

Her eyes alighted on a pair of vending machines, one stocked with snacks, the other with cold drinks. Her feet muddy and her arms throbbing, she crossed to the machines and laid her forehead against the cooler one before setting down the carrier with a thump.

The latch popped, and Marigold walked out on shaky legs, looking left and right with a dazed expression. Poor thing. First the cat show debacle. And then a mile's walk in a strange place.

"You need a hug, don't you, baby?" She reached down and scooped up the cat, groaning with the effort of straightening.

The hug was short-lived. Marigold squeezed out of her arms, perched on her shoulder and leaped onto the top of the vending machine. Lane jumped back when an unopened can of soda toppled off the edge of the machine and fell to the ground, barely missing her muddy toes.

"Marigold, you come down here right now," Lane said an instant before she heard the rustle of plastic and the tell-tale sound of enthusiastic munching. Had somebody left food on top of the machine? "Are you eating crackers? You know that's bad for you."

Lane was inches too short to see what was happening on top of the machine, but she got a clue when something small, cylindrical and orange floated to the ground. Lane picked it up and examined it.

"You have cheese curls up there, don't you?" she accused. "Bad girl."

All she got for an answer was a soft meow. She stepped back a few paces to get a better angle. Marigold's head was resting on her paws, her eyes half closed, orange dye from the cheese curls marring the fur around her pretty mouth.

"Marigold, you listen to me." Marigold's expression wasn't so much of defiance as of supreme indifference. Frustrated, Lane stepped forward, placed a hand on either side of the machine and shook it. "Come on, baby. Get down."

"What do you think you're doing?"

She turned toward the shrill voice, expecting to encounter an elderly woman. Instead a burly bear of a man almost as wide as he was tall moved toward her on short, thick legs.

"Can't you read?" He shook a broad finger at the warning printed in small letters on the vending machine. "It says, Don't shake the machine."

Lane was hot, thirsty and tired, a combination that was making her uncharacteristically cranky. She resolved not to show it even though the man's screeching had frightened Marigold into retreating farther back on the machine.

"I'm sorry, but my cat's up there. I'm trying to get her down."

"So you figured the rules didn't apply to you, is that it? I know your kind. You're a scofflaw."

Losing her temper never got her anywhere, Lane reminded herself. "I'm a woman trying to get her cat down from the top of a vending machine," she said as calmly as she could.

"Why'd you put her up there in the first place?" he demanded, his voice no longer shrill so much as it was piercing.

"I didn't put her anywhere." She heard the hint of temper enter her voice and tried to bank it. "She jumped on top of the machine."

"So she's a rule-breaker, too. Ever heard of obedience training, lady?"

Was this guy for real? "She's a cat," she retorted.

"A cat who doesn't play by the rules," he finished.

She rolled her eyes and gave the machine another good shake. "Marigold, get down here this instant."

"Unhand that machine," the burly man shouted so forcefully that she was shocked into obeying. He took a quick step sideways, putting himself between her and the machine. "I don't believe there is a cat up there. I think you're trying to cheat the machine."

"Why would I do that?" she asked, exasperated.

"We've already established you have criminal tendencies. Maybe you do these things for the thrill of it." He gazed down at her muddy shoes. "Or maybe because you're hungry."

Her temper was sliding away, but she made another attempt to rein it back in. "If I was going to steal my dinner, I'd make better nutritional choices than a pack of nabs and a stick of licorice.''

"So you're denying you're a thief." He narrowed his eyes. "But can you deny that you're a trespasser?"

Because he could easily discover it with a couple clicks of the computer keyboard, she said, "I'm not a guest here, if that's what you're asking."

"Then I want you off this property immediately."

The rumbling inside her was so foreign it took a moment to realize it was her temper preparing to let loose.

"I'm not leaving without my cat." She circled around him to the side of the machine and gave it another bang. "Marigold, come down."

"I told you to stop abusing the machine."

"And I told you I'm not leaving without Marigold."

"This calls for drastic measures." He stalked off in the direction of the office, like a sumo wrestler in a very bad mood. Before he opened the door, he threw over his shoulder, "Hothead."

The label left her feeling ashamed. She'd had a reputation for being cool and composed before Clay Crawford had started chipping away at her armor. What was happening to her? Last night, she'd nearly lost herself to passion. Today, she'd lost her temper.

Nothing short of cool logic would get Marigold down off the machine. She thought a moment, realizing she needed a chair to boost herself up. But the most likely place to get one was the hotel lobby. Somehow, she didn't think the manager would grant her request.

The piercing sound of a siren cut through the air,

followed by the sight of red and blue lights revolving in the twilight. Seconds later, a squad car screeched to a halt in front of the hotel.

A tough-looking policeman, chewing his gum like a piece of cud, got out of the car. The hotel manager hurried out of his office to meet the tall cop as he ambled her way.

"What seems to be the problem here?" the cop drawled.

"She's the problem," the hotel manager accused, pointing at Lane. "She's damaging hotel property, disturbing the peace and trespassing."

All over the hotel, doors cracked open and curtains parted. Apparently, the television lineup didn't have half the entertainment value of the law showing up at the Lake Haven Motor Inn.

"All I did was shake the machine," Lane protested, determined to hold her temper this time.

"See, she admits she broke the law," the manager said.

She looked at the cop for help, but he was obviously the strong, silent type. "It's a vending machine, for goodness sake. Not a living, breathing creature—like my cat."

Marigold picked that moment to come to the edge of the machine and peer, slit-eyed, down at them.

"You call that a cat?" Disdain dripped from the manager's high voice. "Looks more like a furry rat to me."

Fire flamed in Lane, hot and angry. She poked the manager in the chest with her forefinger. "You take that back this instant. Marigold is a wonderful cat and I won't have you saying any differently."

"Officer, this lady's assaulting me. I want to press charges."

"If anybody should press charges, it should be me," Lane said. "For...verbal abuse."

The officer removed his hat, revealing one of the most ill-fitting toupees she'd ever seen. He scratched his head. Above him, Lane noticed Marigold getting to her feet.

"Seems to me we could settle this peacefully," the cop said.

"Watch out," Lane yelled an instant before Marigold plopped onto his head. Her claws must have got tangled in his toupee, because it came off when she leaped to the ground.

The officer groaned and clutched his suddenly bare head. Marigold was at his feet, systematically picking at his toupee as though figuring out whether it would be good to eat.

"That cat's a menace to society," the manager yelled. "I demand that you arrest them both."

"You can't arrest a cat," Lane yelled back. "And Marigold is not a menace. You're the problem here."

"The problem is that you're disturbing the peace." The officer raised his voice to be heard above the shouting. "Not only can I arrest *you* for that, I can impound your cat."

THE POLICEMAN'S ANGRY THREAT pierced the once-silent night, causing Clay to pause as he approached the Lake Haven Motor Inn.

He'd headed for the motel because it seemed the logical place to cultivate sources, but he hadn't expected to run into any commotion. He wouldn't turn back now, of course. He'd saunter over there and casually ask a couple questions to determine what the brouhaha had to do with cats.

"Don't you dare touch my cat, buster!"

It was a woman's furious voice, but not just any woman's voice. Lane's voice.

Clay sprinted the rest of the way to the hotel.

The scene that greeted him had him gasping in disbelief. A short man who looked like a weight lifter was demanding that a scowling, bald cop arrest Lane. Cool, always-collected Lane had a face flushed crimson with anger

Only Marigold, who was picking at something that resembled road kill, appeared calm.

The cop reached for his handcuffs, prompting Clay into action. "Hey, wait a minute," he said, stepping into the fray. "Nobody needs to be arresting anybody here."

"You'd best stop right there unless you want to end up in jail, too," the policeman said, giving Clay the full fury of his glare.

He was as bald as a Sphynx, but something around his eyes looked familiar. Not the eyebrows with the Arc de Triomphe curve, although they were plenty distracting, but the raccoon-like circles under his eyes

"Rocky? Is that you?" he asked, breaking into a smile. "Remember me? Clay Crawford from the *Miami Courier*."

The cop's broad-featured face registered first recognition, then pleasure. Never underestimate the power of the press, Clay thought. Especially when the press pretended he'd never heard the cop in question call his precinct captain a "moron too half-witted to do anything but push a pencil."

"Clay, my man." Rocky grasped his hand in a brief shake. "I'd love to catch up, but I gotta arrest this lady for disorderly conduct first."

"I'm not disorderly," Lane yelled and thumped the machine so hard she winced in pain. Clay took the opportunity to wrap his arms around her shoulders.

She stiffened immediately, so he tightened his grasp and whispered in her ear. "If you don't want to end up in jail, be quiet and go along with me on this."

"Do you know this woman?" Rocky asked suspiciously.

"She's no woman, she's a hellcat," the manager cut in.

Clay ignored the shorter man. "She's a friend who gets touchy when someone insults her cat. Rocky, I'd consider it a personal favor if you forget about all this."

"I don't know, Clay," the cop said, scratching his chin. "Her cat did scalp me."

Clay gave Lane's shoulders a warning squeeze before he bent to retrieve Rocky's toupee. Having discovered that she couldn't eat it, Marigold had lost interest and looked in danger of dozing off.

"Personally, I like the bald look," Clay said, handing the hairpiece to Rocky while he regarded him. "It goes with the tough-guy, cop persona."

"You think so? Maybe I'll go without then." Rocky seemed pleased. He even smiled. The radio scanner in his car went off, reporting a jaywalker a couple blocks away. "Gotta go. You and the lady have a good evening, Clay."

The officer strode off in the direction of his squad car, prompting the sputtering manager to turn on them. "Don't look so smug. I'm pressing charges."

"Would this change your mind?" Clay asked, getting out his wallet and producing two fifties. The man hesitated only slightly before snatching them out of Clay's hand.

"I still want you lawbreakers off the premises," he bit off before heading for the office.

"I suppose you think I should thank you for that," Lane said as they both reached down to pick up her cat. She got to Marigold first so he retrieved the soda can she must have dropped. "Throwing money around like that is shameful, especially when he didn't have a case."

Clay stood back, enjoying her as she raved. His suspicion that Lane Brooks was hiding a wealth of passion under that cool exterior hadn't been wrong. Now all he had to do was subtract the anger from the passion and get her to direct it at him.

He frowned. After he beat her out for the *Splash!* job, of course.

"Seemed like he had a case to me," Clay said.

She ignored his comment, buried her face in Marigold's coarse fur and looked at him from beneath her lashes. "You know of course that now I have to pay you back."

"I don't expect you to."

"I refuse to be indebted to you."

"Okay, then." He shrugged. "I can think of a way you can pay me back."

Her head snapped up. "You're deluded if you think for one second that—"

"I'm talking about repaying me with your soda," he said, holding up the can. "Rescuing a damsel in distress works up a powerful thirst."

He popped the tab, which gave off a terrible whizzing sound a millisecond before sticky, dark soda exploded in his face. He blinked, trying to keep the stuff out of his eyes and caught Lane's amused look.

"That wasn't my soda, smart guy," she said as he mopped his face with his sleeve. "Let's get out of here before the manager calls that cop back to arrest you for making a mess of things."

8

LANE'S FACE no longer felt flushed, her blood no longer bubbled and her breathing was as normal as it got when Clay Crawford was in the vicinity.

Unable to help herself, she looked her fill of him. Wisps of his dark hair were matted and his clothes were soiled from the cola that had splashed in his face, but he was still worth salivating over.

It wasn't because of his fabulous body and the contrast of his dark hair and blue eyes. It wasn't even because of the intelligence and compassion that shone out of those eyes.

It was because he was carrying her cat. With Marigold in his arms, Clay was darn near irresistible.

"I can carry my own cat, you know," Lane said, mostly because it was imperative that she keep on resisting him.

"You're carrying the carrier, which isn't as heavy. I'm sure those arms of yours are sore enough." Too late, she realized that she'd given herself away by absently massaging the tender places. She made herself stop.

"I wouldn't have her with me in the first place if it weren't for that demon cat of yours," she said, casting about for some reason to blame him. "Wade says his hotel room wasn't big enough for the both of them."

"I'll talk to Wade when we get back," he said easily. "It's only right that I keep Rover with me tonight since you had Marigold last night."

"No, don't do that," Lane said quickly. He wasn't playing fair, she thought darkly. Not only was Clay attractive, he was thoughtful. "I like having her with me."

They lapsed into silence as they walked parallel to the nearly deserted highway, the quiet occasionally broken by the whirring of an engine as a car passed them. The light of a full moon shone down on them, casting a soft glow over the sidewalk that stretched ahead of them. The night seemed to have secrets, like the man beside her.

"What did you have on that cop back there?" she asked. "It seemed like he owed you a favor."

"It was nothing," Clay said, shrugging. "I was researching a story about the city of Miami PD cutting back on overtime pay, he mouthed off and I didn't print his comments."

"Why not?"

"While words like lily-livered and despicable liven up a quote, I didn't see the point in jeopardizing a man's career over them."

"Oh." She grew quiet again, but the silence nagged at her. He'd called in a favor because of her, which deserved a heck of a lot more than silence.

"Thank you," she said after a moment.

"You're welcome." He gave her a sideways smile and nodded toward a side street. "We'll get back sooner if we go back that way."

"How would you know about a shortcut in Lake Haven?"

"I spent a couple weeks here when I was in high school."

Lane couldn't get that to compute. What would a rich kid like Clay be doing in a second-rate town hundreds of miles from home? "Whatever for?" she asked.

His hesitation was so long she thought he wasn't going to tell her. "Some teens from my church donated our time to a group building homes for low-income families."

"But I thought you—" she stopped abruptly, realizing hers were thoughts that shouldn't be shared.

"Unless a cat's got your tongue, why don't you say what's on your mind? Although I can guess. You thought I spent all my summers at the country club, didn't you?"

His voice held an edge that made her want to defend herself. "You do come from money."

"My dad comes from money, my mother doesn't." He kicked at a stone, sent it flying into the night. "She met my dad when she was working as a waitress in Hialeah. She's never been comfortable with all the wealth that surrounds us so she made sure I grew up with a strong work ethic."

"Is she the one who didn't want you to go to an Ivy League school?"

"Are you kidding? After the way she pushed me to get good grades? I was the one who picked a public university. It was where all my friends were going and where I felt most comfortable." He paused. "And before you ask, I don't live in a waterfront mansion. I have a condo in Coral Gables."

This glimpse of him was so different from her

preconceived notions that she was having a hard time digesting it.

"What about you?" he asked, taking her arm as they crossed another street. The touch was so thrilling that she felt bereft when they reached the sidewalk and he released her. "Tell me the story of Lane Brooks. Have you always wanted to write for a newspaper?"

"Always. A kind of thrill goes through me when I pick one up, knowing all that information's at my fingertips." She wasn't sure why she was telling him this, only that she wanted to. "When I was in fifth grade, I even shortened my name from Elaine to Lane."

"Because you wanted to write for the *Daily Planet*," he guessed. "Like Lois."

She smiled at him. "Exactly. I was crushed when I found out it was a fictional paper, so I set my sights elsewhere. I started a newspaper in elementary school, was editor of the high school paper and wrote a column in college."

"So you're doing exactly what you always wanted to do?"

She nodded, aware that the logical follow-up question would be why she was vying for a magazine job. She wasn't sure how to answer so she turned the conversation.

"How about you? Did you always want to write for a newspaper?"

"I always wanted to write, but the newspaper part was pre-ordained. I'll tell you one thing, though, writing for a newspaper isn't nearly as important as making a name for myself."

"The Crawford name has already been made."

"I'm talking about the name Clay Crawford, not Charles Crawford."

"But why would the heir to the throne care about what anybody else thinks?" Lane asked and then stopped herself when she saw his face fall.

"So you've heard the Prince Willy nickname?"

She bit her lip, thinking it would be worse if she denied it. "Who hasn't?"

"That's exactly what I mean. I want to be respected because of my reporting and writing, and I don't see that happening if I stay at the *Courier.*"

"I respect your reporting."

She did? In a year of competing side by side with him, that thought had never entered her conscious mind. Now that she'd spoken it, however, she knew it was true. He slanted her a skeptical look.

"No, really. I've seen the research books on cat shows in your room and watched the methodical way you go about reporting a story." She swallowed, because the next part was hard to admit. Even to herself. "I've always known you were a quality reporter."

"And here I got the impression you thought I was a yellow journalist. Or at the very least, a lazy one."

She waved a hand. "Only because I didn't want to give you the advantage. Daddy always says if you butter up the competition, you might as well hand over the piece of bread."

He didn't respond, which gave her time to think over the past year and the rotten things she'd accused him of.

"You didn't know I was a reporter that first night we met," Lane said.

It was more of a statement than a question, but he answered anyway. "Nope."

They continued the rest of the walk in silence, Marigold gently purring in his arms, while Lane thought about the realization she'd come to.

All these months, she'd been blaming Clay for something that wasn't his fault. Even if she'd gotten wind of the mayor's corruption, she couldn't have pulled together a story for the next day's edition. There simply hadn't been enough time.

The reason she'd used Clay as a scapegoat was as clear as the water she left out for Marigold. Once she stopped blaming him, there was nothing keeping her from the other things she wanted to do to him. And with him.

"I'll carry Marigold to your bed," he said once they'd gotten off the elevator and reached her door. "I think she's asleep."

Lane used her key card to unlock the door and trailed him in the darkness. He laid the cat gently on the bed while her heart drummed inside of her, anticipation building to fever pitch.

Tonight was the night she'd make love to Clay Crawford. There was nothing to stop her.

When he straightened, his face was just inches from her, his mouth so close that all she had to do was lean slightly forward and their lips would touch.

"I've thought a lot about what you said last night," he said. She felt his breath on her lips, smelled the curiously sexy mix of man and cola.

Here it is, she thought. Here's where he reiterated his familiar refrain about their professional relationship not having to interfere with their personal one. She waited, holding her breath.

"You were right, Laney. I want that job too badly to let anything personal between us cloud the issue."

He touched her cheek and disappeared through the connecting door, leaving Lane staring after him in shocked dismay.

CLAY CLOSED HIS EYES, shutting out the auditorium and its hundreds of cat-happy occupants. After last night, he felt more like growling than purring.

He rubbed his brow, damning himself for the hundredth time as an idiot. The worst part was he had only himself to blame for acting like one.

He'd sensed that the thaw had finally arrived when he'd walked Lane back to her room the night before. That this time she wouldn't stop him from making love to her. She'd trembled in his arms and gazed at him with affection instead of asperity.

Then, instead of going with the flow and luxuriating in the swift current of their passion, he'd said that incredibly stupid thing about agreeing they shouldn't sleep together and lain awake the rest of the night.

As though self-sacrifice was making any difference.

He didn't know what progress Lane had made on the cat-show corruption story, but he had a big, fat zilch. As far as he'd been able to determine, Pup Doggett ran a squeaky-clean cat show.

"Meow." It was Rover, who'd been staring at him for ten minutes with a supercilious expression on her small face, as though she enjoyed his discomfort.

He shook a finger at her. "Don't you meow me."

Something purple and fluffy tickled his face and

he jerked backward, afraid it might be a new breed of cat before he realized it was the tail of a purple feather boa.

The woman wearing it had a face caked with makeup and white hair piled on her head in an elaborate topknot. She was dressed in a flamboyant grape and yellow caftan and frightfully high heels. The jewels around her neck were so ostentatious he was nearly blinded by the glare.

She looked like Carol Channing about to break out into a rendition of "Diamonds are a Girl's Best Friend."

"Hello there, dahling," she said, and it took a moment for Clay to realize she was talking to him. The wrinkled, ring-heavy hand on his arm was the big tipoff. "I've been meaning to talk to you the entire show. I have seldom seen a more exquisite body."

Clay blinked in shock. Because men were in the minority at a cat show, he'd naturally been the target of female attention. But this was the first time a woman had been this forward.

"So muscular. With such short, satiny hair."

Her grip tightened on his shoulder. He touched his hair, which didn't feel like satin to him. The woman continued in the same breathless voice.

"Such large eyes and strong legs." She sighed. "And such tiny feet."

He eyes dropped to his size twelves, then back up to the woman, who was looking at...Rover?

"Your little one is the cat's meow," she said, removing her hand. He wasn't sure whether to feel relieved or foolish, so he settled for a little of both.

"Exactly how many ribbons did she win?" She

studied the cage, which was festooned with so many satiny awards it was difficult to see past them to the cat inside.

Too many to count. "At least one from every judge."

"She certainly deserves to be named one of the ten best in the show, but you never can tell how these things will go."

Something about the way she phrased her opinion put Clay's reporting instincts on alert. "Are you saying that the best cats don't always win?"

She cast a quick, furtive glance around their immediate vicinity. Then she flipped the feather boa back over her shoulder, revealing that she held a hairless cat. A Sphynx, like Marcus Miller's Prune.

"That's not what *I'm* saying, but there's a rumor going around about the Daytona Beach FFF show." She lowered her voice even further. "I hear that a Grand Champion entered and came away with nary a ribbon."

Clay swallowed his excitement and kept his voice neutral, "Was this cat a Sphynx?"

"Why, yes she was. With a silly nickname. Something like Raisin. Or Apricot."

"Prune?" he supplied.

"That's it." She pursed her painted pink lips. "You've heard the story already, haven't you? Harry Martinelli has a bigger mouth than the intracoastal waterway."

"Actually, I don't know the guy," Clay said. "Would you mind pointing him out?"

The woman smiled, revealing teeth so perfectly white they must have cost thousands in dental bleaching, and indicated a tall man dressed completely in gray. With his dark hair slicked back from his face, he might have resembled an old-time gangster if it hadn't been for his goofy grin. He was directing it at a perky redhead, who took one step back for every step he advanced. They were covering more ground than a lawn mower.

"I'd do anything for you, dahling," the woman with the purple boa said, drawing his attention away from Martinelli. Her smile was predatory. "I do so love a handsome man with a tiny cat."

Five minutes later, having miraculously extracted himself from the woman with the feather boa, Clay approached Harry Martinelli. Before the redhead had walked swiftly away from him, Martinelli had been laughing so loudly he seemed in danger of breaking a rib. Now his lips were set in a tight line.

It probably wasn't the best moment to question him, but Clay didn't have the luxury of time. Only hours were left in the cat show.

"Clay Crawford," he said, sticking out a hand.

Martinelli stuffed his hand in his pocket. His eyes hardened and his bottom lip curled. "So here you are, the competition: up close and personal."

Clay glanced at the gray-and-white Sphynx in the cage behind Martinelli. "You've got it wrong, pal. My cat's a Singapura, not a Sphynx."

"Cut the crap. You think I haven't seen you hitting on every woman in sight? Who do you think you are? Me?"

"I'm missing something here."

Martinelli came so close Clay could smell... onion? In the morning? He reeled backward. Martinelli should either rethink his omelet choice or use mouthwash after breakfast. No wonder the redhead had fled.

"Don't play dumb with me. We both know you've figured out a cat show's the best place to score with the babes. They're crawling all over the place."

"I'm here because of the cats," Clay denied, which got an onion-scented snort of disbelief from Martinelli. "In fact, I wanted to talk to you about the Daytona Beach show."

"Talk to the cat," Martinelli said, indicating the Sphynx, "because its owner ain't gonna listen."

He strolled away, smoothing back his greased hair as he honed in on another target: a quiet brunette reading a mystery novel with a cat on the cover. The woman looked up when Martinelli spoke to her, then did a backbend in her chair.

Clay stroked his chin while an idea formed. Martinelli was clearly partial to the fairer sex and no female in the building compared to Lane in either brains or beauty. Or, most important, reporting skills.

Telling Lane that Martinelli could be the key to breaking the story might not be smart, but what choice did he have? He went off in search of Lane, which, after all, was what he'd wanted to do all morning.

He found her as she was finishing up a conversation with Pup Doggett, a compact bulldog of a man whom Elliot had introduced to them days ago. Lane's features were composed in their usual cool mask, but when she turned away from the FFF president the corners of her mouth turned slightly downward before she yanked them back up.

He knew her well enough by now to tell that Pup hadn't given her any useful information.

From the way her shoulders tensed and her chin lifted, he also knew the moment she spotted him. She would have walked past him with a nod if he hadn't put out an arm to stop her.

"Laney, wait. I have a proposition for you."

"So now you want to sleep with me, is that it?" She looked down at the hand curved over her upper arm, then into his eyes. Her cool gaze seemed to melt like chocolate in the sun but her voice was hard. "Has it even occurred to you that now it might be too late?"

"No," he said, intending to explain he wasn't talking about that kind of proposition.

"Just because I find you incredibly sexually attractive—"

She did? "You do?"

"Doesn't mean I'm going to hop in bed with you because you suddenly have a hankering for me," she finished with spirit.

He leaned closer, enjoying the color that flushed her cheeks. "I do have a hankering for you, but I also have a hankering for your help," he whispered. "On the story."

"That's the kind of proposition you were talking about?"

He nodded, enjoying her discomfort.

"I didn't mean what I said about sleeping with you," she said quickly.

"Oh, yes you did. I'm a newspaper reporter, remember. I have an uncanny ability to remember quotes. And I distinctly remember you saying that you find me unbelievably sexually attractive."

"Incredibly," she snapped. "Incredibly sexually attractive, not unbelievably."

"Six of one, half a dozen of the other. You say tomato, I say to-mah-to."

She cleared her throat and seemed to collect herself so that her gaze was once again chilly, her body language poised. "So what kind of a deal are you proposing?"

Clay had seen the crack in the dam of her self-control and was tempted to chip away at it. But there was time for that later. For now, they needed to concentrate on the story.

"I'll be straight with you. At this moment, I don't have a story. But I do have a lead," he said, leaning conspiratorially forward and telling her the rest of the story. The faint stain of color on her cheeks told him she wasn't immune to his nearness.

"So you're proposing I talk to Martinelli and we pool our information?"

"Exactly."

"And what makes you think I'll tell you what he knows instead of taking the ball and running with it?"

"Because I trust you," he said simply.

His revelation seemed to strike her dumb. He read confusion and something softer in her eyes before she straightened her shoulders and retorted, "You're not too smart then, are you?"

He grinned as he watched her walk swiftly away from him and up to Harry Martinelli, enjoying her spunk. But he did trust her. Completely and unequivocally.

The smile quickly faded when he read interest on the other man's face, which wouldn't have been all that bad of a face if it hadn't been attached to Martinelli's personality. Harry Martinelli, he didn't trust.

But Lane didn't seem at all put off by Martinelli's abrasiveness. Or his onion breath. Clay had observed her interacting with others and knew she had a way of listening that made people want to tell her things.

Martinelli put a hand on her arm as they talked, and she let it stay there. She laughed at something Martinelli said, making Clay suspicious that she was enjoying the other man's attention.

And what if she were? What if Martinelli was more her type than Clay? What if, by sending Lane to Martinelli, Clay had blown his own chances?

Lane must have said something amusing, because at that moment Martinelli gave forth such a goofy guffaw that at least a dozen cats around them meowed in what sounded like fright.

And that's when the truth hit Clay. If he could get jealous of a guffawing Cat Show Romeo, he didn't only want to get Lane into bed.

He wanted to get into her heart, because, like it or not, he'd fallen in love with her.

LANE WORKED HARD to contain her excitement as she walked back to Clay, but the thrill of the chase bubbled inside her. Harry Martinelli hadn't given her enough to write an exposé on cat-show corruption, but had provided her with a solid lead. To a reporter like Lane, that was golden.

It had even been worth the fifteen minutes she'd spent fending off Martinelli's passes while she'd tried not to breathe. To think she'd been avoiding him for days when he was exactly the source she needed to mine.

Once she told Clay that all Martinelli had were suspicions, she could chase down the lead. She was aware that Clay trusted her to share what she'd discovered, but she'd only promised to tell him what Martinelli knew.

Because Martinelli didn't know what had happened at the Daytona Beach show but had directed her to someone who might, in the strictest sense she intended to follow their agreement.

If Clay got burned, too bad. He should have known better than to trust a competitor in the first place.

She was composing her opening sentence when she noticed that something about Clay's expression seemed off. As though he might be coming down with something.

She increased her tempo and laid a hand against his cheek. It was cool to the touch. "Are you all right? You look a little peaked."

"If looking peaked makes you want to touch me, I'll try to look this way all the time," he said, turning his face and pressing a kiss into her sensitive palm. A thrill coursed down her arm. "Find out anything?"

Confused, she let her hand drop. This wasn't the way the conversation was supposed to go. She swallowed.

"He was more than happy to share the mysteries of the Sphynx with me. Even though Prune was the best of the Sphynxes, not one of the six judges placed her in the top three in her color class."

"Yeah, but we already knew that from Marcus."

"But Harry went so far as to say he thought the show was rigged."

"Does he have any proof? Any motive?" Clay asked the same questions Lane had presented to Harry.

"No." Lane shook her head for emphasis. "He has nothing."

Clay's wide mouth drooped and his beautiful eyes filled with disappointment. "So the interview was a dead end?"

She stared at him, thinking about how easy it would be to nod and walk away. Even if the source to whom Martinelli had directed her proved fruitful, Clay need never know how she'd found her.

Nod and walk away, she told herself, but her head stalled in mid-bob and her feet felt weighed down with concrete. She couldn't do this. Not even with the *Splash!* job dangling within reach.

"It wasn't a dead end. Harry thinks Pup Doggett's secretary knows what happened. Her name's Marisa."

Clay's smile started out small and grew until it lit up his entire face. "I was right to trust you with the ball," he said.

She broke eye contact and looked down at her feet, wondering what in the heck had just happened here. "You're probably faster than me anyway," she said, mumbling. "Stacy has all the speed in my family."

"Excuse me?"

"It's just something Daddy always says." She hazarded a look at him. Oh, dear, why did he have to be so handsome? "If you take the ball and run with it, you better be faster than the guy chasing you."

If possible, his grin grew wider. "So you've finally figured out I'm chasing you?'' he whispered, running a hand down her arm. Not wanting to give her body time to react to his caress, she snatched his hand up in hers and tugged.

"Come on," she said, "we have a secretary to interview."

The sane part of her brain knew there was something inherently wrong about collaborating with an opponent, but darned if she could figure out what it was.

9

LANE HEARD THE LAUGHTER before she saw Pup Doggett's secretary. She was sitting at a desk in a back room of the cultural center, one shapely leg crossed over the other as she gabbed on the phone.

"So Mark wants to know, 'How come Benny's kissing you if he's your cousin?' Remember, that's what I told him after he saw us together. So I go, 'He's one of them kissin' cousins you're always hearing about.'"

Marisa's trilling laugh echoed in the room as she swung her leg, dangling a high heel on her toe. Lane thought she would have been pretty if she hadn't gone to so much effort to appear as though she were.

The dark hair she'd styled in great, rolling waves was too big for her face and her makeup was so heavy it was hard to see the woman underneath.

Still, she was a curvaceous little thing, as she'd made sure everyone knew. Her red dress was tighter than Ebenezer Scrooge's wallet.

Lane turned toward Clay, prepared for the inevitable gaping men did whenever an attractive woman showed off her assets, but Clay's eyes were fastened on her. His eyebrows were raised in a can-you-believe-this-woman arch.

"Then Mark goes, 'Kissin' cousins, huh? Maybe I can find me a cousin to try that on.'"

She cut her laughter short with a sneeze so inelegant that the sole paper on the desk lifted, then fluttered back down. She reached for her red leather purse, only then spotting Lane and Clay in the doorway.

"I'll call you back later, girlfriend." She hung up the phone as she pulled out a handkerchief and dabbed at her nose.

"Excuse us," Lane said. "We're looking for Pup Doggett."

Her red-rimmed eyes lifted to them but settled on Clay. So did her smile. "Pup split. He went out for a dog." She laughed at their dumbfounded faces. "I mean a hot dog."

"Maybe you can help us." Clay approached her desk in that confident, sexy way of his. "I'm Clay Crawford and this is Lane Brooks. We're working on a story about cat shows for a new magazine set to debut in Florida called *Splash!*"

"And you think I can help?" Marisa pressed a long-fingered hand to her chest. "Nah. Cats don't do it for me." Her eyes swept Clay's length. "It takes more than felines to get my motor revving."

"I'm sure you know a lot about cats," Lane said, trying so hard to maintain a friendly expression that she was getting a face ache. "Why else would you be working for the FFF?"

"Because Uncle Pup knew I was hard up for a job. I thought I'd wait around 'til something better came by and I could blow this joint." She shook her index finger. "But don't you be telling him that."

Something told Lane her uncle had probably already figured it out.

"We wouldn't dream of it," Clay said. "We certainly don't want to get you in trouble."

"Aren't you just the sweetest thing?" Marisa looked like she wanted to lick him all over so she could find out. "Uncle Pup handles just about everything but the phone and some of the computer stuff. And I haven't exactly gotten the hang of that yet. But just ask away and I'll help if I can."

Clay slanted Lane a quick look that clearly told her he had a plan for proceeding with the interview. She nodded to let him know she understood and listened as he asked the secretary a half-dozen questions about cat-show procedure.

It was a standard interviewing technique among investigative reporters. Ease the source by asking the unimportant questions first, then zap them with the pertinent ones.

Because the secretary had yet to knowledgeably answer an easy question, Lane doubted it would work.

"Any idea how a cat that was a Grand Champion in one organization could fail to win a ribbon from the FFF?" Clay finally asked.

Marisa let out another earsplitting sneeze and did the dainty handkerchief dab again. "You mean there's more than one outfit that does cat shows?"

"I know of at least eleven," Clay said.

"You don't say?" she said. "Guess that makes sense. Look how many beauty contests there are. Miss Teen USA, Miss USA, Miss World, Miss Universe..."

By the time she'd finished reciting her list, Lane was convinced they were wasting their time. Harry Martinelli, it seemed, had led them to a dead end.

"Uncle Pup's the man you want to see," Marisa said when she came up blank on yet another question. "Come around later. For now, how 'bout I print out some of the stuff he keeps on the computer about cat shows? Maybe that'll help."

Lane doubted it, but stood by politely while Marisa tapped on the computer keyboard, periodically pausing to sneeze so powerfully it took all Lane's restraint not to cover her ears.

"I hope your cold gets better," she said when they had the computer printouts in hand.

"Cold? What cold?" Marisa asked. "I'm sneezing 'cause I'm allergic to cats."

As she wrote out her name and phone number on a card she handed to Clay just in case he had more questions, Lane found herself wishing Marisa was allergic to men.

Clay pocketed the card, but the minute they got into the hall it was obvious he was more interested in the printouts than Marisa's phone number.

"We could have gotten more information out of a cat than we did from Marisa Doggett," Lane said as Clay shuffled through the papers.

"Maybe not." Clay stared intently at one of the papers he'd pulled out of the stack, then handed it to her. "Get a load of this. I think it's an e-mail from one of the judges."

The top of the printout was dated two weeks ago, which coincided with the Daytona Beach show. Lane recognized the name as belonging to one of the FFF judges who was at Lake Haven.

Re: Shaved Sphynx, the subject header read.

Lane's eyes quickly dropped to the body of the e-mail.

Pup: Will do as you ask. If the Miller cat's been shaved, she doesn't deserve to win. Don't worry. Will keep this on the QT.

CLAY ENJOYED CHASING a good story, but it was obvious Lane thrived on it. She seemed to have forgotten her aversion to touching him as she dragged him across the cultural center in search of Wade McCoy.

They found the cat wrangler sitting by Rover's cage, his hat pulled low over his eyes. Lane handed Wade the printout of the e-mail, then waited with barely contained excitement as he read it.

"That's just plumb crazy," Wade said, peering out from under his hat. "I've known that man for going on ten years, and he don't shave that cat."

"But what if he did?" Lane asked. "What would that mean in terms of the cat show?"

"Disqualification," Wade said. "The less hair a Sphynx has, the better. You pluck it, shave it, clip it or depilatate it, and your cat's out of the running. But I was at that show and nobody told Marcus they were disqualifying Prune."

"I knew it." Lane clenched a fist. "I knew this was the break we'd been waiting for when I saw that e-mail."

Wade tapped his cowboy hat and rubbed his forehead. "Could be. Seems to me that Pup Doggett told his judges they had a shaved cat in their midst and they believed him."

"Shouldn't the judges have been able to tell it was a lie?" Clay asked.

"Maybe not," Wade said thoughtfully. "A Sphynx isn't truly hairless. It's covered with a fine down the naked eye can barely see. Prune's got less down than most, just like one man has less hair than the next.''

''So they blackballed her,'' Lane said, and Clay could see the wheels turning in her head. He was sure she was thinking about how to approach the judge who'd sent the e-mail and the others who had been at the Daytona Beach show. If any of them confirmed the blackballing, *Splash!* had itself a story on cat-show corruption.

''What are we waiting for?'' Lane's eyes sparkled as they met his. ''We've got some judges to interview.''

The Daytona Beach event had been a six-ring show with six judges, but only five were present in Lake Haven. After the judge who'd sent the e-mail refused to speak to them, Clay and Lane split up.

An hour later, each of them had persuaded one of the four remaining judges to admit that Prune had been blackballed because of unproved allegations of cat shaving. The judge Clay had talked to was self-righteous, asserting that the FFF couldn't condone cheating cats.

''Pup got wind of what we were doing and split,'' Lane said when they got back together to compare notes. ''Elliot thought it would be better for the FFF if Pup gave his side of the story, but he told his grandfather he had no comment.''

''We have confirmation from two judges and the e-mail,'' Clay said. ''*Splash!* doesn't need Pup's co-operation to run with the story.''

''Then I guess all that's left to do is write it,'' Lane said, her eyes holding his. He thought he read something deep and sorrowful in her gaze before she broke eye contact. "So we're done here."

When she flipped closed the reporter's notebook she'd been consulting, it seemed symbolic to Clay. Their collaboration was at an end so she was shutting herself off from him. Just like she'd closed herself off after that magical night on the beach a year ago.

"I've got to get back to Fort Lauderdale," she said, her lips not quite forming a smile. "Maybe I'll run into you sometime."

A line of static came over the public-address system that felt analogous to what was happening inside him. That's what the kiss-off did to you. And she was giving him the kiss-off without the kiss. Except he couldn't let that happen. Not this time.

He started to speak but was interrupted by a loud squeal on the PA system. "Attention... Attention... Will the owners of the ten best cats in the show assemble in ring one for the award presentation."

Lane gave him a tight smile. "Rover's one of them, isn't she?"

Wade had corralled Clay about forty-five minutes ago to tell him that Rover was up for an additional honor, but Clay had hardly paid attention.

"I guess so," he said, "but—"

"Then you better get her up there. You don't want Rover to miss the presentation."

She leaned forward and this time did kiss him, so lightly and sweetly that the contact was over almost before it began.

"Goodbye, Clay," she said before pivoting and walking swiftly away.

He touched his lips, already missing the feel of

hers on them. The kiss-off was even more wrenching with the kiss.

LANE SHIFTED MARIGOLD in her arms as she slipped inside the hotel room and pulled the door shut behind her with a resounding bang.

"Oops," she said, then lowered her voice to a whisper. "Didn't mean to do that. Remember what I told you, Marigold. We need to be quiet so you-know-who doesn't hear us."

Her eyes scanned the room, which the maid had yet to make up since Lane had checked out of the hotel that morning.

"It was nice of the desk clerk to let us come up here and look for Squeaky, wasn't it?" she asked in a loud voice, then covered her mouth with her hand. "Oops again. I better be quiet or Clay will know we're in here."

Her eyes did a cursory scan of the room as she searched for Marigold's toy mouse, which she'd discovered wasn't inside the cat's carrier when they were barely a half hour outside Lake Haven.

Sure, it was possible that she'd packed Squeaky inside one of her suitcases, which were securely nestled in the trunk of her car. But pulling off the highway and stopping to search the bags seemed as much of a bother as turning around and heading back to the hotel.

She could have checked the bags when she reached the hotel parking lot, but by that time it seemed just as easy to search the room.

The sight of Clay's car in the lot wasn't altogether unexpected because she'd overheard him that morning at the front desk asking for a late checkout time.

He was probably in his room, looking impossibly studly as he packed his bag. She didn't want to run into him, of course, but she needed to risk that in order to retrieve Marigold's beloved toy.

She stooped and let Marigold out of her arms, prepared for the chorus of meows that sounded from the cat whenever she changed environments. But Marigold made her soundless way to a chair and hopped onto it.

"What? No meows?" Lane put her hands on her hips, then let her arms drop to her sides. Maybe the cat hadn't been gone from the room long enough to feel uncomfortable. "Not that I want you to meow, of course. We must be very quiet."

She pulled back the ulphostered chair at the small dining table so vigorously that it crashed against the wall.

"Oops yet again," she said, then waited with bated breath for a knock on the connecting door. One minute passed, then two.

"What is he? Deaf?" she muttered under her breath.

She bent down, lifted the quilt and took a quick glance under the bed. No Squeaky, which probably meant she was ensconced in the suitcase. Lane repositioned herself and her hip bumped the bedside table as she straightened. The alarm clock fell to the floor, but this time it didn't blare.

She stopped, again listening for sounds from the next room. She thought she heard faint rustling but couldn't be sure. Maybe he'd already gone, she thought as she gazed at the door that separated them.

"Good riddance. Right, Marigold? But I probably

should check. That way we'll know for sure that the coast is clear.''

She crept to the door, remembering what Clay had said about keeping his side unlocked. Slowly, she turned the knob on the dead bolt and yanked open the door.

Clay was standing beside the bed, not a stitch of clothes on his long, hard-muscled body. The hair on his head and on his chest and on his—oh my!—was damp, telling her he'd just gotten out of the shower.

Her eyes swept his length before coming to rest on his beautiful ocean eyes, which were gazing at her in surprise.

''Laney?'' he said, prompting her to do the only thing she could.

She slammed the door and braced her back against it.

''Laney?'' he said again. She could clearly hear his voice through the plywood of the door. ''Did you want something?''

''No,'' she said quickly. She couldn't want him. She mustn't, she told herself even as she imagined his body in all its naked glory mere feet from hers.

''Then why did you open the door? You must want something.''

''I wanted...'' She frantically searched her brain for something to say and managed to sound normal saying it. ''...to find out what place Rover came in at the cat show.''

There was a significant pause before he answered. ''Open the door and I'll tell you.''

She closed her eyes against the desire to do exactly that, but thought about how luscious he looked naked and knew she couldn't trust herself to resist him a second time.

"Are you decent?" she asked and heard the rumble of his laughter before something she thought sounded like, "Too much for my own good."

Louder, he said, "It'll just take a minute for me to put on some clothes."

It was less than that when one loud knock sounded on the door. Bracing herself, she pulled it open. Clay was no longer naked, but dressed in snug-fitting blue jeans he'd left unsnapped and a plaid shirt he hadn't bothered to button. That magnificent chest she'd salivated over a few nights before was again exposed to her gaze. She dropped her eyes and they fell on his bare feet.

She slowly brought her eyes back up and saw such heat in his gaze that everything inside her seemed to melt and pool low in her body. She schooled her expression and strove for the tone she used when discussing the weather.

"So how did Rover fare?"

His chest rose and fell, drawing Lane's attention to the sexy brawn of it and making her want to strip off his shirt and press her mouth to his flesh.

"I don't want you to think I'm bragging, because she's not my cat." He paused, letting out a heavy sigh. "But she got best in show."

Lane had been prepared for the revelation, but still it stung. "She is a pretty cat," she said.

"Keep in mind that Marigold could beat her in the fifty-yard dash, no contest," he said before he reached for her hand, enveloped it in his and gave it a gentle squeeze. His attempt to cheer her up was so sweet that it felt like he was doing the same thing to her heart.

"It's okay. I've accepted that Marigold's not a show cat. It's like Daddy always says, 'If you're out of your league, you better find yourself a new league.'"

His eyes held fast to hers as she talked. If this was what it felt like to drown in the vast blue ocean, she imagined it wasn't an altogether unpleasant sensation. She blinked, trying to stay above the surface.

"Where is the cat of the hour?" she asked, although what she really wanted to know was why he hadn't released her hand. And why she didn't want him to.

"Wade was driving to Miami to do some business with Marcus and asked if it was okay if he took Rover," he said, his thumb drawing lazy circles on her palm. She managed, just barely, not to shiver. "He's one crazy cat wrangler. He says where he comes from people don't cotton to champagne, so he doused me with beer when Rover won. That's why I had to shower."

Only their hands were touching, but every part of her body felt connected to his. Especially, she thought in abject horror, her heart.

"Was Rover the only reason you came back?" he asked softly. Hopefully?

She gritted her teeth so she wouldn't run her tongue over her lips the way she wanted him to. She could have told him about returning to search for Squeaky but her voice wouldn't work.

"There's something I've been wondering," he whispered. He took a finger and ran it up the length of her arm, creating delicious shivers along the way.

When he got to her chin, he tipped it up and took off her glasses so he could see more fully into her eyes. "Does your father have an expression about keeping your game face?"

"Uh, huh," she said, trying desperately to keep hers. Her lips trembled, her heart sighed and she knew she'd lost the battle. "Let your game face slip and you're gonna get smacked."

"On the lips? As in kissed?" he asked, his eyes smiling into hers. His head came forward, his mouth stopping just inches from hers.

"I'm pretty sure he meant tackled," she answered, amazed that breathless voice belonged to her.

"That can be arranged later. When we're closer to the bed."

The sensual promise in his voice sent her heart tripping against her chest and her blood racing, thick and heated, through her body. She reached up to fist her hands in his thick, dark hair, feeling her game face dissolve the rest of the way.

Then his mouth was on hers and his arms were pulling her against the hard length of his body, exactly where she'd wanted to be since the first time she'd seen him.

His lips were firm and dry, their soft texture teasing her mouth and sending what felt like electric current shooting through her. This time she didn't try to resurrect any distasteful images, because it was useless trying to pretend that she didn't want this kiss. This intimacy. This man.

For almost a year, she'd convinced herself that she was only attracted to his body, but it wasn't lust she felt. It was something warm and wonderful that coursed through her veins and flooded her heart, something only Clay could bring out.

The kiss went on and on, the sensations building, the wonder of it all-consuming. She strained to get closer to him and could feel the heat of his chest through her clothes, the hard thrill of him against her lower body.

His hands skimmed the sides of her chest, tantalizingly near the soft swell of her breasts. He trailed kisses along the side of her mouth to her neck, and she shivered in delicious anticipation.

"All this time, I thought those cool looks meant you didn't want me," he murmured against her skin, his breath like a warm wind.

"I've always wanted you, Clay," she rasped, her head thrown back to give him greater access to the sensitive cord of her neck. She'd thought that surrendering to her desire for him would make her feel weak, but a sensual power surged through her. "Come to bed with me and I'll show you how much."

Almost before she got the words out, she felt her legs leave the floor as he gathered her in his arms and carried her to the unmade bed in her room. She nestled her face in the crook of his neck and smiled.

This is how it feels, she thought, *to be swept off your feet.*

He laid her down almost reverently and kept his eyes on hers as he unbuttoned the crisp white shirt she'd paired with black pants. Underneath, instead of the black lace teddy that Stacy had packed, she wore a simple cotton bra.

But when he unhooked the front clasp and watched as her breasts spilled free, the desire that tightened his features made her feel as though she was wearing decadent red lace.

His mouth fastened on her naked breast, hot and wet, and her inhibitions broke free. She peeled off his shirt, running her hands along his back and anywhere else she could touch.

Sensations filled her that she'd only experienced once before, on that moonlit beach a year ago when she'd lost her sense. And her heart.

"Oh, Laney," he said, doing a sensuous slide up her body until his mouth was even with hers. "We've wasted so much time."

The kiss was wickedly greedy, their tongues mating and bodies straining to be closer still. Long minutes later, when they came up for air, he gave her a mischievous smile.

"Let's race to see who can undress fastest."

They threw themselves into the competition, laughingly removing their shirts and their pants. Clay was naked before Lane could strip off her underwear.

"Hey, no fair," she said. "You weren't wearing any."

But then it didn't matter because she was in his arms again, with nothing between them and nothing to stop them. Except whatever had just leaped up on the bedside table to watch what was going on.

"Meow," Marigold said, settling in for the show.

Clay's head came up and his eyes closed in what looked like pain. "I seem to remember you can't make love in front of Marigold."

"I can't," she said, and gloried in the disappointment that descended over his features. She kissed him softly on the lips. "But I happen to know there's a bed in the other room and a door that closes between this one and that.''

He was off the bed in a flash, again sweeping her up in his arms. ''We better call the front desk and reserve these rooms for another night, because I'm not letting you stop me this time,'' he said near her ear.

She smoothed the dark hair back from his strong, handsome face. ''I seem to remember that it was you who stopped that night on the beach,'' she said, and he stopped moving.

''Only because it was too soon.'' He held her gaze with eyes that had turned serious. ''I wanted you to be sure you wanted me as much as I do you.''

''I am sure,'' she said, running her fingertips over his well-formed mouth.

She watched the smile come into his beautiful eyes before he carried her through the door and they continued what they'd started a year ago with murmurs, sighs and what Lane was beginning to think was love.

THE SUN STREAMING into the hotel room through a crack in the heavy draperies pulled Clay from a deep, satisfied sleep. He came slowly awake, feeling happier than he had at any time in the past year. Because last night he'd made love to Lane.

Not once, but so many times he'd lost count. Their lovemaking had run the gamut from fast and furious to slow and shattering to giddy and greedy.

He stretched, his eyes still closed, his body seeking the heat of the amazing woman he wanted to be with both in and out of bed. His arm came up against something warm, soft and...hairy?

He turned on his side and opened his eyes. Marigold was on the bed beside him, gazing at him out of her crossed eyes.

He laughed and stroked the cat, who arched her back, leaned into his touch and purred.

"You're a sweet thing," he said, "but I'd still rather wake up with Laney in my bed."

But where was Lane? Aside from a hurried room-service dinner at the table for two, they'd hardly left the bed since he carried her into his hotel room the day before.

He was sitting up, running a hand through his tousled hair and blinking the sleep from his eyes, when she came through the connecting door and stopped short.

Her blond hair was damp and her skin rosy, not that he could see enough of that skin. She'd covered her delectable body with a fluffy white robe. The sight of her sent happiness cascading through him like water from the shower she'd obviously taken.

"Oh, you're awake. I was coming in here to find Marigold." She wasn't wearing her glasses, and her brown eyes didn't quite meet his. In the past, she'd either looked at him with coolness or with heat, but she'd seldom avoided his gaze. He was touched to think she might actually be feeling shy after last night.

"She's exactly where you should be: In bed with me." He felt his lips curve into a smile and injected a suggestive note in his voice. "Come back to bed, Laney. It's early."

"Nine o'clock isn't early. Checkout's in two hours." She was obviously trying to sound firm, but her voice quivered, something else that was unlike her.

He ignored the unease that skittered through him, patted the empty space on the bed between him and Marigold and winked. "Then I'll make the next hour and a half worth your while."

He saw her swallow hard before she shook her head. Her gaze still didn't meet his, but her game face was back in place. "This isn't going to work, Clay."

His heart lurched, but he ignored that, too. She couldn't mean it, not after last night. He made his voice light. "As a man who just spent eighteen hours in bed with you, I can vouch for how well it's working."

"It worked fine for a night, but now that it's morning I can't pretend you're not who you are and I'm not who I am." Her teeth caught her lower lip, which he could have sworn had started to tremble. Like her voice.

Clay's unease turned to alarm. "And who are we?" he asked.

She lifted her chin, and that was trembling, too. "Reporters competing against each other for a job."

A job Clay had forgotten about the instant he had her in his arms. A job whose importance was a distant second compared to the love he felt for her. A job that couldn't bring him an iota of the happiness she could.

And she knew that. He could see it in the way her game face kept crumbling before she resurrected it.

"Where's this coming from?" he asked. "You certainly weren't thinking about *Splash!* last night."

"Remember those phone calls we ignored?" She

ran her fingers through the damp strands of her blond hair. "I had a message this morning from Marcus saying he wanted the story turned in by the day after tomorrow." She indicated the red blinking light on his phone. "You probably have the same one."

"So?"

"So how am I supposed to beat you out for a job when I'm sleeping with you?" She cleared her throat when her voice broke. "It's like my Daddy always says, Get in bed with the competition, and you're scr—"

"Don't use that word for what we did," Clay interrupted, swinging his legs off the bed and striding across the room toward her. He cared little that he was naked. He took her by the shoulders. "What we did was make love."

He smoothed her hair back, memorizing the planes and angles of her face as his gaze moved hungrily over her. He could see that she was trying to appear cool and detached, but she looked miserable instead.

A few weeks ago, the most important thing in his life had been securing the *Splash!* job. Now it was Lane. He could no more compete against her for a job than Marigold could compete in the championship division at a cat show.

"I love you, Laney. I think I have since the first moment I saw you on those City Hall steps." His voice was low and insistent. "Love is what matters. Not the job."

He saw her brown eyes soften, but then she squared her shoulders and took a deep breath. "The *Splash!* job is what matters to me," she said firmly.

He was about to tell her she could have it, but then he remembered her reason for shortening her name from Elaine to Lane. It had given him the strong impression that it was *newspapers* that mattered to her.

"Tell me something, Lane," he said, forcing himself to ask the question past the lump in his throat. "Would you want the job this badly if I wasn't up for it?"

Her expression faltered, not a lot, but enough. "What good is a goal if you can't beat somebody to it?" she asked in a small voice.

The truth struck him like a blow to the heart. Although he coveted the *Splash!* job, he'd willingly give it up because he loved Lane. But she wouldn't make the same sacrifice.

Defeating him was what mattered most to Lane. Not the job and certainly not him.

"Don't look at me like that, Clay," Lane said, her voice no longer cold but plaintive. Like her eyes. "After last night, you must know how I feel about you. But a relationship between us can't work when we're in competition."

Her words echoed through him like false hope. He'd thought, hoped, that she loved him. But she didn't. She couldn't. Not if a job was more important to her than he was.

"Maybe we could try again after Marcus hires one of us." She touched his cheek, her voice almost desperate. "Then we won't be competitors anymore."

But what would happen, he wondered, when they had one of the disagreements so common to couples building a life together? Would she be hellbent on winning every argument? Did she even know the meaning of the word compromise?

Slowly, he shook his head and stepped back from

her touch. It felt as if he was moving away from everything he'd always wanted.

"We're in the same field, Laney," he said. "Something like this is bound to come up again."

"You're right, but—"

"Before it does, we should end it right here. Right now."

Wordlessly, they stared at each other. Her eyes, the ones that had long reminded him of a glacier, brimmed with unshed tears and the corners of her mouth sagged. Finally, she nodded.

"Okay," she said softly.

As soon as she uttered her agreement, Marigold let out a sorrowful whine. The cat probably wanted her breakfast, but, for a heartbreaking moment, it sounded like she was crying.

10

LANE HEARD THE DOORBELL echoing through the house as she stood at Pup Doggett's front door, so why couldn't he?

He was clearly home. In the driveway was his Volkswagen, which was so weighed down with cat-power bumper stickers it was a wonder the under-carriage didn't collapse. And the garage door was open, revealing a space jam-packed with so much junk there was barely space to park a bicycle, let alone a car.

She leaned on the doorbell again, determined not to leave until Pup told her to her face that he wouldn't comment on the FFF story.

So far, the cat-federation president had relayed the word through third parties and telephone wires, but it was much harder for a source to say no to a re-porter standing in front of him.

Nothing could stop Lane when she was deter-mined, which was what Clay had discovered the day before.

At the thought of Clay, she got that choked feeling in the back of her throat that made her feel as though she were going to cry.

She'd learned a lot of things about Clay over the past weekend, not the least of which was that he could make her tremble and sigh when she was in his arms.

He was much more than the glib, handsome shell she'd spent a year trying to delude herself he was. He was noble and gallant and hardworking. Sweet and thoughtful and considerate. Not to mention handsome and sexy and darn near irresistible.

Why, oh why, did he have to be her biggest rival?

Her lower lip trembled but she bit down on it. She would not think about Clay now. Her mission was to top his story so she could secure the *Splash!* job.

She'd started writing this morning but had realized the story was incomplete without Pup Doggett's side. They'd established that he'd spread the cat-shaving rumor, but the story cried out for his reason.

When there was still no answer at the front door, she walked to the back of the house. The neighborhood was in far western Miami Dade County, about as close as you could get to the Everglades without stepping in swampland.

The houses were of the cookie-cutter variety, one-story dwellings with stucco walls and tile roofs, but the six-foot whitewashed fence surrounding Pup's backyard distinguished his from the others.

As she approached the fence, she heard masculine laughter and something that sounded like...barking?

"Mr. Doggett, are you back there?" she called through the tall fence. Nobody answered, but again she heard laughter.

She raised her voice. "Pup?"

Again, no answer.

Making a snap judgment that the pursuit of a story warranted trespassing, she unlatched the gate and pushed it open. She'd hardly stepped foot in the yard when a bundle of golden fur came running at her full tilt.

She recognized it as a tongue-wagging, tail-shaking Golden Retriever an instant before it gave a joyful leap. The smooth soles of her low-heeled black shoes slid out from under her and she landed on her rear end.

The dog put its paws on her chest while its flashing tongue coated her face with puppy slobber.

"Garfield, you get off that lady right now," Pup Doggett scolded as he peeled the exuberant dog off her. The animal squirmed in his arms, this time trying to lick him. "Please forgive him. He's only a puppy."

"That's quite all right." Lane got up and brushed leaves and twigs off the seat of her pants. "I wasn't sure I'd get that nice of a welcome."

Pup's dark eyes swung to her, recognition filling them. His heavily browed, pug-featured face contorted in a scowl.

"You!" he said. "What are you doing here?"

"Giving you the chance to respond to the allegations I'm making against you in the *Splash!* article," she said, but he hardly seemed to be listening.

"This isn't my dog," he declared. The Golden Retriever wriggled and squirmed so vigorously that he was forced to put it down.

The puppy immediately ran to Lane, put its fat paws on her knees and tried to crawl up her body. Laughing, Lane bent down to pet it. The tags around the dog's neck jangled against each other, and one of them caught her eye.

"If she's not yours, why does this tag say Pup's Pup?" She noticed an older, more sedate dog lazing in the sun at the foot of the back porch. "And whose dog is that over there?"

"Okay, you got me. They *are* my dogs." Pup's voice sounded tortured. "But you can't tell anyone about Garfield and Tomcat. Oh, please, don't tell. It would be the end of my career if you did."

Lane's eyes raised to his and she read palpable distress. "I don't understand. Why do you care if people know you own dogs?"

"I'm the president of the Florida *Feline* Federation, not the Florida *Canine* Federation."

"Are you saying you don't own a cat?"

"Why do you think I call my puppy Garfield? And my other dog Tomcat? It's so nobody will know they're dogs when I talk about them." Now that he'd gotten started, the words poured from him like water from a broken dam. "It's not that I don't like cats. I do. But I need variety in my life. I spend all day surrounded by cats. When I come home, I need a change of pace."

"Is that why you live all the way out here?" she asked, straightening.

"Do you blame me? People wouldn't understand how I can love my job and still love dogs. I come from a long line of cat men. If it got out that I preferred dogs, my career would be over."

He looked fearfully at her as Garfield ran over to Tomcat on his plump puppy feet. Within seconds, the two dogs were dashing around the yard, playfully chasing each other.

"You're not going to tell anyone, are you? Oh, please don't tell." Pup's plea was so insistent she wouldn't have been surprised had he put his hands together in prayer.

"I didn't come out here to expose you as a dog lover." Although the nugget of information was interesting, Lane didn't see the point in traumatizing Pup by making it public. "I came to find out what you have to say about the cat shaving."

"Do you mean you'll keep quiet about the dogs if I talk to you about the cats?" he asked, hope shining in his eyes.

Lane hadn't intended to offer a deal, but trade-offs were a journalism staple. She figured it wouldn't hurt to agree, especially because she truly believed that Pup would be better off if he told his side of the story.

"I won't tell anyone about Garfield and Tomcat," she said. "I promise."

Relief seemed to seep out of him as he wiped his forehead with the back of a hand. "Then come sit with me on the back porch while I tell you a story."

Ten minutes later, she had a glass of iced tea in her hand and Tomcat's head cradled in her lap. She didn't have Pup figured out.

"Let me say first of all that the FFF is a fine organization that values honesty above all else," he began. "There wouldn't have been a problem at all if Yoda hadn't entered his cat in my show."

Her eyebrows drew together. "Are you talking about Marcus Miller?"

"Did you know that he was bald even back in high school? I think it's genetic, but he claimed he couldn't have hair getting in the way of his thoughts."

"You went to high school with Marcus?"

"Bentley High, due north of Miami. We were in the same graduating class, although he doesn't remember me. I knew that when he walked into the Daytona Beach show.''

''Should he remember you?''

''He had his nose so high in the air I wouldn't be surprised if he didn't remember anyone, let alone the three-hundred pound boy whose high school years he ruined.''

Pup wasn't much taller than her and couldn't have weighed more than one-fifty, but she could detect some sagging skin under his chin that sometimes hinted at a great weight loss.

''I take it you were the three-hundred-pound boy?'' she asked, absently petting his dog.

''You got it. It's not surprising he didn't recognize me. I wore thick glasses instead of contacts. Even back then I was trying to deny my dog loving, so I insisted the other kids call me by my given name of Dawson. Not that anyone called me much of anything. They pretty much ignored me.''

''Then why single out Marcus for revenge?''

Pup's lips drew in a taut line. ''Because he got all the breaks. I was a math whiz, but when we were sophomores he was math-club president. I could argue rings around him but he was captain of the debate club when we were juniors.''

''Was he Valedictorian, too?''

''Of course. But not because he got better grades. I was late for class one morning and a teacher wouldn't let me make up a test. So I got one B on my report card in four years.''

''That must have hurt.''

''It hurt more that Yoda got my spot.''

''So when you saw him come into your show with

his prized cat, you seized the opportunity to get back at him?''

''Exactly.''

Lane closed her notebook, aware that the inclusion of Pup's motivation would catapult her story past Clay's. Unless, of course, Clay had thought to chase down that detail himself.

''Has anyone else asked you about the cat shaving?''

He nodded, and she closed her eyes briefly. Of course reporting ace Clay Crawford hadn't left a question unanswered.

''Your Professional Cat Handler's been here. You know, that guy with the ten-gallon hat.''

Wade McCoy. Lane was confused as to why Wade had chased down Pup's motivation while Clay hadn't, but the bottom line was indisputable. She'd win the position at *Splash!,* just as she'd set out to do.

She waited for the exhilaration to hit her, but in its place was a curiously leaden feeling, as though her heart was sinking.

She lifted her eyes to Pup, who looked as carefree as one of the dogs he'd been named after as he picked up his glass of iced tea and drained it in one gulp.

''I only have one more question,'' she asked slowly, ''Was all this worth it?''

''Of course it was,'' Pup said. ''I would have done anything to make sure Yoda didn't win again.''

Despite herself, Lane understood the sentiment. Nothing was worse than finishing second. Nothing, perhaps, except for the empty feeling she'd had the day before when she'd left Clay alone in the hotel room.

The parallels of her situation and Pup's suddenly blindsided her. She clutched at her notebook, her heart beating hard, because her actions had been so much worse than Pup's.

He'd merely put his job and professional reputation at risk, but she'd jeopardized her very happiness. She'd treated her job as if it were more important than Clay.

Not only that, if she turned in her story, she'd not only have to leave her beloved newspaper but she'd be taking a job away from the man she loved.

Her reporter's notebook fell to the floor and she covered her mouth with her hands. Oh, Lordy. She loved Clay Crawford. And she'd lost him because she couldn't stand to lose.

"Is something wrong?" Pup asked, leaning forward in his seat while Tomcat licked her elbow in sympathy.

Mutely, she nodded. She'd made a dog-gone mess of things and she had no idea what to do about it.

BARELY UNDERSTANDING his motivation for coming, Clay stepped inside Marcus Miller's starkly white penthouse suite after the *Splash!* receptionist announced his arrival.

Marcus was sitting in his armchair, stroking Prune's hairless skin in much the same way as the last time Clay had been in his office.

"Clay! I didn't expect to see you again." Marcus narrowed his eyes. "If you've changed your mind about dropping out of the running, you're too late. I've already made the hire."

"I haven't changed my mind." Clay suppressed a twinge of regret that he wouldn't be working at *Splash!,* but it didn't compare to the agony he'd suffered over losing Lane. "I'm trying to track down Wade McCoy. He has my cat."

It was strange to say the words and stranger still to realize they were true. As of a few hours ago, Rover was his cat.

"So we've turned you into a cat lover, have we?" Marcus asked.

"Something like that." Clay still didn't understand what sort of spell Rover had woven over him. One minute, the little cat was irritating the stuffing out of him. The next, Clay was begging Ted's sister Heidi, the cat breeder, for her papers.

Marcus laughed. "Cats are like women, don't you think? You hardly realize they've found their way into your heart until they're already there."

Like Lane, Clay thought. Except it wouldn't do any good to think about that, not after the way she'd thoroughly dismissed him in the hotel room. He cleared his throat.

"So do you know where I can find Wade?"

"You're in luck. He's down the hall in the photo department." Marcus set Prune down and rose. "I'll walk you there."

The hallways that wove through the *Splash!* offices were as blindingly white as Marcus's suite, but the carpet was the rich blue of the ocean. They passed several photos of leaping dolphins and one of a killer whale before Clay spoke again.

"I guess you got your story about cat-show corruption, then?"

"And an excellent story it is, although I'm having

a difficult time equating the FFF president with that chubby boy from high school,'' Marcus said and briefly filled Clay in on Pup Doggett's motivation for spreading lies.

''What are you going to do about it?'' Clay asked when he finished. ''You can't run a story in your inaugural issue about an injustice that affects only you, right?''

Marcus clapped him on the back. ''I'm starting to feel like the cat that let the canary get away. You have excellent editorial instincts, my boy. Of course I can't run the story.''

''So Pup Doggett gets away with what he did?''

''Not entirely. I'll make noise about taking legal action, but only to scare him. I'll be satisfied with a written apology. I certainly don't want to ruin the man's career over it, but that may happen anyway if word gets out.''

''I hope not,'' Clay said. ''Pup seems like an okay sort.''

''The real shame of it is that the story won't make it into print. The reporting was excellent, but the writing wasn't up to snuff.''

The remark took Clay aback because he'd always considered Lane to be an exceptional writer.

''The hire was a bit of a risk, but I'm sure he'll do better with future writing assignments,'' Marcus added.

''You mean she.''

''He certainly doesn't look like any she I've ever seen.''

Clay screwed up his forehead, because Lane was the quintessential she. Unless... ''Who are we talking about?''

They'd reached the door to the photo department. Marcus swung it wide and indicated the man sitting in the chair smiling at the photographer's camera. A ten-gallon hat was perched on his head, Rover's carrier at his feet.

"Wade McCoy," Marcus said. "The new staff writer for *Splash!*"

"Howdy," Wade said, tipping his hat. "Hope there are no hard feelings, pardner. When I got wind of what you and Miss Lane were doin', I decided to try writin' a story of my own."

"I don't understand," Clay stammered.

"I still love cats, mind you, but I need to get away from all that meowing for a spell."

"No," Clay corrected. "I meant I thought Lane Brooks had gotten the job."

"She probably would've if she'd turned in a story," Marcus said. "But of the three of you, Wade's the only one who did."

Hope radiated through Clay, but realism quickly stamped it out. If Lane had decided not to pursue the *Splash!* job, it was because she'd realized that newspapers, and not Clay, had a hold on her heart.

She'd made it clear in the hotel room that she cared about competition more than she did him. Because neither of them was going to work for *Splash!*, the competition between them was as alive as it had ever been.

The difference was that Clay didn't want to play anymore.

11

LANE PLOPPED DOWN belly first on her newspaper-print bedspread across from her cat and propped her chin on her forearms in an imitation of Marigold's pose.

"So how do you think I should congratulate Clay on getting the *Splash!* job?" she asked. "Should I call him? Ask him to dinner? Show up at his door and pop naked out of a giant cake?"

Marigold's thoughts seemed to turn inward, possibly because her eyes were looking at each other, but Lane knew her cat well enough to read her mind.

"Yeah, I like the last one best, too," she said. "But I'm not sure I have enough flour and eggs to bake a cake that big. Or that Clay would be glad it was me when I jumped out of it."

It had been twenty-four hours since she'd had her epiphany while visiting Pup Doggett and twenty-three hours since she'd let Marcus know she wouldn't be submitting a story.

For one of the first times in her life, she was unsure of her next move. She longed to go to Clay and apologize, but she was afraid that he wouldn't forgive her.

Give in to fear, she heard her father say, *and get kicked in the rear.*

She was trying to figure out if that applied to her

current situation when the doorbell sounded. She crossed her small house and pulled open the door to find Stacy standing on the porch. Her sister had been bathed in smiles the last time she'd seen her, before she'd abruptly left Lake Haven, but now she was awash in tears.

"What is it, honey?" Lane asked as Stacy flung herself into Lane's open arms and sobbed on her shoulder. The cries came harder. "Whatever it is, we can handle it together."

After a few moments of soul-wrenching tears, Stacy managed to gasp, "It's...Teddy."

Recriminations hit Lane so hard she might have reeled if Stacy hadn't been holding on to her. She'd known her sister was falling too fast, too hard, and suspected she'd been heading for heartache.

But instead of trying to slow down the love train, she'd let Clay soothe her worries by vouching for Ted's character. She'd actually believed Clay when he said Ted wouldn't hurt Stacy.

"Why, that low-down snake," she hissed as she rubbed her sister's back. "He better hope he never runs into me, because I'll make sure he knows there's a special place in hell for any man who dumps my sister."

Stacy's head came off her shoulder and she blinked the tears from her big, brown eyes. "Dumped me? Where'd you get the idea that Teddy dumped me?"

Lane glanced down at her wet shoulder. "From the soaking the right side of my shirt just took."

Stacy smiled through her tears. "I'm not crying because Teddy dumped me. I'm crying because he loves me."

She drew back and put both her hands over her heart. "It was so romantic, Lane. I stopped by his office to see if he could go out for lunch. You know that story he's chasing? About the quarterback who's quitting in his prime because a psychic told him to? Well, Teddy says, 'It's one hell of a world when you have to spend your lunch hour with a kook instead of the woman you love.'

"The woman he loves." She jerked a thumb at herself. "That's me."

"Oh, honey. I'm so happy for you." Lane hugged her sister again, this time in sincere congratulations. At least one of the Brooks sisters had a heart that was soaring instead of breaking.

Eventually, Stacy stood back and wiped the tears from her cheeks. "Enough about me. I want to hear about you and Clay. Teddy says you're not in competition anymore."

"So Clay did get the *Splash!* job?" Lane asked, wanting the confirmation even though she was already sure of the answer.

Stacy looked at her oddly. "How could he have gotten the job when he didn't turn in a story? I thought you got it."

Lane shook her head mutely. "I didn't turn in a story, either. But why wouldn't he? He really wanted that job."

Stacy put her hands on her hips and rolled her eyes. "The answer's pretty obvious."

She meant that Clay hadn't gone after the job he'd coveted because he thought Lane wanted it. But what Lane wanted was Clay. What she didn't want was any more competition between them. But how was that possible when she still worked at the *Times* while he was at the *Courier?*

The solution was so simple that she nearly gasped.

"Oh, my gosh," she told her sister, then bit her lip because she had a strong suspicion that Stacy would object to her plan. She took Stacy by the shoulders and turned her around. "Listen, hon. You know I love you, but I need you to leave. Now."

"But I just got here," Stacy said as Lane marched her to the door and opened it. "And I still have to tell you what the psychic..."

Lane gave her sister a gentle push and shut the door on the rest of her words. Then she rushed to the telephone and punched in the number of her editor at the *Fort Lauderdale Times.* His voice mail clicked on.

"Hi, Martin. It's Lane. Listen, I love you a lot. I love the job. But I quit." She stopped to giggle. "Talk to you later. Bye."

A week ago, before she'd been blinded by her zeal to beat out Clay for the *Splash!* job, the thought of leaving her newspaper would have been a stake through her heart. Now, it was the easiest decision she'd ever made.

The information that filled today's newspaper would be old news tomorrow, but her love for Clay was timeless. How incredible that she hadn't realized before now that love was the reason he could make her pulse jump and heart palpitate. It couldn't have been more clear had it been written before her in black and white.

Butterflies in local woman's tummy due to love, the headline would read.

It seemed like forever since she'd stood outside

the coffee shop on the Miami street and yelled at the wing-flapping insects to leave her alone, but in reality it was only a week or so.

Now she wanted the butterflies back. She wanted *Clay* back.

Considering the potential reward, resigning from her job at the *Times* hadn't been difficult at all. She loved newspapers, but she loved Clay far more. What would be difficult—no, impossible—was living her life without the man she loved.

She took ten minutes to put on a pair of short shorts and a halter top in notice-me yellow, figuring she needed all the help she could get after what she'd done.

Then she grabbed her keys, dashed across her living room and pulled open the door. The beginnings of a plan in which she'd beg Clay to forgive her spun wildly in her mind, but she stopped dead as she encountered the strangest sight she'd ever seen.

The man on her sidewalk was holding a leash attached to a cat wearing a strip of neon-pink material wrapped around its tiny body. But it wasn't just any cat or just any man.

It was Rover and Clay.

"C'MON, ROVER, you're torturing me here." Clay scooted down so he was knee to eye with the tiny Singapura, who was sniffing a blade of grass. "You're making a bad idea a heck of a lot worse. Did you know that?"

The cat didn't deign to look at him, but she was so statue-still it was clear that she didn't intend to budge.

Clay sighed. "Okay, I get your point. I could have

told Laney my news over the phone, but do you blame me for wanting to see her one last time?"

This time Rover did look at him, but it was with such a haughty glare that Clay rocked back on his heels. He hoped nobody in the modest Fort Lauderdale neighborhood where Lane lived was witnessing his humiliation.

"Now I know why they say dogs are a man's best friend," he muttered under his breath. "A dog knows who's master."

"Are you trying to do what I think you're trying to do?"

Lane's voice was so unexpected that the leash dropped from Clay's fingers. He swung his eyes toward the sound and encountered a pair of very shapely legs. Slowly, he worked his gaze up her stop-traffic body until they met her brown eyes. She was looking at him curiously, a half smile on her face. He'd given up hope for them days ago, but the sight of her still made him go weak.

"Only if you think I'm trying to walk my cat," he said, straightening to his full height. He held out the neon-blue strip of nylon he'd bought for Marigold. "I thought you might want to try to walk yours with me."

She took the material and turned it over in her hands, looking so adorable he wanted to grab her. "What is this?"

"A Strolling Sweater. Rover's is an extra-small, but I got an extra-large for Marigold."

The half smile on Lane's face turned into a full-fledged grin. "You've got to be kidding."

He shuffled his feet, wondering how to phrase it. "Marigold is kind of...robust."

"I meant you have to be kidding about walking the cats."

"The woman at the pet store said the Strolling Sweaters enable cat owners and their pets to enjoy the Great Outdoors together. Rover's mine now, by the way."

She merely raised an eyebrow and then indicated Rover with a cut of her eyes. "Did she give you any tips on how to get started on all that enjoyment?"

"An instruction booklet." He shrugged. "But I didn't read it."

She nodded. "I thought so. You can train cats to wear harnesses, but sometimes it takes weeks or even months to get them used to it."

"I don't have time for that," he said and got to the point of his visit. "I'll be gone by then."

Lane's heart thudded in her chest so powerfully she nearly cried out in pain. "Gone? Where are you going?"

"I'm not sure yet, but I've decided to leave Florida."

Her throat constricted with fear. Mere days ago, he'd claimed to love her but she'd blown her chance with him with her silly win-at-all-costs attitude.

"What about your job?"

"I quit it."

Her mouth dropped open. The facts were coming at her hard and fast like baseballs from a pitcher who threw one hundred miles per hour. She'd barely processed that he'd thrown away the *Splash!* job before he tossed this doozy at her.

"But your father wants to make you managing editor."

"Yeah, well, we had a long talk at the hospital about that."

"Your father's at the hospital? Is he okay?"

"It was a false alarm. You know Ted's theory about how he was faking his angina?" He shrugged. "Turned out it was true. When Dad couldn't talk me out of quitting, he started clutching his heart so I called an ambulance. It wasn't until we got to the hospital and they ran a battery of tests that he finally admitted he'd been faking it.

"And now, he's finally accepted that he needs to let me strike out on my own if he ever hopes to get me back."

"But then why didn't you turn in a story for *Splash!*?"

"That's the simple part." He lowered his voice. "I don't want to compete with you anymore, Laney. I can't."

"But you don't have to compete with me." She rushed forward to grab his arm. It was important he listen to her, important that he didn't leave Florida. "I quit my job."

He was clearly shocked. "But you love newspapers. That's why you passed up the *Splash!* job."

"That's not why I passed up the *Splash!* job."

He blinked. "What are you saying, Laney?"

"That I've been a fool. That it took Pup Doggett to make me realize I was as blind to what's really important as he was."

His eyes bore into hers. "What's important to you?"

She took a leap of faith. "You. I love you, Clay. Much more than I love to win. Can you ever forgive me for taking so long to realize that?"

He grinned, his ocean eyes unnaturally bright. "Only if you'll marry me," he said and enveloped her in his arms after her joyous agreement.

Their mouths met in a kiss that promised forever and lasted nearly as long, but finally she leaned back and gazed her fill of him. "Everything would be perfect if we weren't unemployed."

"We won't be when you rescind your notice and I accept the offer Elliott Doggett made me this morning."

"Elliott? Pup's grandfather?"

He nodded. "Turns out a major publisher is interested in the family of cat men that founded the FFF. He wants me to write the book. There's only one small catch."

"What?" she asked, alarmed.

"That you collaborate with me. In your spare time, of course."

She smiled. "That's the most marvelous idea I've ever heard. I do believe, Clay Crawford, that this is the most perfect day of my life."

She'd no sooner uttered the sentiment than there was a series of anguished cat noises behind them. She whirled to see Rover, her leash dragging behind her, approaching Marigold.

"Oh, no," Lane cried. "I must have left the door open when I came outside."

Even as she and Clay ran for the porch, Lane knew they wouldn't be in time to rescue Marigold. Her cat's tiny nemesis kept advancing, making guttural noises all the way. And then a curious thing happened.

Instead of retreating, Marigold came forward and

sniffed Rover's dainty nose. Then the two cats rubbed cheeks.

"Well, I'll be," Lane said. "My guess is that Rover's traumatized by the leash, and Mari's comforting her."

"Too bad they're both females," Clay said into her ear as she leaned back against his chest. "It would be nice to have a bunch of kittens around our place."

His arms came around her and she knew that, from this moment on, life was going to be very, very good. Because Daddy had been wrong about how disastrous it was to cozy up to the competition.

Because once Lane stopped trying so hard to win, they both had.

Epilogue

LANE BREEZED into the kitchen, intent on the tray of hors d'ouevres on the counter, when an arm whipped out to grab her by the waist.

Before she could regain her equilibrium, she was in the circle of her new husband's arms. Thankfully, she no longer felt as though butterflies had been let loose in her stomach whenever Clay touched her. She'd long since graduated to bigger, better flutters. She was thinking hummingbirds.

She tilted her head to look at him, and he bent down to give her a sweet, lingering kiss. Although there was soft music and loud conversation in the room adjacent to the kitchen, she couldn't hear anything but the hammering of her heart.

When he finally drew back, it took a moment for her heartbeat to slow and her ears to start working again.

"The engagement party's going great," he said, grinning at her. "I can't wait until we get around to the gifts."

He looked so happy that she struggled mightily with her facial muscles so they wouldn't descend into a frown.

"Tell me again why you're so sure that Stacy and Ted will like our engagement present?" she couldn't help asking.

He laughed, a sensuous sound that made her shiver. "Will you stop worrying about it? It's the perfect gift."

"It's the perfect gift for *us*," Lane amended. "I'm not so sure about them."

He reached down and stroked her cheek. "Then how about we make a bet? If they don't like our present, I'll make love to you tonight. But if they do, you can make love to me."

"You know I can't resist a competition," she said, putting her arms around his neck and drawing closer. The hummingbirds in her stomach went wild. "Do you think we can have another one of those races to see who can strip the fastest? Or kiss the slowest?"

His eyes twinkled. "We can do the kiss race right now."

Their lips were about to meet again when Wade McCoy barreled into the kitchen, sighing in mock horror when he spotted them. "You two cut that out, ya hear? You got an engagement party going on in the other room, not to mention a cowboy who's worked up a powerful thirst."

The cat wrangler went straight to the cooler and pulled out another beer, as though he did so all the time. In actuality, he did. He'd started out visiting Rover and before they knew it, he'd insinuated himself not only in their lives but in Stacy's and Ted's as well.

"We're newlyweds," Clay said, still holding Lane lightly in his arms. "We've only been married a month, so we're entitled."

"That may be so. But I swear, it's a wonder either of you can write a coherent word with the way you carry on. You sure you didn't mix up your canines and felines in that book about the Doggett cat men?''

"That's why we had you proofread the book before we turned it in to our publisher," Clay said. "Seems to me you said it was such good reading that it made you realize you were a cat man after all. Isn't that why you quit the *Splash!* job?''

"I quit the job so you could have it and I could take the vice presidency at the Florida Feline Federation. Somebody needs to keep Pup Doggett in line," Wade said with gusto. More softly, he added, "Not to mention I can't write a lick."

"Writing's not as easy as it seems," Lane said, idly noticing that some of the ever-present ink that smudged her fingertips had ended up on Clay's face. "It needs to be in your blood. The way newspapers are in mine."

She smiled at Clay, aware that she was finally at peace with the way he fit into her life. She was pleased that he'd accepted Marcus Miller's offer to work at *Splash!,* but it wouldn't have mattered had he gone back to newspapers. Never again would she put work in front of love.

Life would be perfect if only Stacy would set a wedding date. She was as effusive about her love for Ted as she'd been when they first met, but she'd been oddly hesitant to make a commitment. Ted considered the engagement a major coup.

"What in the devil is that?"

Ted's shocked voice rang out, prompting their trio to leave the kitchen for the living room. The dozen or so guests at the party were silent, all their eyes focused on the fuzzy ball of fur at the edge of the room. It was of an indeterminate color with long pointed ears. If you looked closely, under the fur, you could see that one eye was yellow, one green.

"I do believe that's a walking dust mop," Wade said.

"It's not a dust mop." Clay crossed the room and scooped it up. He walked over to Stacy and Ted. "It's your engagement present."

At their twin expressions of puzzlement, Lane felt compelled to defend her new husband.

"Clay wanted to introduce you two to the joys of owning a cat," Lane said, keeping a careful eye on her sister. Considering the negative comments Stacy had made in the past about Marigold, she'd been wary of the gift since Clay had spotted the cat in the stray-of-the-week cage in the waiting room at the vet's office.

"Not just any cat, a Himalayan," Clay said.

Lane winced, because the cat was no more a Himalayan than Marigold was an Angora. Clay held out the ball of fluff to her sister. For a moment, Lane was positive that Stacy wouldn't take it. But then she extended her arms, and the cat went into them willingly.

"Oh my gosh. It's just like that psychic predicted," she said, turning to a horrified-looking Ted. "Remember when you were doing the story on the quarterback and she said, 'Pause before you walk down the aisle'?"

Stacy brushed back some of the fluff on one of the cat's legs and held it up. "She must have meant paws. As in cat paws."

Ted arched a blond brow and something that looked like hope leaped into his expression. "Is that why you've been reluctant to set a wedding date?"

"Not anymore," Stacy said. "We got the paws, so let's set the date."

"Allll riiiight," Ted said, pumping his fist.

"I guess this means I win the bet." Clay was suddenly beside Lane, whispering in her ear and making the familiar shivers cascade through her body.

"I guess you do." Lane smiled at the man she would always love while she anticipated fulfilling her end of the bargain.

This was one time she definitely didn't mind losing.

Anchor That Man!

Dawn Atkins

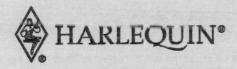

TORONTO • NEW YORK • LONDON
AMSTERDAM • PARIS • SYDNEY • HAMBURG
STOCKHOLM • ATHENS • TOKYO • MILAN • MADRID
PRAGUE • WARSAW • BUDAPEST • AUCKLAND

Dear Reader,

It all started when my single sister, Trudy, was bemoaning the fizzling of yet another romance. She wondered aloud where people got advice on how to make the leap from the everything's-lollipops-and-rainbows phase of infatuation to the happily-ever-after part. In other words, once you hit those old relationship potholes, how do you keep going on the rocky road to love to your happily ever after? I mean, there was *The Dating Game* and *The Newlywed Game,* but what about in between? What about the Making It to Marriage Game?

Hmm... That got me thinking and wondering about what it would take to convince someone burned by love to jump into that sizzling skillet again. It wasn't long before Hawk and Renata were clamoring for me to write their story. So here it is. I hope you enjoy it.

Oh, and I'm happy to report that my sister recently navigated her very own love boat all the way to the shores of happily ever after. Good for you, Trudy. Hawk and Renata would be proud!

Best,

Dawn Atkins

Books by Dawn Atkins

HARLEQUIN TEMPTATION
871—THE COWBOY FLING

To David, who made me believe I could live happily-ever-after, and to Alex, who proved it.

Acknowledgments

Thanks to the crew at KTVK-TV 3 who let me see television up close and personal. My fictional station isn't nearly as much fun! Thanks to the friends who've made this book better along the way: Betsy Norman, Connie Flynn, Laurie Campbell, Amy Dominy, Lisa Plumley, Renata Golden and Laurie White. Thanks, also, to Vicki Lewis Thompson, for that extra spiritual zing. And thanks, too, to my sister Trudy, whose questions about making it to marriage started the story ball rolling.

1

"SO, ARE WE GOING to make it to marriage or not?" Heather demanded, leaning forward from her fairytale throne.

Renata studied the young woman and her boyfriend, Ray—guests on her show—and her heart filled with sympathy. She hated disappointing them, but she had to do the right thing—for their sakes. Even if her producer had a conniption. Denny wanted cheery advice and entertainment value. Renata wanted what was best for the couple. Ever since she'd learned the awful truth, Denny's goal and hers had collided head on.

For strength, Renata glanced at the storybook backdrop that bore her show's name: *Making it to Marriage...with Dr. Renata Rose.* Again, the thrill hummed through her, as it had for the four weeks she'd had this amazing job. She'd managed to squeeze some decent counseling in between the snappy slogans and perky tips Denny required.

Until two weeks ago, that is, when her fiancé, Maurice, had trekked off to the rain forest for an indefinite stay, taking her faith in happily-ever-after with him. Now she knew how dangerous love could be.

Renata took a deep breath and looked back at Heather and Ray. Bright prisms from the foot-high

Cinderella slipper checkered their faces like confetti. Dazzled by the fantasy of love, they didn't realize what was at stake. Their hearts, their futures, everything. Renata swallowed the lump in her throat.

She'd just help them see the bright side. This wasn't the end of the world. She was living proof of that. She'd start with a simple reality check. "Heather, you say you caught Ray in a... What did you call it...? A lip lock...? With another woman at the Kwiki-Mart?"

"That's bad, huh?" Heather asked glumly.

"Well, it's not exactly 'til-death-do-us-part behavior."

"Hey!" Ray objected.

"Maybe if we just made some rules," Heather said. "Like about the difference between *flirting* and *having sex?*"

You poor dear. Renata knew how easy it was to fool yourself into believing the utterly impossible about love. She leaned forward, held Heather's gaze, and spoke gently. "I think we have to be realistic about, um, Ray's commitment readiness."

"My what?" Ray asked.

"It's partly a genetic thing," Renata explained. She scooted closer to Heather and patted her hand, feeling like a nurse at the bedside of a seriously ill patient. "You see, some men wouldn't know monogamy if you tattooed it on their foreheads."

"Hold it!" Ray complained.

"Really?" Heather gave Ray a suspicious once-over, then turned back to Renata. "So, what are you saying?"

"I'm saying..." A flicker of movement beyond

the brightly lit set caught her attention. Denny waved at her like a bad cheerleader. "I'm saying…"

You must lay some tar on the road ruts of love. That's the kind of thing Denny'd want her to say. The kind of thing she would have said two weeks ago, back when she'd naively thought happily-ever-afters grew on trees. You had to plant the seed and nurture the sapling, of course, but she'd been certain that if you applied enough effort and devotion, you could harvest the fruits of your labor—a nice, healthy lifelong love.

But she'd been wrong. The hard truth was that all the planting and pruning and deadheading in the world weren't enough to keep things from going terribly wrong. And she had to protect Heather from learning that the hard way—especially with as much root rot as Ray brought to the garden. "I'm saying," she finished, "that on the rocky road to love, Heather, you two have hit a dead end."

"A dead end? That's a drag," Heather said irritably, as if Renata had given her a peek at the man yanking handles behind the Wizard of Oz after Heather had specifically requested the illusion.

"Don't feel bad, though," Renata continued, going for upbeat. "You're not alone. The fact is, the love boat goes belly up more often than it docks."

"But I already bought my wedding dress. Fifty percent off and everything."

"You can return a dress, Heather," she said, "but there's no money-back guarantee on a bad marriage." Renata glanced up and caught Denny raising his hands in a *why me, God?* gesture. She'd blown it again. This was bad. What if they canceled her show? She'd worry about that later. Right now she had to look out for her guests and their futures.

"So, marriage is out?" Ray asked, sounding relieved.

"You're young, you have time," Renata told them. "Travel, meet people, focus on your careers. You have your whole lives ahead of you."

"But we can still sleep together, right?" Ray asked.

"What about Miss Kwiki-Mart?" Heather demanded.

"I'll go to the U-Tote-Em from now on, okay?"

"Ray," Renata said kindly, "I think Heather is saying she doubts your fidelity factor."

"My what factor?"

"Yeah, I doubt your factor, all right," Heather said.

There was a smattering of laughter from the audience.

The show's announcer, Charles Foster, galloped onto the stage. "Well, well, looks like we'll have to have Ray and Heather back when their, um, *fidelity factor* is all repaired," he said, giving Renata a disapproving look. He cleared his throat. "Next up we'll introduce you to Prince Charming looking for his very own Cinderella in our 'Have Glass Slipper, Will Travel' segment." This part of the show featured a single man looking for Ms. Right. On alternate weeks a woman was spotlighted and the segment was called "Enough with the Frogs Already."

Renata did her best to stay upbeat for the Glass Slipper guest, but by the time the closing music swelled, she was nervous and scared. Helping her couples was hurting her show, and she didn't know what to do about it.

The floor manager counted off the final seconds of taping, and Renata hightailed it off the set, heading for the tiny office that doubled as her dressing room. If she could just have a moment of private time...

"Renata Rose, what is with you?" So much for private time. Her producer sat on a makeup stool, his arms crossed, his expression grim. "Have you been replaced by a pod person—with PMS?"

"I tried to be snappy and perky," Renata said hopefully.

"'The love boat goes belly up more often than it docks?' Come on. We'll be lucky if Ray and Heather aren't signing a suicide pact as we speak."

"At the break, I helped Heather call the bridal shop. She cheered up once she found out she can get a store credit. Plus, I convinced her to come in for counseling."

"I don't get it, Renata. Your audition was great; the first two shows were fabulous. Now—pfft!— you've gone grim."

"I think I've taken love too lightly until now, Denny. It's scary out there. I've been lying awake at night worrying about the couples and all the things that can go wrong for them."

"Cut that out. This is television, remember, not therapy."

"I remember." Though before she'd signed on the dotted line, Denny had told her it could be a little of both. She'd been excited to help couples learn to hold on to love. It was a subject dear to her heart because her parents' mess of a marriage had made her so miserable.

And she'd done great at first. Helped couples work through their troubles and gotten a pile of thankful fan mail. The money was great, too, even at Phoenix's bottom-ranked KTNK-TV 11. If the show worked, she'd be able to quit the teen recreation center and take counseling classes full-time. Without that financial boost, it would take her years to become a full psychologist.

"I'll do better, Denny. I promise. I'm just out of whack, I guess. Kind of haywire."

Denny gave her an appraising look. "It's the Maurice thing, isn't it?"

She stiffened, and her cheeks heated. "What did my mother tell you?"

"Everything. That he typed his Dear Jane note on university stationery—what a romantic!—and sneaked off to save the spotted tree frog."

"He joined an environmental group to do research in the Amazon basin. And he didn't *sneak* off. He made me fresh squeezed orange juice like usual." And *then* he sneaked off. "Anyway, I wish you two wouldn't dissect my personal life over tea." Renata loved her mother dearly, but she spent entirely too much time trying to transform Renata's life into her own version of happiness. Lila Rose, a free spirit who thrived on chaos, had done nothing so much as create in Renata a cell-deep passion for order and calm. She was well-meaning, but completely clueless when it came to her daughter.

"You call that 'tea'?" Denny continued, making a face. "Bleh. She served those carob-kelp brownies, too." He shuddered. "Nasty. I've been peeing green for two days." Renata's mother was famous for her terrible health food snacks. "Anyway, Lila says Maurice wasn't right for you. Too old and boring."

"Not that it's any of your business, but Maurice is only forty. And he is kind, decent and dependable."

"So are my Aunt Lois, my dog trainer and my alarm clock, but I don't date any of them."

"Could we not talk about Maurice any more?"

"You're a lovely woman, Renata. If you'd lighten up a bit, you'd be fighting off the men with a club. Get back into circulation and you'll forget Maurice like that." He snapped his fingers.

"Denny…" she warned. He was completely wrong. Renata had *never* fought men off with a club—or a popsicle stick, for that matter. Most men found her too serious. She'd been content with two college boyfriends—more study partners than lovers—and two other brief, unremarkable romances until she'd found Maurice three years ago. She'd been twenty-seven and it had been time to settle down and Maurice had been perfect. Maurice had appreciated her. Maurice had been the one.

Except then he wasn't.

"Okay. Enough romance advice," Denny said. "Could you just remember your job is to get the couples to marriage, not break them up?"

"What if we broadened the show's concept? Being single is a perfectly good option. We could change the name to *Making it to Marriage…or Not.*"

"Oh, for God's sake." Denny shook his head, making motes of makeup powder swirl in the warmly lit room. "Listen, Renata, the GM's already uptight about getting sponsors for the new sports show. If you don't perk up, he'll nix us for something cheaper.''

"He wouldn't, would he?'' Renata's heart jumped into her throat.

"Think bunny rabbit cartoons. But I'm not giving up so easy. This show is my baby. We're going to push past this snag, one way or another.''

"Thank goodness.'' Renata released her breath.

"I had a good feeling about you. Don't make me regret it.''

"I won't. Really.''

Getting the show had been the happiest moment of Renata's life. The real therapist slotted for the spot had dropped out at the last minute, and Renata's mother, a close friend of Denny's, had convinced him that Renata's finesse with cantankerous teens and quarreling couples made her perfect for the job.

"Wish me luck,'' Denny said on a sigh. "I've gotta go make nice with the GM.''

"Good luck,'' Renata said, biting her lip. "Should I come? Maybe I could help.''

"Oh, no, you don't, Miss Making-it-to-Marriage… or-Not. You've done enough damage already. I *am* going to talk to him about a format change, though.''

"A format change?'' A cold chill ran down Renata's spine. "Please, no more fairy-tale gear. It's bad enough I'm *Doctor* Renata, when I don't even have a degree.''

"*Honorary* doctorate. I cleared it with the attorneys.'' He reached the door, then turned to her. "Just keep an open mind. Stay balls-of-your-feet-ish.''

"Feet-ish?''

"Stay loose. I know that's not easy for someone who puts 'brush teeth' in her day planner, but if you want to keep your show, that's the deal."

"Is there anything else I can do?"

"Fix whatever's wrong with you. Perk up. Are you sure you're *not* a pod person?"

She didn't answer, partly because he had a point. Since Maurice left, she hardly recognized herself. She *used* to be a person who put "brush teeth" in her day planner, but now she didn't know what she might say or do next. It was like a bunch of rubber bands inside her had snapped. All kinds of emotions were flipping and zinging around.

She rested her cheek on the warm counter and thought about the mess she was in. She just wanted what was best for the couples, but now she wondered if she even knew what that was any more. She'd been so wrong about Maurice. She squeezed her eyes shut and pictured him in the big wing-back chair he preferred, studying his research notes, smiling at her from time to time while she dabbed paint on one of her dollhouses. No wild fights or eruptions of mood, just pleasant support. Steady, safe. The sure, secure grip of love. Except Maurice had slipped right out of it, like Houdini from a slipknot.

But Maurice's leaving wasn't the worst thing. The worst thing was her reaction to it. Instead of being heartbroken, she'd been *relieved*. The terrible truth was that Maurice had bored her silly. She'd been lulled into complacency by their similar temperaments and intelligence, their comfortable companionship and mutual respect. They'd planned a life together and if Maurice hadn't chickened out, Renata would have lived it. And that would have been a terrible mistake.

She'd been careful and cautious, and it hadn't been enough. Knowing that, how could Renata advise others to take the plunge? Why should any woman get married when she could end up with someone who would just walk out one day? Or, maybe even worse, bore the life right out of her?

All of which left Renata with a bigger mess. How could she host a show about marriage if she'd lost her faith in it? Sheesh. That was like a minister who stopped believing in God.

She wanted to do what was right. Should she resign? But she couldn't bear to lose her show. It was her best work, her chance to practice counseling, to contribute to the noble cause of lifelong love. And she was no quitter.

She'd just have to buckle down—review relationship theory, study her old texts, touch base with the couples she'd helped already and get some pointers from them.

Maybe *she'd* lost out on a happily-ever-after, but that didn't mean it didn't exist, or that she couldn't help couples get theirs. She'd just get busy and get her faith back—and fast, before Denny implemented some terrible format change, or, even worse, the general manager canceled the show.

HAWK HUNTER STOOD outside Dennis Bachman's door, his résumé folder under his arm, dodging the station staff who bustled by. He was sure he'd nailed the interview for the sports talk show, but for some reason the general manager wanted him to talk to a producer.

Hurry up, Bachman, he thought, sweat trickling down his torso under his Helmut Lang suit. Waiting made him nervous. His only on-air sports experience had been at the university station, it was true, but he was fast on his feet. Flexible and quick to catch on. It was all show business, anyway. He was like an athlete switching sports. He had the main moves. A little practice and he'd nail the finer points.

At the TV station in Albuquerque, he'd been just a news writer. He'd liked it—loved it, really—but Michelle, the image-maker and his mentor, had finagled him this shot at *JockTalk,* a new sports show in Phoenix, and it meant a big-time boost to his career. A boost he wanted so bad it made his teeth ache. He'd never been a patient person, and he was itching to move ahead. Luckily, everything in TV moved fast. Very fast. Everything except this producer meeting....

He smoothed the outrageously expensive power tie Michelle had convinced him he needed. Accessories were the secret handshake in this biz, she'd told him, and he never argued with an expert. He pulled out his wallet to get a business card for Bachman, but he fumbled the flap and the photo of his mother slipped to the floor. He picked it up and stared at it. At moments like this, when he thought fleetingly of a quiet, behind-the-scenes job, it was good to remember his mother. Proving himself to her—or how he imagined her—was what kept the fires of ambition burning brightly in him. It was stupid to still be trying to make her proud—she was gone, after all—but he was hardwired to keep at it.

He knelt to retrieve her photo, just as a pair of female legs in low heels moved into view. As he stood, his gaze followed shapely calves up to a knee-length black dress that hugged nice curves, topped by a serious, pale-as-china face under a helmet of black hair.

"Isn't he in there?" the woman asked him. She stood just at chin level and gazed up at Hawk with dark, almond-shaped eyes. Her face had an elegant, exotic look—the way the young Elizabeth Taylor had looked playing Cleopatra.

"Mr. Bachman? No."

She reached past him to open the door, close enough to smell. Nice. Floral and spicy. A few strands of her hair brushed his chin.

"You can go on in," she said. She had a husky voice that made ordinary words drip with sex, though she didn't seem aware of it.

"Thanks." He slipped the faded photo of his mother into his folder, and stepped into Bachman's office.

The woman followed, then stood beside him, an uncertain smile on her face. She had a nice body—compact and firm as a gymnast's, with great breasts. She was petite, but all there. *All* there. There wasn't a hint of flirtation in her demeanor, however. He'd bet she was one of those women who didn't realize how attractive they were.

"Denny and I were supposed to meet," she said in that smoky voice. She looked at her watch, the door, then him. "Did you have an appointment?"

"Sort of."

"You're here for the show?"

"Yes."

She scanned his face, assessing him, then smiled kindly. "There's no need to be nervous. Our job is to help you tell your story in the most effective way. Just ignore the lights and the camera and be yourself.''

She was mistaking his brief fascination with her appearance for nerves. It was rare for a woman to throw off his rhythm, but she was a rare woman, he'd bet. Taking charge, he flashed his broadcast smile and extended his hand. ''I'm Hawk Hunter. And you're...?''

''Renata Rose.''

''Nice to meet you, Renata.'' He shook her hand. It was cool and slender, small in his grip.

She stilled at the contact, blinked and seemed to hold her breath until he let go. Then she exhaled with relief. He'd unsettled her, he guessed. ''Have a seat.'' She indicated one of two leather chairs in front of Bachman's glass-and-chrome desk, then frowned at the door. ''I don't know what's keeping Denny.'' She turned to him. ''We might as well get you started.''

''Started?''

''Prepared for the segment.'' She leaned over the desk—giving him a nice view of muscled thigh—and retrieved a clipboard. ''Here we go.'' She wiggled appealingly into the leather chair beside him. There was a nice pink in her pale cheeks from bending over, and he caught a glimpse of a white lace bra in the V of her dress. Sensible, but tempting. Just like her. ''So, tell me about yourself,'' she said, her pen poised.

He resisted the urge to flirt, since she obviously had some important job at the station. ''Let me give you a résumé,'' Hawk said. He hated going through the I'm-perfect-for-this-job routine again with both her *and* Bachman—*I've wanted to be a sportscaster since I used to do dodge ball play-by-plays in first grade.* The truth was he wanted to anchor the news—more significant—but this would give him some good clips to circulate and show his skills at banter. Banter was big these days. As he handed her the résumé, the photo of his mother slid to the floor.

Renata picked up the dog-eared square, studied it, then handed it back. "Someone special?" she asked politely.

"Yeah. Thanks." He was mortified that something so personal had appeared in this setting. He wasn't about to explain that the pretty girl in the thirty-year-old high school photo was his mother, pregnant with him at the time she smiled so sweetly for the camera. The social worker had given him this picture after his mother had been killed in a car wreck when he was six. Not long after she'd again been unable to retrieve him from the foster family. *When I get my act together, I promise I'll get you* had been her mantra.

No, he wouldn't explain the faded snapshot to Renata Rose, though it accounted for his success more than anything that appeared on his résumé.

Renata tucked Hawk's résumé under the questionnaire without a glance at it. "So, you're single, I assume?"

He laughed. "You assume?"

"We have to ask, Mr. Hunter. To make sure you're right for the segment."

"Really?" That kind of job interview question wasn't even legal, was it? Even in television where they played fast and loose with the rules. "Yes, I'm single. How about yourself?" He couldn't resist.

"Me? That's not important Mr. Hunter, is it?" She gave him a polite smile. "What things do you like to do? In your free time?"

"Well, I'm into sports, of course."

"So, your ideal woman would be sporty?"

"My ideal woman? What does that have to do with...?" Was this some kind of personality test?

"You're serious about marriage, aren't you?"

"Huh?" There'd obviously been some mistake, but looking into her concerned face, he had the perverse wish to tease her. "Do I need to be?"

She looked uncertain. "Well, yes. If we're going to help you find a wife."

"Find a wife? That's quite a perk. And here I'd be happy with covered parking."

"Excuse me?" She blinked at him, her eyebrows lifted in sweet surprise.

"Just teasing. There's been a mistake, I guess. I'm here to talk to Mr. Bachman about *JockTalk.*"

"Oh, the sports show. I see. I thought you were..." She reddened charmingly. "Oh, dear. You must have thought..."

"That you were running a dating service? It crossed my mind," he said and grinned at her. The idea of a date with Renata Rose had definite appeal.

"Oh. Well. I'm sorry." Flustered and blushing, she stood, clutching the clipboard to her chest. Hadn't anyone ever flirted with the woman before?

"It's all right," he reassured her. "Why don't you tell me about your show? It sounds a hell of a lot more fun than a bunch of sweaty jocks."

"I don't think so," she said. "I'm sorry I wasted your time." She put the clipboard on Bachman's desk and backed toward the door. "I'm sure Denny will be with you shortly... Ow!'' She thumped into the door.

"Nice to meet you," he said as she ducked out. And it was. Surprisingly, because he was generally drawn to tall, lighthearted blondes. But he was curious about what went on behind those dark eyes and that fleeting Mona Lisa smile. He was still breathing wisps of the floral spice she'd left when the door jerked opened and a short, well-groomed man, fiftyish, entered.

"You're Hawk Hunter," he said. There was no question in his voice. "Denny Bachman." He thrust a hand at him.

Hawk shook it. "Nice to meet—"

"I've seen your tape, read your résumé." Bachman looked him over like a lab specimen. "You've got the right look. And a minor in psychology, I saw. You like women?"

"Excuse me?"

"Ever been married? Engaged? Lived with someone?"

Hawk felt like Alice in Wonderland, lost in a nonsense world where everyone was obsessed with his love life. "No, no, and no," he said. "But there's been a mistake, I think. I'm here for the sports show."

"Forget sports, Hawk," Bachman said. "Let's talk about marriage."

Then Hawk knew he'd really fallen down the rabbit hole.

2

"I WANT YOU TO MEET someone special," Denny
said to Renata as they approached a back booth at
Vito's Bistro the next day. Renata was startled to see
Hawk Hunter, the sportscaster she'd mistaken for a
Glass Slipper guest the day before, rise from the ta-
ble, tall, roguish and handsome.

Uh-oh. Knowing Denny and her mother, this
could mean only one thing. They'd been scheming
ways to get her over Maurice, and arranged a blind
date with this handsome single guy. This was
Denny's way to get her back in "circulation," as he
called it. The encounter with Hawk yesterday had
been the warm-up. Oh, dear.

On the other hand, an awkward meal with a
stranger was much better than a terrible format
change, which was what she'd feared this lunch with
Denny was about.

"Nice to see you again, Renata," Hawk said. He
was at least six feet tall, with golden brown, slightly
wavy hair. His features were friendly, his grin infec-
tious, and his eyes engaging—inviting her into the
joke, whatever it might be. There was a wry intelligence in his expression, a smart-alecky, self-
confidence and raw sexiness. In short, he was a lady-
killer. She'd spent little time with men like Hawk,
who might flirt with her a bit, but soon lost interest,

leaving her jittery and relieved, if just a teensy bit disappointed.

She preferred a more straightforward approach, really, she told herself. Maurice had appreciated that about her. Or at least he'd never objected to it.

"Nice to see you, too," she said. She was unsettled to notice that it actually was. She took the hand he offered her. Like the first time, it was surprisingly warm—a heating pad with fingers. Even after he let go, she still felt the heat. She slid onto the bench.

"Oh, that's right. You two already met, didn't you?" Denny said, scrubbing his hands together like he was about to indulge in an illicit treat.

"I thought Mr. Hunter was a guest for *Making it to Marriage,*" she explained.

"Oh, yeah. Hawk and I talked about that. And about you, too," Denny said. "I told him all about you."

"I see." She cringed inwardly, thinking of them discussing her like some kind of pity project: *Take the poor girl out, Hawk. Cheer her up.* She made a mental note to tell Denny and her mother that her personal life was just that—personal. Job One was restoring her faith in love. Dating was way down on her to-do list. Way down.

"So, you're a sportscaster?" she asked Hawk. He looked the part—youthful, energetic and urbane. Exactly the last kind of man for her—if she were dating, of course, which she definitely was not.

"I have been," he said. His eyes, warmly brown, twinkled at her, easing her nervousness, starting up little vibrations all along her nervous system. He was very charming.

"Don't be modest now," Denny said. "Versatility

is Hawk's middle name. He's been a newspaper reporter and a TV news writer, too. He has a degree in psychology.''

''Just a few classes,'' Hawk corrected.

''Hell, you tell her about yourself, Hawk,'' Denny prodded. ''About all that psychology background you have and how much you know about relationships.''

Hawk cleared his throat, looked reluctantly at Denny, then back at her. ''Well, I'm very interested in them—relationships, I mean. What makes them...um...tick and all that....''

Why had he suddenly run out of steam? Renata wondered. With dismay, she realized he must have been put up to this against his will. Her cheeks flamed with embarrassment. She was no bombshell, but she'd been told she was attractive at least. Her seriousness probably intimidated him. That had happened with other men, to her chagrin, until she met Maurice.

Well, she didn't want any man to spend time with her against his will. She had to end this before one more awkward moment passed. ''Mr. Hunter, I'm really not interested in dating right now.''

''Dating?'' Hawk looked blank.

''That's what this is about, isn't it?'' She turned to Denny. ''You asked him to take me out?''

Denny looked sheepish.

Hawk grinned.

Denny cleared his throat. ''Actually, Renata, you know the format change I want to make?''

''Yes?''

''Hawk's it.''

"Hawk's what?" Her glance flew from Denny to Hawk and back.

"Hawk's the format change. We're pulling the frog and slipper segments. He's going to be your cohost on *Making it to Marriage*."

"You're kidding!"

"It's perfect. The man's perspective. Kind of a point-counterpoint thing. Hawk's good on his feet—funny and smart. You two can get a 'man from Mars, woman from Venus,' 'he said, she said,' thing going."

"Man from Mars…? Denny…" She'd thought the worst he'd suggest would be waving a magic wand over her guests. She'd never imagined a cohost. And certainly not a Hawk Hunter kind of cohost. "Two counselors will be confusing, don't you think?" she said, putting the most polite spin on it she could. "I'm working on my tone, like I said, and…"

Denny shook his head.

"Denny, a *sports*caster? No offense, Mr. Hunter."

"None taken. Call me Hawk. And let me jump in here. I had my doubts, too, Renata. I mean, I'm not a therapist, but—"

"We all know that a Ph.D.'s not required, right?" Denny inserted, reminding her of her own lack of credentials.

"But, Denny…" Renata said faintly.

Denny leaned forward and patted her arm. "We're going with this, Renata. I have a feeling."

There was no point in arguing with Denny once he'd had a "feeling." That was what had gotten her a crack at the show in the first place.

"Is there anything that will change your mind?" she asked.

"Audience reaction," he said. "We'll treat Hawk's appearance next week as an on-air audition and let the studio audience vote. Yes, he stays. No, he goes."

Great. Her show, already bordering on silly, would turn into a vaudeville routine, with an applause-o-meter determining its fate.

Just then, Denny's cell phone trilled. He held up his hand while he answered. "Yes?... No!... He what? Did he break anything? Damn. I'm on my way." Denny clicked off. "Sorry, kids. Can't celebrate with you. The GM's gone ballistic over the budget." He stood. "Hawk, will you give Renata a ride home?"

"I'd be glad to."

"I'll come with you," Renata blurted. She rose so quickly the silverware rattled and water sloshed in the crystal goblets.

"Sit, sit," Denny said, waving her down. "Enjoy lunch. The three of us will talk through the details tomorrow. Take your time, get to know each other." He held up a credit card. "The station's buying, so go crazy. Have dessert. The tiramisu is to die for. I already ordered champagne." As if on cue, the sommelier arrived at Denny's elbow. Denny studied the bottle wistfully. "Don't tell me how good it was," he said on a sigh.

"But..." Renata tried again.

"If you want to save the show, make this work, Renata," Denny said. With a final look of warning, he breezed away.

While the wine steward popped the cork, then poured the frothy liquid into two flutes, Renata could only stare, speechless, at Hawk, who looked back at her with warm brown eyes. What *did* they remind her of? Something cozy and familiar. She couldn't figure it out and it bothered her.

After the waiter left, Hawk clinked his glass against hers. The fine crystal rang prettily in the air between them. "Here's to working together," he said.

She touched her glass to his without echoing his words, then took a big swallow, hoping the alcohol would calm her nerves. The bubbles tickled her nose and went fizzily down her throat.

"That wasn't so bad, now, was it?" Hawk said, low and sexy. *Come out and play,* his eyes coaxed.

"Very nice." It did have a lovely finish. And Hawk had a persuasive smile. She envied him his easy-breezy way. His features seemed made for smiling. He had those nice crinkles at the edges of his eyes. She could get lost in eyes like that.... For one second, she almost wished they *were* on a date.

No, no, no. Was she losing her mind? The man was horning in on her show, not asking what her sign was. Maybe it wasn't too late to talk him out of it—her show, not the date. He probably didn't even know what he was getting into. "Have you seen *Making it to Marriage,* Hawk?"

"Bachman gave me some tapes and explained the premise. Let's see if I've got it..." He spoke as if from a script, "'*Making it to Marriage* picks up where dating shows leave off—after the first blush of love fades and the daily disappointments of relationships take over. We help couples over the bumps and ruts on the rocky road to love.' How's that?"

"Impressive," she said.

"Rocky road to love…. Very cute." He chuckled.

"The show has a silly aspect, I know, but it's still serious work," she said, trying not to sound defensive. "We're talking about people's happily-everafters here."

"It's television, Renata."

"I think of the entertainment as the spoonful of sugar that helps the counseling go down," she said. "The fairy-tale stuff brings in more audience, so we can help more people."

"Right," he said, winking. It was all a joke to him.

Before she could explain further what she meant, the waiter brought them focaccia for starters and took their lunch orders.

"What happened to the sports show?" she asked Hawk when the waiter had gone, "If you don't mind my asking."

"The sponsors crapped out," Hawk said, tearing off a hunk of bread and dabbing it in the seasoned olive oil. "It would have been great, but…" He shrugged, took a bite and chewed for a moment. "Sports isn't my target, really, anyway. I want to anchor news in a big market —New York, L.A. or Chicago in five years. I'm just building my portfolio, getting some good clips. Besides, your show sounded fun." He grinned like a kid offered a choice between bungee jumping and hang gliding.

"*Fun* would not be the word I'd use, Hawk."

"So I gathered," he said, going for more oil. "Bachman said you've gone grim."

"That's not true. I've just realized that relationships can be riskier than they might seem."

"Oh, I get it. You just had a breakup."

"Excuse me?"

"A relationship crash-and-burn. And now you're skittish."

She swallowed hard. "Did Denny...?"

"Tell me that? No. You just talk like someone who's checked into Heartbreak Hotel."

Her cheeks flamed because he'd picked up so easily on something so personal, though he'd mistaken her crisis in faith for a broken heart. "That's not what happened. You see—"

"Was he playing around on you?"

"Of course not." Maurice didn't *play* at anything. "We just had mutually incompatible goals."

"Ah. He was a jerk."

"Not at all." Though it was nice that Hawk had jumped onto her side without knowing either her or Maurice.

"You got burned, and now you're scared," Hawk said. "You just have to learn to roll with the punches."

"Roll with the punches? Is that your idea of good relationship advice?" she asked wryly.

"Works for me."

"Have you been in many relationships?"

"A few." He shrugged.

"Anything serious?"

"Not really." She wasn't surprised. Only someone who'd never been nicked by Cupid's arrow could be so cavalier about the topic.

"And do you plan to get married ever?"

"Hard to say. From what I've seen, marriage tends to zap the life right out of love."

"Not the best attitude for someone on a marriage show, don't you think?"

Hawk shrugged. "If people want to give it a try, who am I to kill the thrill? So, did you plan a trek down the aisle with Mr. Incompatible?" he asked her, offering a hunk of torn bread. She took it, her fingers tangling briefly with his, an act that sent more unsettling vibrations along her nerve endings.

"As a matter of fact, I did," she said, "except we were wrong for each other, and I didn't —" She stopped. Why was she telling him this? They'd barely met, but something about Hawk had her blurting private thoughts. She'd better change tacks or she'd find herself confessing she'd always disliked the way Maurice took time to fold his clothes before sex. "Anyway, the only people who can 'roll with the punches,' as you say, are people who are only interested in a roll in the hay." Not a bad play on words, considering how nervous Hawk made her.

"You think that's all I'm interested in?" His crooked smile was full of mischief. "A roll in the hay?"

"I wouldn't know, now, would I?" She returned the smile with a teasing one of her own, except it felt bigger than she'd intended, as if Hawk were a puppet master who'd tugged her strings. She was flirting with him, for heaven's sake! This was so *not* like her. Her insides felt like a washer load set on heavy duty—agitating madly.

"Actually, you're right." He stared at her a long time, his twinkling eyes steadying for a moment. "I'm in no position to get serious right now. But when my career's right and the woman's right, then poof! I'll fall in love." Casually, he dipped more bread.

"Poof, you'll fall in love, huh? I'm afraid that

only happens in the movies, Hawk. In real life, love takes work and time and you have to be careful to—"

"Careful?" Hawk stopped chewing and stared at her. "Renata, people *fall* in love. They don't tiptoe in." He shook his head like she'd said the most ridiculous thing in the world.

"For someone who's never been in love, you seem pretty sure about how it works," she said. Before she could press her point further, the waiter arrived and placed Hawk's steaming salmon and her exotic salad before them.

"This is great," Hawk said, surveying their food, then Renata's face, as if she were part of his pleasure. "A terrific meal and lovely company."

A blush shot through her. He was just being charming, she knew, and she couldn't flirt her way out of a paper bag, but she buried her nose in the champagne glass to hide her grin all the same. More tickling. A funny tingling in her toes. This was entirely too pleasant.

"Mmm," Hawk said. "This salmon is delicious. Want a taste?" He held out a forkful of fish, steam wisping above it. He was ready to feed her off his own fork. It was so intimate, so, so...

Inappropriate. That's what it was! But sweet. Definitely sweet. "I'm fine with this." She held up a forkful of salad.

"It'll put meat on your bones."

"My bones are just fine."

He caught her gaze and held. *I know, and I'd like to jump 'em.* The message struck like an electric shock, zapping her to the floor. Of course, it was just a generic flirtation, she was sure, but potent just the same.

To hide her reaction, she stuck the forkful of salad in her mouth, but the jolt to her system had turned the raspberry vinaigrette to water and the radicchio to a limp blob.

"Lighten up, Renata. You look like you're about to lose your lunch," Hawk said, misreading her reaction. "We'll be okay. I can help your show, I think. I know a lot about television, and a little about people. And what I don't know I'm willing to learn. You willing to teach me?"

"Teach you?" For a second, hope rose. If he was willing to listen to her, maybe she could keep him from ruining the show.

"Yeah. You teach me some counseling..." He clinked his champagne glass against hers. "...and I'll save your show."

Oooh. The man was so full of himself. "I don't think you realize that if the audience doesn't like you, you're out."

"Oh, I realize it, all right. Maybe you don't realize that if I'm out, you're out."

"That's not true." But it might be. Denny had looked serious and the GM was a man of action. Would he really replace her show with bunny rabbit cartoons?

"It's in both our interests to make the best of this situation, don't you think? It's sink or swim, Dr. R. What do you say we start dog-paddling?" He lifted his glass for a toast. "Here's to working together."

He was right, Renata realized. She was bobbing on choppy waters and Hawk Hunter was the only life preserver she had. What else could she do but grab hold? Raising her glass to meet his toast, Renata mustered her bravest smile. "Here's to it."

"Good!" Hawk said. "Now let's order some of that killer tiramisu and you can tell me how to make it to marriage."

3

THE DAY BEFORE THE SHOW, Renata arrived at her mother's house on a mission—keep the IRS from throwing the woman in prison. Lila didn't take her taxes any more seriously than she took anything else in her life. Renata knocked, but there was no answer. She tried the door. Unlocked! A thief could just walk in. Of course, that would be his mistake. Lila would force-feed him her tofu-toffee cookies and chamomile lemonade, and he'd turn himself in just to escape.

"Lila!" she called, noting that her mother had set up a huge wooden loom in the middle of the cluttered living room. Yarn trailed from the beginnings of a weaving—signs that her mother was off on another creative kick.

"Be right there," came her mother's muffled call.

An acrid smell of burnt metal and wax sent Renata racing into the kitchen, where smoke blossomed from the oven. Coughing, she grabbed a mitt and removed a tray filled with a smoking mass of tortured plastic shaped vaguely like stars.

Lila glided in at that moment, her gauze skirt skimming her calves, her face slathered with green cream. "Oh, phooey! I forgot about my stained glass." Lila took the tray from Renata and, with a shrug, tipped its contents into the trash.

"Are you ready to get started?" Renata asked. "Did you organize your receipts for me?"

A piercing squeal interrupted her. The smoke alarm above the stove had gone off. Without blinking an eye, Lila grabbed a broom, poked it upward, dislodging the alarm, which she caught, and, with a practiced move, emptied of its battery. Blessed silence.

"I started to," Lila said. She indicated a large basket on the kitchen table brimming with crinkled paper, topped by a tennis shoe and an empty pizza box.

"What's with the shoe?" Renata asked.

"To remind me that I donated a bunch of clothes to the Salvation Army. The pizza box was because I brought forty pizzas to the homeless shelter on Halloween. That's deductible, don't you think?"

"If you have receipts." Renata sighed, and sat at the table. Her mother had done her best, at least. But Lila was Lila. "Let me see..." She reached for the basket.

"We can do this later," Lila said, moving the basket to the floor. She sat across from Renata, cupped her avocado-mask-encrusted chin in her hands, and leaned forward. "Tell me more about your hunky cohost. Denny loves him."

"Denny would. They're like blood brothers." She sighed. "I, on the other hand, have not been able to get through to the man all week." She was the only one at the station Hawk hadn't charmed the socks right off. He took an interest in everything and everyone, chatting with the technicians, camera crew, even the secretaries. They all loved him. All except her.

"Lighten up, sweetie. This'll be good for you. You've been so sulky since that old stick-in-the-mud Maurice left. You need something to wake you up, get you out of your rut."

"Right." Her mother was always after her to try new things—like nudist camps and past-life regressions. "Just because you like chaos, doesn't mean everyone does," Renata said. "At least I've never had anyone sic a collection agency on me."

"You always bring that up. A simple misunderstanding. No biggie." Lila waved away the disaster like a fly at a picnic. "Things worked out. They always do."

And that attitude was exactly what had made life with her mother so impossible. Because some things *were* biggies and not everything worked out. The hand-to-mouth existence her mother took so nonchalantly had worried Renata as a young girl. She'd never gone hungry or been at a loss for love, but that didn't change her fear that she might. She'd hated the moves from rental house to medium apartment to studio and back, depending on her mother's income. Worse than that was her father's comings and goings. That had made her frantic for stability—the need was deeply engrained in her. The orderly life she'd created for herself gave her peace and comfort. And that's the way she liked it.

"So, are you all set for the show?" Lila asked.

"I'm as ready as I can be." She'd watched the tapes of her first shows, read case studies of marriage recovery—even got tips from two happy couples she'd helped. No matter what, she'd look on the bright side, be hopeful and positive. "Now, if I can just keep Hawk from ruining everything, I'll be back in business.''

"Life is full of surprises, sweetie," Lila said, her smile cracking her avocado mask. "Enjoy the ride."

"SO HOW GOES THE transformation?" Michelle asked Hawk when she called the day before the show. "Hawk Hunter, Sports-Weather-Whatever Guy becomes…Hawk Hunter, Master of Love!"

"Jeez, Michelle, you make it sound like I just burst from a phone booth in a porn flick."

Hawk lay back on the bed to endure Michelle's teasing. She'd become his mentor after he took her image class and they'd hit it off. She was like the older sister he'd never had.

"So how's it going?"

"Not so hot. My cohost makes Walter Cronkite look like a chucklehead. So serious."

"I've never known you to have trouble with women."

"I'm not trying to sleep with her, Michelle. I'm trying to work with her." He had rules about sleeping with women on the job, but he'd found a little flirtation always smoothed the rough spots. That had been a vital lesson of his years in foster homes, where teasing compliments and affability reduced the tension and loneliness and made things feel okay, even if they weren't. But Renata seemed immune to his charms.

"So maybe you should," Michelle said. "Sleep with her, I mean."

Hawk burst out laughing.

"That's funny?" Michelle asked.

"Not really. It's just the thought of how Renata

would react to the idea.'' Her eyebrows would shoot up, her dark eyes would go wide with surprise and she'd back into a door or something. Why did he enjoy startling her so much? Because then he caught a glimpse of the fun-loving girl inside her, below all that reserve, and he wanted to coax her out to play.

But there was no point in that. ''I've just got to stay focused,'' he said, frowning.

''Right. New York, Chicago or L.A. in five years,'' Michelle said, reciting his oft-repeated goal.

''That's the ticket.'' He did miss news writing, though, and TV news was pretty shallow. Still, TV was where the action was, news-wise, and anchoring was the top of the game, so that's where he was headed. Whenever he had doubts, he just took out his mother's picture and thought about making her proud.

''So, if you're not going to sleep with her, then what?''

''I'll work it out. Somehow.'' He'd find a way to get through to Renata. She needed him on her show, whether she realized it or not. Tomorrow, he'd prove it to her.

THE DAY OF THE SHOW, Renata smoothed her blue silk blouse with trembling fingers and waited for Hawk to join her on the set. She was so nervous her tongue stuck to her lips when she tried to moisten them. In direct contrast, Hawk sauntered into the studio, relaxed and confident. He nodded a greeting to the floor manager, said something to one of the assistant producers, then stepped onto the raised set and approached her.

Her heart rattled in her chest like a moth trapped

in a lamp shade. This happened every time Hawk got close to her. It was pure loneliness, she guessed. After losing Maurice, male attention naturally felt good. She might be the most sensible person in the world, but she was still human. And a woman.

"Hi, Renata. Nervous?" Hawk asked, lowering himself into his matching red-velvet throne. Unlike how foolish she always felt in it, Hawk seemed to take command of the chair.

"No," she lied.

"I'm scared spitless." He looked so regal in the throne, that was hard to believe. Maybe he was saying that to make her feel better. Charming to the end.

"It'll be okay," she said, to reassure him. "Just follow my lead. You can add some ideas, but don't say anything silly."

"Don't say anything silly? That's an odd request from someone sitting on a fairy-tale throne with a giant glass slipper on the table, but I'll do my best."

The theme music kicked in—sort of a calypso version of "Flight of the Bumblebee"—and Renata braced for what was to come. She'd just do her best to be her old self and pray the audience didn't like battling counselors. Then Hawk would be gone like a bad dream. She just had to hang her hopes on that.

Charles announced the show, explained Hawk's presence—to the audience's apparent delight—then introduced the first guests, Christine and Jeff, dubbing their story, "Don't Fence Me In."

The couple entered, Jeff wearing a cowboy hat and Christine a gingham dress—costuming suggestions from Denny. Christine's light southern accent had led him to choose a boy-howdy tone for the segment. Charles explained in a country accent that

Jeff needed "wide open spaces" in his love life and Christine wanted to "lasso him into her corral."

The audience applauded, the couple sat on their thrones, and Renata took a big breath and began. "So, Christine, what's keeping you and Jeff from your happily-ever-after?"

"Well, Dr. Renata, every time we get close, Jeff pulls away," Christine said. "He won't even let me plan menus for the week because he might want to go out with the guys."

"Darn it, Christine," Jeff said. "A man needs some elbow room. You're closing me in."

"Um, excuse me," Hawk said, nervously clearing his throat. "Men do have a need for space."

Renata gave him a sympathetic look. He *was* a little scared, she could see. "That may be true, Hawk," she said, "but, let's hear what Christine has to say."

As Christine detailed more of Jeff's failings, Renata could see clearly that Jeff was not good enough for her. She'd promised Denny—and herself—that she'd stay positive, whip out some snappy you-can-do-it bromides, but she looked into Christine's confused face, and felt those rubber bands of emotions flipping and snapping again. She couldn't sugarcoat the truth just to save her show. She had to be true to Christine.

"It sounds to me, Christine, like you've laid out a hand-prepared banquet of love, but Jeff would rather have a TV dinner on a paper plate," she said.

"Exactly!" Christine said.

"Hang on," Hawk said. "What about love making the world go 'round?"

"Not relevant," Renata said to him. Snap. Flip. Snap.

Hawk gave her a look. *Don't do this.*

But she couldn't stop herself now. "Getting a man to settle down is like putting a gorilla in high heels," she blurted. "You can do it, but it's not natural, and in the end you'll just ruin a perfectly good pair of pumps."

Renata caught Denny's violent headshake off stage. At least the audience had laughed. "It's a case of the age-old conflict between men and women," she continued. "Women nest, men hunt. And they're not hunting window treatments."

"That's harsh, don't you think, Renata?" Hawk said, a little too loudly. His eyes widened, brows lifting to signal *roll with me on this.*

She ignored him. "The point is, Christine, that your happiness doesn't have to depend on a man."

"I don't know...." Christine looked puzzled.

"We're going for perky here," Hawk whispered.

Renata ignored him, focusing instead on Christine's fledgling self-esteem. "Repeat after me, Christine, I don't need a man to be complete."

"But—"

"Just say it out—loud and proud—I don't need a man to..." She gestured for Christine to fill in the blank.

"...be complete?" Christine finished faintly.

"Excellent. You're getting it. A woman without a man is like a fish without a bicycle!" She heard some puzzled noises from the audience, along with male groans, but it didn't matter. She was on a roll now. "A woman without a man is like a...a...camel without a rowboat!"

Hawk stared at her. "What"

"You get the idea."

"That's it," Hawk hissed through his teeth. "I'm taking over. You can thank me later." Then he raised his voice for the audience's benefit. "I'd say we've heard enough of the 'I am woman, hear me roar' pep talk for today. I don't think Christine's quite ready to hang ole Jeff in the town square."

The audience applauded wildly. The part of Renata that knew she was out of control felt a wash of relief that Hawk had taken charge. The rest of her just wanted to smack him. Who did he think he was?

As she watched him smile confidently at the audience, then at the couple, pausing with just the right mix of humor and authority, she knew exactly who he was: Mr. Television. Exactly what she was *not*—even before she'd lost her faith in marriage.

"Now, I'm no expert," Hawk said, with endearing humility, "but here's what I'm thinking, Jeff. Maybe you don't mind getting, *broke to the saddle,* but you need some time to get used to the *bridle.*"

The audience hummed pleasantly.

"Explain it more." Jeff's eyes shifted nervously, and he stretched his neck out of his collar. He *did* look a little like a stallion about to bolt from the paddock, Renata saw.

"Men get nervous about sudden changes," Hawk said. "We don't even like to share the TV remote, let alone an apartment. Am I right, Jeff?"

"Oh, yeah," Jeff said. He gestured at his girlfriend. "Like, she's doing all kinds of…stuff…in the bathroom at my place. She put smelly dried leaves in a dish."

"That's potpourri, you big slob," Christine interjected. "It's classy."

"It gets all over everything. Then, she put this fuzzy cover on the toilet lid and every time I, you know, use the facilities, the cover's so thick the lid bangs down and sprays you-know-what over everything."

"Ouch." Hawk said, hunching his shoulders. He shook his head at Christine. "You've got to slow down a little. Let Jeff get used to you shaving your legs with his razor before you start decorating his fixtures." The audience laughed and the handful of men in the audience woofed.

"Yeah, I've given up a lot for you," Jeff said. "I let you put dust ruffles on the bed, for God's sake."

"What about that poster of babes in bikinis over the bed?" Christine asked him. She turned to Renata. "Can you believe he wants to ogle women right where I'm sleeping?"

"Unbelievable!" Renata said.

"Let's give Jeff some credit," Hawk interrupted, gripping Renata's hand hard, the way you'd kick someone under the table to keep her from saying something stupid. His heating-pad hand warmed her to her toes.

"Keeping up that poster doesn't mean he *wants* those women," Hawk continued. "He just doesn't want any change in the scenery. In other words, it's not about cheating, it's about—"

"Interior decorating!?" Renata finished incredulously.

"Damn straight!" Jeff said, grinning at Hawk. "It's a scenery deal."

The audience burst into surprised applause.

Raising her voice to be heard over the noise, Renata said, "There's more at stake here than posters and TV remotes, Hawk. Those things are symptoms of a bigger conflict. Hanging posters of naked women in his bedroom is a symptom of Jeff's unwillingness to commit to Christine. Not to mention his objectification of women."

"That's right," Christine said. "His objectifi-whatsits." She wagged a finger at Renata. "What she said."

Hawk leaned toward Renata, as if confiding in her for the audience's benefit. "Come on, Dr. Renata, lighten up a little. You gotta have fun in love."

The audience exploded with laughter.

"But you're ignoring..." Renata's energy dropped, and her words faded. "...so much."

"How about if I try to *round up* an answer here," Hawk said to Renata, "while you kick back a sec. Would that be all right?" he asked her, his eyes saying *follow my lead...or else.*

Somewhere inside her, she knew he was right. It was sink or swim and she was going down for the third time. With a sigh, she gave in. "Go ahead," she said to him. "Be my guest."

"My pleasure." He turned to the couple. "Jeff, why don't you tell us some things Christine does that makes you feel like the bit's too tight," Hawk said. "And, Christine, maybe you can come up with some ways to get what you want without giving Jeff here saddle sores."

Oh, brother, Renata thought. *That is so phony.* But Hawk kept talking and by the end of the segment, though Christine still looked confused, Jeff had begun to look positively cheerful. This would only delay the inevitable breakup, but Renata was the only one who seemed to realize the danger.

At the end of the show, when Charles asked the audience if Hawk should stay or not, Renata wasn't a bit surprised when they erupted like a bleacher full of football fans.

"That says it all," Charles said, clapping Hawk on the back. "Welcome to *Making it to Marriage.*"

"Yes," Renata managed to say. "Welcome to the show."

The audience applauded delightedly, the closing music swelled, and after a few excruciating moments it was all over.

Renata pushed herself to her feet, desperate to get away, but Hawk caught her hand in his warm one, and pulled himself up beside her. He braced her back with his palm. How did he know she felt like she was about to fall down? "We did it," he said. "We saved the show."

"No," she said heavily. "*You* saved the show. You did what Denny wanted. I just can't go through the motions any more." She felt defeated and weary and completely out of place.

Hawk looked at her closely, his hand still warm on her back. "Don't give up, Renata. It'll get better. We just have to get a rhythm going." His warm eyes were full of concern, a melting brown... And in that instant, she realized what they reminded her of. Caramel.

That was it. Like the caramel apples her mother used to make every October. The ritual of melting the candy squares in the double boiler, dipping and twisting the apples, then slurping up the tart, chewy confection was one of the few childhood moments she cherished. She felt herself soften, then smile at Hawk. "My word," she said in amazement. "I think I believe you."

"You should. With me, what you see is what you get. Just take a look."

She did. She looked right into the eyes of Mr. Playful, Mr. Silly Name, Mr. Nothing is Serious, and saw that he meant it. He wanted to help her.

"You think we can do it?" she asked shakily.

"I know we can."

"I hope you're right." She pulled away, headed to her dressing room to collect herself, to see if she'd lost her mind to trust Hawk Hunter with her precious show. Her hand still tingled from his grip and the imprint of his palm on her back burned hot as a brand, and as she walked, she felt hope rise in her heart. The warmth in Hawk's caramel eyes had melted her doubts and she felt good for the first time in three weeks. Maybe Hawk *would* help her get back her faith. Maybe everything would be all right.

She opened her dressing room to find Denny waiting for her.

"We've got to talk," he said.

"I know, I know. Go ahead and say 'I told you so' about Hawk."

"No, Renata, listen. The GM cut the budget."

"He what?"

"The numbers were wobbly, and he's on a rampage."

"What does that mean?" Renata's heart thudded in her chest.

"It means we can only afford one host."

"One host? So Hawk has to go?" She had a flicker of compassion for him, almost a sense of loss.

He *had* saved her show. And he'd added something. And he had caramel eyes...

"Look, my preference is to keep you both," Denny said, "but it's a no-go unless the ratings jump big-time. I'm on your side, Renata, but you're not bouncing back, and everybody loves Hawk."

"You mean...?" Her throat locked on a breath, anticipating the worst, which Denny proceeded to deliver.

"You've got four shows to change the GM's mind. Otherwise, it's done. We give *Making it to Marriage* to Hawk."

4

SUDDENLY DIZZY, Renata sat down—hard—onto a makeup stool, which squeaked in complaint. Her heart, so full of joy just seconds ago, tightened into an aching knot inside her.

"I know it's a blow, Renata," Denny said. "I tried to talk him out of it, but he's ticked about the sports show, and his wife's hounding him about a French cooking-aerobics show. Burn the calories while the soufflé rises. A staging nightmare. But that's my problem, not yours."

"Oh, Denny," she said faintly.

"Sorry, Renata. Sometimes I hate this business." He patted her shoulder. "I still think you two would make a good team… And I know I could squeeze some money out of the budget if the GM would let me." He sighed, as if that were impossible, then headed for the door. "I've got to go tell Hawk." He stopped and turned to her. "If you'd pick up a few of his techniques, you could take over, you know."

She didn't answer him, just waved as he left. *You two would make a great team.* For those brief seconds at the end of the show, looking into Hawk's warmly confident eyes, she'd thought so, too. Now Denny had dropped his bomb and vaporized her hope. Once her ambitious cohost learned they were in head-to-head competition, he'd pull out all the stops. This was a stepping-stone on his career path. He'd be nice about it—his eyes were kind—but he'd push her out of the way all the same.

Should she just give up, get used to the idea of not having her show? She still had the teen center and her counseling classes. Without the income from the show, it would take her longer to earn her Ph.D.—a lot longer—but she could still do it.

She thought for a minute of what the show would be like in Hawk's hands. Saddles and bridles and lame comments about interior decorating. Ridiculous! The show needed her expertise—and so did Hawk—even if she was more cautious than she used to be. In her current frame of mind, though, she knew she couldn't outshine the sparkling, witty, ever-optimistic Hawk Hunter.

No, she couldn't beat him. Damn.

She rested her forehead on the countertop and squeezed her eyes shut in frustration, as she took several calming breaths. *Think, think, think.* She was no quitter.

Then it came to her. She lifted her head and stared at herself in the mirror. Color lit her cheeks and there was a glint of determination in her eyes. Maybe she couldn't beat Hawk, but why couldn't she join him? Sure... If they were good together—make that fabulous—the GM would have to keep them both, wouldn't he? If Denny thought there was money to be squeezed from the budget, then there must be *some* flexibility. And Denny could be indomitable if he needed to be.

Her only problem would be getting Hawk to see past his ambition to what was best for the show. No easy task. She'd just have to be persuasive. She'd manage somehow. If she could talk Rico Romero, a gangbanger who came to the rec center, into writing poetry, she could talk Hawk Hunter into sharing the spotlight.

She had to get to him quick—before he planned his takeover. She leaped to her feet intent on catching him in his dressing room before he left. She hurried down the hall and pushed open his door, but it thumped into something.

"Ow!" The muffled exclamation came from the other side of the door.

One hand to her mouth, Renata slowly opened the door to find Hawk rubbing his forehead, his face in a grimace.

"Oh. I'm so sorry," she said. Starting a discussion about teamwork by braining her teammate wasn't ideal. "Are you okay?"

"This is getting off easy," Hawk said, rubbing his head, a pained smile on his face. "After what Denny just told me, I thought you might clobber me with that glass slipper."

"No, but I do want to talk to you. Can I come in?"

Hawk stepped aside, Renata shut the door, and he dropped onto the wheeled makeup stool. She chose a wooden chair a few feet away, but Hawk rolled right over to her. She wished he didn't feel the need to get so close. With only a foot between them, she could see the creases in his lips, darker flecks in the golden brown of his eyes—and the rosy bump in the middle of his forehead where she'd conked him.

She swallowed hard and launched into her proposal. "Look, Hawk. I know you want this job. I know you saved the show for me. And I know you think that taking over the show will boost your career. I understand that. But what you have to realize is that without the solid foundation of my counseling experience *Making it to Marriage* would crumble like…like…'' she fumbled for an image, flummoxed by how closely he watched her face. ''Like a sand castle in the tide…or a cookie in milk…or Roquefort in a salad…or a crouton underfoot.''

''Renata—''

''Okay. You get the point.'' She glanced into his caramel eyes long enough to see that he looked amused. Amused! She was fighting for her show and he thought it was funny. ''I know you're entertaining and charming and witty and you know television,'' she continued, ''but you need me, too.'' The expression on Hawk's face was too much. ''What is so funny?''

''You. You're cute when you're arguing with yourself.''

''Surely you realize that without me, the show would be like a bad talk show or some goofy sitcom with a laugh track. We have to…'' Finally, his words sank in. ''Arguing with myself?''

''Yes. Renata…'' He rolled a few inches closer. Now she noticed the laugh lines at the sides of his mouth, the smile crinkles around his eyes and streaks of blond in his brown hair. ''…I want us to do the show together.''

''You do?'' She widened her eyes, completely thrown off.

''I meant what I said before. The show needs two perspectives. It'd be lame with just one of us. The GM's wrong. It needs the back-and-forth, yin-yang, man-woman thing.''

"You think so?" She couldn't believe he would give up so easily. "But this could be your own show...."

"Nah. It was yours first. It'd be better together."

"You mean it?"

He nodded.

"Denny said he thinks he could squeeze some money out of the budget," she said hopefully.

"If we're good enough, they'll pay for us. That's television," he said. "We just have to blow 'em out of the water and they won't dump either of us."

"Right. Great. That's exactly what I was thinking." It seemed impossible Hawk could mean what he'd just said, but there was no duplicity in his eyes.

"We just have to prove that we belong together," Hawk said.

Renata's breath hitched. *We belong together*. The words hovered in the air between them like beautiful butterflies.

"On the show," Hawk finished, shooing them away.

"Sure. Of course. The show."

"Good." Hawk reached to shake on it, his eyes holding hers. She took his hand. Warmth zoomed through her, faster, on nerve pathways prepared by past experience. His eyes held hers, his gaze a heat lamp warming her all over. Her heart thumped in a strange rhythm, her skin tingled and her toes went numb.

He was even closer now. Fleetingly, she noticed the crispness of his collar's crease, the tan of his skin under the pancake, the flex of his neck muscles, the melting brown of his eyes. His cologne filled her head, and she felt breathless and a little woozy.

Hawk tilted his chin toward her and she noticed more things. His teeth were very white, his jaw straight and strong, he had a hint of a dimple on one cheek and he wanted to kiss her.

He wanted to kiss her. Omigod! Panic seized her and she pushed herself back into the chair, as if she were on a carnival ride.

Someone knocked at the door. Renata yelped, and Hawk turned his stool toward the door, the wheels squeaking sharply in the tense air. The door opened and the willowy blonde who anchored the six o'clock news—Tabitha Walker—peeked in, a lovely grin on her perfectly made-up face. "Caught the taping," she said, her gaze glued to Hawk. "You were great, Hawk."

"Thanks," he answered, not reacting to her once-over. He must be used to it, Renata realized.

"Nice touch for your show," Tabitha said to Renata. "We'll talk later," she said pointedly. *About Hawk's marital status, no doubt.* Tabitha wiggled her nails in airy farewell. Until that moment, Tabitha had never even spoken to her.

It was a perfect interruption, though, reminding her that Hawk Hunter was Tabitha's kind of man, not hers—if she'd had any inclination to make anything of that fleeting sexual moment, which, of course, she didn't.

"So, where were we?" Hawk asked, trying to catch her gaze.

She avoided his eyes, afraid to find he still wanted to kiss her—or that he didn't, she wasn't sure which—and jumped to her feet to pace. "We were about to make a plan for a great show."

"Right," he said, with a team-spirit fist thrust. "A

great show." He sounded relieved to be back to business.

"The first thing we need is to get you up to speed on marriage counseling," she said. "I have a number of books and videos you should study, and—"

"Hold it."

She stopped pacing. "What?"

"Renata, the first thing we need is to get you to lighten up. A lot."

"But we agreed that we need balance."

"Balance, sure, but when a couple is trying to dig themselves out of a hole, you can't keeping throwing shovelfuls of dirt on their heads."

"I'm just being realistic."

"Nah. Your problem is you've lost your flair."

"My flair?"

"Yeah. I've been studying the tapes of your first shows. You had flair and now you don't."

"You watched my tapes? Oh. Well." Her voice wavered. He'd been studying her? The thought made her feel strange and oddly flattered. She sat in the chair across from him again.

"So, forget the research," he continued. "If you cheer up, we'll be fine."

She shook her head and corrected him gently. "If you're more serious we'll be fine."

Hawk pulled a quarter from his pocket and flipped it. "Heads, we do it my way, tails yours."

"You're flipping a coin over the show? Why not just arm wrestle for it?" she said dryly.

"You into wrestling?" he asked, his brows lifted suggestively. "Mud is nice."

"Hardly." She felt a little charge all the same.

"Not a bad idea really," Hawk went on. "It could

be like Wide World of Wrestling. We battle it out on the mat.''

Despite her frustration, Renata's mouth darted into a smile. ''You mean Mad Dr. Renata versus Killer Hawk Man.''

''Hey, a joke!'' Hawk smiled at her. ''That's progress.''

''Just because I'm serious about my work doesn't mean I don't have a sense of humor.''

''Then use it more. Your smile lights up your whole face, did you know that?''

''Oh. Thanks.'' His compliment sent heat rushing through her. Why couldn't she get used to Hawk being Hawk? Flirting was second nature to him. ''Anyway, we have to work at this.''

''I have a better idea,'' Hawk said. ''How about we play at this?''

''What?''

''Spend some time together. Not argue our philosophies. Just have fun.''

''Have fun? What good would that do?''

''If we get to know each other better, we'll get some rapport going. Corporations do that kind of thing all the time to build teams.''

''You mean a retreat?''

''Exactly. Think of this as a *Making it to Marriage* team retreat.''

''I don't know....''

''Got a better idea? I mean besides a smack-down next Wednesday?''

What she wanted was for Hawk to study. But she knew that even if she gave him her entire relationship library, he probably wouldn't read a page. On the other hand, if she went with him and brought her books along... And familiarity *was* important to personal comfort, that much was true. "Okay," she said, "on the condition we go over some theory, too."

In answer, he clasped her hand, yanked her arm into an arm-wrestling position on his thigh, and grinned. "Sure you don't want to go two out of three?"

"No," she said, stunned by the playful strength in his hot-pad grip and his wicked grin. She tugged her hand away and reminded herself to breathe.

"Just as well. You gave me a good one here, Mad Dr. R." Hawk rubbed the bump on his forehead, a rueful expression on his face. "You're stronger than you look. You'd probably take me in two."

No, she was weaker, she realized, softening all over under Hawk's warm gaze.

"We'll spend Saturday together," he said with a wink. "I'll pick you up at ten."

"The whole day?" she said weakly.

"Relax. It'll be fun."

Fun. The last thing she should have with Hawk is *fun.* She had to work with him, not play with him. She'd just have to keep her wits about her, her mind on the show and her body under strict control.

Something told her she should have gone for the coin toss.

DESPITE HER VOW TO MAKE Saturday a workday, when the doorbell rang at ten, Renata's heart leaped to her throat like she was on a first date. She lunged for the door, the legs of her crisp new jeans scraping together like sandpaper. Pressing a hand to her heart, she opened the door to Hawk, handsome in a shape-hugging golf shirt and jeans, a mischievous smile on his face and a huge spring bouquet in his hand. "For you," he said, presenting them to her. "Pretty flowers for a pretty lady."

"They're lovely." She inhaled the cool perfume of the bright blossoms. "You shouldn't have." Now she really felt like they were on a date.

He tried to hold her gaze, but she pulled her eyes away before that sizzling sensation could start. She'd have to be on guard if she expected to keep her promise to herself—all work and no play. Well, just enough play so the show would succeed.

"Come in." She backed up, letting him enter.

"Nice place," Hawk said, turning slowly. She watched him take in the living room of her small town house—the entertainment center's shelves loaded with books, miniature dishes and porcelain treasures, her needlepoint-pillow-laden couch and the bank of whatnot shelves that held her doll houses. "It's got so much...stuff."

"Thanks." Having lots of things around her, each in its own spot, made Renata feel safe. It had started when she was a child, as a way to distract herself from her dad's departures. A picture to cross-stitch or a dollhouse to decorate comforted her. Later, of course, she learned that security-conscious people tended to be collectors. To the outside world, it was probably all a little too precious, she knew, but she couldn't help it.

"You make all this stuff?" Hawk asked.

"Most of it." It was a creative outlet, too. A modest one, compared to her mother's brash, splashy approach—wall-sized oil paintings, rug-sized looms, tuba lessons. Renata preferred small things she could manage.

"It must be hell to move."

"Oh, I wouldn't move," she said, startled at the thought. "I love it here." She'd had more than her share of new addresses to memorize as a kid. "I'll just put these in some water." She wiggled the bouquet, then headed for the kitchen. She hoped Hawk would sit down and wait, but he followed her, his steps creaking on the wooden floor. He felt too big—like a giant tromping around in one of her miniature houses.

She was filling a crystal vase with cold water when Hawk abruptly loomed over her from behind, his breath on her neck, practically touching her.

"You missed this," he said and grabbed her backside.

"Whaaa-t are you doing?" She whirled to face him, splashing water from the vase into his face.

With just a blink of shock, Hawk said, "New jeans?" He held up the cardboard price flap he'd ripped from her back pocket. Water dripped from his nose and hair.

"Oh. I'm sorry," she breathed. "I didn't know what you were doing." She set down the vase and dabbed his face with a towel.

"You bought new jeans for me," Hawk said. "I'm flattered."

She stilled the towel on his face. "Don't be silly. I just needed some new ones."

"No one *needs* new jeans. Jeans last forever." He grinned at her.

"Think what you want." She was annoyed, not because he was right, which he was, but because he was so sure about it. Uncomfortable with Hawk watching her every move, she decided to trim and arrange the flowers later and just plopped them into the vase, which she placed on the table. "Very pretty," she said, admiring them.

"Yeah," Hawk echoed, but when she turned, she saw he was looking right at her.

"So, shouldn't we get started?" she said, embarrassed, turning to hurry into the living room, aware of his eyes on her the whole time. She'd have to control this stupid inner fluttering that started up whenever Hawk did things like that. It was just knee-jerk flirtation. She certainly wasn't his type. Just as he wasn't hers. He was only being kind. Or else he couldn't help himself. At the door, she turned to him. "So, what are we doing today?"

"I thought we'd just keep it loose." Hawk shrugged.

"Keep it loose? Don't you have a plan? It's a whole day."

"Relax, Renata. We'll have fun."

"And work on our show," she said firmly. "We agreed." She picked up the three relationship books she planned to go over with him from the entry table, then handed them to him.

He sighed, hefting their weight. "I suppose it's too much to hope that you want to drop these off at the library on our way?"

"You agreed we would study."

"Right," he said. "Just the thing to do on a perfect spring day—crack the books." He tucked them under his arm and held the door for her. "After you, Dr. R."

Not surprisingly, Hawk's car was hopelessly impractical—a red convertible sports car. Too small to be useful and the black canvas top wouldn't last one brutal Arizona summer. The tiny half back seat was piled with balls, mitts, tennis racquets and helmets.

"I just threw in some stuff we might want," Hawk said. He opened her door for her, then made space for the books among the sports gear.

"Today?" She gulped. "I'm more of a Ping-Pong person myself."

"Nothing too intense," he said, grinning. "Maybe skydiving if the wind's right."

"Oh, no." Then she saw he was teasing. Sunlight gleamed in his hair and flashed in his eyes. His smile tugged at her. "Oh, you," she said and let him hold her hand as she lowered herself into the bucket seat. The warmth of the sun-soaked black leather matched the lingering heat of his hand, making her skin prickle with goose bumps.

Hawk went around to the driver's side and sat down. Even with the roof off, he seemed too close. Renata leaned nearer the door.

"I thought about taking you to the Phoenix Art Museum or the Pueblo Grande Museum," Hawk said, leaning closer. The man had no sense of personal space.

"Those sound great." They did. Calm, quiet, interesting. And safe.

"Nah. Too much like a field trip. I thought of something much livelier." Hawk turned up the stereo. Rock and roll thundered, the bass so loud her seat vibrated. Thumping the rhythm on the steering wheel, Hawk whipped out of the driveway, and they roared off.

Livelier? What did that mean? Renata grabbed the handhold and fleetingly considered donning one of the helmets in the back. She already missed the art museum.

5

SO FAR SO GOOD, Renata realized when Hawk pulled into one of the parking lots of the sprawling Encanto Park on Phoenix's west side. Then she spotted the merry-go-round. "You're taking me to kiddieland?" she asked weakly. Amusement parks held sad memories for her.

"Relax," Hawk said, turning off the engine. "We're just walking through it. Wouldn't want to OD on the fun or anything."

"Sorry. I just like to know where I'm going. I like to—"

"Have a plan, I know. Okay, how's this?" He reached behind his seat and pushed aside the sports equipment to reveal a small ice chest. "Lunch," he said, tapping the chest. "I threw a picnic together. How's that for a plan?"

"Very nice. Thank you. I don't mean to be difficult. I guess I'm a little nervous."

"Understandable," he said, and patted her knee. "So, how about we get rid of those jitters with—" He rummaged in the back seat, then held up an ominous-looking black boot with wheels.

"In-line skates?" She gulped a dry swallow. "I've never actually tried that."

"You'll get the hang of it. Easy."

Easy. Famous last words, she learned. After some

wild minutes of flailing, flopping and falling, she managed to work up just enough speed to wind up in the lagoon—she'd neglected to ask how to stop the darn things. To make her feel better about the dunking, Hawk handed her his wallet and jumped in, too.

They dried off, thanks to fistfuls of napkins from a dispenser at the hot-dog stand, a blanket from Hawk's trunk and the spring sun. Renata rinsed her hair in the rest room sink, and they headed back to the car to get lunch. Those sandwiches better be darn good, she thought grumpily, feeling like the Creature from the Black Lagoon, and walking like it, too — her legs stiff from the strain of in-line skating. She wouldn't leave until she'd accomplished her goal, though. They could study over lunch.

As Hawk put away the skates and pads at the car, Renata noticed his shirt was missing a button. "What happened?"

He looked down at his chest. "When I dragged you out of the lagoon, I guess the button popped off."

"I can fix that," she said.

"Oh, yeah?"

She took her purse out of the trunk and removed her tiny sewing kit.

Hawk laughed, his teeth white against his tan. "What else you got in there? Kitchen utensils? *TV Guide?*"

"I believe in being prepared," she said. Okay, maybe *too* prepared. Thank goodness he hadn't noticed the miniature office supply pouch complete with mini stapler.

"You can't prepare for everything, you know,"

Hawk said. "Some of the best things in life are surprises."

"You sound like my mother," she said, her back
to him while she threaded the needle and extracted
the tiny button. "She's big on spontaneity. My personal opinion is that surprise is very overrated." She
turned to find Hawk sitting on the car, patting the
space on the hood between his legs, where she realized she'd have to stand to sew the button.

"Surprise!" he said softly.

Uh-oh. She'd forgotten how intimate this procedure would be. Reluctantly, she moved into place.
"This will only take a minute," she said, as much
to herself as to him.

"Take your time," Hawk said, grinning wickedly.
His knees held her snugly by the hips. She held her
breath and slipped a hand between his shirt and chest
so she wouldn't stick him as she worked. His skin
felt warm against the back of her hand. The lagoon
water had made no dent in his pleasant smell. She
had to hope the same was true of her.

Her gaze slipped out of control and dashed up the
line of his neck to his mouth, little more than a kiss
away. Farther up, she saw his eyes had gone smoky
with emotion—the color of coffee with two creams.
He was as aware of her as she was of him. Her heart
thudded so loudly in her ears she hoped he couldn't
hear it, too.

What if he kissed her?

"Ow!" Hawk said.

"Sorry." She'd slipped and pricked him. Com-
manding her nerves to settle, she pushed the needle
in and out of the holes in the tiny white button from
her kit. Hawk looked past her while she worked, but

the way he swallowed—his Adam's apple dropped and abruptly bounced back—and the unevenness of his breathing told her he was feeling the same tension she was. Finishing quickly, she ducked her head against his chest to bite off the thread. When she raised up, Hawk looked stunned.

"Beautiful Hair."

"Th-thank you."

"Your shampoo, I mean. The brand is Beautiful Hair, right?"

"Oh, the brand. Yes, that's what I buy." She laughed, feeling silly. "I'm surprised you can smell anything but pond water."

"Did you know that men find the smell of a woman's shampoo more arousing than her perfume?" he said, sounding dazed.

"I didn't know that," she murmured, equally caught in the moment.

"I read that researching a feature story." He looked like he wanted to bury his face in her hair and she had the absurd wish that he would.

She patted his chest with a shaky hand. "There. All better." She pushed back.

"Yeah, thanks. Now I know what Girl Scouts grow up into."

That was how Hawk saw her, she realized with dismay—all prim and proper, coloring inside the lines, following the rules. "Don't laugh. First aid comes in handy," she said, making a joke to cover how foolish and boring she felt.

"And I'll bet you can start a fire without matches, too," he said, his voice husky with unmistakable suggestion.

Electricity shot through her, along with ridiculous

relief that even though he saw her as an uptight Girl Scout, he was still willing to flirt with her. "Yep, if you're ever lost in the woods, I'm your girl."

"I'll say."

She smiled, feeling redeemed, then returned her sewing kit to her purse and her purse to the trunk, before picking up her books from the back seat. "We can study over lunch," she said to Hawk's questioning look.

"You're sooo strict," he said, then hefted the ice chest. "Wait'll you taste these sandwiches. And the potato salad. Mmm."

Unfortunately, the sandwiches were mush and the potato salad soup, thanks to melted ice. They were sitting on the grass on a blanket because Hawk had insisted picnic tables were for sissies. Evidently, so were sealing plastic baggies.

While Hawk headed for the refreshment cart, Renata lay on her back on the blanket and took stock. Her back itched from lagoon muck, blisters on both heels stung, her legs throbbed from the strain of skating and when the breeze was right she got a faint whiff of algae from her hair, Beautiful Hair shampoo notwithstanding. As if that weren't enough, her attraction to Hawk was becoming more and more troublesome. His flirtation and attention were wearing her down.

She cheered herself with the thought of the studying they'd do now, after which she could go home and have a hot bath. The clouds were pretty, she saw, through the lace of swaying eucalyptus leaves. The breeze felt good and the park sounds cheered her—birds twittered, children shouted and someone's radio played jazz. She loved jazz. For a moment she closed her eyes and basked in the pleasure of it all.

"You're having fun," Hawk said triumphantly, startling her.

Her eyes flew open, and she sat up and smiled. She *was* having fun.

Then Hawk thrust a shriveled hot dog so old it looked shellacked at her. "Lunch," he declared.

"Oh. Wow. I haven't had a hot dog in a long time." She gulped, then took a bite. "Mmm," she said, grinding through the rubbery meat while Hawk watched her. Satisfied, he handed her a soda, then dropped onto his side, propped on one elbow, to gnaw on his own dog.

Forcing down a second bite, Renata opened *Conflict in Marriage* to one of the pages she'd marked with a stickie note to discuss with him, then turned the book. "Read this section."

"Not while I'm eating," he said.

"It's about establishing intimacy."

"You mean sex?" He perked up.

"Sex is part of intimacy, but—" Seeing his grin, she stopped. "Could you please think like a counselor for a minute, instead of a...a..." *Sex god.* That's what he looked like lying in that pose—like a male pinup model, except with clothes on. Very provocative.

"A man?" he finished. "You want me to stop thinking like a man?"

"You know what I mean. We need to focus."

"Okay, but only if you let me apologize." Hawk reached into his back pocket and pulled out a silk daisy on a wire stem, which he held out to her. "I'm sorry this day isn't going like I'd hoped."

"How pretty!" she said, accepting the flower. Their fingers tangled briefly, and she got that rush of heat again. *Stop that,* she wanted to say, though what control he could have over his body temperature, she didn't know. She tingled all the same. "You don't need to apologize."

"Just a sec." Hawk took the daisy, bent the stem into a curve, and then gently tucked the flower behind her ear. "Now *that's* pretty."

She blushed.

"Even more now. Like I said, your smile lights up your face."

Renata's heart flipped like a fish out of water. She quelled her reaction. This was ridiculous. She was acting like a schoolgirl with a crush. "Let's get down to business, shall we?" She tapped the book in front of him.

"This *is* business, Renata. You already look more cheerful."

"Now I'm a cheerful Girl Scout, huh?" She wanted to joke away his attention—he made her feel too *seen*—but Hawk kept his eyes on her.

"So what was his story, anyway?"

"Excuse me?"

"Your boyfriend. The guy who made you hate men."

"I don't hate men." She frowned.

"'Making a man settle down is like putting a gorilla in high heels.' Not exactly an ode to manhood."

"It was just a simile illustrating Jeff's problem." Hawk's eyes probed, digging in. The man had no sense of personal space. At least Maurice always allowed a comfortable safety zone. "Look, I'd rather not talk about Maurice."

"Maurice, huh? With a name like that, no wonder you ditched him."

"People can't help their names," she said, though she couldn't help smiling. It was a pretty stodgy name. But then Maurice was a pretty stodgy guy. "Besides, I'll bet your parents didn't name you Hawk."

She caught a flicker of something dark in his eyes—hurt or sadness—but he immediately smiled it away, a kid taking a tumble from his bike, dusting himself off, mugging for the crowd. "I needed a professional name—something solid and masculine with flair. It works, don't you think?"

In a meaningless-sex-r-us kind of way, Renata thought. Then she stopped herself. She had no business thinking of sex and Hawk in the same breath. Though it was only natural to be curious about him. "It doesn't matter what *I* think. What do you think?"

"I think it works."

"In what way?"

He looked at her quizzically, then grinned. "Are you analyzing me, Doctah Rrrrenata?" he asked in an exaggerated German accent. "Want me to say the first thing that comes into my mind?"

No. Judging from the suggestive look on his face, she didn't dare. She wished he would realize he was lying too close to her. He should wear a sign like those truck mirrors that warned when things were closer than they appeared. "I'm not analyzing you."

"No need to. With me, what you see is what you get. I'm an open book, Dr. R." He held her gaze. "Completely open." The sexual suggestion was clear.

She couldn't squeeze out a word.

"Unlike you. You're a woman of mystery. So, tell me all about this Maurice."

"I really don't see the point. I mean, it doesn't seem…"

"Come on. Spill." He rested his chin on his upturned palm, and she looked into his interested eyes, open and smart, and realized he wouldn't let her alone until she talked. She took a deep breath and launched into the story of Maurice's resigning his university post to devote himself to research in the Amazon basin.

When she'd finished, Hawk was quiet, considering her story. Finally, he said, "At least when he left, it wasn't for another woman. It was for a higher purpose."

"True." She laughed. "But the real problem was that I realized I was glad he was gone. I'd been fooled by how comfortable we were together, how compatible. We liked the same activities, held the same beliefs. It should have worked. We had everything going for us."

"Except sparks."

"What?"

"It's obvious what was wrong. No fireworks. No sparks."

She frowned. "We had something more important than *sparks*. We had mutual respect. Fireworks fizzle, you know. Love lasts."

"Without sparks, Renata, all you had was a roommate who didn't argue with you over the phone bill."

Maurice hadn't overwhelmed her with passion, it was true, but she wasn't that kind of woman anyway.

Her interests were more cerebral. Intellectual rapport was much more important to her than ordinary lust. Her parents had sparks, all right, but that hadn't kept her father from leaving. "Sparks are highly over-rated," she said.

"You wouldn't say that if you'd felt them," he said, his voice low and serious, with an edge that gave her chills and made her wonder if he was right.

"And I suppose you have?"

"I'll know it when I do," he said with supreme confidence. He stared at her. "And I'm not afraid of it." *Like you.*

"I'm not afraid," she said. But his eyes held her so calmly, she knew he could see that she was. She felt lost and lonely and scared she'd always be that way. She felt like she had as a child when her love hadn't been enough to keep her father around. She fell back onto the blanket, stared up at the sky and sighed. "I don't know what I think any more," she said softly. "I found a good man, I worked hard to build a life with him, and it wasn't enough." She lay still. The blue sky above seemed empty and end-less.

Then Hawk's face was over her, sober, intent, all joking gone. "Don't give up, Renata. You'll fall in love. Real love. Not this namby-pamby, we-have-so-much-in-common, we-like-the-same-music kind of thing, but real love. And passion. Passion so deep all that other junk—comfort and compatibility—won't matter one damn bit."

Was it true? Could love be so strong she'd know it for sure. Could it overcome differences and make two people one forever? A violent hope nudged her rib cage and for that moment, with Hawk's gaze gently holding her, she wanted it to be true.

"How can you be sure?" She raised up onto her elbow so that now she and Hawk were inches apart, lying parallel to each other, looking into each other's eyes, close as lovers.

"I just am. Love is big. You know it when it hits you, and it always finds a way. You meet the right person, the time is right and..."

Renata's heart sank as she realized what he was going to say. "Poof! Happily ever after," she finished for him.

"Exactly."

Pure fantasy. Pure fairy tale. Hawk was like a psychotic person saying something profound, and then in the next breath declaring he could walk on water. He was as unrealistic as her father, who was always pretending everything was fabulous, when it really was empty and sad.

The fledging hope that Hawk had a handle on how love worked gave one last flutter, then plunked to the pit of Renata's stomach. "You're dreaming. Love isn't fairy dust someone sprinkles on you."

"I didn't say it was. But it's not a battle of wits or compatibility calculations, either."

"I guess we'll have to agree to disagree about love," she said softly. She wanted to believe as he did, but she couldn't. On the other hand, what had realism done for her? She thought of the stack of books she'd read and reread, making notes in the margins, underlining key points. It all felt so useless. Just so many words and theories, when real love was as elusive as a butterfly, as slippery as a bar of soap.

Tears filled her eyes. She was confused and sad,

and those rubber bands of emotion snapped and flipped inside.

"Don't cry, Renata," Hawk said, resting a hand on her shoulder, and then patting, as if to soothe her.

"I'm not crying," she said, blinking rapidly. "I have allergies."

"You're just trying too hard," he said. "We don't have to solve this mystery in one afternoon. We're supposed to be having fun, remember?"

"Sure." She gave him a watery smile and sat up, quickly brushing each cheek.

Hawk sat up, too. "I think it's time for my secret fun weapon." He reached behind the ice chest and retrieved a plastic bag filled with a pastel-colored mass. "Ta-da!"

"Cotton candy?"

"That's right. Spun fun." Hawk tore open the plastic, releasing a puff of cherry scent.

"I haven't had cotton candy since I was little." She watched him tug off a feathery tuft.

"No wonder you're feeling blue. You've been deprived of the food of the gods. Did you know that it was invented by accident? I did a story on that once." He took a deep sniff. "Mmm. Just one more of life's sweet surprises," he said, waving the fluffy cloud of pink sugar close to her face.

"You're just full of newsy tidbits." She reached for the treat, but he playfully lifted it out of reach.

"Open wide."

"Just give it to me." She frowned in pretend annoyance.

He shook his head. "Uh-uh. Open up." He waggled the candy teasingly under her nose. "Quick, before you faint dead away from cotton-candy deprivation.''

She giggled, surprising herself, then did as he asked.

But the moment became instantly erotic. Her mouth was open, receptive, wanting the delicacy that Hawk gently fed her. His eyes seemed completely absorbed in the sight of her accepting his gift. She licked the airy sweetness, bringing it fully into her mouth. Her tongue brushed Hawk's thumb.

At the contact, Hawk jerked in a ragged breath and his steady hand trembled. ''You missed some,'' he said huskily. He showed her where with his finger and when she licked the fleck of sugar her tongue brushed him again. His gaze went hot. She made a small sound.

''Renata,'' he breathed and leaned forward.

Her heart rose in her throat as his mouth met hers, soft and warm, lovely and tender. The world around her disappeared until her only awareness was a rushing sound in her ears and the taste of Hawk's mouth.

His lips fit hers perfectly—their mouths two halves of a whole. Their tongues touched with a familiarity that startled her, and she felt the comfortable hunger of longtime lovers with hours of lovemaking before them.

Except then Hawk pulled up and away from her. The air on her wet lips felt cool and unwelcome. She opened her eyes to see what was wrong.

''Quite the secret weapon, huh?'' Hawk's eyes twinkled.

He was playing. The kiss that had rocked her to her toes was just a bit of fun for him. That was what this day was about, right? Showing her how to have fun? How quickly she'd forgotten. One kiss and her good sense had dissolved…like the cotton candy on her tongue.

6

"YES, UM, GREAT," Renata said. She busied herself to hide her awkwardness and began to gather their trash. "We should get going, don't you think?" She crumpled the hot-dog paper into a tight ball.

"What's the hurry?" Hawk asked.

She couldn't meet his gaze, so she brushed the crumbs off the makeshift tablecloth and dumped the ice chest's water onto the grass.

Hawk gripped her arm to stop her. "Don't think so hard, will you? It was just a kiss. In the spirit of the moment."

"Right." She managed a crooked smile.

"Chalk it up to being under the influence of cotton candy."

"Sure." But she was the only one who'd gotten tipsy.

"Good." Hawk sounded relieved. He looked past her. "Look," he said, indicating a couple sitting a few yards away engrossed in what appeared to be a heated argument. "Feel like talking them into marriage yet?"

"Very funny."

"Just checking the flair factor," he said. "Looks like we need some more work. The hot-dog guy says there's a craft fair on the other side of the park. Let's check it out."

"But I'm such a mess." She scratched at a streak of dirt on her forearm, and pushed back her dusty hair, longing to go home.

"Nah." Hawk reached out and adjusted the silk flower behind her ear. "There. You look perfect." He was so hard to argue with. He reached down for her hand, and she let him help her up, steeling herself against the warmth of his hand and pulling away as soon as she was on her feet.

Soon, they were wandering among canvas-topped booths admiring the wares of artists, potters and other craftspeople. Renata tried to coach Hawk as they strolled, mostly to distract herself from how nice it felt to be at his side, their steps in sync, their shoulders bumping companionably. "The two most important elements in a successful relationship are respect and honesty," she said, while Hawk ran a finger along the edge of a gleaming ceramic bowl. "This is especially critical when a couple begins to quarrel. One true test of a relationship is right fight behavior."

"Look at this," he said, plopping a velvet hat with a floppy brim on her head and moving her in front of the mirror. "Audrey Hepburn in *Breakfast at Tiffany's.*"

"Very nice," she said, removing the hat and continuing with the lesson. "I urge couples to use 'I' messages in sharing their feelings. For example, 'When you say this, I feel that.'"

"As in, 'When you ask me if you look fat in these jeans, I feel like I'm in deep weeds'?"

"Hawk." Then a flash of color in the sky caught her eye. Three hot-air balloons hung, as if by magic, in the air above then. "Oh, look!"

Hawk looked upward. "Cool."

"I've always wanted to go up in one of those," she said.

"Albuquerque has a huge balloon festival every year. I covered it for the station."

"Did you get to go up in one?"

"Oh, no. I'm not big on heights."

She sighed. "It seems so free. So magical. I used to have dreams where I could fly, too."

"Freud would have something to say about that, I'll bet. Doesn't flying symbolize repressed sexual feelings?"

"Oh, probably. Everything symbolized repressed sexual feelings to Freud."

"I know how the man feels," he said, holding her gaze.

A thrill surged through her she tried to ignore. Why did he have to be so naturally sexy? "So, what about you? What do you secretly long to do?" Whoops. That hadn't come out right.

"I don't think you want the answer to that."

She gulped. "Well, I know you like sports," she said, determined to stick to safe topics. "What else?"

He released her gaze. "Oh, I like to travel, meet people, explore places and their history."

Big, open, active things, she noticed. The opposite of her. She liked small, close, quiet things. Except for hot-air balloons—her one dangerous dream.

"And music," Hawk said, stopping in front of a booth full of handmade wooden instruments—xylophones and zithers on a table, flutes and panpipes hanging from hooks overhead.

"Me, too," she said. "I love music, too."

Hawk picked up a small stringed instrument—a ukulele.

"You play?" asked the ponytailed man inside the booth.

"A little." Hawk pressed the strings into a chord and began to strum softly with his thumb.

"So, you're a musician, too?" Renata asked.

"I dabble. A little piano and this."

"You and my mother. She was always playing off-key guitar or honking a tuba."

"So what instrument do you play?"

"Oh, I don't. I just appreciate music. I was always afraid—" She stopped. She wouldn't admit she'd been afraid to fail, to bungle the notes. "—I'd keep the neighbors awake. A tuba is not a subtle instrument."

"The ukulele is pretty easy. Want to give it a try?" He waved the belly of the ukulele toward her.

"Oh, no. I have no knack for it."

"You'll do fine. Give yourself a chance."

"Buy it and teach her," the man in the booth urged.

"Would you let me?" He kept his eyes on her, while his fingers made three swift chord changes. "It's only four strings and they're very soft."

"I couldn't." Longing sped through her, though, like quicksilver. Hawk stared at her questioningly, continuing to play.

She watched his fingers, tender and careful, as if the wooden instrument were a living thing from which he coaxed its sounds. *Come on, be beautiful for me.* For a shuddering instant, she wanted his hands on her that way—touching, stroking, coaxing.

"I think I'll buy it," Hawk said suddenly. "I need

something to do with my hands.'' She looked up, startled at the huskiness of his tone and saw in his eyes he'd read her reaction. A shiver rippled through her. Again. The rushes of desire Hawk kept sending through her were wearing her down. She felt like she was trying to stand against an ocean wave. She just wanted to bend her knees and go with the flow.

The instrument was expensive, but Hawk didn't hesitate once he'd made up his mind. In his own way, he was as stubborn as she was.

As they headed to the car, she saw that sunset's purple and gold had squiggled along the horizon. The day was over at last. Thank goodness. Her physical complaints—aching legs, blisters, sunburn and pond scum—were nothing compared to this softness she felt toward Hawk. The day had smoothed the rough edges between them. She felt comfortable and easy with him and the natural attraction seemed stronger. It was hard to tell herself this good feeling was bad for her, though she knew it was. Where was her brain? The cotton-candy kiss had made it all mushy. Not to mention the flash of longing she'd felt watching him play the ukulele. She had to get home for some private time.

Hawk held her door for her. As she sat down, she said briskly, ''Well, that was a busy day. Thanks for everything.''

''Don't thank me yet,'' he said. ''I'm thinking Mexican food.'' Leaving her openmouthed, Hawk went around the car and climbed in beside her.

Two hours later, after Renata'd consumed a fish-bowl-size margarita and a huge chimichanga, and Hawk had paid the mariachi band to bellow a song to her, they finally left to mistaken exclamations of happy birthday from neighboring diners. Renata plopped, worn out, into the soft leather seat of Hawk's car. At last she could go home. She was exhausted from trying to coach Hawk and resist him at the same time.

As Hawk went around to his side of the car, she looked at the Polaroid photo he'd paid for as a souvenir of the evening. A woman had plunked a huge sombrero on her head and Hawk had squatted beside her for the snapshot. She couldn't believe how terrible she looked. All day Hawk had said she looked perfect. Was he insane? Her hair was gray with dust, mascara had smeared under one eye and a streak of dirt traced her chin. The silk daisy looked ridiculous behind her ear. She was surprised the restaurant hadn't booted her out as a vagrant.

But flattery was Hawk's way, she knew. Just like her father, always telling her she was prettier and smarter than she really was, always pretending things were better than they were. Beside her in the photo, Hawk grinned, happily oblivious.

She tucked the snapshot into her purse, not wanting to be reminded that she wasn't a fairy-tale princess at a ball, but a bedraggled woman who'd taken a dive in a swamp.

Hawk landed beside her with an energetic thump. "Now, how about some dancing?"

"No!" She sat bolt upright. "Please. I can't."

"You can't dance? No prob. I'll teach you."

"That's not what I mean." Being in Hawk's arms would be too cruel. Maybe it was all fun and games to him, but it was complete sensory overload for her. "I'm just whipped."

He looked her over. "If you're sure."

"Oh, I'm sure."

"Okay, home it is then." He sounded disappointed.

She was deeply relieved. Catching sight of the tumble of books in the back seat—they'd barely touched them—she wondered what they'd accomplished during the long day of skating and dunking and ukulele playing and kissing. Hawk's face in profile looked content. He'd had fun, she knew, so he was probably quite satisfied.

She, on the other hand, had a knot in her stomach the size of a fist. What had they done to be sure they'd knock 'em dead as a team on *Making it to Marriage*? Nothing. They'd hardly cracked a book and every time she tried to do some mock interviews, he changed the subject or did something annoyingly appealing. In fact, they'd done exactly what she'd dreaded—they'd had a date. A fun date. A date that made her feel more comfortable with Hawk and more attracted to him than ever.

When they pulled up in front of her town house, Hawk turned to smile at her, and it got even worse. This was the part of the date where the woman asked the man in for "coffee," or they exchanged a kiss promising more the next time.

She gulped. The spring breeze was sweet with citrus blossoms. The wind had tousled Hawk's hair so he looked completely endearing. Moonlight blanketed him in buttery light. Her neighbor Myra's lights were out. Duke, Myra's rottweiler, gave a half-hearted woof, then Renata could only hear crickets. They were very much alone.

"Did you have fun?" Hawk asked softly.

She nodded, unable to speak.

"Me, too. I can still taste cotton candy. How about you?"

Instantly, she did. Reflexively, her tongue skimmed her lips.

Hawk took a harsh breath. "We shouldn't do this," he said on a groan, but he moved closer, the leather creaking under him, until he was so close she felt his body heat and smelled his skin. His lips were inches away, his face tilted at a perfect kissing angle.

"No, we shouldn't," she murmured, her eyes drifting closed. She wanted this kiss, though, so much. It was only a kiss. She'd survived the first one...

But barely. The second one could push her over the falls. She had to stop. "We should really...really..." With a burst of self-control she pushed Hawk to his side of the car. "Study! We should really study." She grabbed a book and flipped it open, upside down.

Hawk began to laugh. "Renata Rose, you are something else." He covered her hand with his hot palm and used it to close the book. "We've studied enough. Test me."

"What?"

"Ask me a question. See if I know the answer."

"Okay," she said hesitantly. Was this a trick just to get her to bed? Oh, she hoped so. No, no, she didn't. She'd take it seriously. "Okay, if the man says he's bored with the relationship, what would you advise?"

"A red lace teddy."

"Sex?" She squeaked the word. "Sex doesn't cure everything."

"Can't hurt," he said.

"Forget that. Okay, what if the woman says the man doesn't appreciate her?"

"Then I'd tell him to appreciate her."

"Okkkkkay…"

"Appreciate the way her lips are soft and easy to kiss, the way her voice has this great husky sound like pure sex."

He was talking about *her,* Renata realized, and heat rushed through her. She had to get away before she became putty—no jelly, no syrup—in his hands. She became aware that the door handle was poking her in the ribs, so she gripped it. She should get out of the car, except she was so sluggish, hypnotized by the moment. Ready or not, here Hawk came. In a final spasm of good sense, Renata's hand convulsed, the door opened and she hit the sidewalk with a thump.

"Whoa," Hawk said, leaning across her seat to look down at her. "Was I crowding you?" His eyes were playful, but still molten. "Wanna go inside for the final exam?"

Luckily, the jarring thud onto the curb had cleared Renata's head. "Bad idea. We have to work together, Hawk."

He looked at her a few seconds, giving her a chance to change her mind, and then he sighed like a kid refused a cookie. "You're right." His eyes stopped smoldering and just like that he was his old self. How could he be so casual about something so big? Her whole body ached with disappointment…and in-line skating blisters. She pulled herself to her feet.

"So no hands-on training?" he asked, looking up at her.

"Oh, for heaven's sake. Don't you take anything seriously?"

"Not really," he said, obviously trying—and failing—to tame his smile.

"Well, take this seriously." She lifted *Conflict in Marriage* from her seat and plopped it onto Hawk's lap.

"Easy there," he said with a grimace.

She blushed, realizing she'd whacked him on what must be a swollen spot.

"Sorry. But please study, Hawk. It's important."

"You're the doctor," he said, with no sincerity whatsoever.

But she was too tired and too tense to argue further. "Good night then, Hawk."

"Don't worry, Renata. Everything will be fine now."

"So you say," she said. "Just study." She turned on her blistered heels and limped up the walk, feeling Hawk's eyes on her the whole way. How could it be fine? There was no way this day had helped their show. Hawk only made jokes—or passes—and it was more clear than ever that she didn't know how love worked. Not to mention that all that flirtation was getting to her.

Once inside, she sagged against the closed door for a few deep breaths before she made a beeline for the bathroom. In a few moments, she sank with a groan of relief into a scalding hot bath. She let the fluffy bubbles rise high and felt the heat draw out her aches and her worry.

But as she soaked, pictures floated through her mind—Hawk grinning at her over the fishbowl margarita, Hawk jumping into the lagoon so she wouldn't feel so stupid dripping with muck and the look on his face when he put that flower over her ear. She felt herself grin, and reached up to touch the flower. It was gone and she felt the loss like a stab.

Oh, for heaven's sake. Here she was getting all dewy-eyed about Hawk giving her a flower. He'd just been trying to cheer her up, get back her "flair," as he called it. He surely wasn't pining for her right now. He was probably on his way to a club to find a woman who, unlike Renata, would dance—the horizontal mambo.

What about the show? That was what she should focus on. They had to make it work. Tomorrow she'd call Hawk and insist he cooperate with her. Over the phone, she wouldn't be distracted by his laughing eyes and mischievous grin, and she could state her case more plainly. Yes, that's what she'd do, she concluded, and ducked under the water, luxuriating in the warmth that washed over her. Now if only she could rinse away the taste of cotton candy...

WAY TO GO, IDIOT! Hawk told himself as he drove off. He'd been thinking below the belt there for a minute and pushed too far. The idea had been to perk her up, get back her hope, not jump into bed with her. It was always tricky sleeping with a woman he worked with. The problem was he just kept tasting her mouth, warm and cotton-candy sweet. And so kissable—her lips puffy, her skin soft. And her body so firm and right. Under all that cool restraint, she was one hot woman. And that voice—so sexy it turned ordinary words like "how are you?" into "let's get naked" in his mind.

She was just different from the women he was used to—so careful and serious. She pondered everything—even his teasing. She blushed and her eyes got big. You'd think no one had ever played with her before.

He liked how she made him feel—on his toes and fully alive. The whole day he'd scrambled to find things to amuse her. He liked how her eyebrows shot up and her mouth made a little ''oh'' when he surprised her. And for the whole day, the relentless drive to succeed had faded a bit. He'd almost felt calm. Except when she turned him on.

That was a problem. For a second, the desire to have her thundered through him like an eighteen-wheeler on a downhill.

Honk! The driver behind reminded him the light had changed. He accelerated with a jerk, then shook his head to clear it. *Get a grip, Hunter.* Right now the only business he had with Renata *was* business—their show. She was the kind of woman a man married. And only a certain kind of man would be right for her—a man who stayed put, liked everything just so, and never changed his haircut, let alone his job. Hawk was not that kind of guy. And he wasn't sure he'd ever fall in love so hard he'd risk ruining everything with marriage. Dullsville, Daddy-o. Kiss of death. Marriage killed romance, turned a relationship into mind numbing routine and took the life out of love. He'd learned that from personal experience, having witnessed a variety of marriages as he'd grown up—his own foster families and the families of his friends.

Right there were big reasons to steer clear of Renata Rose's mystical eyes and promising heat. They were at polar opposites in terms of who they were and what they wanted out of life, work and love. He just had to keep that in mind at all times. Maybe if he pictured her with a big international "no" symbol on her body, he'd be able to keep himself in line.

Okay, he was horny. That was normal. He'd better find someone else to play with. That blond news anchor—Tabitha, wasn't it?—had seemed interested in him. She certainly wouldn't expect more than he had to offer—a brief affair before he moved on. He'd make a point of stopping by the news desk, start up something. Yeah, good idea. He flipped on the stereo and the fierce confidence of a rough voice got Hawk instantly back on track. *Rock and roll.*

Glancing down, he noticed the silk daisy, crumpled and limp, on the floor of the passenger side. When he'd slid the stem behind Renata's ear, she'd smiled a don't-dare-hope smile that had hit him like a punch in the gut. She'd looked makeup-smeared, grimy and utterly charming, like a waif offered unexpected lodging for the night, and he'd wanted to sweep her into his arms and promise her everything she was afraid to ask for.

It figured that she'd left the flower here—she didn't dare hope, after all. He picked it up and brought it to his nose. Mmm. Beautiful Hair. *Watch yourself,* he warned. *Ah, what the hell,* he thought as he stuffed it into his pocket. Some things you didn't think to death, you just did.

7

"LET ME GET THIS STRAIGHT," Eric, the male half of the troubled couple, said to Hawk. "I spent two thousand dollars on a Caribbean cruise, Carol still claims I don't love her and all you can say is, 'men act, women feel'? What's that mean?"

They were five minutes into the first segment of the show and Hawk was falling on his face. And it was all Renata's fault. The day after their date, she'd called and begged him to do it her way. To calm her, he'd agreed—even studied *A Galaxy Between Them: Why Men Send Women into Orbit*—but he seemed to be doing a very bad imitation of Dr. Renata, and it wasn't working at all. His rhythm was off, and there was no sign of the easy confidence that was the secret of Hawk's appeal. Be careful what you wish for, Renata thought, sick inside. Hawk was doing what she'd asked, and it was ruining everything.

"Right," Hawk said uncertainly, glancing at Renata. "You see, testosterone made cavemen wrestle saber-tooths to prove their love to their women."

"So you're saying testosterone made me take Carol on a cruise?" Eric shook his head. "Nah. I think it was the whining."

"Oh, for heaven's sake!" Carol said, throwing up her hands.

"Actually, my point is, um," Hawk shifted in his throne. "Renata, what is my point?"

"You're trying to say something about the differences in the way men and women express love, right?" she said gently. "That men *do* things to show their love, while women *talk* about their feelings?"

"Yeah, that's it." Hawk sounded relieved.

"The problem is obvious," Carol said. "The cruise was nice, but what I really wanted was for Eric to say 'I love you.' Spending money is easy."

"Easy?" Eric exclaimed. "Two G's is hard cash. I wanted that money for a down payment on a speedboat. Instead, I spend it on her and she doesn't know I love her?"

"Three little words," Carol snapped. "I...love... you." She counted it out under Eric's nose. "I dare you. Say those three little words. The prettiest in the English language. I...love...you!"

Eric's face went pink. "I don't have to be carrying on all the time," he muttered. "I show you how I feel. With actions—like that caveman Hawk was talking about."

"Just say 'I love you.' *I love you!*" Carol shouted.

"Uh, Carol," Hawk interrupted, "you're making the prettiest words in the English language sound like something you wouldn't want your grandmother to hear."

The couple turned on him and said together, "Butt out!"

Then Carol began to sniffle.

"Ah, no, not the waterworks!" Eric threw up his hands.

"Women feel, remember?" Hawk said, clearly

nervous. "You've got to let them clear the pipes when they need to. You got a tissue, Dr. R.?" *Help me out here,* his eyes said.

"I was wrong, Hawk," she whispered. "Let me fix it."

Renata took a steadying breath and turned to the couple. She had to get it right. They were all depending on her—Eric, Carol *and* Hawk. She handed Carol a hankie. "Eric loves you," she said. "But, like many men, he has a hard time sharing his feelings."

Carol sniffled into the cloth.

Renata was about to say making a man say "I love you" is like ironing your underwear—you can do it, but what's the point?—when she realized she didn't think that any more. In fact, these two might make it if they could just get past this communication problem. And she could help them.

"The good news is that you can work around it," she said to Carol, excitement growing as she continued. "If you love Eric, you have to listen for his love—not with your ears, but with your heart."

"Really?" Carol asked.

"Really," Renata said, delighted to realize she believed it. "And, Eric, if you want to keep Carol, you're going to have to bite the bullet and say those three little words Carol just screamed at you. Once in a while. It won't shrivel your masculinity and it will give Carol great joy."

"But—"

"No buts about it. It's dollars and cents. If you'd said those three little words six weeks ago, you'd be out on your speedboat at the lake right now instead of here complaining about it."

"I guess so," Eric said.

Carol wiped her eyes. Renata's heart felt light. She sat taller and breathed deeper. Confidence flowed through her. For the first time in weeks, she felt alive and strong—and sure about her advice.

She turned to Hawk, as he had to her the week before. "How about this, Hawk? How about you let me be Dr. Renata and you go back to being yourself, and together we can get these two to marriage. What do you say?"

Silence throbbed for a few seconds, then someone yelled, "You tell him, Dr. Renata!"

"Yeah," Hawk said, "you tell me." His smile lit up his face. He was proud of her. And that made her feel almost as good as maybe discovering her faith in love again.

Renata leaned toward Eric. "So, Eric, how about if you try that now—right here on our show—say it out, loud and proud, 'I love you, Carol.'"

"I don't know…" Eric said, bright red. He looked to Hawk for help. "What do you think, Hawk?"

"I think if you ever hope to get that speedboat, you'd better do what the doctor ordered."

"Okay," Eric said. He turned to Carol. "Carol, I…I…" He swallowed, looked from person to person, then blurted, "IloveyouCarol."

"Oh, Eric!" Carol threw her arms around him. "Was that so hard?"

He nodded violently.

The audience exploded with applause and cheers.

For the next few minutes, Renata successfully guided Carol and Eric through the land mines of their dispute, with Hawk supplying observations as only he could.

"When you get the urge to buy Carol something, stop and ask what that gift would say to her if it could speak," Renata said. "Then *you* speak for the gift."

"Yeah," Hawk chimed in. "Is that diamond pendant saying, 'I think you're beautiful'? Then use the words. Is that black lace nightie whispering, 'Oooh, baby, let's get naked'? Just say it yourself."

"Really?" Eric asked.

"Yeah. Try it, 'Oooh, baby, let's get naked.'"

"Oooh, baby—"

"Uh, that's okay, Eric," Renata said.

"You get the idea," Hawk said. "It'll save you some cash."

"The issue is not the money you spend," Renata corrected him, "because of course Carol would like an occasional present. But the gift that builds a life together is love."

"Yeah...exactly," Hawk said wonderingly, then finished softly, "Welcome back, Dr. Renata."

"Thanks, Hawk." They could do this, she knew then, without a shadow of a doubt. They could be a team that would knock their socks off. She felt it deep inside. And it felt great.

The audience—applauding madly—seemed to agree. As the closing music swelled, Renata looked into Hawk's eyes, expecting to feel pride and satisfaction and relief and team spirit. Instead, she felt a rush of desire, and the taste of the cotton-candy kiss filled her mouth. She swallowed hard, fighting the feeling. Just when things were about to get better, they got worse. Even if Denny told them they'd succeeded in proving themselves, she would have another problem—how to work with Hawk without falling for him.

And Hawk wouldn't make it any easier, she discovered. The minute they walked into the office, he swept her into a tight hug. She tried not to respond to the glorious feeling of his arms around her, his chest tight against her breasts, but the hard tug of attraction pulled her like a magnet. Hawk was like some spectacular dessert that she knew would give her a stomachache, but she couldn't help staring at through the window, longing for a taste…just a taste.

His arms still around her, Hawk pulled back. "You were your old self, Renata. All flair, no gloom." Then he seemed to realize that he held her in his arms. His eyes went smoky and his fingers tightened on her back. "Renata," he whispered. She felt him wanting her with his whole body. He searched her face. He, too, wanted a taste of that spectacular dessert, that gleaming éclair dripping with frosting. He tilted his head and moved toward her.

She smelled him—cologne and mint and makeup and man—and felt his heat like an oven. She baked and burned, inside and out. Automatically, she tilted her face, softened her lips, let her hands reach up his back. Just a taste. One taste…

Their lips met, fitting as perfectly as that day in the park, except the excitement of their show made the kiss more frantic, more hot. His tongue was in her mouth. She moaned, and her knees buckled.

A rap at the door brought her to her senses in a rush. She yelped and yanked away. She caught Hawk's dazed look just as Denny shoved open the door.

"Hey, you two. Great show!" Denny didn't seem to notice their panting or their flushed faces, or if he did, he chalked it up to excitement over the show's success. "I knew this could work. I had a—"

"Feeling about us," Renata finished, still breathless.

"You've got it now," Denny said, pacing. "Keep up this rhythm. That back-and-forth, give-and-take thing."

If he only knew, what had just gone back and forth, been given and taken.

"The audience loved it," Denny continued. "Renata, you're your old self and Hawk...well, just be Hawk, like Renata said. I'll talk the GM into a focus group to prove that this team concept works better than either of you solo. I think I can get him to use some of the advertising carryover to make up the budget gap... And maybe we can lose Charles. We don't need an announcer, really, and he's got his commercial work to pay his bills. This is good. Very good." He stopped pacing and looked from one to the other. "I don't know what you did to fix this, but keep doing it. I gotta go." And he was out the door.

In the sudden silence, Renata was unable to speak. Hawk held her gaze and she couldn't look away.

"So, what time do want me to pick you up Saturday?" he asked softly, with a cozy sexiness in his voice that set her nerves humming.

"Pick me up?"

"Yeah. I'm thinking maybe horseback riding."

"What are you talking about?"

"You heard Denny. We've got to keep doing what we're doing. We need another fun day together."

"He didn't mean that literally, Hawk. And we can't...you know, we shouldn't have..." She put her fingers to her lips, which still felt scalded from his kiss.

"I know," he said, looking sheepish and rakish at the same time. "That was a mistake. You just looked so damn good." He winked at her. A lock of hair fell over his eyes, making him look so earnest and kissable she could hardly stand it. "Don't worry. I won't let things get out of hand. Cross my heart." He made an X over his heart.

How easily he made the promise. It wasn't that easy for her.

"We'll be fine now," she said. "We don't need another Saturday. We can meet for coffee to discuss things, and we can review the tape of upcoming guests together in the studio."

"Come on, don't quit on me now, Renata," Hawk coaxed. "Having fun together was good for the show. Having more fun will be even better."

"Let's leave well enough alone, okay?" She was no more ready to spend another day within kissing range of Hawk Hunter than she was to go hang gliding.

"You were a new woman last Saturday. You were wild on those in-line skates. One more day and I'll have you running with scissors, drinking milk right out of the carton and cutting the tags off pillows."

"I like my pillows with tags, thank you. Besides, I'm really busy Saturday."

"With what?"

"Things."

"What things?"

Her mind raced, searching for some convincing

excuse, but she stalled out and just told him the truth. "I have gardening to do, plus I need to paint one of my dollhouses, and..." That sounded lame even to her. "Well, just things."

"Renata, those are chores, not fun."

"They're fun for me. Look, I'll call you," she said, heading for the door, "and we can meet for coffee." *In some bright, unromantic place.* Not giving him a chance to change her mind, she ducked out. She was determined to spend Saturday as far from Hawk and his caramel eyes as she could.

HAWK PULLED UP TO Renata's house Saturday morning with mixed motives he didn't care to examine. He was just here to keep Renata's flair factor primed, he told himself firmly, like Denny had ordered. Never mind that he'd practiced amusing anecdotes all the way over and couldn't wipe the grin off his face at the prospect of seeing her. It's for the show, he reminded himself. And the show was for his career. *Five years to the top—L.A., Chicago, New York,* he coached himself. *Keep your eye on the ball...*

And your parts in your pants.

Still, he couldn't wait to see her. It had been two days and he missed her serious eyes, lush mouth and sexier-than-sex voice. And the way she listened—really listened—to him.

To his surprise, the woman who answered his knock was not Renata, but a short woman with long gray hair wearing a gauze dress draped with beads. An earth mother with a pink Mrs. Santa Claus face and an open expression.

"Well, if it isn't Hawk Hunter, the man of the hour," the woman said, waving him inside, making her jewelry clink and jingle. He caught a whiff of mint and patchouli. "I'm Lila Rose, Renata's mother."

There was a vague resemblance—the same dark-brown oval eyes and high cheekbones, Hawk saw, but this roly-poly woman with an easy smile and laughing eyes was about as different from serious, exotic Renata as he could imagine. "Nice to meet you," he said shaking her calloused hand. "Renata's mentioned you."

"Uh-oh." Mrs. Rose gave a staged grimace, then grinned like an elf. "She told you I drive her crazy, huh? We're different as chalk and oil, she and I."

"You mean chalk and cheese, don't you? Or oil and water?"

"Whatever. We're opposites. Come in and let me fix you some tea. Renata's off running errands. What's that you have there?"

"Something for Renata to plant," he said, holding up the leafy green thing in a plastic pot he'd nabbed at a grocery store on the way over as his excuse for appearing here.

"How thoughtful." Though her dark eyes perused his face casually, he could see she was sizing him up. He liked her instantly. "Come into the kitchen with me and we can get to know each other."

He followed her. In the kitchen, she poured a murky gray-green concentrate from a bottle into a pitcher of ice water. He got a whiff that reminded him of the Encanto Park lagoon—only stronger.

She poured the mixture into two tall glasses. Very tall glasses, he saw with dismay, as she handed him one she'd expect him to empty, then started into the living room with hers. She sat on the couch and waited for him to join her. "You've sure rattled my daughter's cage, kiddo," she said.

"You think so?" Was that good or bad?

"Oh, that's a good thing," she said, reading his mind. "My daughter needs to be rattled. She's stiff as a board about life. Drink up," Lila said.

Gingerly, he took a sip. A metallic fishy taste filled his mouth. His eyes watered and he couldn't help making a face.

"A sugar man, I can see," she said, sounding disappointed in him. She went into the kitchen and returned with a packet of raw sugar and a spoon.

He stirred in the sugar, braced himself, and took another swallow. Now it tasted like *sweet* metallic fish.

"That's the catnip that makes it sting," Lila said.

Catnip? He paused, testing to see if he had the desire to lick the back of his hand or anything.

Lila seemed oblivious. "My daughter's always been a serious girl. Hell, she started making to-do lists when she was five. She needs some fun in her life. She thinks the world will fall apart if she doesn't hold it in place."

Then she looked at him. "Sooo, tell me about yourself, Hawk Hunter." Her tone was nonchalant, but her eyes gleamed shrewdly, like a robin who'd spotted a fat worm and didn't want to tip it off.

"Well, I've been in television for a year now," he said, glad for something to do besides drink green poison. "My goal is to anchor the news at a big station. I'm just on Renata's show to build my portfolio, and—"

"Tell me about *you,* not your job."

But that's who he was—a television guy. "I'm not

sure what you mean. I'm thirty-two, I grew up in Colorado, but I've lived a lot of places…''

"What makes you tick, Hawk? What makes you happy? What bugs you? For starters, what's your real name?''

"My real name?'' Looking into those intense eyes, he knew there was no point avoiding the question. "Buddy Hodges,'' he said. *Good ole Buddy.* He felt the shame of it all over again. Buddy was a generic name, like Pal or Buster. As if his mother hadn't had time to come up with something special.

"Buddy. Hmm.'' Lila studied him like a gypsy reading his future in those two syllables.

She'd be wrong, though. He'd transformed himself completely from the shy, quiet kid he'd been to the cool, confident guy who rolled with the punches, took chances and always landed on his feet. He'd made his own future. "Hawk Hunter's more me,'' he said.

Lila didn't respond. Instead she watched him. "Tell me about your mother.''

"My mother?'' He could have blown off the question, changed the subject, made up a story, but something about the kindness in Lila's no-nonsense eyes disarmed him, made him *want* to tell her. So he did. He told her about his mother, her death, and his uncertain childhood in a series of foster homes. He didn't get emotional. After all, he didn't blame his mother. She'd done her best, but she'd been a kid herself—inexperienced and unprepared for the responsibilities of motherhood.

He told Lila his story, while her warm gaze, comfortable and kind, gently held him. When he was finished, she didn't say a word. She just leaned over and hugged him hard once, squeezing the breath right out of him.

The gesture stunned him, but it felt good and right. No maudlin sympathy or clucking. Just a hug. Like a pat on the back. As if to say, *After all that, here you are. Well done.*

"So you bopped around in foster homes," she said to him. "That could upset the apple pie on your whole worldview."

"You mean upset the apple cart, don't you?" he said.

Lila shrugged away the confused cliché. "But you're okay." She looked him over. "You've got a bright white aura. A little ragged around the edges— some uncertainty, some contradictory impulses—but you're all there. Your mother would be proud of you, Buddy."

Amazingly, he felt the sting of tears. Like a laser, Renata's mother had honed right in to the deep ache he'd lived with since he was six and his mother had died without giving him a chance to prove himself worth the trouble. It was as if she'd gone right to the photo of his mother he always carried, examined it, and answered his big question with a simple yes.

He blinked rapidly, grabbed the glass of liquid algae and gulped a big swallow so he could claim the tears in his eyes were from drinking the nasty elixir.

But Lila's eyes were waiting for him when he put the glass down. She looked calmly at him, as if bringing a grown man to tears were an everyday thing for her.

It wasn't an everyday thing for him, though. And he felt surprisingly better for it. "Thanks," he said simply.

"Thank *you*," she said, "for coming into my baby girl's life."

Wait a minute. He didn't want Lila getting the wrong idea. "I'm not in her life, really, Mrs. Rose. I'm in her *show*."

"Oh. Right." A smile teased the corners of her mouth, and her eyes twinkled. "And you brought her that philodendron because of the show?" She indicated the ratty plant on the floor by his feet.

"Sure. I mean, sort of. If we spend more time together, we'll make the show stronger."

"Tell you what. How about if I tell you a little about Renata? Just to make the show stronger, of course."

"Of course," he said, grinning at her. She'd nailed him and he didn't mind one bit.

"Neither her father nor I could figure out how we got such a cautious little person, so different from us. We're both pretty loosey-goosey people. I probably would have shielded her a little more if I'd been smarter or more mature, but we were young and in love, and you know how that is…"

He sat back to listen, questions lining up in his mind, loving everything about this delightful woman. Everything except her iced tea.

RENATA OPENED HER FRONT door to find her mother and Hawk sitting in her living room, laughing and talking, thick as thieves. A nitrogen-starved houseplant sat on the floor beside Hawk and two tall glasses half-filled with an ominous-looking drink rested on the table between them. One of her mother's concoctions, no doubt. But Hawk and Lila together were an even more dangerous mix.

"This is a surprise," she said, looking from one to the other.

"I came to bring you some iced-tea, Rennie, and get started with those awful taxes," her mother said. "And look who showed up to keep me company—Buddy."

"It's Hawk, Mrs. Rose," Hawk said, "not Buddy."

Buddy? Hawk's name was Buddy? And how had Lila learned that?

"Buddy's an okay guy," Lila declared, looking at Hawk. "You should let him out to play more." Then she smiled at Renata. "Buddy and I have had a nice visit. He told me all about himself, and I told him all about you."

Oh, no. This was worse than she thought.

Hawk grinned at her. "Yeah, your mother told me you once jumped off your playhouse with twenty birthday balloons to see if you could fly."

"The closest to being like me Renata's ever been," Lila said wistfully. Then she frowned at Hawk. "You've hardly touched your tea."

"Oh, right." Hawk widened his eyes at Renata, out of Lila's line of sight, then lifted the glass in a we-who-are-about-to-die-salute-you toast.

Renata smiled. She knew how wretched Lila's teas could be. She wondered which formulation she'd offered him. She hoped it wasn't that *one*…"

"This blend is for clear thinking," Lila said, watching while Hawk took a big drink, "and virility."

Hawk choked.

Yep, that was the one.

"I'll get you a glass, dear," Lila said and headed into the kitchen.

"No, thanks," Renata called to her.

"Save yourself," Hawk rasped as she hurried after her mother.

"I hope your heart-to-heart didn't include any matchmaking, Lila," Renata said once they were in the kitchen. Her mother insisted she call her by her first name, wanting them to be pals, though blood type was the only thing Renata thought they shared.

"Of course not. Your personal life is just that, personal," she said primly, parroting Renata's words without a drop of sincerity. "But he's a great guy, Rennie. A 'life is short, play naked' kind of guy. A perfect way for you to break out."

"Break out? You make it sound like I've been in prison."

"With that Maurice, you were. That man could sap the fun out of a bathtub full of butterscotch pudding."

"My relationship with Hawk is work related."

"All work and no play…" Lila warned.

"Exactly."

And nowhere more so than in her love life. Maurice may not have been the right man for her, but he was a heck of a lot closer than Hawk Hunter, Mr. Free To Be.

"Well, I'll be off then—let you two do some *work*." Lila winked. "I put some soy-sesame bread in the fridge. It's got ginkgo biloba with a tinge of St.-John's-wort. Keeps you perky yet calm."

"Thanks," she said. She'd feed the bread to the birds later. What the world needed was more perky yet calm birds.

"You won't have time to do my taxes tonight, I can see, what with Buddy here and all. Tomorrow maybe?"

"Tonight will be fine," she said firmly, determined to get Hawk out the door as soon as she could. She already felt him nearby like heat on her skin.

"Give it a chance, Rennie." Her mother crushed her into a hug. She was smothered in softness and mint. It was nice. No matter how many rashes she got from her mother's health food or how many times she had to keep the finance company from repossessing her mother's car, Renata loved Lila with all her heart.

She followed her mother into the living room, where Lila picked up her huge purse and headed for the door, her earrings clinking prettily, her gauze skirt swaying. "Toodles, Buddy," she said, wiggling her fingers. "Oh, and you'll be visiting the bathroom more frequently for a day or two. Don't freak. It's good for your kidneys."

"Right," Hawk said, looking alarmed.

Lila breezed out the door.

The minute the door closed, Renata turned to Hawk. "'Buddy'? Is that your real name?"

"Yeah," he said. "See why I changed it to Hawk?" But his smile didn't reach his eyes, and she could tell the subject upset him. Her mother must have given him the third-degree, she realized, and felt her cheeks blaze with mortification.

"I'm sorry about my mother," she said, coming to sit on the wing-back chair next to the couch. "She can be a little much."

"Your mother's great. Don't ever apologize for her."

"I'm not. I just thought maybe she'd been bugging you."

"Just be glad you have her," he said. "Not everyone is so lucky." His expression was sober, and she realized she was seeing the serious man beneath the wisecracking rake. And suddenly, she wanted to know him better.

But before she could ask him about his own mother, he grinned at her. "If gardening's what you do for a good time, then I'm down for that." He lifted up the root-bound, wilted philodendron. "Something to plant."

"That's a houseplant. You don't really..." No point getting technical. The thought was the gift. "Thanks," she said.

"So, tell me what you want gardened and I'll garden it." He scrubbed his hands together. "We can talk about the show while we work.

"But—"

"What's first?"

"I have some plant food in the trunk..."

Before she could stop him, Hawk was out the door. Minutes later, he was slinging plant food haphazardly among her beds, while she trimmed her roses and tried not to get distracted by how nice it was to have him nearby, strong and sure, and part of her day.

She was choosing carefully where to cut a thick rose stalk when Hawk leaned over her to hold it for her—too close, wonderfully close, his breath on her cheek.

"So, this is what you call fun?" he asked softly, his words sending goose bumps down her arms.

"Yeah," she managed. More so with him here,

she hated to admit. For an instant, she imagined surprising him, turning into his arms, kissing him, the sun bright on their faces. She imagined his muscles, his skin, his mouth, his hot hands on her hot places....

"Ouch!" She'd scraped her arm on a rose thorn.

"Careful there," Hawk said, slow and soft, in exactly the tone she was imagining. "How about if I handle the roses for a while and you go cut something that doesn't cut back."

Before she could protest, Hawk lifted the clippers from her fingers, took her by the arms and gently turned her toward the house. "Go now," he said, patting her on the butt. "Didn't you want to plant those purple flowers out front?"

She wandered away from him, grateful for the reprieve. The farther away she got from him, the more herself she felt. She had to stop fantasizing about him. She didn't take sex lightly and that was the only way Hawk took it. Besides, they had to work together. Sex would only complicate things.

She'd barely planted a half-dozen periwinkles when Hawk was again at her side. "I solved your whole problem," he declared proudly. "Come see."

Oh no. She had a bad feeling about this. Sure enough. Hawk had whacked her carefully cultivated roses into a grim-looking foot tall hedge.

"If you keep them cut back like this you won't have to mess with them so often, and you'll have more free time."

"But I don't want any more free time. I like gardening."

"And, here's this." From behind his back, he pulled a breath-taking bouquet of cut roses, the thorns wrapped in a paper towel. "For you." He handed them to her.

"Oh. They're lovely," she said. Cut too soon, many of them, but lovely all the same.

"Take a sniff," he said. "Each color smells different. Did you know that?"

Of course she knew each variety of rose had its own color, petal shape and scent, but she'd been more interested in growing them strong, healthy and pretty, than in noticing their distinct delights. She smelled each bloom. The red had a dense traditional rose scent, the yellow smelled peachy and the white and orange like lilac and honeysuckle.

"Mmm, you're right." She looked up to find Hawk staring at her.

"You look great with flowers by your face."

"Oh, Hawk." She had to deflect the compliment. "You probably say that to all the girls."

He leveled his gaze at her. "You don't seem to know how beautiful you are." He cupped her cheek with his hand. "Didn't that jerk Maurice tell you so?"

Not like this. Not while really seeing her, as Hawk did now. She felt hot and cold at the same time, transfixed by his touch. The mingled perfume of the roses filled her head and she felt Hawk's fingers on her cheek, saw the muscles in his neck, the way his eyes took her in, cherished her. Maybe there was more going on here than just lust. Maybe this wasn't just a generic flirtation for him. She felt her eyes drift closed.

"Let's go..." he whispered.

Absolutely. To bed. In a heartbeat.

"...back to the park," Hawk finished. "Only, this time, we'll hit the amusement rides."

"Whaaat?" The change of subject jolted Renata like a needle skip on a record.

"Yeah, your mother told me you loved merry-go-rounds as a kid. So, I thought we'd start there."

"I *hated* merry-go-rounds as a kid. I can't believe my mother told you that."

"She said your dad always took you to a merry-go-round when he was in town. It's what you did together."

"Yeah. It's what he thought good daddies did," she said feeling the sadness all over again. She remembered the squeak of her bare leg against the smooth coolness of the horse, the empty cheer of the scratchy calliope music, her heart hollow in her chest, desperate with hope. *Back in the saddle, girlie girl,* he'd say, all jolly and phony.

"I always wanted him to stay, but he never did," she explained, "so I'd always think about how he would be leaving when the ride was over. Merry-go-rounds make me think of that."

"We'll just have to get you over that then."

"I don't want to get over it. I don't need to get over it." Didn't he understand how that hurt?

"Come on, Renata."

"I can't believe Lila told you all that. She doesn't understand me at all. My mother—"

"Loves you," he finished fiercely. "A lot. I would have given anything for—" He stopped abruptly, his eyes full of pain.

"What? Hawk? Tell me."

"Just be glad you have a mother."

"Don't you have one?" Her heart stopped beating.

"No, I don't," he said softly. "And no father, for that matter."

"What happened?"

"My mother got pregnant in high school with me. Her parents kicked her out, her boyfriend left. She tried to make it on her own, but having a baby was too much for her to handle. She had to put me in a foster home."

"That must have been a hard decision for her."

"It was just supposed to be temporary. She was going to get me out when she had enough money, or her life settled down, once she got her GED, a bigger apartment... She had a hard time."

"So, did she? Get you out?"

"She didn't get a chance to. When I was six, she was killed in a car accident."

"So you stayed in foster homes?"

He shrugged. "I did all right."

Renata's heart ached for him. Some of the kids at the teen center were foster children and they bore the lost, guarded look that said they weren't sure they were loved or ever would be. "I'm ashamed I complained about my parents when you don't even have any."

"Nobody's life is perfect," he said. "Some of the families were nice. I always figured out the lay of the land. When the children were jealous of me, I became their best friend. When they were mean, I either outwitted them, avoided them or fought back. I turned out fine." He grinned at her, holding up his hands as if he'd escaped an accident without a scratch. She knew that was impossible. A life like that left marks.

Poor Hawk. She'd had a taste of a father—enough to know what she was missing—and she'd always had Lila. Regardless of their differences, their love for each other had always been strong.

Looking into Hawk's serious face, her heart ached for the lonely, lost boy he had been. No wonder he was so flip, so easygoing. He'd spent his life living on the balls of his feet, living a life where love was an option, not a given.

She suddenly remembered something. "Was that your mother in the photo you dropped in Denny's office?"

"Yeah, that's her." He smiled softly.

"She was pretty."

"I know. When I was a kid I thought she was gorgeous."

"And you always carry her photo?"

"Yeah. It keeps me going, working to be the best. Never settling for second. It sounds stupid, but it's a way to make her proud."

"It's not stupid at all," she said. "And I'm glad you told me. I'm so sorry about your mother, Hawk."

"Don't be," he said firmly. "I made my own way. And you should, too. That's the point, you can't let childhood crap keep you down or make you afraid of things."

"You're right," she said. "But it still affects you, changes your world." Now she could see pain behind Hawk's affability, and loneliness, too. "And you can't pretend that a rough childhood hasn't affected you, either."

He looked at her a long time, but his eyes acknowledged the truth of what she'd said. He was such a brave, dear man. She had to touch him, comfort him somehow, so she brushed his hair from his forehead, then cupped his cheek.

"Guess you analyzed me after all, Dr. R. And you didn't even need a couch," he said, then covered the hand she'd placed on his cheek with his own. He turned his face to kiss her palm. His eyes locked on hers.

The moment went electric, crackling with desire. Alarmed, Renata broke contact, stepped back. There was a flash of regret on Hawk's face, then he smiled. "How about a swim at my apartment? The pool's heated."

She almost said yes. She longed to spend more time with this increasingly interesting man. Hated the thought of him leaving.

"We can talk about the show," he offered, but they both knew that was not what would happen.

"I don't think so," she said as firmly as she could. "I've got more work to do. I'll meet you at the studio on Monday."

"Okay," he said, giving her that wicked grin. "But if you change your mind I'm at Forty-fourth and Campbell. The Fairmount. Apartment two-fifty. There's a hot tub."

She walked him to his car, thanking her lucky stars she'd stayed strong. Still, she caught herself memorizing his address.

No, no, no. That would be a mistake. Considering how much trouble they'd gotten into fully clothed, near nudity in warm water would be too much temptation. And getting intimate with Hawk would be bad. Bad for her. Bad for the show. Bad all around. They'd meet at the studio and plan the next show. No more alone time. Period.

To keep herself from hunting for her swimsuit, she called her mother to confirm plans to work on her taxes. For once, Lila's financial flubs offered a welcome distraction.

"Come over for dinner and I'll make you a special treat," Lila said. "Caramel apples. Doesn't that sound yummy?"

"What in the world made you want to make those? It's not even October." Instantly, she realized what it was. Hawk's eyes. Every time Renata looked into them she thought of autumn's sweet, crisp treat. They obviously had the same effect on her mother.

"So did you have fun with Hawk today?" Lila gently pried.

Not an easy question. Her roses had been traumatized, and she wanted to sleep with Hawk with every fiber of her being. Learning more about him had only made that worse. On the other hand, she felt alive to the tips of her toes, and she had a beautiful bouquet of roses that flooded the house with their mingled scents—scents Hawk had made her stop and smell. "Yeah," she said, surprised, "I guess I did."

8

HAWK DROVE TO HIS apartment, his insides knotted up after spending half a day in Renata's closed-in little world, with her flowers and dollhouses and her to-do lists. She actually had "polish silver" written on her wall calendar. Why polish silver when there was stainless steel? Hell, he'd been using plastic since he got here—and cutting pizza with scissors— because he hadn't unpacked all his boxes.

Thanks to Lila, he at least understood that Renata's need for order was her defense against the "loosey-goosey" life she'd grown up in. But still, the uptight way she lived drove him nuts.

No. That wasn't what drove him nuts. What drove him nuts was how much he wanted her. He fantasized about her all the time, could hardly focus on his work or even his future for thinking of her.

That was no good. He had to keep his eye on the ball, career-wise. The Las Vegas station had written to tell him there were no openings, but they'd keep his tape on file. He had stuff circulating in Seattle, Detroit and Philadelphia. Who knew how long this show with Renata would last? He had to be ready to jump when the time came.

In the meantime, he had to keep the show doing well. And he couldn't even focus on that for thinking about sleeping with her. It was getting to Renata, too, he could see, and she was tightening up like a muscle after a workout. That could hurt the show, too.

There was only one answer. Sleep together. Get it over with. Clear the air between them. By holding out they were making too big a deal out of it. After all, how great could it be? They'd just have sex and get it out of their systems. No question about it. For the sake of the show, he had to sleep with Renata.

Ah, hell. Who was he kidding? It was for his sake, too. It was worse now that he'd told her his story and she'd handled it so well—caring, without being sappy. First Lila gave him a maternal pat on the back on behalf of his own absent mom, and then Renata soothed him with a touch of her cool, calm hand.

And now he had to make love to her. It would be good for her, too. But she was so obstinate. How could he convince her? He'd have to ease her into it, nothing too scary. He plopped onto the sofa and picked up the ukulele he'd bought because of Renata, and tried to figure out how to seduce her for her own good. What would do it? What did she like? Not merry-go-rounds, that was for sure. She liked balloons... and music.

Yeah, music. Her eyes had gone all misty when he'd played for her. She liked hearing him play. Hmm... This had possibilities. Definite possibilities.

HAWK PARKED A COUPLE OF units away from Renata's town house so she wouldn't hear his car. The porch light was on, but he skirted its glow and headed for the fence to the backyard. He carried his ukulele by its neck, music playing in his head.

His heart thumped and his palms felt sweaty. Why was he nervous about playing? This wasn't Carnegie

Hall. This was just a romantic serenade under Renata's window. He'd deliberately picked fun, old-fashioned songs—nothing too serious—just enough to romance her socks off...and the rest of her clothes, of course.

The night was beautiful, he noticed. The three-quarter moon gave everything a magical gleam, and the air felt soft and smelled of flowers. When Renata looked out her window and saw him singing in her moonlit yard, she'd run down to him and throw herself into his arms....

Okay, that was dreaming. Renata didn't throw herself into anything. She'd tiptoe down—gingerly—and he'd have to sweep her off her feet. No prob.

He reached the low picket fence that marked off her backyard, and lifted the latch.

"Woof!"

He jumped at the sound. There hadn't been a dog in the neighbor's yard when they'd been working in the garden. And by the deep sound of it, it was huge. "Shh!" he hissed.

The dog kept at it.

Shutting the gate, he hurried into Renata's backyard. He located what must be her bedroom on the second story, its window lit by golden light, probably her bedside reading lamp. Her mother said she was always in bed by ten.

The idea of her tucked under a light sheet, maybe in something lacy, heated his blood unbearably. He couldn't swallow for the sudden dryness of his throat. He wondered what kind of bed she had. She wasn't the type for a pillow-top mattress, his favorite, but he didn't care if she slept on a tatami mat on the floor. He'd be there in a heartbeat. Well, as soon as she invited him. And if things went according to plan, that should be soon.

He plucked at the strings, nervous about playing. He cleared his throat and sang softly.

His fingers might be suffering from performance anxiety, but below-decks he was all warmed up and aching to get on stage. Yeah, this would work. It had to.

First, he had to get her attention. He grabbed a fistful of decorative stones from one of the flower beds, stood and flung them upward. They pinged and rattled against the window, but the curtains didn't move.

"Renata?" he called softly. Nothing. The neighbor's dog gave a low growl. He put the ukulele on the patio table and headed for the garden for a dirt clod. The well-tilled soil netted only a couple decent-sized lumps. He tossed first one and then the other. Each made a soft thud and dissolved into powder. Not noisy enough. No curious face and dark hair peeked out at him. He had to find something bigger and harder.

He pawed the dirt under the oleanders along the side fence and found a lump that turned out to be a bone. Perfect. Suddenly, with a scramble and a woof, the dog crashed into the chain-link fence from the neighbor's side, barking hysterically.

"Relax, Rover," he said. "I'll give it back when I'm done."

At the window, he tossed the bone in an easy arc, but he'd underestimated its heft. "Jeez!" A thud and tinkle of glass told him he'd have an apology to deliver along with his serenade. He waited for Renata's alarmed face, but seconds passed and no Renata bobbed into view. Maybe she was watching TV and couldn't hear him. "Renata?" he called a little louder.

Nothing.

"Renata!" he shouted.

The dog set up a frantic barking. Hell, that should wake her if nothing else. These houses were close together.

"Come out, Renata!" He heard a car coming down the street.

Maybe he had the wrong window. He grabbed the dog bone from where it had landed and went to the far side of the house. The window there was dark, but he threw the bone at it, with less force this time. No glass tinkled. But no Renata, either. The dog barked wildly.

"Renata!" he yelled. "Are you there?"

He was just about to give up and go to her front door, ruining the surprise, when a flashlight's glare blinded him.

"You want to explain what you're doing, sir?"

Hawk blinked and shielded his eyes from the blazing light. The flashlight moved downward, away from his face, until he could make out a large man in uniform standing on the other side of the fence.

"Officer, uh, hello." Feeling foolish, he rubbed his hands at his sides as he stepped forward. "I was just getting my friend's attention."

"Ever hear of the front door?"

"That wouldn't be a surprise. You see, I'm trying to…uh…" Under the cop's suspicious glare, his plan to serenade Renata sounded downright goofy. He didn't even have his ukulele to prove his good intentions—he'd left it on the patio table. He was glad the cop didn't know about the broken window.

The officer crossed his arms. "Go on...."

"I was going to...uh, play a song for her. If you'll let me get my instrument." He turned toward the backyard, but the cop stepped forward.

"No, sir," he said sharply. "You'll stay right there."

Hawk stopped moving and felt the urge to raise his hands.

"I'll need your name, sir."

"Hawk Hunter. Listen, I know this looks bad, but I just wanted to be sure I had her bedroom."

"Her bedroom?"

That sounded worse. "I'm not a pervert or anything. I'm a friend. Actually, I work with her."

"You work with her, and you followed her home to surprise her in her bedroom. I see. What's that in your hand?"

"A dog bone. I was throwing it at her... Never mind." The ground seemed to shift beneath him as he got mired in the quicksand of his lame explanation.

"I'll need to see some ID."

Uh-oh. Hawk had seen enough police shows to know that meant the cop meant business.

"Sure, no problem. Glad to cooperate." Hawk fumbled in his back pocket for his wallet. With a jolt of dread, he realized his five-year-old driver's license still held the name Buddy Hodges. Not planning to stay anywhere for long, he hadn't gotten around to changing it. Slowly, he flipped open the leather billfold, slipped out the card and handed it forward.

"I just moved here, Officer, and there's been a

name change. And, um, about those parking fines in Albuquerque…''

He could almost hear the clang of steel bars.

EARLY THE NEXT MORNING, Renata stood on her front porch and rubbed the knot in her neck. She hadn't slept well on her mother's rock-hard health pillow and the rooster Lila preferred as an alarm clock crowed too early even for Renata.

Her mother's taxes had taken her longer than she'd expected—they'd stopped to make caramel apples—so she'd spent the night. She didn't mind. Making order out of the chaos of her mother's basket of receipts and deductions scribbled on cocktail napkins had distracted her from thoughts of Hawk. He was in her head all the time now. At night she dreamed of him, and when she took a shower, she imagined him there under the pounding water, his hands on her, his body hard and strong, his mouth everywhere. *Everywhere.* She felt like some strange, sex-starved creature, her nerves scraped raw, aching for his touch, hungry for it.

As she fished for her keys, she remembered his eager expression when he held up the droopy philodendron, his grin when he handed her the roses, his serious look when he'd told her about his childhood. Despite her best intentions to keep him at arm's length he'd gotten cozily tucked into her heart. All she could think of was touching him, being touched by him, hearing more about his life and dreams, telling him about hers…. But sleeping with him was out of the question. They had to work together, and he wasn't her kind of man.

Heaving a sigh, she put her key in the lock just

as the porch light—on an automatic timer like her bedroom light—clicked off.

"Renata!"

She turned to see her neighbor hurrying up the walk.

"I'm afraid I made a mistake last night," Myra said, pushing her glasses up her nose. "I thought he was a prowler. Duke was barking so loud, and he seemed to have a weapon. What was I to think?" Behind her thick glasses Myra's eyes seemed huge with remembered alarm.

"What are you talking about?"

"There was a strange man in your backyard, so I called 911. The police came, but once I got my binoc—I mean, when they got out by the police car under the streetlight, I could see that it was the man from your show—the one who took you out last week."

"You mean Hawk?"

"You can hardly blame me, though. He was throwing rocks at your window and everything. When the cop arrested him—"

"He got arrested?"

"Well, there were no handcuffs that I could see, but he didn't look happy and the officer was checking his ID in the police car a lo-o-o-ong time, and then they drove off, so I can only assume..." She pushed her glasses up again.

Renata was stunned.

"You don't blame me, do you?" Myra said. "I just think neighbors can't be too careful. That's why I'm the Block Watch captain."

"I'm sure you did the right thing," Renata said, her mind whirling.

"I'm so relieved you think so," Myra said. "Let me know if I can help. If there's a lineup or anything. I really like lineups."

"Sure," Renata said dazedly. "If there's a lineup, you'll be the first to know. Bye now." She shut the door on Myra, wondering what on earth had happened to make Hawk throw rocks at her window. If that was what he'd been doing, Myra's vision being what it was.

She went straight to the phone to call him, then noticed she had two messages on her machine. The first had come at 11:00 p.m. and consisted of a heavy, frustrated sigh—Hawk's voice, she could tell. The second was Denny at 2:00 a.m. "Call me the minute you get in," he'd said, laughter in his voice. "Wait'll you hear what happened."

Denny picked up the phone after several rings. "Hel...lo?" he muttered sleepily.

"Sorry to wake you," Renata said, "but you said to call the minute I got in."

"Yeah. That's right." He cleared the sleep-fog from his voice and resumed in his normally terse tone. "Hawk call you yet?"

"No, he hasn't. And what in the world did—"

"He's probably not up yet. We didn't leave the police station until after one. Then I dropped him at your house to get his car, and he still had to drive home."

"How did he end up at the police station?"

"You weren't home to verify his identity, and his driver's license was out of date, so they took him in. He called me to come get him."

"What was he doing here throwing rocks?"

Denny paused, then chuckled. "I should let him tell you."

"Denny, for heaven's sake!"

"Okay, okay. This is rich. Hawk came to your house to—catch this—*serenade* you."

"Serenade me?"

"Yeah, can you believe it? With a lute or something...I forget."

"A ukulele?" she said softly.

"Yeah, that was it. Anyway, he was throwing rocks at your window to get your attention and your neighbor thought he was a Peeping Tom."

She hardly listened while Denny explained more about the Block Watch report and bail and Hawk's name change. She was too stunned by the idea of Hawk below her bedroom window in the moonlight...with his ukulele...*singing* to her.

What a lovely thing to do! Her heart pinched tight, but it was a sweet pain. If only she'd been there to greet him, to listen, to say...what? What would she have said to him? She didn't know, and the thought sent her heart into a spasm.

What did he mean? Just three days before he'd promised not to let things get out of hand. Certainly, a serenade in the moonlight was out of hand. It was out of this world, actually, in the way of tender gestures. Not like a roll-in-the-hay at all.

Denny's chuckle brought Renata back to the conversation. "Hawk is so gung ho," he said. "I knew I was right about him. He'll do whatever it takes for the show."

Whatever it takes for the show. At the words, Renata's heart, which seemed about to pound its way out of her chest, stopped dead. "What?"

"Hawk thought a serenade would help you be less serious, keep up your—"

"Flair?" She went cold inside.

"Exactly." Denny paused. He must have heard something in her voice because he said, "Now, don't give him a hard time. He didn't intend to get arrested. He meant well and he's helped you a lot, whether you realize it or not."

"I'm sure you're right," she said, indignation rising in her. "I'm just getting tired of people thinking they need to help me. I'm just fine as I am."

"Well, take it easy on Hawk. He had a long night."

"I'm sure he did," she said. But she didn't feel the least bit sorry for him. Hawk was treating her like his own little fixer-upper, and she'd had just about enough of that. He had to understand that he couldn't play with her emotions. She was no Eliza Doolittle and he was no Henry Higgins.

She dialed his number, but his machine picked up. He was probably still asleep. She headed upstairs to take a shower and calm herself down before she called again. The first thing she saw was her curtain flapping against her broken bedroom window. When she went to examine it, she looked outside and saw Hawk's ukulele lying below on her patio table.

She remembered how Hawk had looked playing it that day at the park—so sexy and tender, his fingers graceful but strong. At the time, she'd wanted those fingers on her. If she'd been here last night, she'd probably have succumbed to that stunt. Maybe even thrown herself at him. Then, when he said, "Only kidding. Wasn't that fun?" she'd feel like a complete fool. Her heart felt sharp-edged in her chest, her nerves burned with hurt. It wasn't fun. It was cruel. And it had to end right here. She'd just take that ukulele back to him—wake him up if she had to—and straighten him out, once and for all.

Twenty minutes later, Renata stood in front of apartment two-fifty, gripping Hawk's ukulele by the neck, her heart pounding louder in her ears than his door knocker. Hawk opened the door, wet from the shower, a terry-cloth wrap low on his hips. He looked so good and so nearly naked she forgot for a second why she'd come.

"Where were you last night?" he demanded, bringing her right back to her mission. He had the nerve to sound exasperated, though his bloodshot, tired-looking eyes gave her a twinge of sympathy. His hair was wet and tangled from the shower and he smelled of spicy soap. "Come in." He adjusted his wrap, then backed up, holding the door so she could enter.

"I was at my mother's," she said, "not that it's any of your business."

"I came to see you."

"So I hear. And broke a window. And left this." She slapped the ukulele into his belly.

"Easy, there," he said. He took the instrument from her, a puzzled expression on his face.

"Myra thought you were breaking and entering." Which he was—breaking and entering her heart. She was dismayed by how good he looked shirtless. Water beaded on the hair on his muscled chest, which tapered nicely at his waist. His water-shiny face and tangled hair begged to be touched.

"I wanted to surprise you," he said.

"I know. Denny told me. Yet one more lesson

about fun and flair. I've had about all the flair I can stand, Hawk. It's ridiculous. No, it's cruel. And stupid. You scared my neighbor, broke my window, made me feel like an idiot for thinking that you were... Well, it was just wrong!''

"I know."

She stopped her tirade. "You know?"

"Yeah," he said, and stepped toward her, his eyes holding hers. "I was wrong." He was so handsome, so all there. The only thing that stood between her and the whole naked glorious man was a skinny swatch of terry-cloth. She didn't have the stamina for this kind of excitement, so she took refuge in her indignation—and one more backward step. "Darn right, you were wrong. You can't play with people's feelings like that."

"I know." Hawk matched her backward step with a forward one. "I was trying to do it your way—the way you would like. But there's no point in that."

"Good." She stepped back again. Again he followed. Again she stepped, but this time her heel bumped the door, making further retreat impossible. "Then we're agreed. No more stunts."

"No more stunts," he said. Then he put his arms around her waist and pulled her away from the door and into his arms. The water on his skin soaked through her silk blouse.

"Wh-what are you doing?"

"I'm doing it my way." He held her close—the soft hair of his chest inches from her face, his towel pressed against her hips, each of his fingers a separate warm pressure point on her back.

"Doing what your way?"

"This." And then his mouth was on hers—warm

and strong and sure, and she felt her insides go liquid and her legs turn to rubber, and as the kiss lengthened and deepened, to jelly, then syrup, then water. She would evaporate away entirely if he kept up what he was doing with his lips and tongue and the fingers kneading her back.

She broke off the kiss and pushed back, gasping for air. "But we agreed this was a bad idea." Her pulse fluttered in her neck like a butterfly trapped in a child's hand.

"We were wrong," he said. His mouth was a breath away, his eyes hot on her, holding her. "I went to your house last night to convince you of that—your way."

"But you told Denny it was for the show."

"What else could I say? You think I'd tell him how I feel about you? I had a lot of time in the police station to think. It's amazing the way obscene graffiti, unmentionable smells and four tattooed bruisers make you stop kidding yourself about what you really want. And what I really want is to make love to you. My way."

Looking up at him, Renata felt a sizzling sensation inside, like an antacid dropped in water. She knew instantly what it was—sparks. "I don't know what to think," she said, breathless and scared, and so excited she had no feeling in her fingers or toes.

"Don't think." The look on his face stopped her heart. Gone was the easygoing Hawk, replaced by a man who knew exactly what he wanted and expected to get it. No man had ever looked at her that way before.

Without another word, Hawk captured her mouth. Renata made a little surprised sound and began to tremble. Her hands slid up Hawk's back and her fingers slipped through his wet hair—it was silky and thick and heavenly. Hawk's lips parted and his tongue pressed against hers. With a wild thrill, she opened to him, letting his tongue move inside her mouth.

It felt so good and so right. She seemed to know what she was doing, too, she discovered, when her tongue reached to meet his and Hawk groaned. She was turning him on, and that made her feel powerful and sexy. He slid his hands down to grip her bottom, tugged her to him, then lifted her so she stood on his insteps. He turned and began to walk with her, kissing her all the way down the short hall into the bedroom.

Don't think. Don't think, she told herself as she rode his feet. Her legs hit the edge of the bed and she fell back.

Hawk landed right on top of her.

"This is too fast," she said. "I'm not prepared at all. I didn't plan—"

"This isn't the kind of thing you put in your day planner, Renata," Hawk said. "Just go with it."

"But what about—"

"Protection? Got it."

"No. I mean what are we doing?"

He looked at her seriously. "We have to stop fighting this, Renata. It'll be good for us both. Just don't think about it." He resumed kissing her neck, his breath hot. She fought the desire for him that twisted inside her like twine. What was she doing? This was insane. It couldn't possibly mean the same to Hawk as it did to her. She wanted it more than he did, and that was terrible. She should stop, get up. She should…

Hawk stilled, then lifted his head. "Cut it out."

"What?"

"You're thinking again."

"Sorry."

"Let this happen," he whispered against her skin. His fingers moved to her buttons and began to undo them. She opened her mouth to speak, except his tongue found an amazingly sensitive spot on her throat, and she couldn't make a sound. Her vision went gray for a second and everything inside seemed to hiss and tingle. *So this was sparks…* And Hawk had been right. Maurice and she had never had this flash fire of sensation, this stinging burn, this ache.

It was wild. And wonderful. The new, startling taste and touch of Hawk swept her away. He was everywhere, touching, kissing, stroking. Cool air on her skin told her Hawk had opened her blouse. Then his lips reached the lacy edge of her sensible bra. She wanted to ask him if he felt sparks, too, but she only made a strange sound in the back of her throat.

Hawk groaned in response, making her even hotter. Every little thing Hawk did twisted her insides tighter and tighter. Every nerve seemed about to snap.

Her vision darkened again, her breath came in quick, incomplete gasps, and she felt faint. To feel so much at once for the first time was just too scary. "Hold it a minute," she said, pushing at him.

"What's wrong?" He raised up, his eyes bleary with lust.

She slid out from under him and sat up. "I have to catch my breath."

Hawk chuckled low in his throat, sat up, too, and pulled her into his arms. "No rush. We've got all day."

She opened her eyes, panting desperately, and, to orient herself, focused her gaze past his shoulders to the walls of the room. The room was neat, but un-lived-in, she noticed. There was nothing on the walls, for one thing—only a couple of framed posters propped against the bureau—and packing boxes formed twin towers at the end of the bed.

"Are you moving?" she asked.

Hawk's mouth stilled on her collarbone. "What?" He twisted to see what she was looking at.

"All the boxes."

"Nah. I just haven't unpacked everything." He started to kiss her again, but she pulled back.

"Oh," she said. "That makes sense." Too much sense. Hawk hadn't been in town long, but he wouldn't be here long either, she realized. Part of her wanted to blank out, lose herself again in the swamp of sensation, but she couldn't block out the truth. "I can't do this," she said abruptly. She turned on the bed, planted her tingling feet on the floor and began to button her blouse.

"Sure you can. You're doing it." Hawk reached for her.

She avoided his hand and got to her feet. "I'm not the kind of woman who can just have sex, Hawk. I'm sorry. I've got to go." She turned and left his bedroom, headed for the front door, but she felt him follow her and when she reached the door he put his arms around her from behind. "Give us a chance, Renata. We don't know what will happen."

"Yes, we do," she said to the door, afraid to look

into the handsome face that wanted her, that could trick her into staying. "You'll be gone and I'll be here. I don't know what I was thinking." She turned the handle and pulled.

Hawk's hand reached past her and kept the door from opening. "You weren't thinking. That was the whole point. Just this once, could you just go with how you feel?"

"I can't," she said and yanked at the door. She couldn't bear the hurt of being abandoned. It was the lesson of childhood she knew best of all. If she stopped this before it got started, she could save herself all that pain. "Please," she said, not turning.

Hawk sighed heavily and released the door.

Renata pulled it open, and ran out, holding in the tears until she reached her car.

Damn! Hawk slammed his fist against the door after Renata closed it, then grimaced. In the movies, that move looked so dramatic. In real life it just hurt. He cupped his bruised fist in his other hand and shook his head. For a strong-willed woman, she had such a skittish heart.

He threw himself onto the couch, tossed one arm over his face, and tried to collect himself. His skin still vibrated from the feel of her, like a frayed electric cord, and he still smelled her on him. Maybe he'd come on too strong. He'd gone on instinct, which he trusted. And, dammit, he'd had enough of tiptoeing in. She was the most stubborn woman....

Quick footsteps on the landing caught his ear. Then his door opened. He sat up to find Renata standing there, her dark eyes shiny with tears and panic, her hair tangled and sexy. Her chest heaved beneath her misbuttoned blouse, arousing him instantly.

"You're back," he said stupidly.

"This is the dumbest, craziest, the absolutely most reckless thing I've ever done," she said hoarsely, her eyes wild. He watched her chest shudder upward, the silk stretching over her tender flesh. She ran her fingers through her hair, messing it up, making it even sexier. "This can only be temporary, while you're here, so I know it's nuts, but it doesn't matter. I've never felt this before. It's *sparks,* like you said. And I want to feel them again. So let's do it, let's take a chance because it would be..." She faltered and bit her lip, a nervous gesture that always charmed him. "It would be..."

"Good," he finished for her. "It would be good. That's what it would be." He scrambled to get off the sofa, but his toe snagged in the fabric. He stumbled, took two unbalanced steps and crashed into her, making them both fall down in a heap.

"You don't have to tackle me. I won't run this time." Only his remarkable Renata could manage irony when she was so scared. Her heart pounded like a trip-hammer under him.

He got to his knees, slid his arms under her and lifted.

"Oh, dear," she said as he wobbled to his feet holding her, but she threw her arms around his neck and let him carry her back into his bedroom, where he laid her on the bed and wrapped his arms around her, hugging her tight. He couldn't believe she'd come back and was in his arms and his bed.

"Renata." Her name was a breath and a prayer on his lips.

"I'm scared," she whispered into his neck. A delicate trembling started up in her so he held her tighter.

"I know. It'll be okay." He kissed her mouth and her trembling slowed. She blew out a breath.

With great care, he began to peel off her clothes, reassuring her as he went. She helped him, slipping out of her silky blouse, her pants, her filmy underwear, like a mermaid sliding through water. He held her close against him, so she wouldn't feel vulnerable or awkward. Then she was naked. He pushed his towel-wrap off, and the feeling of his erection against the velvet of her thighs sent a jolt of lust straight to his brain. He struggled for control, aching inside and out.

"Oh my," she said softly, her face flushed with arousal.

"You can say that again." He reached down to hold her lovely backside, wondering at its smooth perfection.

Worry darkened her features.

"Don't think," he warned.

Her face cleared and she gave him a hesitant smile.

Silently, he vowed he wouldn't rest until he'd erased everything but desire from her face. He'd take it slow and easy and be careful not to alarm her.

He pressed his mouth to hers for a lazy kiss. Then slowly, he slid his hand down to cup her breast. Round, compact and perfect, it shaped itself to his hand like it had been waiting for his touch. He lowered his mouth to kiss its softness. Renata gasped, so he caressed her nipple with his tongue. She rewarded him with more little helpless sounds.

He felt himself move against her thigh, so he changed the kiss to a soft sucking. She groaned his name. His heart seemed to be pounding a hole in his rib cage.

He ran his hands along her torso, down her hips, then skimmed the inside of her thigh. The skin there was so delicate he feared his pressing fingers would bruise her, but her answering groan, filled with pleasure, told him she wanted more.

She slid against him, her fingers squeezing his buttocks, then she reached for him, and he groaned. How the hell could he be gentle, take it slow when she was this hot? His mind kept blanking out and he wanted inside her so bad...except once there—in that hot, soft place—he knew he would never hold out. No amount of thinking about baseball would keep him from thrusting hard and climaxing instantly. He pulled back to say something, to try to slow down, but Renata shoved her fingers into his hair and yanked him down.

"Don't stop," she gasped. "I might start thinking." She pushed her tongue deep in his mouth and rubbed her sweet hips up against him and he knew there was no use fighting it.

So he didn't.

A TICKLING SENSATION woke Renata the next morning. Still half-asleep, she scrubbed at her nose, then realized she was lying on warm, hair-covered skin.

Hawk's chest, she realized. In an instant, the wildness of the past twenty-four hours rushed over her with a wallop. She'd been ferocious. A wild woman. She raised her head and saw thin red marks on Hawk's shoulder. She'd scratched him with her sensible nails. And was that a hickey on his neck? Renata Rose had delivered a hickey?

Mortified, she closed her eyes to figure this out. With Maurice sex had been pleasant, if a little predictable. And she'd always felt in control. She'd assumed she just wasn't the kind of woman who went crazy for sex, but in Hawk's arms, she'd become a savage tigress. She felt a smile curve her lips. She was mortified, all right, but also a little proud.

She looked at Hawk's handsome face, tan against the pillow, his hair adorably ruffled. Part of it had been Hawk's remarkable skill. He seemed to know her body better than she did and pinpointed her pleasure spots with unerring precision.

Oh, yes. Right there. Right there. Her remembered cries came back to her in an embarrassing rush. It was as if Hawk had unleashed a lifetime of pent-up desire in her. He'd met her frenzy head on, over and over, hell-bent on fulfilling her every desire.

And fulfilled she was. Fulfilled to the tippy-top. They'd made love all day and deep into the night until finally they'd slept—sweaty, exhausted and fully satisfied.

But now, in the milky morning light, she wondered what had possessed her to take this chance. What if she was in love with him? Hawk was not the kind of man for her. Even if he loved her back. It wasn't by accident they'd agreed to disagree about love. He didn't even believe in marriage. Marriage killed passion, he thought, and passion was all you needed.

But Renata believed in marriage, wanted it for herself. And love took more than passion. Love took work and compromise. And you had to want the same things. Her parents had had passion, all right, but her father kept leaving anyway. Renata could never live with a love like that. She wasn't that kind of person.

She wasn't a sex maniac, either. How could she face Hawk after how she'd behaved? What would he think of her? Embarrassment filled her.

She was about to get out of bed when Hawk opened his caramel eyes and his smile curved, sleep-soft, against the pillow. "Hi, there," he said huskily.

"Hi."

"How'd you sleep?"

"Fine, and you?" She sounded like a flight attendant. She scooted away to make space between them.

But Hawk wouldn't let her go. He threw his long arm across her body and pulled her on top of him.

Now every inch of her body touched every inch of his. "I slept great—with you as a blanket," he said.

She wobbled unsteadily on top of his muscular frame until he squeezed her tightly, snuggling under her. His chest hair chafed her breasts, tender from the night's embraces, pricking her with renewed desire. She was enveloped in the musk of his skin, which she loved, and she felt his neck muscles beneath her cheek, which she'd nipped in the night to the music of his lusty groans.

"You were great," he murmured, his tone husky and sensuous.

"I hope I wasn't too...um, loud." Blush heated her cheeks.

"You were perfect." He released a heavy, satisfied breath, then kissed the top of her head. Maybe they would just cuddle.

Then he wrapped his legs around hers and pushed up against her with an easy stroke that made her suck in her breath. Uh-uh, no cuddling here. Renata closed her eyes as the sensations rolled through her, and her desire began to coil. Soon they'd be off on another wild ride.

"Hawk, I'm afraid this was a bad idea," she whispered.

"Rennie, please. Let's not think this to death. Let's just feel how we feel, okay?" His eyes were full of caring.

Rennie. It was what her mother called her. Usually that annoyed her, but hearing it from Hawk made her feel good and safe. She let herself sink into the moment, let the heat in his eyes dissolve her doubts. "Maybe you're right," she said. She wanted him to be—at least her body did. She felt herself soften on top of him, melt into his shape.

They fit so perfectly. Hand-in-glove. Two halves made whole. All the clichés worked. She began to move with him. She couldn't fight this lovely quicksand that sucked and pulled at her with promises of pleasure and fulfillment. "I'll probably regret this when I come to my senses."

"I'll just have to see that you never do."

RENATA SPENT THE NEXT few weeks in a happy haze, sleepwalking cheerily through the days, living for the moments in Hawk's arms. The show seemed to benefit from their togetherness, too. When the second show went as delightfully as the first, Denny had easily convinced the GM to keep them both. Now things were so smooth Renata could hardly believe she and Hawk had ever quarreled. They were a perfect tag team of relationship advice.

Plus, taking the risks she had with Hawk had motivated Renata to take other chances, too. She'd arranged a counseling internship through the university that allowed her to counsel a few of the families of the teens who came to the rec center. The college credits put her closer to her Ph.D., but the best part was helping the teens she cared about.

Four weeks after that fabulous first fall into Hawk's arms, Renata was in her office at the teen center studying for an advanced psychology exam, when Hawk popped in.

"Hey, babe!" he said. "Isn't it about time you clocked out?" He wore a tank top and skimpy basketball shorts, and he had a whistle around his neck and a ball in his hands. His bare shoulders glistened with sweat—he'd been playing basketball with the kids. "I think you're about due for another ukulele lesson." He waggled his eyebrows at her.

That was code for making love and a rush of lust raced through her. "Mmm," she said. Hawk actually was teaching her to play—in between lovemaking sessions. He would snug his naked body up against hers, wrap his arms around her, intimate and cozy, and use his fingers to guide hers along the smooth neck of the instrument and the soft ridges of the strings.

As a result, Renata now could strum through a lazy version of "You Are My Sunshine," erratic in rhythm, with pauses for laughter when her fingers misbehaved, while Hawk whisper-sang the words in her ear. She felt sensuous, womanly and powerful when she played. *And* when they made love.

It was glorious. Music and learning and sex got all mixed up in her mind. Now, as Hawk stood there spinning the basketball on his fingers, his hips thrust slightly forward, she couldn't help imagining those same fingers on her skin just so, those hips moving against hers. With every fiber of her being she wanted to go home for a "lesson."

But she had responsibilities. "Felicia's mother's coming in for a session in a bit. My advisor's going to sit in."

"Oh." Hawk looked disappointed, then he studied her. "You nervous about your advisor looking over your shoulder?"

"Not if it makes me a better therapist."

"You're a great therapist already. Look at all the couples you've helped on the show."

"*We've* helped," Renata corrected. "We're a team, remember?"

But instead of agreeing with her, Hawk frowned. "You know, Denny thinks we've gotten too predictable lately. He wants a little more edge to the show."

"More edge? We're a well-oiled machine. What's he talking about?" Denny was too easily bored.

"It's television, Renata. Constant change. You have to roll with it. We can look over the tape of next week's guests and maybe come up with something to shake things up."

"Okay," she said, but she was distracted by the edge of red silk she saw above the waistband of Hawk's basketball shorts. "You picked out my favorite boxers."

"Easy enough. I just pulled them out of the red section. I can't believe you color-coordinated my underwear."

"I just like things organized," she said, flinching at the mention of her weakness. The truth was whenever she got nervous about Hawk leaving, she did something to make his presence seem more permanent. Besides organizing his underwear, she'd emptied all his packing boxes, hung art prints on his walls and filled his apartment with houseplants, including a window ledge herb garden for his kitchen. Nothing like having a garden to tend to make you feel settled.

She didn't fool herself about what she was doing—turning Hawk's place into a safe haven like her own made her feel like he couldn't leave. Color-coordinating his underwear was probably over the top, but establishing order also kept her from thinking, which had become her enemy. Hawk helped, too. Every time she slipped into thought, Hawk was there with a kiss, a touch or a look, and so she let herself believe things would be all right.

"At least you found my pizza cutter," Hawk mused. "And it's nice to have all my books out." He leaned down and kissed her on the forehead. She never tired of his touch. The brush of his lips made her shiver with longing.

"There were so many, how could you ever find anything?" Most of the stacks of boxes she'd unpacked had been full of books on a wide range of topics—natural science, psychology, history, politics—proving it wasn't by accident Hawk was in the information business. Reading was the one quiet pleasure they enjoyed together—along with lovemaking and music and the show. Renata wouldn't allow herself to think of their differences—there were too many.

"I can't stand it," Hawk whispered abruptly. With a quick look to be certain no teens were in sight, he bent and kissed her mouth this time, his lips tender, slow, full of the promise of hours of pleasure ahead. He broke off the kiss. "I want you," he whispered, his face filled with the look she loved—adoration built on a bedrock of lust.

"Me, too," she whispered back.

"Hurry home. I want to work on your fingering technique."

The suggestion zinged along her nervous system and left her breathless. Hawk Hunter was without a doubt the sexiest man on the planet. She was so lucky to be with him, so glad she'd taken the risk. He was all hers. No one knew him the way she did.

No one knew they were together, either. It was a delicious secret.

"You bet," she whispered. Somewhere inside, she knew this was dangerous, that it couldn't last forever, but for now the sheer joy of it was enough. The show was going well, after all. Oh, they'd need to spice it up for Denny, but surely Hawk would be here for a while. They would have more time.

What about afterward, Renata? Hawk's having fun and you're falling in love. Part of her knew she was setting herself up for a terrible heartbreak. But like Scarlet O'Hara, she wouldn't think about that now. Right now, she'd just think about her upcoming "ukulele lesson," and that would be enough.

"WHEN YOUR LOVE BOAT springs a leak, there's no need to panic," Renata said to John and Mary, on the show two weeks later. "While one of you bails water, the other one should..."

"Hammer a cork in the hole," Hawk finished.

"Exactly," Renata said. "And if that doesn't work..."

"Go for a rowboat," Hawk finished.

"Of course," Renata said, beaming at him. This was the third time they'd finished each other's sentences.

"But she keeps nagging me to get a better job," John said.

"And he belches in front of company."

"And her mother wants to move in with us."

"She'll be fine. She'll watch the baby," Mary argued.

"What baby?" John went pale.

"I've been meaning to talk to you—"

"You're pregnant?!" John jumped up. "Oh, my God!"

"Sit down, you dope. I'm just planning ahead."

"Now, now, you two," Renata said. "Sounds like your little love boat's floundering."

"You both need to start paddling in the same direction," Hawk said.

"Nice image, Hawk," Renata said.

"Thanks. It just came to me."

Renata grinned at him. How had she ever doubted him? She turned to her guests.

"Now, Mary—"

"Now, John—" Hawk said at the same time. Their eyes met and they burst out laughing.

"After you," Hawk said.

"No, don't be silly. You were doing great."

"But maybe you have a better idea."

"Could we just get on with it," John snapped. "I'd like to hear some solid man's perspective on this thing, Hawk. How about it?"

"Actually, when you're in love, your differences don't matter," Hawk said. "Right, Dr. Renata?" She could tell he was trying to keep his expression professional, but she saw tenderness in his caramel eyes. "When you're in love, you listen with more than your ears. You listen with your heart."

"I couldn't have said it better myself." Renata felt extra hot under the lights. Of course he was talking about the couple, but maybe he meant more....

"But what about our differences," Mary insisted. "John has to change."

"*I* have to change? I don't think so. *You* have to change," John said.

"Now, now," Hawk said. "You'll both have to

board the Change Train. Right now you're standing on the platform trying to push each other onto the tracks.''

The audience gave a halfhearted laugh for the first time this show. Lately, the audience had seemed sluggish. Meanwhile, the floor manager signaled they should close out, so Renata jumped in: ''We'll take a quick break, then see if we can get these two a transfer from the Change Train to the Love Express.''

Hawk guffawed. He even loved her jokes. What a perfect man.

An hour later, Renata pushed the makeup stool in a circle, spinning around just to feel that light-headed feeling. She'd be in Hawk's arms in a few moments. How she loved the thought. She stopped the stool with a squeak and glanced at herself in the golden light of the makeup mirror. Good Lord, her face looked soft, almost—could it be?—cuddly. Renata Rose cuddly? She laughed at the idea, marveled at it, and she wasn't a bit sorry.

Denny burst through the door. ''You have got to stop this.''

''Stop what?'' she asked.

''Making moon eyes at each other all the time. The couples practically nod off. The show's a complete snoozeroo. Aren't you two about due for a lover's spat?''

''What are you talking about?'' Afraid Denny might cook up some terrible stunt to exploit their closeness, Renata had convinced Hawk to keep their relationship a secret from everyone at the station. ''We're not…um, we're not…''

''Not sleeping together? Come on, Renata.''

Had her mother told him? Renata had had to tell Lila, since the woman bopped in and out of her house constantly, but she'd extracted her mother's promise not to say anything to Denny. Lila'd been so pleased that Renata was "playing naked" with Hawk, that she'd agreed to fight her inclination to tell all.

"Hawk and I are just professionally compatible," she said.

Denny stared at her. "Okay, pretend if you want, but the show needs some juice in a quick hurry."

"But you said we're a good team," Renata said. "You wanted teamwork, remember?"

"Teamwork, not diabetes. You're so sweet to each other I get cavities just watching. Where's the tension? Hell, you used to admit a love boat capsized now and then."

She was about to point out that that attitude was what had gotten her into trouble in the first place, when she saw the look on his face and knew this wasn't Denny's usual cranky restlessness. "You're serious, aren't you?"

"Yeah. Work on it, okay?" he said.

After he left, Renata's stomach tightened. They had to do something, she and Hawk. Maybe they could invite back some of the couples from previous shows and see how they were doing. Or reenact a couple's quarrel, providing reconciliation techniques. Yeah, that would be exciting. Like Jerry Springer, except the guests would end up happy, instead of throwing chairs at each other. All she and Hawk had to do was put their heads together. They could work this out. They had to. The show was what kept them together. She didn't want to think about what would become of them without it.

10

"THE NUMBERS STINK AND we lost a sponsor," Denny said to Hawk later that afternoon.

Hawk was sitting in the same chair in Denny's office he'd sat in that first day three months ago, when this whole crazy thing had started. Now, this whole crazy thing appeared to be circling the drain.

"What are you saying?"

"I'm saying if you don't come up with something new, the show's DOA."

"What did you have in mind?"

"I dunno. I'm running out of ideas," Denny said. "I've been working on the news package redesign. My energy's sapped." He yawned.

Denny running out of ideas was a very bad sign. He'd been the show's advocate with the GM all along. Hawk broke out in a sweat. "Something new, huh?"

"Yeah. Spicy or flashy or fresh."

"Okay, okay, let me think." Hawk's mind raced. He and Renata had talked about a few ideas, but none seemed very novel. "What if we got local celebrities on the show? We could bring back the 'Enough with the Frogs Already' segment. Tabitha Walker, the news anchor, would be perfect for it."

"Possible, but that woman's about as interested in marriage as she is in knitting."

"Then how about we have guest therapists—famous ones—on the show. Isn't Dr. Laura on the circuit promoting her new book?"

"Long shot."

"How about a remote broadcast at home with one of the couples? We could counsel them in their natural habitat."

"Expensive."

"Then what?"

"I don't know. I told Renata you two should have a lover's quarrel on the air, but she nixed it."

"You what?" Hawk said.

"I know Renata wants to pretend you're not an item but that's an angle we could use."

"That's crazy."

Denny shrugged. "Just brainstorming."

"Here's an idea. Renata just got a postcard from one of our couples—Carol and Eric—the couple who went on the cruise instead of saying 'I love you'?— saying they've set the date. Maybe we could have them back on the show."

"No conflict. On the other hand, if they'd get married on the show…that's news. News is good. If we can get news coverage, we've got an instant spike in ratings." Denny pushed to his feet. "I gotta go. Just come up with something. I really don't want to have to tell Renata her show's canceled."

"It'll break her heart," Hawk said softly, thinking of the way her eyebrows would lift and her face would pale at the news. "And Saturday's her birthday." He had a great surprise planned for her— something she'd always wanted to do—and he didn't want this bad news to ruin it. "We'll come up with something," Hawk said. "We have to."

Denny gave him a long, thoughtful look. "How serious are you two, anyway?"

"Serious? We're not...I, um...I don't know." They were serious about the show. That was all he needed to know right now. They had to come up with something. Something big. And something fast.

Half an hour later, Hawk pulled into his complex's parking lot and headed to his apartment to grab a change of clothes before going over to Renata's for the evening.

Inside, he found a message on his machine from Michelle, and headed into his bedroom to call her back. Just the woman to talk to about creative ideas for saving the show. He threw himself onto the bed and picked up the phone. Renata's scent lifted from the pillow and made him feel good and a little aroused, but also set him worrying again.

"Hey, Michelle," he said when she answered.

"Have I got some great news for you, Hawk-man!" she said before he could lay out his problem. "I scored an invitation to a party next week in L.A. The big boys from the NBC affiliates in southern California. Very exclusive. You can circulate your tapes."

"Maybe you could do it for me," he said. "I've got my hands full here. That's why I called. I need your help with the show."

"What?" She sounded stunned, but he was too worried to figure out why. He explained the crisis he and Renata were in, ending with the ideas Denny and he had kicked around for the show.

Michelle was quiet.

"Hello?" he asked.

"You must be in shock," Michelle said. "That's

the only way to explain it. I tell you you've got a crack at L.A. and you want me to help you save that backwater show? That's crazy. It's only luck I got this invite. You have to come. It's your career.''

"My career's here.'' Part of him couldn't believe he'd just said that.

"What happened to L.A., Chicago or New York in five years?'' Michelle asked in amazement. "This Phoenix thing was temporary, remember? It's a no-where market. You've got good clips. It's time to move on.''

"Don't be so sure,'' he said, hearing how ridiculous he sounded even as he spoke. "We had a fifty share at one time, and if we can extend the run of the show, who knows what can happen? Maybe syndication.'' He stopped talking. Michelle was right. Three months ago he would have done anything for a chance like the one she'd just presented. He should be packing up tapes and résumés right now. Instead, he was trying to talk himself out of going.

"Why don't you want to go?''

Renata. Just Renata and that was everything. He needed to hear her, see her, touch her every day to feel right with the world. He thought about holding her in his arms and how he felt around her—Buddy blended into Hawk and he felt whole. He couldn't leave her, not now.

And he suddenly knew why. He sat bolt upright and his head hit the headboard. "Ow! I'm in love, Michelle. Ouch. Wow.'' He rubbed the bump on his crown.

"Love hurts?''

He laughed. "Nah. It just hit me over the head.''

"So, you're in love with the sad therapist?''

"Yeah," he sighed. "I'm in love with Renata." It felt good to say it, if a little scary. He wasn't supposed to fall in love until his career was set—not now, when he was a nobody. But here it was, ready or not.

It hadn't happened "poof" like he'd expected, either. They were as different as chalk and oil, as Lila said. All her fussy stuff and restraint and planning drove him nuts, but he couldn't imagine life without her. Besides, the only thing that could possibly explain why he wasn't making reservations for a flight to L.A. right now had to be love. True love.

"Well, what do you know," Michelle said, laughter in her voice. "I'm proud of you, Hawk, I guess. Blowing off ambition to be happy."

"I'm not blowing off ambition. Nothing's changed. I still have my career plan. I've just got to make this show work right now. So, help me figure out something to fix it. Denny wants some excitement. Something to make the news."

"I'd say cohosts on a marriage show tying the knot is pretty newsy."

"Tying the knot? I barely figured out I'm in love with her. Nobody said anything about marriage. Hell."

"I'll bet Renata will have a lot to say about it. Women always want to get married."

Of course she was right. He knew all the things Renata wanted and marriage was right up there. But people didn't necessarily get married right away. That's why they had engagements, wasn't it? They'd just have a long engagement. An engagement could be newsworthy, if there was human interest and novelty to it…

And then it dawned on him. His birthday surprise for Renata. The perfect opportunity. It would thrill her and save the show at the same time. Figuring it out as he talked, he explained the idea to Michelle. "What do you think?"

She was quiet for a very long time. "Don't you hate heights?" she finally asked.

"Forget about me. What do you think Renata will think?"

"As near as I can tell, she'll either be the happiest woman on earth or never speak to you again."

"Very funny." He was positive this was the right thing for Renata. For him, it meant a leap of faith that it would all work out. Maybe marriage didn't have to kill love. They both just needed time to find out, and this plan would buy them time. His instincts said go for it and Hawk never fought his instincts.

"HEY, RENNIE." HAWK'S soft voice dragged Renata from sleep while it was still dark. "Happy birthday, sweetheart."

Renata opened her eyes to find him leaning over her. His voice and scent—soap and cologne— washed over her in a delightful wave. He was naked and still damp from the shower. "Are you feeling okay?" she asked him.

The night before, Hawk's stomach had been upset. "Better, I think," he said with a slight frown. She could see he was putting up a good front. She blinked to see him more clearly. "What time is it?" she asked.

"Time for your birthday surprise."

"My surprise?"

"You'll love it. I promise." His eyes twinkled with mischief.

"Okay." Two months ago, she would have demanded an itinerary. But now she knew Hawk knew her through and through. He respected her, did what she needed. If Hawk said she would love the surprise, she would.

"We've got to get going, so get dressed," Hawk said, patting her. "Wear something comfortable but nice-looking." He bounced off the bed and headed for the bathroom.

Renata ran her fingers through her tangled hair and watched Hawk brush his teeth at the sink. Such an ordinary act, but he looked so sexy doing it she just sat and watched. He looked so right in her bathroom...and her living room...and her kitchen...and especially her bedroom. When he'd first come to her house, he'd seemed oversized, out of place thumping around, rattling her plates—and her. Now he belonged. She couldn't imagine her doorway without him in it.

Despite her excitement, as she stepped into the shower, worry assailed her. The fact was, four o'clock wasn't such an unusual time for her to be awake. Lately, it had been her worry hour. Now that the show was on shaky ground, she'd begun to wonder what would happen between them.

The truth was, she was getting kind of tired of the show and had gotten more excited about finishing her degree. But the show was what kept Hawk and her together, and she didn't want to lose Hawk. It panicked her to think their relationship might run its course along with their show.

The truth was, she was in love with Hawk.

Deeply. The feeling had magically sprung up like Jack's beanstalk or Rapunzel's hair, twining around her heart, sending tendrils everywhere. Did he love her? She thought so, but she was afraid to ask. Would he stay with her? She had no idea. Slowly, she soaped her legs and arms, then let the hot water sluice down her body.

He hadn't talked about his career at all since they'd begun sleeping together, so maybe he'd changed, just as she had, she thought, rubbing shampoo into her hair. Maybe if the show folded, he'd settle down here in Phoenix. He seemed so much calmer since they'd been together. She'd changed him— helped him appreciate a quiet life. Maybe he was getting the television lust out of his system.

"Hurry up or I'll have to come in there and soap you myself," Hawk warned lovingly, making her shiver. "And then we'll never make sunrise."

Maybe everything would be all right, she thought, rinsing quickly, skipping the cream rinse. She'd trust Hawk. He'd been right before. He was here, wasn't he, filling her life with surprises? Steady and solid and full of passion? Yeah. She smiled, pushed away her worry, and ducked her face under the hot shower spray for a last quick rinse. She couldn't wait for Hawk's surprise.

A half hour of driving brought them northwest of town, past the newest subdivisions until they reached open fields and undeveloped desert. Hawk swallowed a gulp of stomach remedy, then referred to a scrap of paper on which he'd scribbled directions.

"How's your stomach?" Renata asked him.

"A little queasy, but this helps," he said. "I'm sure it was the shrimp last night. I'm just glad you

didn't have any of it. Whoops, here's the turnoff."
With a jerk of the wheel he steered his sports car
onto a narrow dirt road, raising dust on either side,
making her glad they'd kept the ragtop on.

Soon she saw people clustered around a couple of
pickup trucks and something else she couldn't quite
make out. As they got closer, she saw it was a bil-
lowing expanse of brightly colored nylon cloth.
"That's a hot-air balloon!" she cried. "Oh, my
gosh! You didn't!"

"I did." Hawk grinned at her. "And we're going
up in it. A champagne toast as the sun rises. Happy
birthday, Renata."

"Oh, Hawk!" She squealed, a sound she hadn't
imagined she could make, then rushed out of the car
and ran a few steps forward. "I've always wanted to
do this," she said to Hawk when he joined her.

"I know, sweetheart. Why do you think we're
here?"

"This is so romantic," she said. She threw her
arms around him and kissed him, tasting coffee and
mint, then pulled back to look at his face, lit with
the soft glow that appeared whenever he made her
smile. And in the time she'd been with him, she'd
smiled more than she had in her whole life.

Dizzy with joy, she looked around. Hints of a
pink-and-yellow dawn lit the bushes and cactus
around her. The air was cool for a summer morning
and smelled of tangy creosote and damp earth. A
mourning dove gave a comforting coo, abruptly
drowned in the roar of the balloon's gas jet. She
watched the striped balloon puff upward and felt a
rush of excitement.

"I can't wait!" She felt as delighted as a child

about to get the pony of her dreams. Hawk was always making her feel young—pulling her back to childhood, but making things right this time.

"I know," he said, "and this is only the beginning." He looked at his watch, then her, his eyes twinkling with promise. Before she could ask what he meant, he tugged her hand and they hurried toward the balloon, now fully inflated and suspended magically over the gondola. It seemed so fantastic, almost impossible, that it could rise into the air, colorful and fragile, and carry them across the sky.

On the ground beside the gondola, a man wearing a weathered captain's cap, a wrinkled navy blazer, and a quarter-inch of stubble shook their hands. "Captain Dave," he said, chewing on a battered cigar as he looked them over, "and this is Champagne Over the Desert—the best in high-altitude romantic escapes." He handed each of them a card.

"Ladies first," he said, then held Renata's hand as she climbed a small stool, then swung a leg over the leather-covered edge of the wicker gondola, and stepped onto the basket's floor. Hawk climbed in after her, then hugged her against him. The basket shifted a little. Hawk made a sound. "Wish I'd brought the stomach stuff." His face was pale.

"Are you sure you're okay?" she asked him.

"Fine," he said, but his smile looked strained. "I wouldn't miss this for the world." He glanced at his watch.

"Oh, look," she said, pointing at an ice-filled plastic tub. "There's our champagne. Even strawberries."

"We're off," Captain Dave said to the three-person crew wearing Champagne Over the Desert T-shirts who were stabilizing the basket. He adjusted a valve, the gas jet roared loudly, the crew let go and the balloon began to lift.

"Whoa, there," Hawk said as the basket creaked. His hand gripped Renata's waist like a vise.

"What's wrong?" she asked him.

"I'm not big on heights," he said with an uneasy smile. He swallowed audibly.

"Plus, you're not feeling well." Renata brushed his hair from his forehead. "You poor dear man."

"I'm okay," he said, glancing at his watch.

"Why do you keep checking your watch?"

"Oh, no reason. I just want to be sure we don't miss sunrise," he said, his eyes holding some of their old twinkle. He had a secret all right. Renata was so transfixed by the experience, she decided not to probe. Why spoil her birthday surprise?

They headed smoothly upward and, when the jet blast stopped, a strange silence filled her ears, as if the desert held its breath to be sure they made it. She couldn't believe she was actually here, skimming through the air, her long-held wish fulfilled, and with the added glory of being tucked in the arms of the man she loved at the same time. It was almost too much to bear.

She looked up at Hawk to see if he was enjoying the view, but his eyes were shut tight. Worry shot through her. "Hawk, are you okay?"

Was he okay? Hawk asked himself, clammy with sweat, his stomach cramped and queasy. "Sure," he said. *Except for having my life pass before my eyes.* He'd been fighting nausea and now he was zooming through space. He felt like Jimmy Stewart in *Vertigo.* The things you did for love. He opened one eye to see that Renata's face glowed with delight. He steeled himself against his misery. It was worth all of it to make her this happy.

"Look down and you can get your bearings," Renata said.

And that was his biggest mistake. Looking down, he saw that the cacti he knew to be tall as flagpoles looked like twigs on a child's train set. They were hundreds of feet in the air, with nothing holding them up but the skill of the crusty captain and the flaming butane that roared way too close to the thin skin of the balloon.

His stomach sank like he'd taken the biggest dip on the Cyclone, and he dropped like a stone to the floor of the basket.

"Oh, my gosh." Renata crouched beside him. "What happened?"

"Just got a little dizzy," he said. Jeez! What was he, some kind of wuss? How was he going to propose to Renata curled in a ball of terror and nausea?

"You'll be fine, pal," Captain Dave reassured, showing teeth that had been capped and not very well. "Usually it's the ladies that lose their cookies." He chuckled and winked at Hawk. "Feedin' the quail, I always say."

"Yeah, well, I had some bad food last night," he said, lowering his voice to sound more masculine.

Captain Dave chuckled.

"Don't worry, Hawk," Renata whispered. "I'll just talk you through it, like you helped me with in-line skating."

He managed a crooked smile. "Yeah. I helped you right into the lagoon."

"It's nice to be the one who's helping for a

change.'' She patted his cheek, then stood up, so her knees were at his eye level. "This is so breathtaking," she said.

I'll say. He wouldn't take a solid breath until they touched down. Right now, he had to get busy if they were to be ready for the surprise that would meet them on the ground. He reached up, took Renata's hand and tugged her down to him.

11

"RENATA, I WANT TO TALK…uh…" Nausea swept through Hawk. The bad shrimp cocktail was mixing with his vertigo in a killer combination that could very well lead to feeding the quail, as Captain Dave so colorfully put it.

"Don't talk now," Renata said. She patted him on the shoulder, and stood again. "I'll tell you what I'm seeing."

"Wait," he said weakly, feeling green. He tucked his head between his knees, trying to get enough control to stand up and propose.

"This is so perfect," she called to him.

Right. He was tucked into pass-out posture, too sick to move, let alone propose. Just perfect.

"So, you want I should pour the champagne?" Captain Dave asked.

"That would be lovely," Renata said. Then she squatted down. "Is that okay, Hawk?"

"Sure," he said. "Great." He managed a queasy smile.

She sat down facing him, her legs crossed. "I'm so sorry you feel sick." She brushed his hair off his forehead. "Should we land? This can't be fun for you."

"No, this is important," he said, rallying with a ragged breath.

Captain Dave bent to hand them each a plastic champagne glass. Golden, frothy liquid dripped from the glasses to the dusty floor of the basket.

"Thanks," Renata said.

"Hang on," Captain Dave said. He plopped a strawberry into each glass. "Whoops!" He plucked a bit of leaf from Renata's flute, then licked the champagne from his fingers. "Nice bouquet," he said.

Hawk rolled his eyes. Ignoring Captain Dave, he tapped his plastic glass against Renata's with a flat click. He had to tell her how much she meant to him, that he loved her, that he wanted to be with her. Except it took all his concentration to keep his stomach in place and his head from spinning. He took a deep breath, "Renata, I—"

"So, how's the upchuck urge?" Captain Dave asked. Hawk looked over to find the man had seated himself on the ice chest like he expected to be part of the conversation.

"Could we have a moment?" Hawk asked.

"You want privacy?" Captain Dave chuckled. "Maybe I should dangle over the side?" When neither of them laughed, he cleared his throat. "Gotcha. Duty calls." He stood and moved to the other side of the basket. The gas jet roared.

Hawk turned back to Renata and twined their forearms for a toast.

"This is the biggest thrill of my life, Hawk," Renata said. Her eyes shone with excitement. "You did this because it's my childhood dream, even though you're deathly ill and afraid. You sweet, sweet, romantic man. I've learned so much from you about having fun, and about love, and about what really matters. I've learned to throw caution to the wind and run with scissors. I've—"

"You paid for this sunrise, folks, you really ought to look at it," Captain Dave called.

"Oh, yeah." Renata jumped up. "Oh," she gasped. "It's beautiful. Come up here, Hawk."

He looked up at her, but nausea swirled and he saw a double image where her face was. He'd just make it short. *I love you. We belong together. Will you marry me?*

"Never mind," she said. "You stay there and I'll describe it to you." Hawk had never seen her so bubbly. Just wait until she heard the real surprise. "It's all pink and gold," she called to him. "The cacti are so tiny, like toys. And there's the balloon truck driving up. And, hey... Is that a KTNK truck?" She looked down at him.

Hawk groaned. They were early, and this wasn't how it was supposed to go.

"What's a TV truck doing here?" she asked him. "Hawk?"

"That's what I wanted to tell you about." He dragged himself to his feet, desperately woozy. "Renata, will you—?"

The gas jet's roar blotted out his words.

"What?" Renata asked.

"Renata, will you—?" Hawk began again. Again the gas roared.

"Do you have to do that?" Hawk yelled at Captain Dave.

"Unless you want us to smash against the rocks, yeah."

Better get this over with, roar or not. Hawk gathered his energy, stilled his roiling stomach, and bellowed, "Renata, will you marry me!?" Except the roar ceased just as he spoke, and he found he'd shouted into the silent desert air.

"What?" Renata stared at Hawk, her mouth open. Had she heard right? Had Hawk just proposed to her? She wasn't sure because he looked so gray and miserable, and he'd sounded almost angry.

"Uhhhhh." Hawk clung to one of the balloon lines, his face now ashen.

"Oh, honey, sit down," she said, helping him to the floor of the balloon. She sat with him. "Did you just ask me to marry you?" She was so stunned she could hardly get the words out.

Hawk nodded.

It was hard to believe the happiest words in the world when he looked so unhappy saying them, but she wanted to. With all her heart.

"We're heading down," Captain Dave called to them.

"It's so sudden, Hawk," Renata said. "I don't know what to say...or...or what to think."

"Don't think. Just say yes," Hawk said. "Quick."

"Quick? Why quick?" Abruptly, doubt shot through her.

"That's the rest of the surprise," Hawk said weakly. "We're supposed to make the announcement on the air."

"*On* the air? You mean *in* the air, don't you?" She smiled. Then it hit her. "Oh, no. That's what the TV truck is here for, isn't it?" Dread chilled the warmth in her heart.

"We're supposed to announce our engagement on *Arizona Today News*."

"Why on earth would we do that?"

"To save the show, of course. We're dead if we don't do something fresh. Denny said we should make news somehow. I already had this surprise balloon ride planned for you." He paused and closed his eyes to breathe slowly, obviously fighting dizziness. "When I realized I was in love with you, everything just fell into place. Associated Press may pick up the story and the publicity will at least extend the show, and maybe—who knows—get us syndicated."

"But this should be between you and me, not you, me and a television audience." She began to feel dizzy herself. This was wrong. Very wrong.

"But it makes a great teaser, don't you think? 'TV marriage counselors take own advice. News at six.'"

"A teaser? I don't care about teasers. You asked me to marry you. That's what I care about. We haven't even talked about marriage before, or what our relationship means. We need to talk this through."

"That's exactly why I did this. To buy us more time together. So, say yes, okay?"

"Whether I mean it or not? Whether I'm ready or not?"

"Look, I'm not ready, either. But I love you. I know that much. And you love me, don't you?"

"Yes, but—"

"Then say yes... Ohhh." He paused and bent over. "Let's just make the announcement, okay? I'm sick and the timing's off, but let's do it," he said on a queasy-sounding breath. "We can sort all this out when we get home."

"You asked me to marry you as a TV stunt?" she

said slowly, as the idea became clear. She couldn't believe it. Wouldn't believe it.

"It's for the greater good, Renata. For us. For the show. Don't think about it, just do it."

He was always saying that. *Don't think. Stop thinking. You're thinking again.* But this was one time when thinking was essential. This was their future, their life together, their happily-ever-after.

"I don't know…"

"We're landing," Hawk said, still looking green. "Just let me do the talking, okay? Please? And agree with me."

Finally, she just nodded, hoping he was right, trying to fight the doubts that gnawed at her joy. Was this just a performance? Did he even *want* to marry her?

"Look happy, okay?" Hawk asked, clearly struggling to smile himself.

She stared at him, stunned and confused, wanting to be happy, but how could she be? Hawk wanted her to put on an act for TV, like putting on makeup. The balloon reached ground level, Captain Dave's crew grabbed the lines, caught the basket and ran it to a stop.

Immediately, Tabitha Walker and a cameraman ran up to the wobbling basket. "Look who's here— Hawk Hunter and Renata Rose, cohosts of TV 11's *Making it to Marriage* show." Tabitha was looking at them, but her attention and glittering smile were for the camera. She was all television.

Like Hawk, Renata realized with a pang. Hawk was all television, too.

"Looks like we've caught you two on a secret balloon getaway." Tabitha thrust her microphone toward them. "So, you have some news for us? An announcement, perhaps?"

"We do, but just a sec…" Hawk said shakily. "Uh-oh.…" Abruptly, Hawk leaned over the side of the basket and threw up.

"Euuuw!" Tabitha squealed and jumped back. "Cut!" she said to the camera guy, who smirked. "You got some on my shoes!" she said to Hawk, outraged.

"Sorry," Hawk managed. "Vertigo."

"Three-hundred-dollar Italian leather. Ruined."

"I feel better now, thanks for asking," Hawk said, but his humor was lost on Tabitha. "Roll tape," he said to the camera guy. "Ask me again, Tabitha."

Tabitha turned on her TV smile, aimed the mike their way, but her enthusiasm had clearly waned. "So what's the scoop? You have an announcement?"

"As a matter of fact, Tabitha, I just asked Renata to make me the happiest man on earth. I asked her to be my wife." He sounded so TV-phony, Renata's stomach turned.

"Well, well. That's really *something* coming from the cohosts of a *marriage* show." Tabitha had rallied and winked for the camera.

"We think so," Hawk said, putting his arm around Renata. The embrace felt strange and empty of feeling. She felt like a cardboard cutout.

Tabitha shoved the mike in her face. "And what about you? What did you say when Hawk asked you to marry him?"

Renata looked at Tabitha, then Hawk and tried to form the words they wanted her to say: *I was thrilled. Of course I said yes.* But she couldn't. It felt too fake. Even if she wanted to say yes to Hawk, she couldn't do it on television. They'd have to figure out some other way to save the show.

"I'm sorry. I can't," she said to Hawk. "Not like this." She hiked one leg over the gondola's edge, and Captain Dave helped her to the ground. "Told you he'd feed the quail," he muttered to her with a wink.

"Renata, what are you doing?" Hawk said. "Wait here, Tabitha."

"No, forget it, Tabitha," Renata said.

"Will you two make up your mind?" Tabitha said irritably, the microphone flopped carelessly from her limp wrist.

Renata stumbled toward the car, her heart aching, needing to get away, to clear her head. The time had come at last to think. To *really* think. Hawk chased after her. As they passed the TV 11 truck, a technician leaned out, holding a cell phone. "Tabitha, phone," he called. "It's Dennis Bachman."

They all stopped. Denny probably wanted to know how the scheme had gone. Denny's words came back to her: *Hawk will do anything for the show.* Those two were on the same wavelength, all right.

"Yes?" Tabitha said. "How did it go!? How did it go!? Well, for starters, Hawk hurled on my shoes." She gave Hawk a hateful look. "Yeah, they're still here." She handed the phone to Hawk. He kept his eyes on Renata as he spoke to Denny.

As Renata watched, his face, which had regained its color once they'd returned to the ground, went newly pale. "Are you sure?" he asked soberly. "Is there anything we can do? I see…. No, I'll tell her. Thanks."

He handed the phone to Tabitha, then walked toward Renata, holding her gaze, his face full of sadness.

"I'm sorry, Renata, but *Making it to Marriage* has been canceled. Next week's the last show."

"You're kidding." She felt like the bottom dropped out of her stomach. "How could they do that?"

"The GM's bored with us." He sighed. "I'm sorry. This news spot wouldn't have done any good, anyway, it turns out. Denny said it was a done deal."

"So, I've finally been replaced by a bunny rabbit," she said woodenly.

"Huh?"

"Nothing. Just an old joke." Tears swelled in her eyes and her head felt like it might explode. She turned away, and began to run toward the car, tears streaking her cheeks. Her legs felt wooden beneath her. Hawk had proposed, but it was only a stunt, and she'd lost her show. It was all too much.

Hawk caught up with her at the car and folded her into his arms, tight and secure. "I'm so sorry. I thought we could save it."

She felt the familiar warmth of his body, the comfort of his arms around her, the wonderful way they fit together. She knew she should resist him, but for just a minute she let herself feel how much she needed him, loved him, wanted him.

"It'll be okay," Hawk said. He pulled back and looked at her. "Michelle thinks I've got a chance in L.A. There's a cocktail party with some muckety-mucks with NBC I've been invited to. It could turn into something."

"What does that mean?"

"It means it's time for me to move on, I guess. We knew the show could only last so long."

"That's right," she said softly. "So you'll go to L.A." She knew this could happen—*would* happen eventually. She just didn't expect it so fast.

"If it works out. And if I don't get something in L.A., then somewhere else. And you'll come with me."

"Come with you? How can I do that? Everything I have is here—my house, my classes, my mother and…and the rec center…and everything."

"I know it's sudden. But we'll be fine. We'll get an apartment, and find you a job, get you signed up for classes. You can organize everything the way you like it."

Even if he meant what he was saying, when she thought about leaving everything she knew and loved, it seemed impossible—completely out of her realm. "I'm not like you, Hawk. I can't live on the fly, with everything in boxes and nothing stable. I'm not that kind of person."

"Sure you are. You underestimate yourself. It'll be an adventure."

An adventure? Renata felt an eerie déjà vu. Instantly, she realized why. Sometimes when she seemed especially sad about her father leaving again, he'd ask her to come with him to wherever he was headed—Sacramento, Las Vegas, Tucson. He'd call it an adventure, too. But they both knew she couldn't come. She had school and a life. It was just his way of assuaging his guilt for leaving her. Her father didn't really want her. He wanted his work, his travel, with a little family on the side.

Just like Hawk. The truth flashed through her like

frost, chilling her to the bone. She could only stare at Hawk, as cold numbness spread inside her.

"Maybe you won't come right away, if that's too hard," he said.

She remained silent.

"We can still get married," he offered.

"Still?" He made it sound like a consolation prize.

"If that's what you want."

"What about you? Do *you* want to get married, really?"

"I'm willing to give it a try. I just want us to be together."

Disappointment rocked her. It had been a stunt, just like she'd thought. Did he even really love her? And if so, how much? Sick at heart, she tested him. "Why don't you just stay here?"

"Stay here? What would I do? The show's gone."

"You could get a job as a newspaper reporter or a copywriter at one of the other stations. The NPR radio station does some excellent work. The pay's not great, but…"

"Be realistic, Renata," he said.

"I am being realistic," she said heavily. "What's realistic is that you want your career more than you want me." She'd known from the beginning that nothing was more important to him than his ambition. All the herb gardens and bookshelves in the world wouldn't keep Hawk here if his career beckoned.

"My career's important to me, sure, but so are you. We can have a great life wherever we go. If we have each other."

"It's not that simple. And I can't just drop my life

and go with you. We both have to be realistic.'' Her voice shook. ''We've had a wonderful time, but it's time for it to end.''

''We can make this work, Renata. I asked you to marry me. To come with me. Don't brush that off like it's nothing.''

''It won't work, Hawk. Stop it.''

He stared at her, his caramel eyes pleading with her.

After a long, painful silence, she said, ''Take me home, please.''

Anger flickered in his eyes, and a muscle danced in his cheek, making her shiver. ''You are too stubborn for your own good,'' he said, jerking open the door for her. After she sat down, he slammed it, got in himself and spun gravel as he roared off, scaring her a little. She'd never seen Hawk angry before. Another bit of proof they couldn't get married. The most important measure of couple success was right fight behavior and they hadn't even practiced. This was just crazy dreaming on Hawk's part. She couldn't risk her whole life and all she'd built just to prove it to him.

He didn't speak, and she was glad for the silence. It gave her time to get used to the truth she'd just realized. She'd been floating in a dream world of ''not thinking it to death,'' where Hawk had taken her, and now she had to get her feet firmly back on the ground.

She was numb with shock, luckily, so she knew she wouldn't cry. That was best. Her sensible side had come to her rescue again. Maybe Hawk and she loved each other, but love wasn't enough. They were just too different from each other. Their goals were different. Their personalities were different. Everything about them was different. The only thing they had in common were sparks, and sparks weren't enough for a happily-ever-after. Sparks fizzled. Hawk would realize it once he came to his senses.

By the time Hawk pulled up in front of her house, Renata felt dead inside, but resigned, and so distant from Hawk he seemed like a handsome dot on the ground she was looking at from the dizzy height the hot-air balloon had reached.

Hawk stopped the car and turned to her, anger, disappointment and yearning warring on his face.

"I know this is hard," she said softly. "But surely you can see to push things further would be fooling ourselves. You have your career. I have my life." Her voice started to shake. She swallowed. "You have to move on. I have to stay."

"Can't you at least try? Bend a little for once?" His face was pale with anger. "What do you want from me? I asked you to marry me. You think that was easy?"

"Yes, I do. Because you said it on impulse. Because of the show. You haven't thought about the day-to-day struggle of a life together—me with my dollhouses and you living out of boxes, always on the go, obsessing over your career. You think that someone waves a wand and like magic everything works out. It's not that easy. Love is work."

"No kidding. This hasn't been any wave of the wand so far, Renata. I've had to drag you kicking and screaming into this relationship. I've worked hard. And I've been there for you. And, okay, you're right—marriage is a little intimidating. But I know I love you and that's enough for me to take a chance. It ought to be enough for you.''

"We've been in a dream world, Hawk. We don't want the same things in our lives." *And when you realize that, you won't love me any more, and I won't be able to stand to see that in your eyes.* "I know I'm right, and you will, too, if you're honest with yourself. I have to go," she said. And fast, before the hurt in his caramel eyes made her lose her nerve and take it all back.

"Renata, don't!" he said, grabbing her hand.

"I have to." She pulled away, brushed tears from her cheek, yanked open the car door, and hurried up the walk to her door. As she fumbled with the lock, she felt Hawk waiting there in the car. Why didn't he just leave? Did he think she would change her mind? Run back to him? As much as her soul ached to believe, she didn't dare be seduced by his fantasy. She opened the door and quickly shut it against him. What she saw inside the house made her gasp.

Balloons. The living room was filled from floor to ceiling with helium-filled balloons. Red, yellow, blue, pink, green globes—at least two hundred of them—bobbed and dodged in the moving air, dangling bright, gently curled ribbons.

He must have arranged for someone to inflate the balloons while they were gone—maybe Lila. Stumbling forward into the room, Renata found some of the ribbons had been tied into a gigantic balloon bouquet. A large card attached to the knot read, "Here's to a life full of balloons and music. Love always, Hawk." And below, tied to the ribbons, but resting on the table, sat—of all things—a ukulele.

She turned slowly to stare in wonder at the room's

whimsical, bobbing balls of color. The sight was impossible—and too lovely for words. If only balloons and music were enough. She closed her eyes against the glorious sight of the bright globes.

Bang! A balloon popped. She started, and her eyes flew open. It must have bumped the hot ceiling light and burst. Her dream had popped like that balloon. Pow! Just air and shreds of color, as fragile as cotton candy. Pain welled up inside her and her throat closed down. Her heart felt tight as a fist in her chest. There was that impossible ukulele waiting for her, like a promise unkept, like music unplayed.

COME OUT. COME OUT. Come out, Hawk silently implored Renata. *For once in your life, take a chance.* Surely, when she saw the surprise he'd arranged for her with Lila's help she'd get past her fear. It was only fear, he knew, but it hurt all the same. And as the minutes dragged, and hope turned to hurt, then anger, he realized he was the biggest schmuck on the planet.

Okay, she was afraid. So was he, but he was willing to try. Why wasn't she? He shouldn't have to fight so hard for something that should be as easy as breathing—two people who loved each other making a life together.

As ten minutes turned to thirty, his anger solidified. He wasn't a lovesick fool who sat around pining for a woman too afraid to love him, no matter how much he loved her. Nothing he did for her would be enough, that was obvious. He couldn't be a different person. And, really, neither could she. It *was* impossible, he finally saw, sick inside, but not because of him, but because she wouldn't even try.

Well, he wouldn't mope over Renata. He learned that lesson in foster homes. You didn't get your heart too set on things, because things changed. You just got it together and moved on. He'd stick with his plan. Go with what he knew. Try to get past this pain in his chest so big it made it hard to breathe. He'd give her five more minutes...

An hour later, angry and aching, Hawk drove off.

12

THE DAY BEFORE HER LAST show with Hawk, Renata returned from the teen center, feeling that familiar knot of loneliness in her stomach. She hated returning to an empty house. Hawk had ruined that for her—the joy of being alone in her home. Without Hawk taking up space with his size and boundless energy, the place seemed to echo.

It was probably just garden-variety depression after the breakup. Everybody felt that way at first. It would be better after Hawk left. And he would leave Phoenix after the last show. He had gone to L.A. and, sure enough, gotten a job as a part-time sportscaster at a big station.

When he told her about the job he left long pauses in the conversation, as if waiting for her to change her mind, but the excitement in his voice when he talked about L.A. kept her from saying anything that was in her heart. He was reaching his goal. She was happy for him.

Every now and then she thought about changing her mind, offering to go with him. But that was just the "bargaining" stage of grief, she knew. She'd get over it. She'd get over Hawk. She had to.

They'd see each other one more time—the show tomorrow. The last show. She dreaded it, but promised herself she'd be strong.

She'd just sat down to do some studying when the doorbell rang. For a second her heart pounded, thinking it might be Hawk. She remembered how her new jeans had scraped together when she hurried to open the door to him on their first date. Now she looked through the peephole and found her mother bearing a soup tureen and a determined look. Uh-oh. Lila on a mission.

"Chamomile-tofu soup," she said, swishing into the house, trailing the scent of mint and patchouli, her beads rattling. "Full of potassium and B vitamins. Depression reversal," she said. "I laced it with some tincture of St.-John's-wort, too."

The last thing Renata needed was strange-colored urine, but she knew her mother meant well. "I'll get some lemonade," she said turning toward the kitchen.

Lila gave a soft whistle. "This place looks empty. Where are all your dollhouses?"

"They were getting dusty," Renata called back to her, having reached the refrigerator. "I put them out in the garage. I've been too busy studying." And too busy with Hawk. Now only the studying remained, and she planned to redouble her efforts there. On top of everything else, she'd lost interest in her hobbies.

"And you got rid of that awful leather chair," Lila said, setting the soup tureen on the kitchen table.

"Yeah." She laughed a little. "I realized I'd bought it for Maurice and never really liked it." She took down two glasses, two soup bowls and spoons and placed them on the table.

"Good for you," Lila said, ladling out the soup while Renata poured the lemonade.

At least being with Hawk had taught her never to

settle, like she had with Maurice. Now she knew she was a passionate woman as well as an intellectual one, and would never be with a man who didn't share that intensity. She should thank Hawk for that. Maybe tomorrow on the show. No, that would make her cry.

"I see you kept some of the balloons," Lila said. She indicated the half-dozen shriveled balls that still hovered a foot above the floor, trailing their ribbons. Renata had kept them around as a reminder of Hawk and what might have been, bittersweet though it was. "Yeah. I should throw them out."

"Try the soup," Lila said abruptly. To her credit, Lila hadn't hounded her about the breakup.

Renata sat and took a spoonful, trying not to make a face as the bitter tang filled her mouth. "I'll let it cool a little," she said, setting down her spoon.

"Honey, why don't you call him?" Lila said.

"I don't want to talk about Hawk, okay?" She washed the nasty taste down with some lemonade.

"All right." She could see Lila struggle not to probe. "Then how are you feeling about the show being canceled?"

"I'm fine," she said, aimlessly stirring the soup she had no intention of eating. "It's for the best. My heart's not in it any more anyway." Her heart wasn't in anything these days, least of all happily-ever-afters. Whatever grief she felt for the show obviously had been overshadowed by her misery over Hawk. "It was a good experience, and now I can afford to take classes full-time next semester and just keep the teen center for the counseling experience."

"Renata Rose, don't try to make a silk purse out of a black cloud."

"You mean a silk purse out of a sow's ear...or every cloud has a silver lining."

"Whatever. Silk purse, silver sow, I don't care. You're miserable. Let yourself feel it."

"I *am* feeling it, Lila. I'm just not dwelling on it."

"Oh, sweetie. You've always been such a soldier." Lila stood, patted her shoulder and headed to the refrigerator for ice. "Well, look at this," she said.

Renata looked up and saw that Lila held the Polaroid photo of Hawk and her in the Mexican restaurant on the evening of their first date. She'd stuck it on the refrigerator and forgotten about it.

Lila carried it to the table. "This is a great picture," she said, her surprised gaze flying from the photo to Renata. "It's so *not* you."

Renata looked at the picture. At the time, she'd hated the embarrassment of having it taken, but now she saw how fun it had been, how playful. Hawk looked so happy and hopeful. Her heart clutched in her chest.

"You two look good together," Lila said. "You should have smiled."

She took the picture from her mother and studied it. Hawk had said she was beautiful, but she'd only thought about how bedraggled she'd looked. She could see now what he meant. She looked grimy but festive, with that silk daisy over her ear and that goofy sombrero on her head. She should have smiled.

If she had the chance to do it again, she'd smile. She'd smile as if her life depended on it. And sing along with the mariachis, while she was at it.

She closed her eyes and when she opened them they fell on the ukulele Hawk had given her, lying on the bay window bench where she'd left it. Its graceful beauty reminded her of all Hawk had shared with her, opened up to her. Suddenly, it was too much. She began to cry.

Lila looked up. "Oh, pumpkin," she said, hurrying to pull Renata into her arms.

"I don't know what to do any more," Renata said through her tears. "I miss him so much."

"Of course you do, Rennie. You love him."

She cried even harder.

Lila patted her back. "You'll know what to do."

"I don't see how."

"You will." She sighed and kept patting. "It's so nice to be able to comfort my daughter," she said. Her earrings softly jingled as she patted. "I've wanted to do this for years. I suppose living with me made you hold everything in."

"I'm just different than you," she said, pulling away, collecting herself, sniffling.

"But you still need love. Why don't you try to work things out with Hawk?"

"It's impossible."

"Where there's love, nothing's impossible."

That made her angry. Her mother was as unrealistic as Hawk. "Excuse me for saying this, Lila, but I would think you, of all people, would understand. I mean, Daddy abandoned you."

"Abandoned me?" She laughed incredulously. "Daddy didn't abandon me."

"You always denied it, but what else would you call it?"

"Honey, if your father stayed too long he got on my nerves. I always told you that."

"But I didn't believe you." Though the subject had been painful to her as a child, sometimes she couldn't help asking her mother about it.

"It's true. Did I ever look miserable when he left?"

"No, but you were just being brave for my benefit."

"Uh-uh. I wouldn't lie to you about a thing like that. I didn't then and I wouldn't now."

Renata stared at her mother. She *was* telling the truth. How had Renata been so blind?

"I loved your father and he loved me, but he was a restless guy, and I could only take him in small doses." She got a serious look on her face. "I know it was hard on you, Rennie. We tried to make it up to you as best we could."

"But weren't you lonely?" Renata couldn't get her mind around this new view of her parents' relationship. Her mother *wanted* her father to leave? It seemed impossible.

"I was busy with you, and I had my projects, my music, my jobs, my charities, my friends. And your dad when he was in town. It was a good life, except it was so hard on you. That was my only regret. His, too."

"I was always so sad when Daddy left."

"I know. Maybe being the kind of people we were, we shouldn't have had a child, but we didn't realize you'd be such a serious little person. We both loved you very much." Lila stared thoughtfully at Renata. "You're not running away from Hawk because of Daddy, are you? I couldn't live with myself if we'd caused you to give up your happiness...."

"No. Of course not." But was that what she was doing? Assuming Hawk was acting like her father always had? Her throat felt so tight she could hardly speak. Her mother's words had tipped her on her head. "Could we not talk about this any more?"

"Okay, but only if you play me something on your ukulele," Lila said brightly, clearly offering a distraction.

Renata took the small, light instrument into her hands. Suddenly, she saw Hawk's face as it had looked when he taught her to play. Full of tenderness and delight. And love. Lots of love. He'd done everything he could to make her feel safe and loved. And she'd been too scared to believe it.

Hawk was not her father, ready to lose interest in her and leave. And she wasn't a lonely little girl afraid her father didn't love her. She was all grown up, capable and strong and able to give love and receive it—from Hawk, who loved her back, steady and sure. And suddenly, she wasn't afraid any more.

"Okay," she said, blinking back her tears, smiling at her mother, knowing she had to make things right with Hawk. "But I only know one song. And I'm not very good."

"You have to start somewhere," Lila said, sitting back in her chair.

"Yeah," she said. "And I'm starting right now." For once her mother was absolutely right.

THE NEXT AFTERNOON, Renata sat in her throne, waiting for Hawk to join her on the set, her heart in her throat. She'd tried to reach him the night before and this morning, but he hadn't been home. She looked at her watch. They were minutes away from rolling tape. He'd never been late before. What if he wasn't coming? What if he'd just stayed in L.A.? Her heart fluttered in her chest.

And then there he was, bounding across the studio, headed right for her. Her heart pounded the familiar tattoo. How she loved him!

"The plane was delayed out of L.A.X.," he whispered, his breath warm on her, his eyes taking her in. He looked so happy to see her. It was as if nothing had come between them.

Doubt assailed her. Could she really give up everything that was familiar and move somewhere new just to be with the man she loved?

"God, I've missed you," he said, his eyes full of love.

Oh, yes, she could. She absolutely could.

"You've missed me, too," Hawk said, reading her face. "Thank God."

"We've got to talk," they both said at once. "After," they said together. They grinned at each other just as the opening music chattered its calypso beat and the show began—the very last *Making it to Marriage…with Dr. Renata Rose and Hawk Hunter.*

Renata could hardly peel her eyes away from Hawk long enough to greet Luis and Gloria, the troubled couple who felt they were too different to make a life together.

"Love shouldn't be such a pain," Gloria complained as the segment began. "We argue all the time. I like Chinese food, he wants Italian. I like hip-hop, he digs heavy metal. I like movies, he's into sports, sports, all the time sports."

"That ain't fair," Luis said. "I went to a chick flick with her—subtitles even. The least she could do is go to one wrestling match."

"Those are disgusting. And they're fake."

"They are not."

"Are too."

"Are not."

"Are too... Dr. Renata, are you listening to us?"

"Uh...huh? Oh, yes." She'd been staring into Hawk's caramel eyes, longing to be in his arms. She had to tell him how she'd changed, what she'd realized. "Actually, Gloria, I think that when you love each other you have to open yourself up to new experiences—like wrestling...or Chinese food...or learning to play a musical instrument." She reached behind her throne and brought out the ukulele she'd brought with her. "Like this one, for example."

"Renata," Hawk said tenderly.

"A musical instrument?" Gloria looked confusedly at Luis. "I don't see what that has to do with wrestling."

"We're not starting a band here," Luis said. "I just want someone who's easy to be with. I don't want to work so hard just to get along."

"I know what you mean," Hawk said softly. "I used to think love was 'Poof! Happily ever after.' But it's not like that. It takes effort and commitment and you have to make sacrifices, but it's worth every bit to be with the person who makes your life worth living."

"Oh, Hawk," Renata said softly.

"I said 'no' to L.A., Renata. Flat out."

"You didn't!" she said, startled.

"I did."

"But that's your dream. You can't give up your dream."

"You're my dream, Renata."

The audience buzzed with interest.

"What's the deal?" Luis asked.

Hawk turned to Luis, as if seeing him for the first time. "You know that happily-ever-after thing you're after?" Hawk asked him. "Watch and learn." He turned to Renata, set aside the ukulele and took her hands in his warm ones. "You're the first thing I think of every morning, Renata, and the last sight I want to see each night."

"Oh, Hawk." She felt his words in her soul and all she wanted was to give back the love she saw in his eyes. "I can't stand in the way of your career."

"Forget my career. I had this crazy idea that I had to be the best to prove myself to my mother. All these years I thought it was my mother's approval I needed. What I wanted was her love. Love is what makes people happy, not jobs, not success. It's love. And now I know I need your love to be happy."

"Oh, Hawk. I'm sorry I didn't trust you. You're not like my dad checking his watch at the merry-go-round. You're my Hawk, the man who thinks I'm beautiful even with pond scum on my chin. The man who taught me how to play music. Let me show you."

With shaking fingers, she lifted the ukulele from her lap. The hot lights had put the ukulele slightly out of tune, she noticed, when she shakily strummed, but she was too nervous to fix it. Plus her palms were so sweaty, she could hardly hold the neck in place. She gathered her courage, played the introductory chords and began to sing the only song she knew—

"You are my sunshine." Her fingers fumbled a bit, then found the new chord. It was slow, awkward and embarrassing and her voice wavered like mad, but when she saw that Hawk's eyes brimmed with tears and pride, she knew it was worth all the humiliation in the world.

And then she couldn't finish because Hawk was kissing her.

Someone squealed in the audience. Applause began slowly, then grew like thunder. Then the lights, the audience, her guests, everything slipped into the background. Nothing existed but the warm circle of the two of them and what they meant to each other.

Renata broke off the kiss. "It'll be great in L.A.," she said, her voice thick with tears of joy. "There's UCLA and tons of troubled teens. It'll be fun in an apartment, cutting pizza with scissors and pounding on the ceiling when the neighbors are too loud."

"L.A. can wait, Renata. You can't. Maybe I don't even need TV. Maybe I can get a reporting job right here, like you said. Or hell, I can be a librarian. Or wash cars or sell widgets. I don't care. I just want to be with you."

"Yes, you do care. I *want* to go to another city. No, I *have* to go. Really. I'm getting too complacent. It's time to run with scissors."

"But you're settled here. You're working on your degree. And you love the teen center. I'm the one who should make the sacrifice."

"No, Hawk. I'll go."

"I'll do it."

"Dios mío!" Gloria said. "Could you quit arguing and just get it over with."

"Get it over with?" they asked simultaneously, looking at each other.

"Propose, for God's sake," Gloria said. "You're showing us how it's done, aren't you?"

"Of course," Hawk said. He slid off his throne and onto one knee, still holding her hand. "I love everything about you, Renata. I love the way your eyebrows crook when I say something crazy and even the way you color-code my underwear. I love how smart you are, and how funny and how wise. I love the way you introduced me to myself—the parts of me I'd left behind. I love the little girl who comes out to play with me and the woman I make love to every night. Renata, will you marry me?"

His words vibrated through her like music on the ukulele strings, echoing inside her, making her nerves sing.

"Yes," she said, "I'll marry you. I don't care where we go—L.A. or the Amazon. As long as I have you, I'm happy."

Then Hawk pulled her into his arms and kissed her, warm and sweet as the caramel of his eyes and she melted and melted. Their hearts pounded in rhythm to the rolling waves of applause that washed over them.

Hawk broke off the kiss, turned to Gloria and Luis, who were holding hands and smiling at each other. "And that, my friends, is how you make it to marriage."

Everyone laughed. The audience cheered, and the show was over. When the floor manager waved them off the air, Denny rushed onto the set. "Fabulous show, you two. Great theater!" Denny touched his eyes, where moisture gleamed. "You got my old heartstrings throbbing."

"Glad we finally gave you a show you loved," Renata teased.

"Oh, I'm sure there'll be more," Denny said. "In a year, I figure you'll be ready for a concept I'm playing with—*Making it to Parenthood.*"

Renata and Hawk looked at each other and burst into laughter. Then Hawk's mouth caught hers in a warm kiss. Most people heard bells, but, with healing clarity, she swore she heard the joyous calliope of a merry-go-round—an overture to her very own happily-ever-after.

Princes...Princesses...
London Castles...New York Mansions...
To live the life of a royal!

In 2002, Harlequin Books lets you escape to a world of royalty with these royally themed titles:

Temptation:
January 2002—*A Prince of a Guy* (#861)
February 2002—*A Noble Pursuit* (#865)

American Romance:
The Carradignes: American Royalty (Editorially linked series)
March 2002—*The Improperly Pregnant Princess* (#913)
April 2002—*The Unlawfully Wedded Princess* (#917)
May 2002—*The Simply Scandalous Princess* (#921)
November 2002—*The Inconveniently Engaged Prince* (#945)

Intrigue:
The Carradignes: A Royal Mystery (Editorially linked series)
June 2002—*The Duke's Covert Mission* (#666)

Chicago Confidential
September 2002—*Prince Under Cover* (#678)

The Crown Affair
October 2002—*Royal Target* (#682)
November 2002—*Royal Ransom* (#686)
December 2002—*Royal Pursuit* (#690)

Harlequin Romance:
June 2002—*His Majesty's Marriage* (#3703)
July 2002—*The Prince's Proposal* (#3709)

Harlequin Presents:
August 2002—*Society Weddings* (#2268)
September 2002—*The Prince's Pleasure* (#2274)

Duets:
September 2002—*Once Upon a Tiara/Henry Ever After* (#83)
October 2002—*Natalia's Story/Andrea's Story* (#85)

Celebrate a year of royalty with Harlequin Books!

 Available at your favorite retail outlet.

HARLEQUIN®
Makes any time special ®

Visit us at www.eHarlequin.com

HSROY02

eHARLEQUIN.com

| | | | community | membership |
| buy books | authors | online reads | magazine | learn to write |

buy books

Your one-stop shop for great reads at great prices.
We have all your favorite Harlequin, Silhouette,
MIRA and Steeple Hill books, as well as a host of
other bestsellers in Other Romances. Discover a
wide array of new releases, bargains and hard-to-
find books today!

learn to write

Become the writer you always knew you could be:
get tips and tools on how to craft the perfect
romance novel and have your work critiqued by
professional experts in romance fiction. Follow
your dream now!

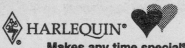

HARLEQUIN®
Makes any time special®—online...

HINTLTW

TRUEBLOOD, TEXAS

Coming in June 2002...

THE RANCHER'S BRIDE

by

USA Today bestselling author

Tara Taylor Quinn

Lost:

His bride. Minutes before the minister was about to pronounce them married, Max Santana's bride had turned and hightailed it out of the church.

Found:

Her flesh and blood. Rachel Blair thought she'd finally put her college days behind her—but the child she'd given up for adoption haunted her still.

Could Max really understand that her future included mothering this child, no matter what?

Finders Keepers: bringing families together

HARLEQUIN®

Makes any time special ®

Visit us at www.eHarlequin.com

TBTCNM10